Nanagin

Copyright © 2023 by H. C. Kilgour and Owl Talyn Press

ISBN: Paperback   979-8-218-24783-6
       Ebook   979-8-218-24784-3

This work is fiction. Names, characters, places, and incidents either are a product of the author's imagination or are used fictitiously, and any resemblance to any actual persons, living or dead, events, or locales is entirely coincidental.

First paperback edition August 2023

Front cover design by Aleska Kirsten
Back cover art by Judas Iscariot
Map by "aja"

OWL TALYN PRESS
First published in the United States by Owl Talyn Press in the United States
www.owltalynpress.com

Nanagin

H. C. Kilgour

*For Gina
for always knowing when I could do better,
and pushing me to do so.*

Mountains
Westerlies
Xieng River
Javin Lake
Upper River Fort
Grech
Grev
Whendell
Tratolek
Suilenroc
Agrielha Castle
Tatat River
Lake Romann
Agrielha
Drath
Grenadon
Bouyne
Middle River Fort
Revod
Suttan
Ohvenail
Greyault
Aylentowne
Bowtilmer
Móverth
N

Albiera River
Averit Volcanoes
Wynsh River
Icchota Lake
Glensung Plains
Port Ligola
Edreba
Yarav Forest
Illeria Mountains
Port Clire
Haggard Land
Nueweba River
Igress
Eastern Ocean

CHAPTER 1

Soldiers filled the hallway, forcing Aron to push past them to follow his father and older brothers. Outside, lightning illuminated the night sky, quickly followed by a deafening clap of thunder while rain steadily drummed against the windows. At the end of the hallway, the throne room loomed like a cavern, its doors hanging from their hinges, the wood blackened and warped. The stench of burning flesh permeated the air.

Aron peered through the doorway, speechless. Everything was charred and covered in a thick coat of ash. Guardsmen lay scattered about, dead or dying, their agonizing cries heart wrenching. A hazy layer of smoke filled the air, causing his eyes and lungs to smart.

Caius, his father and king, strode across the room, stepping consciously over men who cried for help. Following, Aron could just make out the shape of something that did not belong in the center of the room. It was a young woman, dressed in a black shirt with sleeves stopping above the elbow, dark blue pants of a coarse-looking fabric that hugged her legs, and black shoes with white stars on the sides. He had never seen such clothing, nor was he inclined to believe anyone in Arciol had. This girl should not be there, yet… there she was.

Drawing nearer, he studied her features. Curly brown hair, riddled with hints of red, was splayed across the floor and over her shoulders. Freckles dotted her pale skin like haphazard constellations. She was a tiny thing, no taller than an adolescent, and from between her slightly parted lips the sounds of her breaths were slow and steady. Given the generous curves of her body, Aron assumed she must be used to a life of luxury.

Kneeling beside her, he swept a strand of hair from her face, while his eldest brother, Braxton, prodded the girl's shoulder with the tip of his boot. She did not stir.

Looking over his shoulder, Aron found Caius was walking towards a nearby solider who barely clung to life. He was surprised Caius was not more interested in the girl, then realized it was not out of character for his father to ignore the subject of concern.

Kolt, the second of the three Alagard boys, followed their father.

The soldier's skin was cracked, the red of his flesh showing, and his breathing was labored. "Your grace," he croaked, "water, please."

"What happened?" Caius demanded.

"Water," the man begged.

Caius's expression was as blank as slate as he knelt beside the man. "Answer me and you will have your water."

The man reached toward him weakly. "Please."

Anger flashed across Caius's face. "Answer the question!"

Fear sparked in his eyes and the man began to speak. "We were standing guard…" He coughed. "When a bright light filled the room." Another cough. "There was… an explosion…"

The man gasped and the words died in his throat as his chest ceased to rise and fall.

"Useless." Caius straightened and returned to the girl. Grabbing her wrist and, satisfied with what he saw—or did not see—let her arm drop limply. Leaving the throne room, he ordered the nearest guards, "Put her in a cell. If her condition changes, alert me at once."

Braxton and Kolt followed silently after their father while Aron lingered.

He looked at the girl again, a pang in his chest as he realized any innocence she had was about to be stripped away. Two guards came to remove the girl and Aron strode after them, wishing there was something he could do to save her.

✝✝✝

As Braxton followed his father and Kolt through the castle, no words were spoken. The girl… young woman—she was no child, but certainly not older than his twenty-four years of age either—was mysterious and questions raced through his mind. Where had she come from? How had she survived the blast? Who was she?

He shook his head to dispel the questions and pushed open the door to his bedchambers. Foregoing a candle, he slipped from his clothes and crawled beneath the covers, which were in a state of disarray from his hasty departure.

Tired as he was, it was difficult to find sleep. There was something about the girl, though every time he thought he understood what it was, the idea slipped away.

His dreams were strange. He started in a void, where he could hear nothing, see nothing, and feel nothing but the weight of existence. Pigments slowly added to the dark backdrop, seeping in like sunrise; they were dusky colors, mostly blues, browns, and grays. Slowly the bolts of stain pulled into rough shapes.

When those became clear, he could see two people holding hands as they ran; he instantly recognized the girl. Fear was etched into every pore. She pulled against the person leading her, as if afraid, and began speaking.

Whatever words she said were muffled and in a foreign tongue.

He tried to focus on the person she was with, but their face was blurry. The only thing he could see was an intense pair of blue eyes that felt familiar. As he concentrated on them, they began to cloud. Then the world around him faded to shapes again, then to color, then to nothing.

When he stirred, sunlight was pushing through his window.

There was a knock at the door.

"Give me a moment," he called, throwing back the covers and dressing. Standing outside his room was a soldier. "What?" Braxton demanded.

"The girl's awake."

A shiver raced down Braxton's spine and, hating himself for what he was about to do, he began making his way to the dungeon.

✜✜✜

Morning light filtered through the barred window, casting shadows over Keegan. She was warm underneath the covers and happily blanketed in sweet serenity. In a state of pseudo-sleep, she yawned, stretching her arms above her head.

She bolted upright with the realization she'd overslept and was going to be late for class. It took her mind a moment to start racing in bewilderment as she glanced at her surroundings. Her eyes darted around the barren room, which appeared to be a dungeon cell. She pinched herself. With the sting of pain, a disquieted feeling rose in her stomach like bile. But she refused to believe this was real.

Warily, Keegan rose and walked to the door, holding back a wave of panic. Finding no way to open it, she pounded against the wood. After several minutes and no response, her hands could take no more. Doing what she could to hold back panic, Keegan stood on her toes and was just able to look through the small, barred opening in the door. She saw the backs of two men who wore black tunics underneath sleeveless shirts of chainmail.

"Hey," she called, trying to convince herself this was all some elaborate creation of her mind, "where am I?" She really hoped the answer would be "In a dream."

One of the men started to turn, but the other must've given him a hard look, as he returned to staring forward.

Realizing they'd give her nothing, she backed away to sink onto the cot, eyes wide, mind reeling, a lump stuck in her throat. This wasn't a dream. The details were all too rich, too lifelike. She couldn't deny the truth any longer.

Time slowed, each minute stretching into what felt like eons. There was no one word for what she felt—a pit of unease sat in her stomach that swallowed her up; a blanket of shock shrouded her in empty, chaotic thoughts; a fear of the unknown that led to only one outcome: death. Waves of emotions threatened to break free from their cage and form into salty ribbons that would stream down her face.

No. Keegan rose to her feet and began to pace, refusing to let herself ugly cry. *Breathe. Think of something happy: puppies, chocolate, diving... Oh, God, what if I die here? No. Focus. Snow, piano, reading on a rainy day... There has to be a logical explanation.*

She eventually noticed the sound of footsteps—and they were getting closer. Racing back to the door and peering through the opening, she found the guards had moved apart to reveal a man.

He was tall, easily reaching six feet in height. His black hair was close-cropped, and his eyes were a sullen blue, as if they'd given up hope. The thick, white outline of a scar followed the contour of the bottom of his left eye.

As he inserted a key into the lock, Keegan scrambled away from the door. She desperately wanted to believe the sword belted around his waist was for show, but she knew it was lethal. Alarm threatened to have her curling into the fetal position, but she likely had one chance to escape—and crying in a corner was not it.

"Who are you? What do you want?" she demanded.

The man ignored her, stepping forward.

Her eyes darted to the still open door; it was a long shot, but she *had* to try. As she ran past the man, he wrapped his arms around her torso and swung her around until she was back where she'd started.

"Stop," he commanded, pushing her against the wall. His body was flush against hers, his hands pinning her wrists to the cold stone. "Please, do not resist. I do not want to hurt you, but he will make me."

Keegan wasn't given time to consider his words as a second man stepped into the doorway. He had paling blond hair, a similar hue of stubble marking his square jawline, and brown eyes that stared cruelly.

"What have I told you about showing kindness, Braxton?" the older man drawled.

Braxton said nothing and pulled her forward.

Blood pounded in Keegan's ears. "Who are you people?"

The man turned his attention to her. "I am Caius Alagard. Who might you be?"

Keegan ignored his reciprocated query, instead focusing on prying the hand off her arm.

Braxton dug his fingers into her bicep, eliciting a yelp. "Answer him."

"K-Keegan," she stammered.

"Keegan," Caius repeated, lifting her chin with the tips of his fingers, "you—"

"Don't touch me," she bit, jerking away.

Caius grabbed her chin forcefully. "I shall do whatever I please."

With her free hand, she dug her fingers into the underside of Caius's wrist and wrenched his hand away. Standing rigidly, she had the gall to stare him down.

Caius gave her a look of contempt before striking her.

Her eyebrows knitted together as her hand rose of its own accord to brush her now stinging cheek while tears welled in the corner of her eyes.

"If you wish pain upon yourself, it can be arranged."

The malice in his voice sent spikes of fear through her and Caius's lips pulled into an unsettling smile, leaving her with no doubt he'd live up to his threat.

"You can't do this! I haven't done anything wrong," she blurted.

Caius gave a foreboding chuckle as he walked from the cell, leaving her with Braxton.

"Do not push him," Braxton warned, releasing her arm, taking his leave too.

She didn't have to check if they'd locked the door; she'd heard the bolt sliding into place.

Tears began sliding down her face and she wiped them away with a shaky hand. But more kept coming and refused to stop.

✠✠✠

Braxton stood outside the cell again, this time alone. It had been all too easy to see the terror on the girl's face before and he hated himself for having taken part in its cause. Steeling himself, he pushed open the door. As it scraped across the floor, Keegan bolted up, the same expression of fear already on her face.

He gently took her by the arm, causing her to flinch, and he could feel her trembling. She lashed out and he quickly spun her around, wrenching her arm behind her back. Pushing her from the cell, he could not bring himself to look at her.

After rounding a corner, the girl instinctively began fighting upon seeing the soldiers waiting outside the door further down. One did not have to live in the castle to know the malice in the room behind.

"They're waiting," a guard said, an air of nervousness in his voice. It was a warning.

Inside the room Braxton found his father, along with Kolt.

A chair sat in the center of the room and Keegan strained against Braxton; it would have taken a blind man to overlook the gaping scars in the wood and the deep red stains. Various instruments designed to cause pain hung from the walls and chains dangled from the ceiling.

As Braxton forced Keegan into the chair, Caius said, "You know better than to keep me waiting."

He bowed his head. "I apologize, father."

Keegan looked between them, questions filling her hazel eyes. Plucking up her courage, she asked, "What do y'all want with me?"

"Do not speak unless spoken to," Caius snapped, anger pulling at his features. Turning to Kolt, he asked, "Would you care to deal with this?"

"You will show us respect," Kolt shrieked at the girl.

Keegan responded to the verbal assault by shrinking into the chair.

"You are nothing," Kolt spat, placing his hands on the chair's armrests. "You will do as we say. Understand?"

When her eyes did not lift, Kolt flung her from the chair.

Keegan landed on her hands and knees and quickly tried to stand, seeming to know what was coming next. The kick caught her in the stomach all the same, leaving her winded and curled in a ball.

Knowing the beating would continue unless he stepped in, he moved between them as Kolt went to kick again; his brother was mindlessly cruel.

"Stop." The blow landed on Braxton's shin, and he winced. "She did not challenge you," he said through gritted teeth.

Kolt shoved him aside and knelt beside the girl. "Do you understand?"

With watery eyes, she gave a slight nod.

Kolt shoved her back into the chair then clutched her chin and drew close. He gave a wicked smile, running his thumb along her lips before retreating to where their father stood.

"Where do you hail from?" Caius asked with a knowing smile.

"Charlotte," she answered meekly.

Braxton was taken aback; most times, Caius asked a question, then made his way into people's minds and answered himself to further mystify and baffle them.

Frustration pulled at the corners of his father's lips and confusion knitted his brows. "Where is this Charlotte?"

"North Carolina."

"North Carolina," Caius repeated, as if trying the words out. "How curious, I know of that place, but not of Charlotte."

Though his father seemed not to be entirely confused, Braxton was; there were no such places as Charlotte or North Carolina in Arciol.

"Where are you from?" Caius repeated.

"Charlotte."

"There is no such place."

"Yes, there is."

"Where are you from?" Braxton knew the false calm about Caius was a subtle sign he was becoming increasingly agitated.

"Charlotte. But I go to school in Wilmington," Keegan offered.

"Tell me about Wilmington."

"Uh… It's a college town on the Cape Fear River."

Braxton stood quietly to the side, waiting for Caius to move to the next question.

Do it, boy! he heard his father yell in his mind, clearly dissatisfied with Keegan's answer.

Hating himself, Braxton struck the girl.

Caius turned his back to them and was replaced by Kolt as the interrogator.

"How did you get here?"

Keegan shook her head. "I have no idea."

"What do you know about the Lazado?" Kolt continued. "How were you planning to kill my father?"

"The who? And- and what?"

Kolt prepared to strike and she raised her arms in defense. Infuriated, he grabbed her hand and, before Braxton could intervene, pulled her little finger sharply to the side.

Her cry tore at his heart and he clenched his fists, retreating within his mind; he had to, for his sake. Stealing a glance at her finger, he was relieved to see it was merely dislocated.

"Tell us what we want to know," Kolt demanded, placing his hand around the girl's throat.

"I am," she wheezed, kicking him back. She would rather endure pain than face death. But she had little idea exactly how much pain they would make her endure.

The screams the girl emitted as they continued their interrogation were painful to hear and Braxton stared at the wall, refusing to look at what was happening.

By the time he returned Keegan to her cell, a few cuts and quickly forming bruises were already marring her features.

Walking into the cell of her own accord, Keegan curled into a ball on the cot, staring blankly at the wall, the hand with the dislocated finger cradled against her chest. Braxton stood and watched her until the guards made their evening rounds, bringing trays of what could barely be called food.

✣✣✣

Aron wandered past the cell slowly, peering through the small, barred window. The girl lay on the cot and appeared to be asleep, dark bruises mottling her face.

10

As he made his way through the castle, his heart tore in two. Aron wanted to help the girl, but he feared his father. His thoughts were dragged away from the girl as the dread of what he was about to face began to overwhelm him. Most evenings, he ate in the kitchen with the staff—at least they tolerated him. While he always had a place at the king's table as an Alagard, he was not truly welcome. He shuddered, recalling his three broken ribs from the last time he had dined with his family. The only reason he was braving them tonight was because he wished to learn more about the girl.

Since birth, he had been nothing more than a nuisance to his family—like a forever-present itch. As a child, he had struggled to understand why. When he turned five, Braxton had explained: he was the reason their mother died.

Kolt, two at the time of their mother's passing, had not understood why she was no longer present, but had realized it was Aron's doing—and had yet to forgive him. Braxton had been four and, while he too had been upset, understood Aron was not to blame.

As Aron grew, he began to look like his mother; it was one of the few reasons his father tolerated him to the extent he did, but also the reason Caius wanted nothing to do with him. Both were blessings.

While Braxton did not loathe Aron, he was being pulled in two different directions. He had lived long enough to be nurtured by their mother, but, as the only elemental of the three boys, was under the cruel tutelage of their father. Not to mention one day he would be king. Never had Aron wished for the life Braxton led.

The dining hall's large, double doors loomed ahead and the guards outside gave each other enquiring looks as Aron approached.

His brothers were already inside. Kolt sat with his feet propped on the table, cleaning his nails with a knife. He glanced at Aron, giving him a look of disgust. Braxton barely acknowledged his presence with a quirk of his brow.

Aron chose a seat at the far end of the long table, well outside of Kolt's reach—or so he hoped. No one spoke and a strained silence fell around them until their father arrived.

"Get your feet off the table," he snapped at Kolt, after pausing upon seeing Aron, "you were not raised in the fields."

Food was brought out and Aron ate slowly.

"Keegan," Kolt started, "is—"

"A problem," Caius finished. "I gathered after I was unable to hear her thoughts."

"How were you not able to get past her wall?" Braxton questioned, genuine surprise and concern in his voice.

"Royik if I know," Caius answered. "But she *will* tell me what I want to know."

"She did," Braxton said quietly.

"Charlotte does not exist," Kolt barked.

"I am having doubts," Caius said. "It has been well over two hundred years since my Nanagin."

Aron quickly recalled everything he knew about Nanagins, which was not a great deal. They were rare magical portals, requiring one to be in just the right place at just the right time, that transported a person to another world. In Arciol, it left behind a destructive blast. Throughout history, there were only a handful of occurrences when an Arciolan had returned; Caius being one of them. When they did return, they boasted accentuated powers, well above the abilities of others. From what could be determined, the more time spent in the other world, the greater the augmentation.

"What does that have to do with anything?" Kolt asked.

"When I went to the other world," Caius began, "I was taken to a port city called Wilmington… in North Carolina. Quite a lot of time has passed; it is possible much has changed. Including the major cities."

Braxton nodded in agreed.

"You would be stupid to believe her," Kolt sneered at Braxton.

Caius shrugged. "Either way, everyone has their breaking point."

"Breaking point for what?" Braxton demanded while Kolt commented, "With Braxton that could take months."

"Time is of no consequence," Caius said, ignoring Braxton and addressing Kolt instead, "but if she is not broken within the week, you may take over if that suits you."

Kolt grinned sinisterly.

"Of what importance is she?" Aron asked boldly.

The way Kolt's face turned red suggested he was liable to fly across the table and beat him.

"He poses a good question," Braxton remarked, shifting the attention away from him.

"Of what importance is she?" Caius said. "She is the key to finding the Child of Prophecy. If she is not the child herself."

The Child of Prophecy—or the bane of Caius's existence—was their father's obsession, spanning longer than Aron's nineteen years. Anytime something unusual happened, his father blamed it on the Child of Prophecy. And if he could find the person that caused the event… it usually did not end well for them. Though Caius was the strongest elemental in the world, the Child of Prophecy was said to be the one person who could end his reign. While Aron, and most of the world, did not think that was such a horrible thing, Caius had devoted years to finding and destroying the child. He bordered on paranoia now, believing any exceptional magical occurrence might have a connection to the Child of Prophecy.

Standing quietly, Aron exited; it was best to leave while his father and Kolt were preoccupied, and he had heard enough. Keegan would reveal the whereabouts of the Child of Prophecy or die.

Leaning against a windowsill outside the dining hall, he gazed over the plains surrounding the castle. The sun had set, casting pink hues into the sky. While he wished no harm upon Keegan, to help her would mean a world of pain for him.

CHAPTER 2

Hiding in the shadows of an alcove outside the dining hall, Aron hesitated before following his father when the doors pulled open, and Caius sauntered past.

After a few minutes, he realized his father was going to visit the Blind Prophet. He was the man who knew the answers to the questions Caius would ask long before he voiced them.

Caius stopped outside a plain wooden door on one of the lower levels of the castle, removing a key from around his neck.

When his father was safely inside the room, Aron crept forward, pressing an ear against the wood.

"You know why I am here," Caius stated.

"As always," came Alyck's raspy voice. "However, I cannot answer what you wish to ask."

"And why is that?"

"To know, I must first understand—and the girl remains *well* outside my realm of understanding."

"Then understand her," the king snapped.

"An ant can no more understand the actions of man than a man can understand the actions of an ant. Bring her to me."

There was a moment of silence before the door handle began to turn. Aron scrambled back into the shadows.

"The tide has returned, brother," Alyck said as the door creaked open, "and you shall be swept away in the undertow."

Caius slammed the door in frustration. With an irritated growl, he punched the wall, then sucked in a deep breath, cradling his now misshapen hand. Enraptured in pain, Aron's father stalked away, forgetting to lock the door.

Aron bided his time until he could no longer hear Caius's mutterings.

"You are lucky tonight, Little King," Alyck said after Aron had slipped inside the room. His uncle sat in a chair, arms crossed loosely—he knew Aron had been eavesdropping. "Anger has always made my brother forgetful. You want to know about the girl."

He gave a curt nod.

"There is nothing I can tell you that you will not learn in due time."

"Can you not be straightforward?"

"No, for nothing is."

Shaking his head, Aron reached for the door handle.

"Tsk, you give up too easily, Little King."

"Then are you going to tell me?" Aron asked, a hint of frustration in his voice. The only way to get information from Alyck was to refuse to play his games.

"Contrary to what I told Caius, I know many things about the girl, but there are very *few* things *you* need to know currently."

Aron refrained from rolling his eyes. "And what would those be?"

"Firstly, she needs your help."

"Why would I do that? Should my father find out, I..." He shuddered at the possibilities.

"Because you need her help, too."

"How so?"

"That, you will discover for yourself."

Aron made to leave again.

"Help her, as right now she is the *only* person who can help us."

Back in Aron's bedchamber, a small fire burned in the hearth and the window was open. Aron sat on the edge of the bed, torn. To go against his father… was that something he was willing to do?

‡‡‡

Sleep did not find Braxton easily and, when it did, the dreams it brought were unsettling. He was again surrounded by darkness, the world swallowing him up. Dark colors began to appear, painting a hazy scene and Keegan's face took form.

She pulled back, as if ripping from someone's grasp, and a set of indigo eyes appeared. Above them, a pair of black brows formed. Braxton focused, trying to discern to whom they belonged—but he could not tell, despite their familiarity.

Words that he could not understand were exchanged.

The pair of startling blue eyes began to move away, and Keegan followed.

He chased after the two of them, but found himself falling through oblivion, the breath sucked from his throat. Braxton jolted awake, momentarily disorientated as the feeling of falling followed him into the realm of light.

Pale sunlight shone through his window, and he realized it was morning. He would have gladly returned to sleep for a while longer, but the dream had his nerves on edge. Throwing back the covers, he began to pace, his stomach tumbling.

What could this mean? Would his dream come to pass?

He passed his mirror and looked at his reflection. Stubble marked his jaw and he appeared worn, more so than usual. The scar under his left eye smiled cruelly.

He looked at his own eyes. They were the same as the ones he had seen in his dream. Was he…?

Pulling away from the mirror, he continued to pace. But his mind kept going back to the fact he was going to be the source of Keegan's fear. Yet… if the dream came to pass, would he not be the one to save her? Could he do that?

Finding himself only becoming more anxious, he went to his desk and pulled out a sheet of parchment and a stick of graphite. As he drew, his worries melted away, presenting themselves on the page rather than in his head.

‡‡‡

Keegan was ready to make a bid for freedom as soon as Caius entered her cell. She slid past him stealthily, but, as her foot crossed the threshold of the cell, her body froze mid-stride.

"Where do you think you are going?" Caius demanded.

She struggled against the invisible bonds that held her in place. "Let me go!"

Caius came to stand in front of her. "Let you go; why not?"

Her body was released, and she careened into him. Caius grabbed her wrist and began pulling her down the hallway like a misbehaving child. She kicked at his knees and yanked her arm free. As she turned to run, hands on the back of her shoulders threw her to the floor.

Caius placed a heavy boot on her shoulder. "Did you *really* think you could escape?"

Defeated, she asked, "What do you people want with me?"

He pulled her to her feet without answering.

She noticed he was taking her into the depths of… wherever the hell they were, before stopping outside a door along a weakly lit corridor.

Inside the room, from the shadows, a dusky voice said, "Leave, brother, if you want your answers. She will not escape from here if even I cannot."

Caius wavered, then released her and retreated outside, shutting the door.

A man stepped into the torchlight. Thin strands of greasy black hair intermittent with gray hung past the man's shoulders and framed a haggard face. She could just see the blue of his irises underneath milky cataracts. He appeared to be in his late thirties.

"I mean you no harm, child. I only seek to answer your questions."

"Where am I?" Keegan stood rooted in place.

"Agrielha."

"Wh-where's that?"

"Agrielha is the capital of Arciol."

Her eyebrows furrowed. "Those aren't real places."

The man moved closer. "Do you not wonder why my brother does not know where Charlotte is?"

"I- I don't- I don't know." She backed against the wall, praying he wasn't cruel like the rest of his family.

"You need not fear me, child."

Her heart pounded furiously. "Just tell me where I am. *Please*."

"I did."

"Those aren't real places!"

"Who is to say simply because they do not exist in your world that they do not in another."

Her mind was unwilling to grasp the concept. "What?"

"Exactly as I said."

"Are you trying to tell me I'm in a different world?"

He nodded.

"*Impossible*."

"What is possible and impossible is entirely relative."

Keegan sank to the floor, running her fingers through her hair. She fully believed this all had to be some kind of drug-induced trip—it was the only logical explanation. And these people had proven they weren't above drugging her.

"This can't be happening," she muttered.

The man sympathetically placed a hand on her shoulder. "But it has."

She jumped to her feet. "Don't touch me."

"I have no intention of hurting you, Keegan."

Her gut clenched in fear. "How do you know my name?"

"I am the Blind Prophet. I know all, Keegan Ilene Digore. Or should I say Keegan T—"

"I just want to go home; what do I have to do to get there?"

"You are home," he said.

"Please." Tears began to collect in her eyes. "Please, how do I go home?"

"You already are."

"Why am I here?"

"To right the wrong."

"How the *fuck* am I supposed to do that?"

She didn't like the wicked glint in his eyes. "Kill a certain man."

Shaking her head in dismay, she asked, "Why me? There are seven billion people on the planet; why me?"

"No one else is powerful enough."

She motioned to herself. "And *I am*?"

"Not yet."

"And I'm supposed to do this alone?"

"Three shall join your plight. Brother in arms, brother in blood, brother in heart. Together, strong enough to move the stolid hearts of broken men; alone, forever cursed to remain nothing but a distant memory in the endless flow of time."

"What does that mean? What the fuck is wrong with you people?"

The Blind Prophet gave her a suggestive smile before slipping back into the shadows.

Behind her, the door burst open. Keegan didn't resist, her mind in disarray, as Caius took her back to the cell. She expected him to push her in and leave her be; Instead he threw her up against the wall.

"What did he mean?" Caius asked.

"About what?"

"Everything."

"I don't know."

Caius delivered a backhanded slap, the ring on his finger scratching away skin on her cheek. "You feign ignorance."

She could feel blood gathering at the new seam and gritted her teeth. "I promise, I don't know. And even if I did, I damn well wouldn't tell *you*." She instantly regretted her words; this was not the time to be snarky.

Caius grabbed her wrist. "What did he mean?"

Feeling a burning sensation, she clenched her fists. "I don't know."

"Look at me," Caius growled. When she didn't, he grabbed her jaw, forcing her to stare at him. "Tell me."

Her nails dug into her palm, and it was all she could do to stop herself from crying out. "I. Don't. Know."

"The sad thing is, I *almost* believe you."

Suddenly the pain was no longer contained to her wrist. It radiated through her body, the blood in her veins turning to liquid fire. She could feel it coursing through her and was barely aware a scream escaped her lips.

"Tell me."

Keegan sank to her knees as the blood reached her chest, the fire circulating in her heart. "Make it stop."

Caius stared down at her.

"Please," she whimpered as the blaze made its way up her neck.

"Groveling suits you."

The blood found its way to her brain and the world imploded.

✝✝✝

Aron tried to walk inconspicuously down the row of cells, but the subconscious need to check over his shoulder made it difficult. He had almost reached Keegan's cell when Caius stormed from it. Quickly, he turned on his heels, hoping his father would overlook him.

"Coming to check on the girl?" Caius called.

Aron froze.

"Come see." Caius bore a nasty sneer as Aron joined him. "Look at her."

He peered through the window in the door. Keegan lay pressed against the wall, one arm folded awkwardly under her body while the other was cast haphazardly in front of her. Knowing Caius was waiting for a reaction, Aron tried to conceal his emotions, but disgust and hatred flashed across his face.

"Does it make you mad that we have tormented her?" his father taunted.

Clenching his jaw, Aron stared straight ahead.

Caius pulled open the door, all joviality gone from his demeanor. "Go help her."

Aron stood still, unsure of his father's intentions.

Grabbing his shirt at the nape, Caius pushed him into the cell. "Attend to her!"

Aron stumbled and heard the door slam shut behind him. Cautiously, he made his way to Keegan, wondering if she was even alive.

"What is her crime?" he asked, glancing over his shoulder.

"She has committed none. Yet."

"Then why are you torturing her?"

"She may be connected to the Child of Prophecy."

A lump formed in Aron's throat as he recalled Alyck's words. Gingerly, he scooped Keegan up, moving her to the cot.

"And if she truly knows nothing?"

Caius chuckled. "Then you are not my son."

His anger beginning to roil. "You are hurting an *innocent* person to satisfy your lust for bloodshed."

"Hold your tongue, boy. You know nothing of my whims or wants."

Aron gritted his teeth and glared at his father. When Caius started to walk away, he called, "Are you going to let me out?"

"If I am in a good mood, I might instruct the guards to do so in a few days. This way, you get to spend some time nurturing that soft heart of yours."

When Caius was gone, Aron turned to the wall and met it with his foot. A dull pain formed in his toes as he sat back against the wall opposite the cot.

For too long had he sat by while his father tortured, maimed, and killed on whims. For too long he had been afraid. So where did the fear stem from? Was he not untouchable?

Years before, Caius had let it slip that his mother had forced him to make a Death Deal; to break that vow meant Caius's own death. The deal was he could never kill or grievously injure her sons, nor could any being under his command.

Looking at Keegan, Aron finally knew what he was going to do.

Time passed undetected as he schemed and he barely noticed the guards making the evening rounds. Eventually, he heard the jangle of keys and the click of the lock.

The door opened to reveal Braxton.

"Return to your room, Aron."

Aron surveyed his brother, who looked tired, worn, and remorseful.

As he walked past, Braxton placed a hand on his chest. "Do not push him; he will only hurt the girl to punish you."

Aron gave a slight nod and shoved past, making his way from the dungeon hurriedly, his anger threatening to boil over. Nearing his room, Aron slowed his pace, running a hand along the wall, stopping when his fingers found a divot. If he had not known it was there, it would have been impossible to find. He applied pressure and a hidden door opened.

Slipping into the newly revealed passage, he closed the wall behind himself. The way was dark as pitch, but he knew the path well enough to make the trip blind.

Three steps and he took a large stride, knowing the fourth tread had been removed and dropped off into empty space.

Tenth step and he ducked; the ceiling jutted down to about his shoulders. Too many times had he hit his head on the low ceiling or walked face first into the obstruction. On one occasion, he had even chipped a tooth.

Sixteenth step; he hugged the left wall, as along the right-hand side a stone protruded at the height of an average man's waist. When he had first discovered the passage at eight, the stone had been at his shoulders. As he had grown, it had become increasingly painful to walk into.

Twenty-ninth step; he turned right with the hallway.

Twelve more steps and he came to a dead end. In the beginning, he had been disheartened that this did not lead to some mysterious hideaway and had forgotten about it for a while. The next time he returned, he came prepared with a torch and discovered another stone that needed to be pressed.

The door gave way and he emerged into the cool night air. Here, on top of the castle, high above the sentries, where the stars twinkled like old friends, was his sanctuary. The gable was small, only about fifty feet in width and length, but it was all he needed.

A smile played on his lips as he spied someone standing near the edge of the roof, staring at the night sky.

He crept towards her, and she was too enraptured in the heaven's beauty to notice him. Taking a final step, he threw his arms around her.

She jumped, but relaxed as he leaned forward to kiss her cheek and reached to hold onto his arms. "Aron."

"Hello, Shiloh."

She turned in his arms to face him and he kissed her.

Even with his eyes closed he could recount every detail of her: the almost invisible freckles dotting her nose, the dimples that appeared when she smiled, the way her hair felt like silk when twirled between his fingers.

"How was your day?" he asked.

"Oh, you know," she said, running her fingers through his thick hair, "not nearly as great as my night. How was yours?"

His smile faltered and he turned his back to hide a scowl. "I think… I *am* going to do something dangerous and unwise."

"Aron," Shiloh said softly, "you can't run away. How many times have we talked about this?"

"I wish it were that. Honestly, the results would be infinitely better."

Shiloh made him face her. "What are you planning?"

"I am going to help someone. I am going to save her."

‡‡‡

Braxton eased the door open, wincing as the hinges whined. He did not come to this place often.

"Hello, Uncle," he said to the man leaning against the shadow-shrouded wall.

"Hello, Braxton. It is not often I receive a visit from you. But I suppose these are… *unusual* circumstances. You are here to ask about your brother and the girl?"

"Yes, tell me Aron's future."

"I do not understand why you continue to ask that question."

"I need to know nothing has changed."

"It has not."

"Say it, Alyck. Please, I need to hear it."

"Why?"

"Because I promised Mother I would look after him."

"Aron will live a long and prosperous life."

He felt himself calming. "Tell me about the girl."

"*Please*," Alyck scoffed. "She is the one who will shape the future. Her path is along the same road Aron will travel."

His heart sank. "What can I do to help her?"

"It is imperative that you do absolutely nothing."

"But—"

"Absolutely nothing," Alyck repeated.

Braxton nodded and slipped quietly from the chamber. It was the dead of night, the perfect time for secret trysts, and he had the feeling Aron had gone to see Shiloh. He knew of their relationship, but not where or how they had met. While he had no woman to hold, he had friendships of other sorts, and it was to these he headed his steps.

Making his way to the upper levels, he looked for the indentation in the wall. Finding it easily, he pressed the stone, creating a small seam in the wall. He slipped through and let the door close behind him, casting himself into darkness. He climbed the stairs until he reached a dead-end. Pulling a lever, he opened another door that spat him into an anterior room. In the annexing chamber, he could hear rustling and clicking.

Braxton, came Myrish's voice, *tell us the goings-on.*

My father has the inclination he has found the Child of Prophecy, Braxton answered. *Or at least someone who knows something about it.*

Torches cast a soft light over the twelve griffins. The magnificent creatures had the heads and wings of eagles and the bodies of immense cats. He made his way over to Niyth, one of the smaller ones, with a silver sheen to her feathers.

Humph, replied Niyth, *I doubt that. How many times has he found the Child?*

"Too many," he mumbled.

What makes this one different? Niyth shifted her wings, causing a clinking of chains.

This one blew the throne room apart, Braxton said. *One moment she was not there and the next it was a scene of chaos. And in the center of it all, there she was, unscathed.*

The griffins clicked their beaks, speaking amongst themselves in their beastly language that eluded him.

Watch her, Myrish instructed. *Watch her and protect her.*

CHAPTER 3

Stirring, Keegan recalled the events of the previous days. She rubbed the sleep from her eyes, weary with the knowledge that today was going to be just as painful, wincing as her dislocated finger protested against her movement. She'd managed to get the joint back into place, but it was still swollen and sore. Closing her eyes, she took a deep breath as a tear trickled down her cheek. Wiping it away, she swung her legs over the edge of the cot, wondering when someone would come for her. She wasn't kept waiting long.

"How are you?" Braxton asked softly as he approached, genuine concern in his voice.

She looked him in the eye. "Why do you care?"

"I am not merciless like my father and brother—regardless of what others think."

"Coulda fooled me." She internally groaned, wishing her mouth didn't have a mind of its own.

"Do you think I have a choice?"

"Yes."

A mix of shock and offence showed on his face. Unable to formulate a response, he roughly pulled her from the cell.

Braxton took her to the same room as before, again forcing her to sit in the chair at the center. She breathed a sigh of relief when she saw Kolt was absent. While Braxton did strike her, he did so in a way that allowed him to soften the blows. Kolt, on the other hand, reveled in causing her as much damage—physical and psychological—as possible.

"Where are you from?" Caius asked.

"Charlotte." She desperately wanted to add that no matter how many times he asked, her answer wouldn't change.

"How did you get here?"

"Don't know."

"What do you know about the Child of Prophecy?"

"The who?"

"Tell me what I want to know."

"I am. Or at least I'm trying to." Her response was met with a blow from Caius.

"What do you know about the Lazado?"

"The what?"

"This will stop if you tell me what I want to know."

"I have been," she yelled, clenching her fists. Her words became unchecked. "You're just too thick to get that."

She saw Caius's fist coming and remembered nothing more.

‡‡‡

By her count, three days had passed since she'd first awoken in the cell, which should make it the night of April 24th. Since arriving, Keegan had amassed more cuts and bruises than she cared to count. She lay on the cot, unable to sleep, the cell as dark as her prospects. Listening to the sounds of the night, she heard little more than her own heartbeat. Then the clash of metal on metal and a dull thud outside the door caught her attention.

The door opened and a bright strip of light gushed forth. For an instant the light was blocked, then reappeared. As her eyes adjusted, she could just make out a figure approaching her. She remained still, unsure of what to do. Not for the first time, she wished she could melt away.

A hand covered her mouth and without thinking, she bit down, the taste of iron flooding her tongue.

A man muttered a strange curse, then whispered, "I am here to help you."

She sat up. "What?"

"Shhh." The man found her hand and dragged her to her feet. "Come with me."

Keegan resisted, though not enough to waylay the man. "Who the hell are you?" Upon seeing the two guards laying in pools of blood outside the cell, she pulled away violently. "Who are you?"

The sound of footsteps echoed from further up the corridor.

"Do you trust me?"

"No!"

"Too bad." He took her hand again and pulled her along.

Keegan knew she shouldn't trust the man, but he was helping her, and, for the moment, it was enough. As they ran, she studied him.

His features were sharp, reminiscent of someone she'd seen before. Blue eyes, deep as the ocean, sat beneath heavy black brows, and shaggy, pitch-black hair covered the tops of his ears. She could feel rough callouses on his palm.

He led her through the warren of hallways to a worn timber door and pushed it open, leading her onto a grassy knoll.

Stars twinkled in the midnight blue blanket of the sky above and she breathed in the fresh air, letting it fill her lungs. Looking behind, Keegan stared up at a large stone wall. In the gloom, she was just able to make out turrets.

"What the…" She wasn't given time to question further as her companion didn't stop and the castle became lost in the darkness.

They ran across the expanse of grass, quickly reaching a low, wooden building with a thatched roof. Inside were long rows of stalls filled with slumbering horses, who snorted at the disturbance. They went down a row, stopping outside a stall that housed a large, black stallion.

"Why are you helping me?" Keegan asked cagily as the man began tacking up the horse.

"Does there need to be a reason?"

"Yes. I don't even know who you are."

"Aron."

"Okay, *Aron*, why are you helping me?"

"Because."

"'Cause what?"

"My reasons are my own."

She crossed her arms. "Not when they involve me."

"Would you rather I take you back?"

Her silence was her answer.

Aron finished saddling the horse and, grabbing its reins, led them outside. In the distance Keegan could see flickering torches and hear shouts.

"Get away from here as fast as you can," Aron said, helping her onto the stallion.

"Where do I go?"

"Anywhere you like, as long as it is far from here."

"Aren't you coming with me?"

"No. Good luck." He slapped the horse's flank, sending it running.

Looking back, her savior was already lost in the night. Turning around, she let the horse gallop into the unknown, her auburn hair streaming freely behind her.

✠✠✠

He was in darkness again. Colors appeared and he could tell his dream was set in the castle's dungeon. The world was still and silent, like death. Two figures began to approach; one was Keegan. He turned his attention to the other person, hoping to discover his identity.

The same blue eyes were clear, mocking, and above them were dark brows. He reached up to touch under his left eye. Beneath his fingertips he could feel the scar; looking at the unknown person, he realized there was no scar. This was not him.

A banging awoke him abruptly.

He sat up groggily, trying to orientate himself. "What?"

"The girl," a guard called, "has escaped."

Cursing, he threw back the covers and dressed quickly, grabbing his sword as he opened the door.

"Tell me what happened," he instructed, starting down the hallway.

"Someone helped her."

"Who?"

"We don't know, sir; no one saw them."

But Braxton had—at least, a portion of his face. "Are they still in the castle?"

"No, they made it to the stables and stole a horse."

"*A* horse?"

"Yes, *a* horse," the guard repeated unsurely.

"Then one of them is likely still here. Tell Kolt to search the castle. I am going after the girl."

"Your brother's already begun the chase, sir."

"On horseback?"

"What other way is there?"

Braxton shook his head. "He will never catch her that way."

"Why?"

"He is an awful tracker when he can see; I do not expect him to get any better in the dark. Search the castle and take into custody anyone who is where they should not be."

✠✠✠

The castle was in confusion as Aron made his way back to his room, making it take longer than he would have liked. He had just slid into bed when a guard was banging on the door.

Aron cursed, throwing back the covers; he had hoped Keegan would have more time. Pulling on a shirt and pair of boots, he followed the guard who led him to Keegan's cell. The dead sentries had been removed.

Aron stepped into the cell. On any given day, he despised and avoided his father, but seldom did he fear for his own safety. And though Caius could not kill him outright, there were countless atrocities he might commit to punish him. Aron had no doubt that should his father discover his involvement in Keegan's escape he could be certain of a torturous life that would only end when he himself took it.

Caius paced furiously across the cell while Braxton leaned against the wall.

"Where is Kolt?" he whispered to his brother.

"Leading the search," Braxton answered, eyes never leaving their father. "Or a mockery of it."

Realizing Aron was there, Caius turned on him. "Did you have anything to do with this?"

"No," Aron said, keeping his voice flat. "I was asleep."

Caius stared at him, fury in his eyes, then turned towards Braxton, lashing out. "She was your responsibility! You had best pray to Sola and Lunos that Kolt finds her."

Aron knew how this would go; he and Braxton would stand against the wall while their father paced. Occasionally, Caius would lash out at whoever he deemed to be the guilty party in that moment. From experience, he would bear the brunt of it.

Night faded to dawn and dawn to day. When Kolt returned without Keegan in hand, it was he whom Caius assaulted.

When the tirade was finally over, Kolt said, "She is too far gone for me to track. Only the Vosjnik can do it."

"Guard," Caius roared. The man came quickly. "Fetch them."

Aron felt his stomach clench. If the Vosjnik went after Keegan, there was only a small chance she could evade them.

Time passed and eventually the eight members of the Vosjnik filed in: Connery Sray, the telepath and leader; Dax Ockloun, the water elemental; Thahan Havidray, the archer; Finlay Cralter, the fire elemental; Guthrie Urvent, the air elemental; Vitia Gorell, the life elemental; Brennian Thandov, the swordsman; and Kade Tavin, the earth elemental. These were the strongest, most ruthless, and bloodthirsty group of people in Caius's arsenal; they had to be, for to become a member the person previously holding the position had to die.

Caius gave orders, but Aron was not paying attention—he already knew what they were: find Keegan and bring her back *alive*. Aron studied the Vosjnik's faces and began to lose faith. While they were monsters due to their physical abilities, they were also monsters for blindly following orders. It was rare for one of them to think on their own; though it did happen it was not nearly often enough.

He recalled the story about one from before he was born. The man, Rosh Broyker, had been a spy for the Lazado, infiltrating the Vosjnik for six years before being discovered. Aron prayed there was a spy amongst them now.

"Dismissed," Caius said. Turning to his sons, he snarled, "Get out of my sight."

Aron needed no further cue and quickly made his way to his rooftop paradise. It looked different at dawn. He could see for miles across the grassland surrounded the castle from the south, west, and north. To the east was the sprawling city of Agrielha proper a mile away.

Shiloh was waiting for him.

"The deed is done."

Her countenance dropped. "You never listen, do you?"

"I do listen," Aron said, approaching. "I just find that it's best to listen to Alyck."

"*Alyck*. He's the last person you should take counsel from. Do you know what the other laundresses say about him? He's a snake that only serves the king."

"They are wrong."

"I find that hard to believe." Shiloh cupped his face in her hands, "But, it's done, and the most we can do now is pray to Sola and Lunos your father never finds out."

Aron wrapped his arms around her, pulling her close. "When I leave…"

She looked up at him uncertainly.

"I want you to come with me. I love you; I will not leave you here with these… monsters."

Shiloh placed her head on his shoulder. "Just say when and we'll go to the ends of the earth."

✝✝✝

Kade followed Brennian from the cell, his heart racing.

"Be in the stable yard in an hour. Bring your armor. Cuirasses are to be worn when we ride," Connery instructed.

There were a few grumbles as the Vosjnik briskly made their way to their living quarters.

Once the door to his room was shut, Kade packed quickly. When done, he surveyed the small space that had been his home, a smile sitting upon his lips.

In the stables, Connery, Dax, and Vitia were already tacking up their horses. Kade made his way to his horse's stall, passing the one that should've housed Caius's black stallion, Darkheart. The girl was either brave or stupid; maybe both. He quickly saddled hi dun and led the horse to where the others stood.

Vitia had pulled her hair into a braid, making the tops of her horns visible. At a glance, she seemed human, but she was far from that; the woman was an Alvor.

"This damned girl," Dax grumbled. "I had plans today."

"Stop whining," Vitia said. "It's been too long since our last mission."

"We got back two days ago!"

There was a malicious gleam in Vitia's brown eyes. "Like I said, too long."

While all members of the Vosjnik were bloodthirsty killers, Vitia went a step beyond. She played with her prey before one of the others took pity on the bastard and put them out of their misery. She'd kept her last victim alive for weeks, breaking his mind and abusing his body.

Guthrie joined them.

"What's so important about this noxþ girl?" Dax asked.

"The king did not say," Connery answered, "and it is not our place to ask."

Cralter arrived and began playing with a small ball of fire in his hand.

"Put it out," Guthrie said uneasily. "You'll burn down the stables."

"I will not," he argued, the flame reflecting in his pale blue eyes. "And it's Finlay; I hate being called Cralter."

There was a gust of wind and the flame disappeared. "Now you won't, *Cralter*," Guthrie said coolly.

"Why must everyone spoil my fun? No one bothers Vitia when she wants to play with something."

"Stop moaning," Vitia said apathetically, rolling her eyes. "And I've earned it."

"Guthrie's right," Dax said, crossing his arms. "Things do tend to burst into flame around you."

"He's a fire elemental," Kade said flatly. "What do you expect?"

"For him to have some royiken control," Thahan said, joining the conversation.

They continued to banter until Brennian arrived.

As they led the horses from the stable, Cralter approached him, "Thank—"

"Don't thank me, Cralter," he snapped. "I only pointed out the obvious. I'd suggest you quit acting like a child. Or have you forgotten members don't just get replaced when someone stronger comes along?"

‡‡‡

"Two visits in as many days," Alyck said gleefully. "What is the world coming to?"

"You knew someone was going to help her escape," Braxton stated.

"Of course. My brother does not keep me locked in this noxþ room for nothing."

"Is she safe?"

"She will never be safe as long as Caius lives."

"And Aron?"

"As always, his fate remains unchanged."

"Is the girl really as important as my father believes?"

"Even more so."

"How?"

"Wait and find out. Is that all for today?"

Braxton considered telling Alyck about his dreams, but decided against it, as they could easily just be his subconscious trying to satisfy his desire to help the girl.

"Yes," he said, turning to leave.

As the door closed, Alyck said, "See you… soon."

Braxton made his way through the castle, heading to the griffin stable and finding himself strangely at ease. Standing at the open face of the wall, he could see far into the distance. Below, he watched the Vosjnik disappear over the horizon.

He sent the monsters after her? Varley asked, though it was more of a statement.

Braxton nodded.

The griffins talked amongst themselves, sometimes in his language, other times in their own.

The fates were decided long ago, Crowlin said soothingly, nudging him with her beak. *No amount of worrying will change them.*

I know. Braxton turned away from the opening and came to stand beside her, running a hand over her soft feathers. *But it is what humans do; we worry when we cannot control the outcome.*

Humans, such strange creatures. Thinking will get you nowhere; actions move you forward.

Braxton sighed; she had given similar lectures before. *I know. But you must think before you act—lest you make things worse.*

CHAPTER 4

During the day, the Vosjnik caught up to Keegan. As far as they could tell, soon after Kolt had given up, she'd stopped to rest. Her trail led west towards Lake Romann.

Now, with the sun making its descent, they could see her on the horizon. Darkheart proceeded at a slow trot, indicating she'd yet to notice them.

"Cralter, Thahan, Guthrie," Connery ordered, "flank her from the left. Kade, Brennian, Vitia, from the right. You know what to do from there."

"Yes, sir," they responded, spurring their horses.

Kade's hair whipped about his head as Aros raced across the grassland.

The girl glanced back and he swore she locked eyes with him. She stared for a moment, then realized the seriousness of the situation and frantically spurred Darkheart into a gallop.

Kade, came Connery's voice.

With a slight movement of his hand, Kade raised a column of earth in Darkheart's path.

The warhorse balked and Keegan pulled frenziedly at the reins; Kade was surprised she managed to remain in the saddle. Though from the way he could see the tightness in her muscles, it might have been pure panic. Once control was regained, she quickly led Darkheart around the column. Kade was close enough to hear her yelling, "Go, go, go!"

Darkheart was a magnificent horse, but even he had limits, and ever so slowly, the three groups closed in.

"Vitia, go," Kade yelled.

Vitia pulled ahead of their group; on the other side, Guthrie did the same.

Shadows grew longer as the rusty orange sun sank below the landscape. Kade knew the girl understood what they were doing and had no choice but to move forward. Veering off to either side meant running into either him and Brennian or Cralter and Thahan—and turning back wasn't an option. Vitia and Guthrie were beginning to pull ahead and would soon turn to face her.

And so it was done as the sun's form sank beneath the ground.

Keegan spun Darkheart around, looking for a way out. As tears welled in her eyes, a wind launched towards her.

Kade looked to Connery, unsure of what was happening.

"Hold your positions," Connery called.

As the wind intensified, the horses scrambled backwards to avoid being drawn into the gale. A whistling began to sound from the strength of the squall and light exploded into existence. The wind reached a climax and shattered outwards.

Kade hunkered down on Aros, bracing for impact. The explosion, though it was more sound than anything, was so intense that he felt the reverberations in his bones. Once his eyes readjusted to the darkness, he realized Keegan was gone and the area was coated in a layer of ash. The only thing proving the girl had been there were tufts of upturned grass.

He stared in shock; he'd heard stories about Nanagins but had never imagined he'd witness one.

‡‡‡

The sun was just touching the needle-like tops of the pine trees when Jared Sieme arrived back at the clearing. He dumped his armload of sticks, gazing about; trees surrounded a small expanse of grass no more than forty feet in diameter. It wasn't much, but it would do for the night.

Kneeling, he cleared away the debris at the center of the clearing and grabbed a handful of leaf litter. Striking his flint, he sent a spark jumping into the tinder. It began smoldering and he blew on it gently, letting it burst into flames.

He set the burning foliage down and placed small branches on top. As the flames grew, he added more kindling until he had a roaring fire. Satisfied with its size, he set about making a spit. That done, he retrieved the rabbit he'd caught earlier, which he skinned, gutted, skewered, and placed on the spit, leaving it to roast while he buried the entrails at the edge of the clearing.

The smell of cooked meat wafted through the air, making his stomach grumble. Once it was done, he removed it from the skewer and ate ravenously, juices rolling down his chin. Cicadas and crickets chirruped in the background as the last rays of sunlight succumbed to the night. His hunger satiated, Jared leaned back on his hands.

Behind him, a branch cracked, and he jumped to his feet, pulling the knife from his boot. He waited apprehensively for a beast to appear but, when none did, sat back down, feeling on edge.

These royiken woods, he thought, stabbing his knife into the soft earth. *Why did Lucas have to decide he's too good to run errands?*

Their mother was a seamstress in Suilenroc, and though there were others who also qualified in the village, with even more in the nearby city of Tratoleck, she was the best and the ladies of both paid highly for her work. Lucas, being the eldest, normally delivered items to clients in Tratoleck or was sent to buy cloth and dye when needed. But he'd suddenly decided Jared was better suited for the job. He might have forgone the duty to his younger brothers, but

Nico was too young and Carter irresponsible. This was his first trip and, thus far, he couldn't understand how Lucas had managed them for so long.

The hustle and bustle of the city was overwhelming compared to the small village he was accustomed to. More than once, someone had tried to pickpocket him and the simple fact he'd kept a hand on his purse had saved him. Once inside the foyers of clients' homes, he was treated like filth by butlers and manservants. When forced back onto the streets, he found the smell of sewage and waste assaulted his senses, threatening to make him sick. But despite all the city's downfalls, he preferred it to the forest when alone.

Jared moved closer to the fire, its warmth making him feel protected. Slowly, his eyelids began to feel the day's weight and, as they closed, his head dropped forward to rest upon his chest. The pop of a log brought him back from the brink of sleep. He tried to calm his nerves but found his muscles tensing regardless. Another snap from the forest made him pull his knife from the earth and spring to his feet.

He realized the entire forest was quiet; not even the cicadas thrummed. A light wind began to ruffle his hair, which quickly grew into a storm. There was a sound like thunder, and he was thrown back, slamming against a tree. He sat slumped against the trunk, head throbbing as pale blue and yellow spots floated across his vision.

Brewer pulled against his tether, braying frantically. After a few moments, Jared's sight cleared, and he made his way to the large Clydesdale to calm him.

He quickly rebuilt the fire, making it larger than before to ward off this new, mysterious creature. As he finished, the underbrush across the clearing began to rustle. It was then he realized he'd lost his knife in the blast and scrambled to find it as a dark horse pushed through the undergrowth.

Jared relaxed at the sight of a harmless creature, but approached with caution nonetheless. The horse snorted and tossed its head as Jared grabbed the reins. It was then he noticed the young woman on the animal's back, slumped against its neck haphazardly.

The horse shifted and the girl began to tumble. Jared dropped his knife to catch her, laying her gently on the ground.

She had a rounded face with freckles dotted across her skin. It was possible she was quite pretty, but the shallow cuts and dark bruises made it difficult to tell. He could only wonder who was shameless enough to beat a woman. As he studied her, he realized she wore clothing he'd never seen before, along with shoes that appeared to be made of canvas with soles of a material much more durable than leather.

Gently, he checked her wrists. There were no markings of any kind, so he knew she wasn't an elemental.

The horse snorted and he went to tether it next to Brewer. Then, retrieving his blanket from his saddlebag, made his way back to the girl and unfurled it over her.

He sat beside her for a time, surveying her, questions running through his head. With a few movements of his fingers, he made the earth swell and cover her wrists, trapping them against the ground; she could be dangerous for all he knew.

Jared leaned against a tree, content to let his mind wander into the wee hours of the morning.

✝✝✝

Keegan awoke to the sounds of a crackling fire and twittering birds. Opening her eyes, she found herself staring skyward, the branches of pines fringing the blue. Bolting upright, she remembered all was not right with the world—*especially* hers. She found she could only raise herself halfway up, as something pinned her hands to the ground. Looking down, she saw the earth had encased her wrists like manacles.

"What the hell?" she mumbled.

Soldiers corralling her was the last thing she recalled. They must have caught her; it was the only explanation for the current situation.

She then noticed the young man tending the fire. Even sitting down, she could tell he was of a decent height, with rich brown hair and matching eyes. He didn't appear overly muscular but looks could be deceiving.

As she began pulling against the earthen restraint on her right hand, she realized he wasn't one of the soldiers that had been chasing her.

"Take it easy," the man said, raising his hands. "It's all right, I'm not going to hurt you."

She continued to pull against the cuff, noticing shallow fissures running through it.

"Where am I?"

"Between Tratoleck and Suilenroc."

"How'd I get here?"

"I was going to ask you that."

She glanced down to see the cracks in the restraint had widened to the point it would soon crumble.

The man approached slowly and knelt before her. "Will you tell me your name?"

Keegan gave one last pull, her hand coming free. She swung wildly, aiming to catch the man with a right hook.

He caught her punch and forced her arm back to the ground, using a well-placed knee on her bicep to hold her down. "Who are you?" he demanded.

She didn't answer, struggling under his weight, and drove her knees into his back, sending him flying forward. Rolling onto her side, she worked to free her other hand.

The man quickly pushed her down again and sat on her chest, his knees squeezing her ribcage. Earth rose to cover her arms up to the shoulders.

"What the hell did you do?" she screamed. "Get it off me!"

"Who are you?"

"Get it off me!"

"Tell me who you are!"

The cold feel of steel presented against her throat and felt herself shutting down as memories of her time with Caius raced through her mind. She gritted her teeth, trying to hold strong but felt the prick of tears as distress coursed through her.

"Keegan Digore," she replied.

The pressure from the knife lessened.

"Where are you traveling from?"

"I- I don't know."

"Where are you going?"

"I don't know." She knew the man was becoming aggravated with her lacking answers as she saw the muscles of his jaw tense. "I don't know. Please, believe me!" She could hear the desperation in her own voice.

"Are you working for the king?"

"I would *never* work for that bastard." Given the chance, she'd happily repay him in kind for her warm welcome to this strange and devastating world.

The man stood and she eyed him warily for a moment.

"Are you gonna let me go?" she asked cautiously.

"Why should I?"

"I haven't done anything to you."

"You tried to attack me."

"And you wouldn't't've done the same thing?"

He began to feel around the waistband of her pants.

"What are you doing?" she blurted, instinctively jerking her knee up.

The man stopped her knee before it made contact. "Checking for weapons," he said, running his hands down her legs.

She knew he meant what he said when his hands lingered no longer than necessary and didn't dig into her flesh.

Satisfied that she had no hidden weapons, the man returned to the fire. As the earth covering Keegan's arms receded, he motioned for her to join him.

She rose and looked over her shoulder. She might make it into the woods before he caught her, but then what? She had no idea where she was headed, and she'd lose the horse. For better or worse, this man was the only "good" option at the moment.

The man handed her a piece of bread as she joined him. "I apologize, but it's best to be cautious. I'm Jared Sieme."

When she didn't respond, Jared made his way to the horses, nervously adjusting the straps on his saddle.

Once done eating, Keegan quietly untethered her night-colored horse.

Jared surprised her by asking, "Do you have a place to stay?"

She gave him a searching look before shaking her head.

"Do you need one?"

She took a moment, weighing her options, before nodding sheepishly.

"You're welcome to stay with my family," Jared continued, kicking dirt over the dying embers of the fire.

"Why would you offer that to a stranger?"

Jared gave her half a smile. "Because it looks like you could use some kindness in your life."

✝✝✝

Kade finished untacking Aros and found Connery waiting for him outside the stables. The sun was at its peak, blinding him slightly, and he stifled a yawn; he wasn't fond of riding through the night.

"Ready?" Connery asked.

"No," Kade answered bluntly. "There's no good way to tell Caius what happened."

Connery nodded solemnly as Kade followed him across the grass. "Be ready to become leader of the Vosjnik."

With a failure like this, there was a good chance Caius would imprison Connery—and that was thinking optimistically.

Connery led the way to the throne room, the doors still missing from Keegan's explosive entrance.

A guard outside stopped them. "The king isn't here."

"I can see that," Connery growled, displacing his mounting fear with anger. "Where is he?"

"Dining hall."

On the way there, Kade spotted Aron, who, upon catching sight of them, paused and turned to follow them. Of Caius's three sons, Kade disliked Aron the most; at least the other two had spines.

They finally reached the dining hall, only to be stopped again.

"The king isn't to be bothered unless it's urgent."

Connery shoved past. "I would not be here otherwise."

The king and his other sons sat at the far end of the table.

Seeing them, Caius stood with a smirk. "Which cell is she in?"

"None," Connery said, not one to prolong things. "We were unable to capture her."

Fury contorted the king's face as he slammed his hands upon the table. "How did she evade you?"

"She experienced a Nanagin," Connery started, going on to describe the force of nature preceding the girl's disappearance.

When Connery was done, Caius reached for the nearest object, which happened to be a metal water pitcher, and threw it across the room, the clatter of its impact echoing off the walls.

"Tell me why I should not execute you?" snarled Caius.

Calmly, Connery answered, "I believe it is still possible to detain her; we simply need to consult the Blind Prophet."

Some of Caius's anger dissipated as he stalked from the room, ordering, "No one leaves."

Kade and Connery both pulled out chairs.

When Aron tried to do the same, Kolt snapped, "Who said you could sit?"

Aron looked to Braxton, but he only stared back blankly. As Aron slowly pulled out the chair, Kolt sprang up. Holding up his hands and backing away, Aron did what any normal person would do to diffuse the situation. But Kolt wasn't normal; he struck out with a punch, catching Aron on the jaw.

As Kolt reared back to strike again, Braxton spoke up, "Let it go."

Kolt turned to him, a red flush creeping up his neck.

"Let. It. Go," Braxton repeated.

Scowling, Kolt returned to his seat in a huff, leaving Aron to lean against the wall, rubbing his jaw. Apparently, his younger brother wasn't worth the effort today.

You would think by now Aron would have learned, Connery commented, pushing his thoughts out to Kade. As a telepath, he could force his thoughts into others' minds as well as hear theirs.

Hmph, Kade returned, *let them fight; fewer imbeciles to deal with.*

Be careful to whom you say that.

Time passed slowly.

When Caius returned, he said, "Suilenroc," before storming back to his seat.

Connery said nothing, bowed, and exited.

As Kade neared the doors, Caius called, "If Connery fails again, you will be leading the Vosjnik."

Once Kade's back was turned, he let a smile cross his lips.

✝✝✝

Jared led the way, Keegan quietly following, her mind still reeling from recent events. Occasionally, he tried to strike up a conversation, but she responded curtly, wishing to be left alone. Thankfully it wasn't long before he took the hint.

As the sun dipped below the horizon, they climbed the last hill towards a picturesque, two-story house. Jared guided them around back, approaching a wooden barn. He dismounted and heaved open the doors on groaning hinges.

Inside, the floor was littered with hay, stalls were filled with farm tools, goats and sheep occupied pens, and chickens roosted in the rafters. Towards the back were two empty stalls in which Jared tethered their horses.

While he untacked the animals, Keegan found a pile of hay that looked like a comfortable place to sit. She could've easily fallen asleep if she weren't so nervous about meeting the Sieme family and their reaction to her, which would dictate her future.

When Jared was done with the animals, she extracted herself from the hay, yawning and pulling strands of straw from her rust-tinted curls. Outside, the sky was dark, a few stars twinkling high above. Rolling thunderheads obscured the horizon.

The wooden steps leading to the porch creaked in slight protest under their feet. Jared pulled the door open and ushered her inside. She glanced at him for reassurance and, with a deep breath, stepped over the threshold.

Inside, a family of five sat around a table with a single empty chair, plates of half-eaten food before them. Noticing her, they grew quiet.

"Mother, Father," Jared said, approaching the table, "may I talk to you?"

His parents stood and followed him into the kitchen, giving each other nervous and confused glances.

Keegan leaned against the wall by the door, crossing her arms, and pointedly stared at the floor so as to be as unintrusive as possible.

Jared's brothers began whispering and she could feel the wary glances they stole at her.

The minutes ticked by slowly.

When Jared returned, he motioned her over. "You can stay."

She breathed a sigh of relief, the tension in her shoulders evaporating. "Thank you."

"Would you like something to eat?"

She shook her head. "I'd rather get some sleep."

"Give her Nico's bed," Jared's mother instructed.

The youngest boy started to protest, though a look from his mother silenced him quickly.

Jared led her up a set of narrow, wooden stairs.

As she climbed, her vision began to distort. She blinked a few times until the world returned to its normal clarity. It only worked for a second. Her heart started beating faster and, when she reached the top of the stairs, she felt dizzy. A ringing began in her ears and she could barely see down the landing.

"Are you alright?" Jared asked.

She nodded, unwilling to admit she wasn't, especially to a near stranger.

As Jared opened a door, her legs became weak, and she fell to one knee. She placed a hand on the wall to steady herself, but her body became like stone. The last thing she recalled was the cool feeling of the wooden floor on her cheek and a muffled yell for help.

CHAPTER 5

Jared anxiously paced the hallway, the familiar creak of the floorboards having a calming effect. He couldn't fathom what was taking Lucas so long to fetch the town healer after Keegan's collapse.

He started another round down the hallway when he heard the front door slam shut. Rushing to the top of the stairs, he saw his mother and the healer's son ascending.

"Sorry for the delay," Jameson began, "Ma's delivering Caara's baby and could only spare me. Not that I mind—thought I was going to go deaf from all the screaming."

Behind them, Lucas stomped up the stairs, his thick brown hair hanging in wet strands. The storm on the horizon had finally arrived.

Jared watched silently as Lucas went to their bedroom, slamming the door behind him. He sighed, knowing he'd have to reconcile with him later, and entered Nico and Carter's bedroom.

A single tallow candle on the bedside table offered light. Keegan lay beneath the covers, sickly sweat beading on her brow.

"Can you tell me what happened?" Jameson asked, gingerly examining some of her bruises.

"She just… collapsed."

"You spent some time with her beforehand, is there anything else you can tell me?"

"She was like that when I found her," Jared growled, understanding the implication.

Jameson nodded placidly, placing a hand on Keegan's forehead. "She has a fever. Fetch some wet rags, please."

In the kitchen, he rummaged about for a cloth. Carter and Nico still sat at the table, talking quietly.

"How is she?" Carter asked.

"I don't know," Jared said without glancing up.

Hearing heavy footfalls on the stairs, he looked over his shoulder to see Lucas coming to join them. His brother had changed into a dry set of clothes.

As Jared returned to his task, Lucas poured himself a cup of water and leaned back against the counter.

"How is she?" his brother asked.

"Don't know," Jared restated brusquely.

A tense silence followed.

"You shouldn't have brought her here."

Finding a rag, Jared asked, "Why not?"

Lucas took a drink. "You're endangering everyone."

"How so?" He reached around Lucas to grab the pitcher to wet the rag.

Lucas took another sip. "You hardly know her. She could be a spy."

"Could be but isn't."

"How can you know that for sure?"

"I asked her."

"And if she lied?" Lucas cautioned. "You and Nico will be in a world of hurt."

Jared glanced at his wrist, the outline of the earth symbol stark against his light olive skin.

"I have more faith in people than you do," he said, walking away.

Lucas stepped in front of him. "Faith has nothing to do with it. You've seen more of the world than just our little town. People lie and hurt others simply 'cause they can."

Jared drew himself up, almost matching his brother in height. "Not everyone."

Lucas pushed him backwards. "You've endangered everyone in this house!"

He shoved his brother in return. "I have not."

As they converged on each other a force separated them.

"Enough," their father roared, holding them at arm's length. "Both of you stop acting like children."

They scowled at each other.

"Lucas, quit being so cynical, people can be trusted. And Jared, you need to guard yourself more—you have too much faith in the morals of others."

Lucas lunged at Jared but was stopped again.

"Enough! And wipe that look off your face, boy," Jude snarled, knocking Lucas upside the head.

Back upstairs, as Jared was about to enter the bedroom, he stopped to listen.

"I can't imagine what must've happened to her," Jameson said quietly.

"Is there anything you can do?" his mother asked.

"No. Neither the burn nor the cuts are infected. The only thing to do is to let the fever run its course."

"What could've caused this?"

"I'm not sure. I've never seen anything like this. I'll ask Ma about it when she's free. But even then…"

There was a pause. "Will she live?"

"I can't say. If her condition changes, let me know."

"Of course. And thank you for making the trip."

Hearing them approaching the door, Jared stepped back as they emerged into the hall. "I have that rag."

His mother nodded. "Go on in while I show Jameson out."

He approached the bed slowly. Keegan's body was still, but her eyes moved rapidly beneath closed lids. He placed the rag on her forehead, feeling the raw heat radiating from her. Grabbing a chair, he moved it to the end of the bed.

Outside, thunder clapped and rain pelted angrily against the windowpanes.

‡‡‡

Aron crept down the corridors, the pads of his leather boots making minimal noise. This time of night, the only people about were the guards—and they had predictable paths.

In his hand, he held a key. A few years ago, it had appeared in his room with a note saying, *Use wisely –Alyck.* Not knowing to what, or rather who, it belonged to, he had placed it aside. A few months later another note had appeared. *Come see me –the Blind Prophet.*

As he made his way down a flight of steps, a rat scurried nearby, setting his nerves on edge. Reaching the door, he looked around, making sure he was alone.

"Well, hello, Little King," Alyck said in a cool, derisive tone once Aron had shut the door.

"You knew I was coming," Aron stated.

"As always."

"Then you know what I am going to ask."

"Have we been spending a tad too much time with Caius?"

"I will *never* be like *him*."

"One can only hope."

"Will you answer my questions?"

"Yes."

He waited expectantly and when Alyck said nothing, asked, "Are you going to or not?"

"You must ask me something."

"Why did you tell my father where to find Keegan?"

Alyck's grin faltered. "It needed to be done."

"Why? By condemning her, you condemn us all."

The Blind Prophet laughed. "You do not know what the future holds, Little King. Only I do."

"Then tell me why."

"Actions are like ripples on the water. The smallest ones can turn into the biggest waves."

"Can you do anything but speak in riddles?"

"Of course, but where is the fun in that?"

Aron sighed and headed towards the door.

"I would not do that."

"What?" Aron asked irately.

"Now is not the time to go gallivanting about the country with your fair maiden."

"How did you—"

Alyck rose from the chair and made his way over. "Have you not learned by now, I know *everything*." He held Aron's face in his hands. "Be patient, Little King. Your time will come and soon you will be free." After staring for a moment longer, he walked away. With a wave of the hand, he added, "Return to your room. And stay away from Shiloh."

‡‡‡

The world around him was blinding and Braxton shielded his eyes until it became tolerable. Studying his surroundings, he found he was in his room. Everything seemed to be in its proper place, and he searched for the glaring light. But, as hard as he tried, he could not find the source, for now there was no light.

About to give up, there was a flash behind him. He spun around, wincing when the burst occurred again, his retinas slow to adjust. The flash came again, but not as bright—yet still it was enough to make him look away.

The light's intensity diminished slowly until he could discern its source; it came from the chest at the end of his bed. There was another flash as he opened the lid, making him cover his eyes.

The light pulsed weakly, emanating from a book, making it difficult to discern the details of it. He heard someone speak behind him and whipped around to find no one was there. The voice came again, and he searched the room, frantically trying to find it with no luck. Annoyed and about to give up, he finally understood what the voice said: *Prophecy.*

Braxton jolted up; everything around him was calm and in dawn's shadow. He was in bed, unsure how he had gotten there, convinced he had been searching for something. But whatever he had been looking for completely eluded him now. A dream, again.

Its vividness had him on edge as he slowly dressed, pressing his mind to recall what it had been about. As he was about to head to breakfast, a single thought resurfaced. Knowing the word *prophecy* meant something, he forwent breakfast and headed to the library instead. It was high time he learnt a little more about prophecies, beside the fact Alyck made them.

✝✝✝

Jared had spent a sleepless night watching over Keegan, the drumming of the rain against the window threatening to lull him to sleep. The storm had broken sometime in the middle of the night and now warm sunlight flooded through the windowpanes. He sat in the chair at the end of the bed, feet propped against the footboard.

The door opened and his mother entered. "Have you been up all night?" she asked.

He stifled a yawn.

"Get some sleep," Alessandra said, kissing his forehead. "I'll watch her." When he took no action, she gave him a stern look. "Go."

Out in the hallway, Nico sat across from the doorway. "Is she going to make it?"

He tousled his brother's hair. "I don't know, but there's no need for you to be concerned."

"You can't do that anymore, I'm fourteen," Nico protested, flattening his hair.

Jared laughed. "You're my little brother, I will *always* be able to do that."

Nico gave him an obscene gesture, which he playfully returned before making his way to his bedroom that now housed four instead of two. Lucas was lounging on his bed, staring at the ceiling. He didn't even deign to glance at Jared.

"I'm not going to fight with you," Jared said wearily, sitting on his bed. "I've done nothing wrong."

"You brought her here," Lucas responded.

"I helped someone in need. What's wrong with that?"

"She's going to get us all killed. People don't beat women for no reason; she's done something to deserve it."

Jared pulled his boots off, gritting his teeth. "She needed help; I did the right thing."

"You're going to need help."

They could argue till they were red in the face, but they'd never agree. And knowing this, Jared turned his back to Lucas and went to sleep.

✠✠✠

A small smile graced Keegan's lips as she turned onto her back, reveling in the warmth of the blankets. Opening her eyes, she found herself staring at a sloping ceiling. The days recently past flooded back and the smile faded. She closed her eyes as dread washed over her. All she wanted was to be home, where the most she had to worry about was getting through organic chemistry.

A door creaked and she reopened her eyes. She watched Nico slink across the room. He had fiery red hair, bright blue eyes, and was as pale as an Irishman with just as many freckles. She found herself going cross-eyed as she followed his movements. He stopped at the end of the bed, and she realized there was someone else in the room.

"Is she going to be all right, Mother?" Nico asked quietly.

"I don't know," a soft voice relied, "but I think we might have our answer soon."

Keegan propped herself up on her elbows, saying, "I'm fine. I think," as her stomach released a loud gurgle.

"You must be hungry. Go on," the woman said to Nico, "get Keegan some breakfast."

The boy left, dragging his feet.

Keegan studied the woman, who had mid-length, raven hair streaked with gray. Her brown eyes were soft and kind, exuding a feeling of ease.

"Thank you… uhh… Mrs…"

"No need for formalities. Alessandra."

"Thank you for your hospitality. Where's Jared?"

"He went to get some sleep."

"How long have I been out?"

Alessandra looked at her, unsure of how to respond.

"How long have I been asleep?"

"Just one night."

Keegan made to push herself fully upright and a dull pain shot through her arms. Looking at her hands, she saw five markings etched in white on the underside of her wrists. There was a tree in a square overlapping four others that contained a stone, a water droplet, a flame, and a triskelion.

"What the…"

Alessandra was quickly on her feet and gently took Keegan's hands. Shock morphed her features. "You're an elemental. And a unique one at that."

"What the— What are you talking about? What's an elemental?"

Alessandra hesitated before hurrying towards the door, saying, "Jared will explain."

Alone, Keegan's mind was unsure of where to go. Her eyes scanned the room, not truly processing anything, refusing to look at the symbols marring her skin. Throwing back the covers, she went to the window. Her fingers gripped the fabric of her t-shirt, pulling her arms close across her chest.

Outside, lush, green grass covered small hills out into the distance until they merged with a dark line of distant trees. The sun beat down from a clear sky, making everything seem bright and cheery.

"You're up."

Startled, Keegan's head snapped up to look at Jared.

He carried a plate of food, which he sat on the bedside table before taking a seat on the bottom corner of the bed.

"My mother said something about you being an elemental." He yawned, struggling to keep his eyes open.

Keegan remained where she stood; it took all her willpower to not crumple.

She must have looked how she felt for Jared pushed himself off the bed and came to her. Her eyes stared blankly at his chest, refusing to lift.

"May I?" he asked softly. When she didn't respond, he gently took her hand and turned it over. "Impossible."

She didn't need to know exactly what he meant. She was a freak. Something to look at. Something to fear. Something to kill. And she had the feeling no one had an answer to her affliction. No one knew what to do with her.

Tears began to spill forth at his incredulity and her knees buckled. Jared wrapped his arms around her, and she buried her head into his chest until she had no more energy left to spend.

CHAPTER 6

Books were piled high around Braxton like a fortress. He had spent the better part of the morning searching for information on prophecies and had finally been rewarded with two tomes that seemed as if they might be helpful. One was a thin volume, bound in dark moleskin, giving the origins of the Blind Prophets; on the front page, scrawled in his father's handwriting, was a spell. The other was nearly a foot thick with worn, yellow pages.

He focused on the latter.

Many of the later pages were blank, while the others recited the prophecies made by the previous prophet, Angela Alaga, and only a few from Alyck; it appeared Caius had seldom deemed a prophecy important enough to record. That or he knew they were all too important to keep available to just anyone.

He looked at the last entry from Angela, the words scrawled in tight script. He cursed under his breath; of course, it was in the Old Language. And, not only that, but droplets of ink scattered the page, making the text difficult to read.

Jyken ey— —eki lunviyda — psod— ri ayþ drackyn, æa— woth viæn nuþ q—lx ayþ æyscs fayo eyar oywn þen. Nackh j—en eya casne, fackyon ictotm, —uh du woth unla ryo iruh ayþ adæmno. —od— woth yarv rhæpn casn— jappec eya. Qalx ayþ bu—a, qalx ayþ —aysne, qalx okæpyio, qa— ayþ payn ri luxyen, —æ ps—æ woth v—æn. Astæm

*egreþer —u woth ry— eyar oywn foylisha g—œ woth —
olcan eyar haycl—n oh kævoka kunyi.*

He transcribed the prophecy and, leaving the library, took the two tomes, not wanting anyone else to stumble upon. Eventually, he knew he would have to return them though.

In his room, he locked the books in the trunk at the foot of his bed. The day was still young, the sun having only just crossed its zenith. Having nothing better to do, he began making his way through the castle to visit the griffins. No one bothered him and he was glad; it was much easier than having to slink around like Aron. It was better than always having to use a hidden passageway.

Halfway to the griffins, he paused. Alyck was only a few years younger than Caius; maybe he knew what the prophecy said. When his father and uncle were boys, it was common for the Old Language to be spoken. If Alyck did not speak the Old Language, Braxton had no doubt he could find someone who could.

✝✝✝

When Keegan woke again, the room was still bright and airy from the sunlight streaming through the window. Jared sat next to the bed, head leaned against back of the chair, mouth wide open as he slept. She turned onto her side and his head snapped up.

"How are you feeling?" he mumbled, rubbing the sleep from his eyes.

She gave him a dejected look.

"Who are you really?" he asked.

"I told you."

"Then what aren't you telling me?"

"Lots of things, 'cause they don't matter." She paused. "'Cause they don't exist here."

"I need to know, if I'm to help you."

Keegan sent a puff of air from her nostrils. "I doubt anyone can help me."

"Regardless…"

"It doesn't matter," she bit, heart aching. "What did you mean by impossible?" she asked, recalling his incredulity upon seen the marks on her wrist.

Sympathy oozed from Jared's eyes. "You shouldn't be an elemental."

"Tell me something I don't know."

"You don't understand…" He sighed. "One doesn't become an elemental overnight. You're one thirty-five days after birth, or, or not at all, and… you can't have more than one element."

"I don't know what to tell you."

Jared pinched the bridge of his nose, blinking a few times. "I'm too tired for this."

"Then get some sleep," she bit.

"Fine." Jared strode from the room, the door closing heavily behind him.

Staring at the door, Keegan drew her knees to her chest, feeling tears beginning to form. She pushed them back; they wouldn't help her survive—never had, never would. A grumble from her stomach reminded her of her gnawing hunger, but the plate of food Jared had brought earlier was nowhere to be seen.

She threw back the covers and made her way downstairs. As she was about to enter the kitchen, she stopped.

"I don't like her," came a voice.

"You don't like anyone," another jibed.

"Whether you like her or not isn't relevant," a deep voice retorted. "We need to decide what we're going to do."

"She needs to stay here, away from prying eyes," Alessandra said.

"I agree," the third man said, "but we'll be hard pressed to conceal a *third* elemental."

"If we turn her away," Alessandra said angrily, "we might as well cast out our sons."

"I didn't say it couldn't be done, only that it'll be difficult."

Keegan felt a tickling in her nose just before she sneezed. There was a pause.

"Keegan," Alessandra called, "come join us."

Abashedly, she came from behind the corner, feeling five sets of eyes boring into her. "I was just, uh…"

The man she presumed was Jared's father motioned her over and she tentatively sat.

"How are you feeling?" Alessandra asked, stroking her hair in a motherly fashion.

"Better," she mumbled, staring at her lap as her stomach released an unearthly growl.

Without a word, Alessandra pushed her chair back and fixed a plate of food.

Keegan shoveled a few mouthfuls in before speaking. "I can understand if y'all don't want me to stay."

Jared's father said, "I can't say you'll always have a place here, but for the time being, you do."

"Thank you," Keegan murmured.

✠✠✠

"Can you tell me what this means?" Braxton asked, holding out the parchment with Angela's prophecy.

"No," Alyck said flatly, not even pretending to look at it. "I am blind, remember?"

Braxton read the incomplete prophecy then repeated his question.

And Alyck repeated his answer.

"But… you know everything."

Alyck gave a small laugh. "While it may appear that way, it is not so. I know everything about the future, but that, *that* is the past. And only half of it."

"But I think it has something to do with the future."

"That does not make it any less of the past."

He gave a frustrated sigh. "Who knows the Old Language?"

"Your mother did." There was a tinge of sadness in the words. "But she cannot help us now. I would recommend going to the place where you have that lovely little scrap of information."

"It will take me weeks to go through the library."

"It should not take you that long if you have any sense. Look for a book covered in purple stone with silver veins."

"A book covered in stone with silver veins? You cannot be serious."

"Purple stone. Silver veins. And I promise it is exactly where I say it is."

✠✠✠

Jared slept for the rest of the day, leaving Keegan with his family. She felt like an outsider as everyone went about their daily life. Through quiet observation, she learned enough about each member of the Sieme family to feel like she had a fair grasp on them.

Jude was a towering man. At least six and a half feet tall, he had bulging muscles, short brown hair, and a bushy, red-tinted moustache. He was a shepherd by trade, as were his sons. Mostly, he was a quiet individual, but when he spoke, his word was gospel.

But it was Alessandra who truly seemed to keep the boys in line—including Jude. Her voice was soft, yet Keegan couldn't help but get the sense you never wanted to cross her. She spent most of the day in her workshop sewing and, by late afternoon, re-emerged to begin dinner.

Lucas was twenty-one and did his best to avoid Keegan; obviously, it had to do with her being dangerous. Sadly, she agreed. In her world, he would've been a heartthrob with his rich brown hair, electric blue eyes, and most of his father's height. To top it off, he had spectacularly defined muscles and beautifully tanned skin. Despite the fact she knew he loathed her, Keegan did catch herself staring a few times.

Carter, at sixteen, was a bit of a conundrum. He seemed to look up to Lucas, yet also seemed to find him grating. She was surprised there weren't regular fistfights—though had the feeling there were and they just occurred outside of Alessandra's sight. Cater had sandy brown hair and a small amount of peach fuzz on his upper lip that he was immensely proud of. He was a few inches shorter than Jared, not as muscular as Lucas, which was probably why he let Lucas win most arguments, and his eyes were a light amber.

Then there was Nico, his flaming hair and freckles completely out of place compared to everyone else's darker hair and complexion. Exceedingly curious and observant, he spent most of the day questioning her between chores. She tried to answer him simply, but he had a way of knowing which parts of her answers to latch onto.

When everyone gathered around the table for dinner, Jared was roused to join them. Dinner was an unexpected but pleasant surprise. Keegan had anticipated a somber event, especially in light of... everything, and was taken aback when it was much like her own family dinners. It was chaotic, it was loud, it was full of banter. It was home.

‡‡‡

A book covered in purple stone with silver veins.

Braxton lay awake, staring into the darkness, Alyck's instructions stalking through his thoughts. *A book covered in purple stone with silver veins.* But as much as it weighed on him, he had not been afforded time to return to the library. And, at this rate, it would be next week before he fell asleep.

Sighing in frustration, he threw back the covers. As he made his way through the dark hallways, he swore at one point he saw a shadow emerge from a wall. But, when he blinked, it was gone. It might easily be Aron returning from one of his late-night trysts, but he ultimately chalked it up to his eyes playing tricks on him.

The bibliothecary had long since retired, but his auxiliaries were still hard at work.

"Can we help you, sir?" one of the older boys queried, seeming self-conscious.

"Yes," Braxton said, wondering how dull they would find him. "I am looking for a book covered in purple stone with silver veins."

The auxiliary stole a fervent glance to the other boys, no doubt wondering what punishment he would receive if he could not locate said item.

"A book in purple stone… with silver veins?"

"Yes."

"There's no book like that here, sir. At least none that *I* know of."

"I presumed as much," Braxton told him, turning to leave. "Thank you for your help."

The boy seemed surprised at his acknowledgement and lack of anger.

"If I were to find a book like that though, I… I'll let you know."

"At once," Braxton said, giving the youth a smile. "I would appreciate it."

Back in his chambers, just as he fell asleep, something struck a chord; Alyck loved riddles. He hoped he had not been given one, as more often than not, they left him stumped.

In his dreams, he found himself going through the ritual of the blinding light. He did not waste time searching, knowing it was coming from his trunk, and quickly pulled the book out. It was familiar, but he could not remember what it was about, nor where he had seen it.

The scene changed and he found himself standing on a field with a purple-black sky behind him. Screams and wind buffeted him. Something tore at his chest and a single word rang in his ears: "Betrayer."

CHAPTER 7

I wanna know about Caius," Keegan stated as she watched Jared slosh buckets of water over the ground.

She had reluctantly agreed to do some training, mostly to see what being an elemental was like. And who knew, maybe it'd help her get home. At the very least, a basic understanding of magic might help her survive this world.

"Why?" Nico asked.

"Know thy enemy, know thyself," Keegan explained.

"What the nastor does that mean?"

"Language," Jared snapped at his brother, "there's a lady present. And you're too young to be using that kind of language."

Keegan laughed. "I'm by no means a *lady*. Honestly, I probably cuss more than y'all. But, if you know your enemy, you know their weakness, which can help you beat them. So… tell me about Caius."

Jared began, "Long ago peace was kept by the Council of Elders. It consisted of the most powerful elemental from each race."

"I'm gonna take a stab in the dark here," Keegan interjected, "Caius was one of them."

"You would be correct."

Keegan ran a hand through her hair. "Great."

"They kept the peace for centuries. Caius joined their ranks and for a few years all was well. Then he turned against the other Councilors and crowned himself king. People were quick to rebel and form the Lazado. There was a battle for the city of Agrielha, but the Lazado weren't strong enough and Caius and the western city lords just about annihilated them.

"Those who survived fled to the Alvor city of Edreba. Caius tried to follow them, but the other races fought off his advances. After about a decade of war, the Council of Elders sacrificed themselves to create the border now separating the other races from us. The Lazado have remained in Edreba for the past two hundred thirty-seven years. Those of us who have remained under Caius's rule have been living in fear that he'll find us if we're elementals."

"Why?" Keegan asked, "And how can he live that long? How old does that make him?"

"To answer the latter, two hundred and eighty. As for how he can live that long, no one knows." Jared straightened up, tossing the bucket aside. "Get in the mud."

"Why?" Keegan drew out the word. "And you didn't answer my other question."

"What was it?"

"Why are y'all afraid of being found?"

Nico put it bluntly. "Because if found, we either join him or die."

"Then… isn't it dangerous to practice magic?" Keegan asked.

Jared shrugged. "It can be. But there are no soldiers stationed here. And our neighbors won't turn us in. Not without risking their own loved ones."

Nico reiterated his brother's statement, "Now, get in the mud."

Keegan cocked an eyebrow. "Uh, again, why?"

"Do you want to learn to be an elemental?" Jared asked.

"I guess…"

"Then get in."

"Fine." Keegan slipped off her shoes, rolled up her jeans, and slowly made her way into the mud patch, the sludge squelching between her toes. She crossed her arms. "What now?"

"Move the mud," Nico said, looking like he knew some secret she didn't.

Keegan gave the Sieme brothers a blank stare. "Isn't that what y'all're supposed to teach me?"

"Yes," Jared acknowledged, "but some lessons are best learnt on one's own."

She placed her hands on her hips. "I don't think that applies here."

"I promise, it does."

"Just teach me. Please."

"No."

"Teach me."

"No."

"Uhgg!" she snapped, feeling a rush of energy triggered by her frustration. "Just freakin' teach me!"

"Fine."

"Good," she said, more pleased with herself than she should've been. "Wait, why'd your answer change?"

"Because you just proved you have the raw potential of an elemental. Turn around."

Turning, she saw a misshapen wall of mud had solidified behind her. "How'd I do that? Did I do that?"

"Magic," Nico answered. She felt he should've said it sarcastically, or at least added a "duh".

"Now you need to learn to control the magic," Jared said.

"And I do that... how?"

"Close your eyes and concentrate on the point between your brows. Look for a small knot of energy."

Nico interjected, "Put your finger here," and tapped the spot above the bridge of his nose.

Slowly, she complied.

"Now close your eyes and look for something that shouldn't be there," Nico told her.

As she began to concentrate, she became aware of a slight pressure and, the more introspective she became, the more it took shape in her mind's eye. It formed into an opaque gem with ethereal swirls of motes contained within.

"Found it… now what?"

"Break it," Jared said.

"How do I do that?"

Jared shrugged. "That's up to you."

She gave him a flat look before becoming introspective again. Gingerly taking the gem, she watched it turn a deep red as it sat in her palm. Keegan readied herself, then tried to crush the gem. Uncurling her fist, she was dismayed to find it was still whole. She tried again with the same result.

"It won't break."

"Keep trying," Jared encouraged.

Biting the inside of her lip, Keegan closed her eyes and returned to her task. After multiple failed attempts, she became exasperated. In frustration, she threw the stone onto an imaginary ground. Time seemed to slow, and she watched as it shattered, sending red shards flying away. As it broke, it felt as if electricity coursed through her body, and she felt the same rush as before. She gasped and opened her eyes, the energy receding.

"Was that it?" she asked, giving a little hop of excitement, and having to steady herself.

Jared smiled. "Yes."

"How did that help me control it?"

"You have to be able to freely access that energy to control an element."

"Oh, well, then I guess I've got the getting to it part down. Maybe. So how do I do the actual controlling?"

"Once you have access to the energy, imagine the earth doing as you wish. You can use your hands as a guide. Eventually, you'll just have to think about what you want to make it happen."

Keegan closed her eyes and struggled to break the gem again. As her body buzzed, she took a deep breath and raised her hands, imagining a glob of mud mimicking the movement. She opened her eyes, and, to her surprise, the mud had risen. In her elation, she lost control of the energy and the ball dropped to the ground with a solid thud.

"You're unsteady, but that was good for your first attempt," Jared said. By the way his eyebrows furrowed together, he seemed to be holding something back.

Keegan smiled mischievously. "So, I guess I've got it then?"

"Not quite; you need to refine the skill. And that can take years."

"Oh. Oh, and what about the other elements? Can y'all teach me them, too?"

"We can't."

"Why?"

"Because we're earth elementals," Nico answered.

"So?"

"That means we can only control earth," Jared said.

"Then who *can* teach me?"

"That will depend on what element you want to learn," Nico commented.

She drew out the syllables of the first few words. "I'll probably need all of them."

"It's not like you'll save the world or anything," Nico joked.

Keegan hated to admit it, but it felt like that's where her life was headed.

"Each element is common to one race," Jared explained, playfully pushing Nico into the mud upon seeing her discomfort at his previous comment. "Life to the Silver Tongues, earth to the Torrpeki, water to the Merfolk, fire to the Dragons, and air to the Buluo. You'd have to go to each of them to learn their respective element."

She looked at him like he had three heads. "All those creatures exist?" She didn't add, "The ones I've even heard of".

Nico got up and threw a handful of mud at Jared, catching him in the face. "Why wouldn't they?"

"Uh, cause they're mythological."

"You little bwint," Jared growled at Nico, wiping the mud off.

"Language," Nico chided.

Jared smacked his brother upside the head, then returned his attention to Keegan. "I assure you, they're real."

Nico took the opportunity to tackle Jared.

Keegan stared at them blankly as they tussled before giving a sharp whistle. "Enough, dinguses."

They stopped long enough to give her a perplexed look and realize they were behaving like children. Jared pushed Nico away and got to his feet, his clothes worse for wear.

"There's no way those…" Keegan spoke, before gesturing with her hands, "whatever the hell you said, exist."

"Magic exists," Jared reminded her.

"Touché."

The two looked at her confused.

"Good point. What about humans?"

"What about them?" Jared repeated, unsure of what the question was.

"What element's common to us?"

"None. We can be any element," Jared made a ball of mud rise and sent the orb careening towards her. "Now, catch."

Keegan raised her hands to stop it, but the projectile hit her in the chest, knocking her into the muck.

She sat up, spitting mud, to find Nico hunched over with laughter. "You're supposed to stop it."

"It's not like I didn't try," she snapped, forming her own mud ball and launching it at Jared. It only made it a few feet before she lost control and it dropped. Her scowl deepened and she crossed her arms.

Jared sent another ball towards her; it crashed into her before she could react.

She snarled a curse.

"Again," Jared said as soon as she'd risen.

The exercise continued for hours, and she didn't notice the passing of time. Eventually, she prepared to catch the next projectile, but none came. Pulling herself from her fervor, she noticed Jared was motioning for her to join them. The sun was touching the treetops in the distance. Shakily, she made her way through the mud, suddenly realizing how drained she was.

Sitting on the grass, she asked, "Why're we stopping? I could do this all day."

"It's time for dinner," Jared said. "And you have been doing this all day."

She rubbed her eyes, too tired to point out the missed sarcasm.

✠✠✠

Keegan had been quiet during dinner and many times had needed to catch her head as it dropped forward. Now with dinner over and the table cleared, they lounged in their chairs, enjoying small cups of borzan before bed. Crickets chirped in the springtime night and for a time the conversation pertained to nothing of importance.

Jared looked over and saw Keegan asleep in the chair, a hand against her cheek, mouth wide open.

"You worked her hard," Carter commented.

Jared shrugged. "No harder than Nico when I trained him."

"She must not've gotten very far then," Lucas said presumptuously. "Was she even able to do anything?"

"She was close to being able to stop the ball by the end of the day."

"You act like that means something to me."

"Stopping the ball took me five months," Nico said, effectively quieting Lucas.

"There's something about her," Jared declared. "I can't place it, but she's something… different."

"A word of advice," Jude said, "don't expect the world of her. She's only one person."

Jared nodded and gently shook Keegan's shoulder, waking her. "Let's get you to bed."

She looked at him groggily and, yawning, blearily made her way up the stairs.

Jared followed, worried that whatever illness had affected her was still at play. He was surprised to find he'd become so protective of her.

She crawled into Nico's bed and nestled beneath the covers. "Thanks."

"For what?"

"Helping me."

‡‡‡

Aron took a deep breath, filling his lungs, the muscles in his arm tensing as he pulled back the bowstring. Exhaling, he released, and the arrow shot forward while the string snapped back with a twang. He watched as the arrow sailed through the air and hit the center of the target.

Beside him, Braxton shot and hit the outer ring.

"You always were an excellent archer," his brother praised.

"I just practice," Aron commented.

"It is about the only thing you do."

"Father never would let me wield a sword." Aron notched another arrow, released, and watched as it embedded itself flush with the other one. "So, this is what I do."

"He has his reasons."

Aron sent another arrow at the target and together they made a line. "And I have mine."

"Be careful when you say that. There is no knowing how father would take it."

"It is as it is, and he can take that however he royiken wants."

Braxton notched another arrow and let it fly. It clipped the target's edge and went tumbling off into the field behind. "Noxþ," he mumbled.

"Set the targets back a hundred feet," Aron said to the men standing nearby, who jumped to do as directed.

"Why are you setting them back?"

"I need a challenge."

They waited patiently while the boards were moved. The arrows protruding like spines were plucked and returned to them.

"Do you think the Vosjnik have found Keegan?" Aron asked, running his thumb along the fletching; it had been two weeks.

"We have not heard from them," Braxton answered, lazily loosing his arrow. It barely stuck to the target. "What makes you ask?"

Aron took his time shooting, only answering when the arrow was rooted in the board. "Curiosity."

"I think it is more than that." Braxton's next arrow missed the mark completely.

Aron chose not to respond.

"Move the targets back," Braxton called.

Aron glanced at him skeptically and prepared his next arrow. "Getting a little ambitious?"

Braxton was quiet and as soon as the men moved out of the way, loosed his arrow. "No," he said, walking away.

Aron stared after his brother, then looked at the target. The arrow was dead center.

✣✣✣

In his dream, Braxton quickly located the book to stop the pulsing light and had a moment to examine it; the cover was a rich purple and the pages silver gilded. His surroundings changed and, though he could see nothing, knew war and turmoil raged around him.

Purple dripped across the background, splattered occasionally with red. Wind began to buffet him and a single word echoed: betrayer. There was a screech and a searing pain ripped through his chest. He opened his mouth to scream, but no sound escaped.

Another shriek pierced his ears and the world turned black. He could feel the covers over his body and the sweat dripping down his forehead. It took a moment for him to realize he was awake. He ran a hand across his chest, convinced he would find oozing wounds, yet found himself sound.

Throwing back the covers, Braxton began to pace, his body too full of adrenaline to attempt returning to sleep. As he walked, his heart slowed and his mind calmed. He recalled something else from his dream, a book, and understood Alyck's riddle. The volume was not literally covered in stone; it was amethyst colored with silver gilded pages.

Slipping on a shirt and boots, he made his way to the library to amend his request. As he returned to bed, a phantom pain manifested across his chest.

CHAPTER 8

They had been traveling for just over two weeks and were finally reaching Suilenroc—which was normally a three-week ride from Agrielha. The town was nothing impressive, merely a collection of houses nestled between a few low-lying hills.

"Split up," Connery ordered. "If you receive any information on the girl's whereabouts, you know how to reach me."

Kade shook his head as the others began going around the main square; for the best fighters and elementals in the world, they weren't the brightest folk. He made his way down a side street until he reached the edge of town, where he about-faced, and headed back.

As he walked, he knocked on doors and talked to anyone he saw. The answer was always the same: no one had seen or heard of the girl. He was almost back to where he'd started when he came across a man carrying what appeared to be jars of salves and creams.

"Have you seen a girl," he asked, "short stature, auburn hair, would've been wearing trousers."

The man's eyes narrowed. *That sounds like the girl Jared Sieme brought home,* he thought but said aloud, "No."

Closer to the center of town, Kade came upon an old woman sitting on a porch. "Do you know where I can find Jared?"

"You'll have to be more specific, dear."

"Jared Sieme."

"Oh, such a sweet young man," she said thoughtfully. "Hmm, his older brother though… Take forty years off me and I'd make him a man."

"Do you know where I can find Jared Sieme?" Kade repeated impatiently.

"Maybe."

Kade reached into his purse, pulling out a bronze coin. She pointed towards the back of the town. "On the hill." Grinning, he tossed her the coin and walked away.

Found her, he told Connery.

‡‡‡

"Ready to go?" Jared asked.

Keegan slipped on her shoes. "Yup."

From the kitchen, his mother called, "Be home early, please."

"Yes ma'am," Keegan answered as the door banged shut behind them.

Jared saw her out of the corner of his eye and had to fully glance at her before his momentary confusion subsided. He still wasn't used to seeing women in trousers—especially a woman in Nico's clothes. Keegan had worried "wear-and-tear" would ruin her trousers—jeans, as she called them. Once Nico's pants had been hemmed, they fit well enough, and she'd shortened the shirtsleeves, so they only came to her elbows. He thought it was indecent, but Keegan seemed comfortable, and he'd learned you couldn't make her do anything she didn't want to.

"Why do we need to be home early?" Keegan asked.

"It's my birthday," Jared said. "Mother probably has a special dinner planned."

She told him, "Happy birthday!"

Jared chuckled. "Thank you."

"How old are you now?"

"Twenty."

"Damn it, you're older than me."

"You?"

"Nineteen. Today's May eleventh, right?"

He nodded.

"I'll be twenty in a month."

"The eleventh?"

"Tenth."

In the two weeks Keegan had been training, the first had been spent practicing in the mud patch outside the barn. As the days progressed, she'd grown stronger and finally a rogue mud ball had hit the barn door, splintering a few of the planks. After that, they'd taken to training near the forest's edge, far from anything they could break—other than themselves.

Inside the barn, the sheep were gone, as Jude, Lucas, and Carter had taken them out to graze. Nico normally went with them but was helping Alessandra with a bit of cleaning.

Keegan struggled under the weight of the saddle as they tacked up the horses, but she managed to get it on Bastille's back. Earlier in the week, Nico had pointed out her horse needed a name. She'd debated between Midnight and Bastille and chose the less stereotypical moniker for a black horse.

On the first day they'd moved location, Jared had discovered Keegan didn't know how to saddle a horse. She'd learnt quickly, but always had him check her work. Leading the horses outside, they mounted.

Keegan spurred Bastille, flying past, calling, "Slowpoke!"

Jared chased after her with a grin.

In the distance, trees that were at first no more than a hazy line, began to gain detail. As they neared, birds hopped to higher branches, tittering.

"What are we doing today?" she asked eagerly as they turned the horses loose.

"Combat," Jared answered, rolling up his sleeves.

Keegan gave him an impish grin. "Any ground rules?"

"No maiming. The point is to subdue the other."

"Okay," she said, causing the earth to encase his feet.

"Wait until I'm ready," he chastised, releasing himself.

Keegan sang, "All is fair in love and war."

Rolling his eyes, Jared sent an earthen ball her way.

She swatted it away. "Come on, you've gotta do better than that to hit me now!"

He sent her another orb.

This time, she stopped it, straining to do so, and returned it, adding three of her own. While he was preoccupied with stopping the projectiles, she tackled him. Maneuvering herself until she had his arm in her grasp, she placed it between her knees and started bending it in the opposite direction.

"Argh!" he yelped, feeling strain in his shoulder and elbow.

Keegan immediately released his arm and rolled onto her knees.

"What the royik was that?" he roared.

"Me winning. And what does royik mean? I haven't been able to figure that one out yet."

"The point of this isn't to win," he growled. "We're doing this to teach you how to use magic defensively. And who taught you how to fight like that?" He rubbed his shoulder. "I think royik is your version of fuck."

"Royik is definitely not an English word," she stated. "What language is it from?"

"The Old Language," he told her, still massaging his shoulder.

"Why cuss in another language?"

Jared shrugged. "Why use the curse words you do?"

"Touché. And, sorry, but winning is totally the point. And you learn to fight like that when you've got four brothers and we all do martial arts."

"What's martial arts?"

"Badass fighting. Shall we go again?"
Guardedly, he nodded.

✝✝✝

Silently, they made their way up the hill. Rounding the back of the house, the Vosjnik dismounted.

"Be prepared for anything," Connery instructed. "Kade, with me."

Kade followed him up the porch stairs and Connery knocked on the door.

A woman opened it. "Can I—" She noticed the griffin emblem on their cuirasses and tried to slam the door.

"You should not have done that, Alessandra," Connery said, retrieving her name telepathically as he pulled her onto the porch.

Alessandra shrieked as she was slammed against the railing.

"Where is the girl?"

"Wh-what girl?"

"Keegan."

"I don't—" she started as a rock smashed through the railing.

Kade shielded his face and, as the debris settled, looked for the source. A redheaded boy stood behind the Vosjnik, several rocks suspended around him.

"His name is Nico," Connery said, hauling Alessandra down the steps.

The boy sent a rock towards Cralter and Kade reached for his magic, letting the stone sail harmlessly by.

Behind him, Alessandra screamed for the child to run.

Instead, the boy attacked again and Cralter reciprocated, sending a fireball towards Nico. The boy dodged, and the fireball sailed onto the porch, setting it alight.

"You should listen to your mother," Kade said.

Nico's scowl deepened as he charged.

He let the boy approach and, before the fight began, had him pinned, even as he tried his hardest to fight back.

"Stop," Kade hissed.

Connery dragged Alessandra towards them and forced her to her knees.

Kade pulled Nico to his feet, twisting an arm behind his back. Grabbing a fistful of the boy's hair, he snarled, "Tell us where we can find Keegan."

"Say nothing," Alessandra instructed.

He drew a knife and pressed it into Nico's side. "Tell us!"

Alessandra shook her head. "I don't know where she is."

Kade studied her face. "She's telling the truth."

Connery clenched his jaw. "What about you, boy, do you know where the girl is? You know something."

Nico wavered and glanced at his mother.

Growing impatient, Connery drew his dagger and prepared to bring it across Alessandra's throat.

"Say nothing," she implored.

Just before the knife touched his mother's flesh, Nico yelled, "At the tree line!"

Connery paused and grinned, then sliced open Alessandra's neck. Her body dropped heavily and Kade knew it would be a relatively painless death.

Nico grew hysterical, fighting desperately, and Kade knew he could become a threat in his distress. He wrapped an arm around the boy's neck and applied pressure. Nico clawed at his arms in vain and slowly became limp.

Kade lowered him to the ground, telling Brennian get him a length of rope

"Just kill him," Vitia growled.

He bound Nico's hands. "No, he'll make an excellent addition to the king's army."

As he worked, Connery began giving orders, "Kade and Brennian, look on the northern edge—"

Kade ignored the rest of the instructions; they didn't pertain to him.

✝✝✝

Jared landed with a thump and found Keegan sitting atop his chest. She kept her body low and placed a forearm against his neck. Her elbows were in the crooks of his shoulders, her hair gathering over one shoulder to hang down like a curtain.

She smiled mischievously, before rolling over to lie on the grass. "You're easy."

He sat up, his body sore; meanwhile, she'd barely broken a sweat. They always began fighting using magic, but it never lasted long.

She propped herself up on her elbows. "You've gotta learn to fight."

"I can fight," he snapped, insulted by the insinuation, "but I won't hit a woman."

She rolled her eyes, letting her head fall back with an exaggerated sigh. "God, there's that stupid rule even here."

"Pardon?"

"The rule that guys can't hit girls. Y'all treat us like we're gonna break."

"I never said you were." He said as she rolled her eyes again. "I most certainly did not say you were going to break."

"You say you can't hit women. Why?"

"Just… It… it's not- women are… delicate."

Keegan rose. "I'm about as far from delicate as you can get."

Jared took a step towards her. "You're taking this entirely out of proportion."

She shoved him back. "Am not."

Out of instinct, he raised a fist.

"Do it! Hit me!"

He clenched his jaw, staring at her angrily.

"Coward."

"I'm not going to hit you."

She began to rant.

He sighed; Keegan was so incredibly hardheaded and hotheaded. Deciding to give in, he let his mind blank momentarily and his fist found its target.

She stared back at him, rubbing her jaw, then, with a wry smile, said, "Good. Now we can have some fair fights."

✞✞✞

Aros tossed his head impatiently, forcing Kade to resituate himself in the saddle as he stared through the foliage concealing them from their target. He didn't know who the man was, but doubted he'd be a problem.

Aros shifted again, causing the foliage to rustle, and Brennian's horse let out a soft snicker.

The man jumped to his feet. "Someone's there," Kade heard him say.

Kade urged Aros through the underbrush.

Keegan said something and the man moved protectively in front of her.

"Give us the girl," Kade said.

"Why should I?" the man asked boldly.

Kade saw through his pretense as he dismounted. "The king wants her and you're ill-equipped to protect her."

"You underestimate us," Keegan said, stepping forward defiantly.

Brennian laughed, dismounting.

"It doesn't matter," Kade asserted. "You'll come willingly."

"Why the hell would I do that?" Keegan bit.

"You have nowhere else to go," Brennian answered brutally.

Keegan paused and he could see the wheels in her head turning. "Jared, where are the others?"

"What do you mean?" Jared asked.

Keegan turned towards him, urgency in her voice, "Where are the others?" She saw the smoke in the distance. "Oh god…"

Jared turned as well.

Kade could only think them fools as grabbed the back of Jared's shirt with one hand, his shoulder with the other, and threw him to the ground.

Brennian dealt with Keegan, pressing a knife against her neck, wrapping his free arm around her shoulders, hissing, "You're coming with us."

She brought her foot up between his legs. "Like hell I am!"

Grunting, Brennian loosened his grip slightly. Keegan tried to take advantage of this, but, keeping his composure, the swordsman threw her to the ground.

Kade heard the breath knocked from her lungs and, before she could get up, caused the earth to pin her. He then focused on Jared, who was starting to fight back. As he blocked Jared's strike, Kade sent a rock to hit the back of Brennian's head, rendering him unconscious. Kade retaliated against Jared's attack with an uppercut to his abdomen. As Jared doubled over, he grabbed his head and smashed it into his knee. Jared fell to the ground, stunned or unconscious—it didn't matter which. Coming back to Keegan, he retrieved Brennian's knife along the way.

"You're an elemental?" she accused.

"Yes," Kade answered, kneeling beside her. "I'm going to release you; don't fight or try to run."

Keegan got to her feet slowly, a hard look in her eyes. She stared at him for a moment before beginning to move her hands.

He stepped aside as a rock flew past his head. With a jerk of his fingers, earth rose, wrapping around Keegan's wrists, and pulled her to the ground.

She collapsed to her knees, hands held awkwardly against the grass. "Why are you doing this?"

"To keep you from Caius."

"Please, don— Wait, what? Why do you wanna keep me from Caius?"

"Revenge."

"For what?" Jared asked, shakily getting to his feet, blood dripping from his nose and mouth.

"Killing my parents," Kade growled.

"Understandable," Keegan said, some of the hatred and panic leaving her voice. "But how does kidnapping *me* accomplish that?"

"I'm trying to protect you. Caius knows where you are, so I'm taking you somewhere safe."

"And where would that be?" Jared asked.

"The Lazado."

Keegan said, "Why didn't you just say that from the get-go?"

"From the what?"

"From the beginning."

Kade motioned to Brennian. "I had to keep up appearances."

"Why should we trust you?"

"Trust me, don't trust me. I don't care." He released Keegan's hands from the earthen bonds and grabbed the front of her shirt, pulling her to her feet. "But you will come with me—one way or another."

"Don't hold your breath."

His fist connected with her nose.

Keegan hurled a strange curse at him. Blood trickled into her mouth, and she turned her head to spit it out, flecking the grass with red. "So, it's go quietly or you beat the crap out of me?" she snapped.

"If that's what I must do."

"Fine, we'll do it your way."

"There is no *we*. Only you."

"Like hell—"

"Show me your wrist," he instructed Jared. When Jared hesitated, Kade pushed the point of the knife into Keegan's neck, drawing blood. "Show me, your wrist."

Scowling, Jared complied, confirming Kade's suspicion.

Withdrawing, he pushed Keegan towards Jared. "Get ready to leave."

"Do we get a name to work with?" she asked as he returned with their horses in hand.

"Kade Tavin. Mount up."

"Not yet." She took a breath as if to gather up her courage. "I have a stipulation."

He couldn't help but laugh. "What would that be?"

"We go help Jared's family."

Kade looked at Jared and noticed the resemblance to Nico and Alessandra. If he had any inkling Nico was still alive, it could—no, *would*—complicate matters.

"By now, there's no one left to help." He shoved Darkheart's reins into her hand. "And now isn't the time to grieve."

"They can't be dead," Keegan said, almost pleading. "We can still save them."

"Stop," Jared said weakly.

Keegan turned to him, baffled. "How can you say that? This is your family!"

Jared pointed at Kade. "Do you see the star branded on the side of his thumb? That means he's a member of the Vosjnik."

"So?"

Kade put it frankly, "We're not known for being merciful."

"But… they didn't do anything!"

"They harbored you. Now, get on the horse before I'm forced to do something you'll regret," Kade told her snidely.

"I'd love to see you try," Keegan spat.

"As you wish." He dropped a shoulder, placing it against her hips, allowing him to easily throw her over his shoulder.

Keegan yelped in surprise as he made his way towards her horse. Over the shock, she started beating against his back and yelling obscenities. As he shifted her onto the saddle, now with some leverage, she managed to get her foot between their bodies and kicked him back before sliding off the horse. Before she could go far, he grabbed her hands. She pulled against him, but his grip was unbreakable.

Taking the reins, he secured her wrists with them.

"Let me go!" she screamed, half pleading.

He stepped back. "No."

She noticed Jared hadn't moved. "Why aren't you helping me?"

"Because he's right," Jared answered. "There's nothing we can do."

Keegan shook her head. "We don't know that!"

"Yes, we do," Kade snapped, becoming impatient. "Now get on the horse!"

"Not until we help his family," Keegan repeated belligerently.

At this point, he knew she wasn't going to go voluntarily. He marched over to Aros.

"Get on the horse," he instructed Jared. When Jared didn't move, he roared, "Get on the royiken horse!"

He rummaged through Aros's saddlebag and pulled out two lengths of rope. When he returned, Keegan was attempting to pull the reins loose using her teeth. He grabbed her foot, hoisting her up, and forced her foot into the stirrup.

"What are you doing?" she shrieked, kicking at him with her free foot.

He tied her foot to the stirrup and stepped back.

She looked over her shoulder, trying to figure out what he'd done and realized he'd made it so she had no choice but to do as he wished. Kegan gave him a look of utter loathing, then swung her leg over the horse and began trying to lift the reins over his head.

Kade lunged forward, grabbing the reins. "Oh no you don't."

"Let go," she said, jabbing her heels in. The horse started forward, but just pivoted around Kade.

He reached up and untied her hands.

At once, she began slapping at him.

Taking the second length of rope, he tied her hands to the saddle horn. A stream of oaths spilled from her mouth, all foreign to him.

"I warned you," he said, taking the reins and securing them to Aros's saddle.

CHAPTER 9

A dark column of smoke marred the otherwise pristine sky ahead. His lungs burnt and there was a stitch in his side, but Lucas refused to stop running. He knew to expect the worst but prayed to Sola and Lunos anyway. He'd never been religious but was shouting out to any god that might be listening now. Behind him, he could hear the heavy breaths of his father and brother as they chased after him.

Lucas reached the crest of the hill and froze. The house still blazed violently, there were deep gouges in the earth, and a body lay in the grass. An excruciating ache entered his heart.

Turning the body over, he stared into his mother's lifeless eyes. He knew he was screaming but could hear nothing. Hands pushed him out of the way and his father took his place. Jude gently rocked as he pulled his wife close against his chest.

Lucas turned away, anguish and anger rushing forth. He clenched his hands as the desire—the need—to hit something struck him. A sob sounded in his throat and could feel his nails cutting into his palms, but he only clenched his fists tighter.

A rider approached.

"What happened?" Jameson asked, swinging from the horse.

Lucas shook his head, covering his eyes with a hand. Hot tears rolled down his cheeks, mingling with the blood from his palm.

"Are any of you hurt?"

"No," Jude answered.

Lucas turned to his father. Tears still ran down his cheeks and into his moustache, but his voice conveyed composure.

"Have you seen Nico and Jared?"

"No. But you need to leave."

Jude brushed a strand of hair from Alessandra's blank face. "Why?"

"This was the work of the Vosjnik."

Jude's head snapped up. "How do you know that?"

"They came through town asking about Keegan."

"Did you tell them anything?" Lucas demanded.

"Of course not!"

"Then how did they know to come here?" he yelled.

"I'm not sure," Jameson told him. "Now, please, you need to go."

Jude wiped his eyes. "We bury her, then we leave."

"Where will we go?" Carter choked.

"East. It's where your brothers would've headed. I hope."

Jameson asked awkwardly, "Is there anything I can do for you?"

Jude picked up Alessandra. "Tell the town we perished in the fire."

"Then you'd best leave now. The rest of the townsfolk will be here soon."

Nodding, Jude sent Carter to the barn to retrieve a shovel and their spare packs.

Carter returned quickly, handing a pack to Lucas, tears still streaming down his face. It suddenly struck Lucas the only things to their names were the clothes on their backs and these few meager supplies.

"Come on, boys," Jude said quietly, "we have a long walk."

Lucas went to stand by his father and looked out over the hills. This land, once so familiar, was now soaked with sadness and blood. Come hell or high tide, he was going to kill those who had done this to him—to his family. They would pay.

‡‡‡

The world was rocking; up and down it went in a steady motion. Nico's head rolled side to side. Thud-ump, thud-ump went horses' hooves. He opened his eyes and saw tree trunks and leaves rushing past. Nico tried to turn, but arms reaching around him to hold the reins stopped him. He remembered what had happened and began to fight.

"Stop," growled a voice.

Nico brought his elbow back and it met a cuirass, "No!" His hand went numb.

"Halt," another voice called.

The horse was reined in, and it was then he noticed the rest of the party. Six men and a woman, seven total. He knew they were the Vosjnik, but it seemed they were missing a member.

The man behind him dismounted, pulling Nico with him.

He stared at the man, who had feathery hair so black it seemed blue, and intense eyes, pale as water.

"Release me," Nico demanded. If his hands weren't bound, he'd already be using magic.

"Drug him," a man commanded.

Nico assumed this was Connery, the Vosjnik's leader, who wasn't what he'd imagined. He was of average height, instead of the giant of stories. His hair was dark gray and in places stark white. Scars crisscrossed his face in deep lines and Nico had no doubt more covered the rest of his body.

"Who has the ether?" the man holding him asked.

"I do," the woman said, producing a bottle of jade green liquid from her saddlebags.

After soaking a rag, she passed it on, and the man pressed it against Nico's mouth and nose.

Nico held his breath, but it only delayed the inevitable. The first breath was the worst; it felt like all the moisture was sucked from his throat. He began to cough and slowly his mind began to feel fuzzy as he lost access to his magic.

"He has had enough, Dax," Connery said. "We will make camp here."

Dax withdrew and Nico collapsed coughing and dry heaving.

"But we haven't found them yet," the woman sniped.

"There is plenty of time to do so, Vitia" Connery said, tethering his horse. "The girl is with at least one unwilling companion; they will be slow moving. Besides, it will do no good to push too far or hard."

Glancing at Vitia, Nico could see she was fuming, and the filed horn stubs protruding from her head only added to her fearsome appearance.

Noticing Nico had recovered, Dax hauled him over to a tree.

"Sit." When he resisted, Dax pressed into the muscle in his shoulder, saying again, "Sit."

Nico winced but remained upright. Frustrated, Dax kicked his legs out from under him and his head hit the tree, sending spots across his vision.

Dax wound a long length of rope around Nico and the tree. When he finished securing him, he returned to his comrades and began setting up camp.

Nico watched their activities, wondering if he could name all members from the tales and rumors, while straining against the rope, which was tight and beginning to chafe his arms.

Based upon exchanges, he knew who Connery, Dax, and Vitia were. He found himself eyeing Vitia's horns suspiciously, wondering if they'd been grown magically. The man who lit the fire had done so with elemental magic, so he was Cralter. The former fire elemental had been something of a nuisance, thus, when replaced, his death was celebrated. He guessed the man with the bow strung across his back and bronzed skin to be Thahan, the archer. The other two, he didn't know. One had thin blond hair that seemed to be constantly blowing in some breeze. The other had a long sword he held as tenderly as one would a woman.

The group ate, then lounged around the fire, while Nico's stomach gurgled loudly enough for them to hear.

Cralter noticed and asked, "Should we feed him?"

Vitia laughed. "No, I want to see how long it takes for him to grovel."

"I will never beg," Nico called, eliciting laughter.

Vitia smirked. "Better men have yielded."

Nico stared at them with a look of determination.

"Whatever helps you sleep at night," the man with the sword sniggered.

✞✞✞

Night had settled, forcing Kade to let them stop, and Keegan waited agitatedly for him to release her restraints.

He approached Bastille, beginning to undo the rope securing her foot to the stirrup. "I did warn you," he said, moving to the rope around her hands.

Free, she dismounted, then turned to Kade, making to smack him.

He caught her wrist. "I don't recommend that." He and swung her around, twisting her arms across her chest, then pushed her forward, sending her stumbling into Jared.

She turned, but, before she could lunge, Jared wrapped his arms around her. "Let me go," she snarled.

"You need to calm down," Jared said. His words were barely a whisper, indicative of someone who was only just holding it together. He likely still couldn't fully comprehend all that had happened.

"I am calm," Keegan said. Even she knew she was lying.

"No, you're overreacting," Kade corrected, standing before her.

"You're under-reacting!"

"There was absolutely nothing *you* or anyone else could've done."

She screamed, "There had to've been something!"

Kade declined to respond and they glared at each other icily.

Keegan took several deep breaths and Jared tentatively unwrapped his arms. Setting her jaw, she stormed away but didn't go far for fear of getting lost. Finding a large pine tree, she sank down against its trunk, her emotions raging, each one vying to be heard. Anger spoke the loudest and kept her cheeks flushed. That faded to sadness and tears leaked from her eyes. Defeat was the last to make an appearance as she realized Kade was right.

Getting to her feet, she brushed away the dirt and wiped her eyes. Back at camp, she took a seat beside Jared. Kade offered her a piece of bread, which she snatched from him.

They sat silently around the fire, Jared staring blankly into the flames, Kade sharpening his knife, and her eying Kade. Now that she was doing that—rather than plotting his demise—she noticed his wavy, red-brown hair with a rebellious curl across his wide forehead. And how his eyes were a hard hazel with piercing shards of green. And the freckles dotting his face that even made appearances on the backs of his hands.

She knew they were going to be water and oil.

‡‡‡

The quarter moon hung low on the eastern edge of the sky, giving them just enough light to see by.

Jude placed the last shovelful of dirt on the grave and stepped back, tears gliding down his face.

"I wish I could've done better for you." With a whisper Lucas strained to hear, Jude ended, "I will always love you."

They might not have been able to give her a proper grave, but Lucas knew his mother would've been satisfied. She rested beneath the boughs of one of the few oak trees in the forest and wildflowers were amok around her.

Jude turned to his sons, pulling them into an embrace, and there they stood, the shattered remains of the Sieme family, lost in sorrow. No words were spoken and slowly they pulled apart.

Lucas shouldered his pack and stared into the dark forest. He'd learned to not dread it, but now it seemed to mock him. Gazing down at the white cloth around his hands, he saw red dots were already pushing through like macabre daisies. He clenched his fists, sending shooting pain through his palms. It was a good pain; it would remind him to keep going, to kill the Vosjnik. Unclenching his fists, his fingertips were lightly bathed in crimson. Gritting his teeth, he stepped past the first line of trees.

Night truly overtook them as the high branches blocked what little light there was from the waxing moon. They were slow-moving and their sullen footfalls snapped branches with shattering cracks. Time took on no meaning, the silence over them only intensifying their dejection.

Well into the night, long after even the night creatures had returned to their roosts, they stopped to make camp. They didn't bother to build a fire, and no one specifically stayed up on watch, but Lucas knew none of them slept.

‡‡‡

They are gone. Jared stared up at the dark underside of the forest. *They are gone.* That single unforgiving phrase repeated itself. He lifted his head and looked around. *They are gone.* Keegan lay beside him, wrapped in the blissful serenity of her dreams. He envied her. *They are gone.* Kade was leaned against a tree, eyes glazed over as they watched the flames finish their dance. *They. Are. Gone.*

Jared stood and slipped into the woods. *They are gone.* Ahead, the forest was pitch-black, only a few streams of moonlight pervading through the canopy. He found his feet leading the way as his mind was overcome. *They are gone.* He was suddenly running, branches whipping him in the face and pulling at his clothes. Finally, he could run no more and sank down against the trunk of a tree, ragged, agonizing breaths shaking his body. *They are gone.*

Tears streamed down his face. From somewhere far off, an anguished, animal-like cry broke the silence. *They are gone.* The sound pulled at his heart, tearing it in two. *They are gone.* He was no longer sitting. He lashed out, punching a tree and he kept punching until his exhausted body could spend no more energy. *They are gone.* He fell to his knees, sucking in the cool night air. Warm blood ran between his fingers and dropped onto the dirt in heavy globules. *They are gone.* The pain in his hands was nothing compared to what he felt inside.

But I am here. He rose from the ground. *I am here.* He kept repeating those words. Tears would do him no good nor raise the dead. *I am here, and they are gone.* As he re-entered camp, he noticed a few strips of bandage where he'd been lying. *I am here. I can make a difference.* He sat, his body dropping like a rock, and wrapped his bloody knuckles, the cloth stinging as it touched the open wounds. *I am here.* He lay back, his hands folded across his chest. *They are gone. I am here. I can still protect Keegan.* He'd taken her in to help her and that was exactly what he intended to do. *I am here. I will protect Keegan.*

‡‡‡

"I solved your riddle," Braxton told Alyck, shutting the door.

His uncle gave him a coy smile.

"You did not mean a book covered in stone, you meant it is the color of stone and the pages are silver gilded."

"I take it you found it then," Alyck said.

"Not yet, but I have the library's auxiliaries searching for it."

Alyck took a moment to answer. "You will never find it that way. This book is… ever-changing, showing each who holds it what they need most."

Braxton frowned. "So, I have to find it myself?"

Alyck rose from the chair. "Correct. And you have been given everything you need to do so."

"It will take who-knows how long to search the library."

Alyck placed a hand on his shoulder. "It is exactly where I say it is."

Braxton gave him a scowl before taking his leave.

The walk back to his room was shrouded in darkness, but before he knew it, he was there. As he opened the door, the pulsing light began and he made his way to the trunk, digging around until he found the book. He blinked and was no longer in his chambers.

Braxton looked around, perplexed and disoriented as he was still in the hallway outside the Blind Prophet's chamber. An uneasy feeling formed in his stomach, and he cautiously began making his way back to his room.

As he walked, he thought about Alyck's words, trying to recall them exactly. Slowly, they came to him: 'I would recommend going to the place where you have that lovely little scrap of information.' *Have.* He began rushing through the halls.

Reaching his room, he dashed to the trunk, throwing open the lid. Alyck had told him to look where he was *keeping* the books, not where he had *found* them. He grabbed the larger tome and stared at it, willing it to morph. After moments of nothing, he placed it on the floor, repeating the process with the thinner book, getting the same result.

He sighed and was about to close the trunk when a blotch of purple caught his eye. Moving an old cloak, he revealed a book. Picking it up, he recognized it as a sketchbook Alyck had given him. Turning it over, he looked at the pages and was pleased to find they were gilded in silver.

As the book began to transform, he dropped it in surprise. Its color slowly drained away, leaving it a warm black. Cautiously, he picked it up and flipped open the cover. The title was written in neat script, *The Evolution of Languages*.

CHAPTER 10

Someone was nudging her. Keegan extracted an arm from beneath herself and shooed them off. The bedroll was yanked away, causing her to bolt up. In the middle of the clearing, the campfire was running on fumes and morning sunlight shone through the canopy of leaves.

"Time to leave," Kade said from above her.

She rubbed the sleep from her eyes. "What time is it?"

"Morning."

"No shit, Sherlock. I meant like what—oh, never mind; y'all don't have clocks."

Kade stared at her blankly for a moment. "Time to go."

"We gonna eat breakfast?"

"No."

"Why not?"

"No food."

"God," Keegan mumbled, "you're unprepared." She didn't regret making the comment but didn't imagine it did her any favors. And it wasn't like she was awake enough to control her mouth currently.

"What did you say?"

Deciding to not hold back, not in light of what Kade had put them through, she said, "I said, you're unprepared." She then noticed Jared, who had dark circles under his eyes and his knuckles were wrapped in bandages.

Seeing her gaze, he looked away.

Keegan wrapped her arms around Jared and told him quietly, "It's gonna be okay."

He didn't say anything, but his tenseness was all the answer she needed. It would never be okay; he'd just lost his entire family.

"It's not like I was able to prepare for this," Kade commented.

"How? You were looking for me. I assume you had to bring food."

"Yes, enough for me."

"Is it that much of a stretch to pack food for three?"

"It would've looked suspicious."

"But—"

"Enough," Jared interjected. "Please."

Keegan let her face fade to a softer expression. "We'll need to stop at the next town."

"We were going to do that anyway," Kade said, adjusting a buckle on his saddle.

‡‡‡

They'd been riding for no more than a few hours when Kade stopped in a clearing.

"Stopping for the day already?" Keegan questioned.

"No. The next town isn't far from here," Kade replied.

"Isn't that a good thing?"

"Do you want to get caught?"

"No…" Her brows furrowed in confusion. "But how will going into town get us caught?"

"The townspeople will see you."

Keegan shrugged. "So?"

"When the Vosjnik come looking, they'll be able to tell them which way we went."

"People aren't gonna remember us."

"Maybe not Jared or I, but you, yes."

"Why would they remember me?"

Jared could see Kade was aggravated. But, however many questions Keegan had, they were valid. And he was too exhausted from the trauma of everything to deal with playing mediator.

Kade said, "You'll be staying here."

"Fine, whatever," she conceded. "Am I staying alone?"

"No."

"Who else is staying?"

"I am."

Keegan scrunched her nose. "I'd rather Jared stayed."

Seeing a potential fight about to start, Jared commented, "It's fine, I'll go. I just need some money."

Kade looked at him surprised. "Didn't you bring any with you?"

Keegan drew out the word, "No." Then she added, "We didn't expect to get attacked by you—" At least she could sometimes stop herself from being antagonistic.

Kade stared at her. "One should always be prepared."

She stared incredulously. "Says the man who didn't pack food!"

Kade started towards her, and Jared stepped in front of him. "Maybe your status as a soldier can help."

Kade's gaze lingered on Keegan for a moment longer before he walked away with clenched his fists.

Jared gave a sigh of relief. With enough provocation, Kade would strike Keegan—repeatedly.

✞✞✞

Although he hadn't planned on going into town, Kade appreciated the opportunity. It had been less than a day and Keegan was wearing on him in ways no one ever had before. It was almost like her mere existence irked him.

Before emerging onto the road leading into the town— which was closer to a village—he donned his cuirass; the sigil would give him credibility. Passing between the small houses, people saw him and rushed inside, no doubt locking the doors. Children's faces peered through shutter slats, watching with fearful curiosity.

As he dismounted, a middle-aged man approached. "Can I help you?"

"Do you represent the people of this village?"

"Yes."

"Taxes are due."

"We just paid them. Two days past, I swear it."

"The king has increased them."

"Again? We barely have enough to live by."

"Taxes or conscripts," Kade offered. "Take your pick."

"Can you give us a few days?"

"No."

"Then we won't be able to pay."

"I'm feeling generous; give me any items of value and I'll sell them in your stead. You have an hour."

The man was well-aware Kade was lying, but the fear of retaliation made him cooperate.

Kade walked away and leaned against a house while the man made his way solemnly to the townspeople who had started emerging from their homes. Faces began to display anger and disdain, but he was immune to remorse; he'd done worse—*much* worse.

Hearing a giggle, he looked around. To his right, a face disappeared behind the corner of the building he was leaning against. He turned back to study the people, watching the house out of the corner of his eye. When it looked like he wasn't paying attention, the face returned; it belonged to a little girl with straggly blonde hair. He looked over and again she disappeared behind the corner.

"I know you're there."

No response.

"Come out."

The girl did as instructed.

"You shouldn't spy on people," he said, squatting down.

"Sorry, 'ister," the girl mumbled. Looking at him, she cocked her head to the side, "What your name, 'ister?"

"Ka—"

She interrupted, "Mamma says soldiers 're scary."

"Are you not afraid of me?"

She shook her head.

"You should be," he said, straightening up.

"Why?"

"Because I'm a soldier."

She wrapped her arms around his thigh. "That not mean you be a bad person, 'ister Ka."

Kade was lost for words; how was he supposed to react?

A woman began calling for a child and Kade pushed her away. "Go."

He expected her to run off. When she didn't, he looked down at her again. She held her hand out as if she wanted him to shake it.

"Mamma says it's polite to shake when you meet a new person."

Kade begrudgingly complied, if only to make her go away.

Slowly, people approached him with a few coins or valuables in hand. By the end of the hour, he'd acquired enough to buy what they'd need in the next town over.

He shouldered the bag he'd commandeered and was about to mount Aros when he paused. "My squad's beginning to run low on food."

"What do you want us to do about that?" someone asked irritated.

"Supply us with food," Kade growled.

"You'll have to pay for it."

Kade pulled out a few ill-begotten coins and the butcher and baker left to shortly return with several loaves of bread and packages of meat.

Kade mounted Aros, saying, "Until next time."

✝✝✝

Lucas was surprised he'd slept, even if it wasn't for long. The same appeared to be true for his father and Carter. No one spoke and the silence was heavy. Carter's stomach gave a soft growl and Lucas rummaged through his pack, producing a few pieces of jerky.

Carter bit at the meat with little gusto.

Finally, Jude stood, beginning the day. Their pace was slow, giving them all too much time to think.

Lucas could feel his anger welling up and clenched his fists to push it down. Opening his hands, he saw more blood had risen to the surface of the bandages.

"You have to stop doing that," Jude told him quietly.

As he walked, he thought of what he was going to do to the Vosjnik. He would beat them into the dust, making their faces unrecognizable to even their mothers. He would flay the flesh from their bones, the whip cutting as deep as his laughter. He would watch as fire melted their forms, the yellow and orange flames turning red with their blood. He would let wolves tear them apart, as beast should destroy beast. He would drown them, the weight of their sins pulling them under.

Lost in thought, he barely noticed the passing of day and only hunger reminded him he was human. Soon enough, night found them again and they were forced to stop. A fire was lit and he watched the flames dance in the dark.

Fire gives light, but it also destroys, he thought. It was something his mother often said, especially when he was angry. Had. As she'd explained it, a bit of anger helped you push through, but you had to be careful to not let it consume you.

He started at his hands. The blood staining the cloth had turned brown. Lucas clenched his fist, turning the spots red once more. He would feed the flames and use them to destroy the Vosjnik.

‡‡‡

Night was upon the castle. Aron was headed to Alyck, and this was not going to be pleasant. That afternoon he had found a note in his chambers. Though only two words—*See me*—it had formed a pit in his stomach.

Hesitating, he opened the door, the hinges protesting.

Inside, Alyck sat, eyebrows furrowed in frustration. "Stay away from Shiloh."

Aron made to protest.

"You do not understand the reality of it."

"But—"

Alyck roared irately, "There will be no happy ending!" Then he repeated in a whisper, "There will be no happy ending."

"You cannot know that."

"I cannot know that?" Alyck roared, rising from the chair. "*I* cannot know that! I know more than you could ever hope to know, Little King. Now, please, listen."

"I love her."

"Then let her go. Or there will come a time when you wished you had."

Aron choked, "I cannot do that."

"But you must. Please, trust me."

"I love her," Aron reiterated.

"Then I cannot help you. Leave, there is nothing I can do for you at present."

"But I did not ask for help. You requested I come."

"Leave!"

Aron set his jaw and slammed the door on his way out. He refused to believe his happiness with Shiloh was fleeting. They would be happy together—he would not entertain any other outcome.

‡‡‡

Nico awoke shortly after first light. He didn't have to watch the Vosjnik break camp for long until the fire was all that was left.

Dax approached him and, scowling, began to undo the rope.

With the ropes slackened, Nico pushed to his feet and tried to run.

Dax was faster and grabbed a fistful of his hair. "Pass me the ether," he snapped to Vitia.

Nico choked and what little magic he'd regained overnight disappeared. He sunk to the ground hacking and heaving, yelping as Dax dragged him over to the horses and lifted him into the saddle.

"Why do I have to look after the kid?" Dax grumbled as he mounted behind Nico.

"Because I say so," Connery answered. "Move out."

Six horses followed the Commander as they made their way through the forest, no one talking.

The day passed slowly. Once, they had to double back because they were following the wrong trail. Another time, they stopped to relieve themselves, which was awkward for Nico with so many eyes upon him and his hands bound.

They stopped at dusk and again he was secured to a tree. His stomach gurgled loudly and Vitia asked if he was ready to beg. He remained quiet.

One by one, everyone retired, leaving Cralter on watch. Eventually, even he drifted off.

So much for that, Nico thought, beginning to strain against the ropes, holding back a cry of frustration when he couldn't break through them.

Resting his head against the tree, he noticed part of the rope had begun to fray where it had rubbed against the rough bark. His heart fluttered and he began moving his body in a sideways fashion to wear through the restraint further. It was a slow-going business as the rope around him and the bark against his back pulled at his body. Finally, a strand snapped.

He eyed the horses and crept towards them. A branch cracked and he froze. Cralter stirred but didn't wake and he began slinking forward again. With care, he made his way through the sleeping bodies and had almost made it across when a hand grabbed his ankle.

"Where do you think you're going?" snarled Dax, as he tumbled to the ground.

Frantically, Nico felt along the ground, finding a rock. Grabbing it, he smashed it into Dax's face, who yelped and released him.

The others roused and groggily drew their weapons, doing their best to not stumble over the uneven terrain.

Nico scrambled to his feet and took off, branches whipping him in the face. Behind, he could hear the Vosjnik giving chase. Soon, his breaths became ragged and a stitch formed in his side—but he dared not stop.

A weight pushed him forward and he fell. Turning onto his back, he stared up into Dax's seething face, blood dripping from a gash in his cheek. Nico fought against him, but his efforts were useless.

Dax looked around. "Where's that noxþox woman? Vitia!" he called. When there was no response, he called again.

This time there was a faint reply.

"Over here," Dax yelled.

A few minutes passed and Vitia appeared from the shadows. Sidling over to them, she handed Dax a length of rope while Nico let insults roll off his tongue.

Vitia kneeled beside him. "Look at this, the little whelp wants to talk like a man." She grabbed his jaw, "Silence."

He went to continue his tirade but found no sound escaped his lips.

Vitia stood, pulling her hair back, hands awkwardly grazing her horns. Her brows creased as she looked at the sky. "Do you see that?"

"See what?" Dax questioned.

Vitia pointed up. "That."

Nico looked and saw the remnants of a trail of smoke.

"Vito," Dax murmured, sharing a look with her, before they took off running, pulling Nico along.

Bursting into camp, Vitia exclaimed, "We found them!"

CHAPTER 11

Jared stared at the dying flames. Kade slept against a tree and Keegan was on her stomach half underneath the bedroll. He grabbed a stick and stirred the embers. It was hard to not cry. If done quietly, no one would know, and he could mourn in peace. But if he let his emotions reign now, there would be no bottling them back up and he couldn't afford that. Knowing the fire would soon die, he added a few branches to its meager flames. As they burned, they sent up pale gray smoke.

The night air was cool and pleasant, and his body was beginning to grow numb. Owls hooted in the trees. There was a call. *Maybe a deer,* he thought, though something didn't feel right. He heard the call again. Could he be imagining it? He listened carefully. The yell came once more and there was no doubt, it belonged to a man.

He rushed to Kade. "Wake up."

"What happened?" Kade questioned, immediately alert, assuming the worst, sword already half-drawn.

"Listen."

Kade listened and heard the yell when it came again. "It's them. Wake Keegan. *Now.*"

"Huh," she mumbled blearily, lifting her head, as Jared shook her shoulder. When she saw it was still dark, she put her head back down.

"Get up," Jared insisted.

"Why?" she grumbled.

"The Vosjnik."

"Crap." Keegan haphazardly bundled up the bedroll and tossed it to Kade, who had already smothered the fire and mounted his horse.

As the sun began to light the sky, Jared turned to look at Keegan. She could barely keep her eyes open—not that he was faring much better.

"Is it safe to stop?" he called to Kade.

"No."

"Can we at least rest for a few hours? Keegan looks as if she's about to fall out of the saddle."

"No."

"But we've put so much distance between us."

Kade reined in his horse. "That means nothing. This is the Vosjnik we're talking about; they are relentless, determined people. It's noxþ near impossible for them to lose a trail once they've found it."

"If that's true, then why are we even trying?"

"I said *near* impossible."

"What do we have to do?"

"Reach Suttan. It'll be possible to lose them in the city."

"Suttan's completely out of the way if we're headed to the Lazado and at least a week's ride from here."

"The *only* way."

"We'll never get there. We'll collapse from exhaustion at this rate." Jared looked back at Keegan. She sat hunched over, forehead resting against Bastille's neck.

"We don't have a choice. But if we can make it across the Tatat River, we may be able to gain some time."

"How far's that?" Keegan asked, drowsily straightening up.

"Half a day, give or take, depending on how many more needless stops we make."

She rubbed her eyes. "Then what're we doin' standin' around?"

"Are you going to make it?" Jared asked.

"I ain't got much of a choice, do I?"

✝✝✝

Keegan was barely aware of where they were going—granted, it wouldn't've mattered if she was sleep-deprived or not. Heavy lids threatened to close and remain that way.

Suddenly, Bastille stopped, causing her to jerk up. In front of her was a wide river, its waters a pale, muddy brown.

"Where's the bridge?" she asked.

"There is none," was Kade's response. "At least not around here."

"Then how're we gonna get across?"

Kade spurred his horse into the river. "Swim."

Bringing Bastille to the edge of the river, she watched as Kade and Jared made their way across.

Eyeing the river, Keegan steeled herself and spurred Bastille in. As the water hit her, she gasped; it was icy cold. As the horse swam, the current gently pulled him downstream.

"Can we stop yet?" she asked, shivering in the noonday sun as Bastille emerged from the water.

Kade shook his head. "We should continue to put as much distance between us and them as we can."

She wrapped her arms around herself. "I thought we were safe once we crossed the river."

Kade led the way forward. "No, we just bought ourselves some time."

This is just like that movie with all the dogs, Keegan though. *What the heck's it called? Ugh, they did that thing where they erased their tracks and co...* She sat open-mouthed for a second. "Oh, my god, we're idiots."

Jared turned to look at her, "Pardon?"

"We're idiots. I know how we can lose them. We can erase the footprints and create a false trail."

Kade looked at her as if she'd lost her head. "There's no time."

"Oh, come on, all three of us are earth elementals; it shouldn't take *that* long."

"She's right," Jared acknowledged.

"Fine," Kade acquiesced. "Jared, erase our trail. Keegan, create a false path on this side of the river."

"Why're we doing all the work?" she complained.

"You're not. I'm going to create another trail on the other side of the river."

"Oh." She was silent for a second. "Have fun crossing the river again."

Kade glared and muttered something under his breath before turning his horse and spurring him back across the water.

‡‡‡

Nico jolted, realizing he'd dozed off. Ahead, the trees were thinning and he could hear running water. They emerged from the forest and the brown waters of a river flowed before them. In the loam, clear footprints could be seen following the riverbank east.

The man with the sword, Brennian, said, "They made our job easy."

"I would not be so sure," Connery responded. "Cralter, cross and check for footprints on the other side."

"Why m—" Cralter began.

"Shut your mouth and do as told!"

"Yes, sir," Cralter grumbled, spurring his horse into the water.

The rest of the Vosjnik waited.

Cralter emerged from the river and his horse shook its hair free of water. "There are footprints over here, too."

Connery cursed under his breath. "Thahan, join Cralter and follow that trail. Brennian and Guthrie, do the same on this side. If you lose the trail or it ends, come back here.

Otherwise, keep going until you find them. After one team comes back, those of us here will regroup and catch up.”

“Yes, sir,” Brennian, Guthrie, and Thahan answered.

Vitia dismounted and pulled Nico from Dax’s horse.

He sat on the ground, legs bowed out in front of him and watched Vitia head into the forest to collect firewood while Dax took the horses to the river to drink. As he sat scowling, his stomach grumbled loudly. He tried to ask for food, but Vitia had yet to give him his voice back.

“Are you hungry?” Connery asked.

Nico stared, confused, but nodded.

Connery chuckled, reaching into his pack, producing a small loaf of bread. “I am a telepath.”

The bread was stale, but he didn’t care.

When Vitia returned and saw him eating, rage crossed her face. “Why’d you feed the boy?”

“Because he is just that, a boy.” Connery answered. “Now, give him his voice back.”

Vitia crossed her arms.

“That is not a request.”

Gritting her teeth, she made her way to Nico and hit him upside the head before stalking off.

As dusk settled, Guthrie and Brennian returned.

“False trail,” they announced, coming to sit by the fireside.

“Get some sleep,” Connery said. “We will leave at daybreak. Vitia, you have first watch.”

Slowly, everyone drifted off and Nico realized they hadn’t tethered him to anything.

Vitia stared at him, her brown eyes filled with hate. “You won’t make it ten paces before I run my sword through you, boy.”

Nico gulped, having no doubt she’d happily live up to her threat.

CHAPTER 12

Morning came all too soon, though Keegan wouldn't have called it that. The sun had yet to rise and under normal circumstances no one could've paid her enough money to be awake at that ungodly hour.

"Can't why sleep longer?" she mumbled. *Goddamnit*, she thought; whenever she didn't get adequate sleep, her ability to speak coherently went out the window. "Why can't we sleep longer?" she corrected herself, untethering Bastille.

"Do you want to get caught?" Kade asked.

"If it means I get to sleep more, yes."

Kade glared, but she knew he understood it was a joke.

"You can sleep in the saddle," Jared suggested. "I'll make sure Bastille doesn't stray."

"Easier said than done," she noted as they left the clearing.

"What did you just call him?" Kade asked.

"Call who what?" she questioned, her brain struggling to follow even this simple conversation.

"Darkheart."

Her brows furrowed. "Who's Darkheart?"

"Your horse."

"Uh… his name's Bastille."

"Who gave him that name?"

"I did. It's a helluva lot better than Darkheart. What dipshit came up with that?"

"Caius."

"Makes sense; he is a dipshit."

"His name's Darkheart, so call him that."

"It's Bastille, so *you* call him that."

"It's Darkheart."

"Bastille."

Exasperated, Jared snapped, "Can you two do anything without fighting?"

Keegan held her hands up. "Hey, I didn't start it."

"Yes, you did," Kade snapped back.

"Did not!"

"What did I just say?" Jared barked.

‡‡‡

Kade stalked through the market of Drath feeling less than amiable. Spending so much time with Keegan had put him in a foul mood. Lack of sleep wasn't helping either.

He'd left them in a clearing not too far from town as now was an opportune time as any to acquire their missing supplies. And maybe a small part of him hoped they'd get caught and he could walk away from it all.

What I really want—need—to do is... Bah, there isn't time, he thought. Looking up, the sun was just starting its decline. *Maybe. Maybe, if I'm quick about this.*

He managed to sell the ill-begotten items swiftly, filling his purse with coins.

In the market, vendors offered their wares: fruits and vegetables for the common folk, meat and fine wines for the servants shopping for their masters, and silks and jewelry for the rich merchants and tradesmen. He ignored most of them until he came upon a stall hawking what he was looking for. The mercer stood behind a little table, cloaks hanging from strings slung between posts while dresses and lavish fabrics covered the table.

As he approached, the man called out, "Maybe a few yards of fine velour for your beautiful wife to make a gown."

"No."

"A shame," the man said. "I sell the finest velvet in the city. Come, feel this. See how soft it is on the skin." He held up a piece of rich, red fabric.

Kade glared at him.

The man slowly placed the bolt back on the table silently, eyes darting about. No doubt, he was unaccustomed to irritable customers. "Is there—"

"I need two cloaks," Kade said.

Regardless of his attitude, the merchant's eyes regained their gleam. "I have many cloaks. This one has rabbit fur lining; wonderful for warmth and beaut—"

"Stop talking," Kade growled; Keegan had worn down his patience and this man was treading on thin ice. "I want two woolen cloaks. Those there." He pointed to two simple, black cloaks hanging at the back of the booth.

"Are you—"

"Yes."

The vendor warily took down the cloaks, folding them neatly. He stood away from the edge of the booth, as if afraid Kade was going to bite.

"Two gold coins."

Kade guffawed, "They're hardly worth that."

"I sell the fines—"

"Everyone says that. Lower the price."

The man stammered for a moment before gathering his mettle. "No."

Kade was about to continue arguing when he paused and picked up an emerald green dress. "Fine. Two gold coins for two cloaks and a dress."

"I can't do that! I'd be cheating myself."

Kade pulled out two coins and made to hand them over. He needed to hurry this along, so he made sure the man saw the star branded on his thumb. He had neither the time nor the patience to deal with this man.

"Tw-two gold c-coins will suffice."

Kade sneered, tossing the coins onto the table. He shoved the cloaks and the dress into his bag and walked away, leaving the man with sweat beaded on his brow. It was only once he left the stall that he realized he shouldn't have shown his brand. Tiredness was seeing he did not think clearly.

Acquiring the rest of the supplies was a simpler task. No one argued with him over prices or tried to sell him unneeded luxuries. He had a feeling word of his presence preceded him.

He leaned against a building, repacking the bag so everything sat nicely and glanced at the sun. It had barely moved from its high perch. Kade smiled to himself; there was still plenty of time to scratch one of his ever-present itches.

He knew little of Drath, never having been in the city before. But Brennian was from Drath and had always bragged he knew the best haunts. There was one bagnio he'd talked about often.

Turning back towards the market, he eyed the merchants, wondering who was sordid enough to frequent the establishment he was looking for.

He approached a wine-seller. "Do you know where I can find Clark Idar?"

The man smiled, revealing discolored teeth. "Take tha' side street ov'r there," he pointed. "Turn down the third street 'n the left and then the alleyway 'n the right."

Kade nodded his thanks and found his way easily enough. When he turned down the alleyway, it smelled of piss and he had to carefully step around the large puddles littering the uneven ground. A mutt hugged the wall, picking at a bone between its paws. Further ahead, women leaned against the wall of a building, pulling at any man who passed by. Their dresses were hardly more than thin chemises, leaving little to the imagination. Just the way he liked it.

The women saw him and a thin brunette with her hair pulled back into intricate braids approached. She bore a flirtatious smile and cunning gleamed in her eyes.

"Is there anything I can do you for?"

Kade let a grin stand as his answer.

She grabbed his hand and pulled him through a doorway.

The inside of the building was nothing grand. A tatty couch and ottoman were pushed against one wall, a few uncomfortable-looking chairs sat idly about, and an iron chandelier with half melted candles hung from the ceiling.

The girl pulled him into the depths of the building and as they passed a tall man dressed in rich velvets with rings hugging every finger, she said, "Hello, Master Clark."

The man gave a slight nod with a toothy smile. "Making money today I see, Marka."

"Yes, sir," she answered without turning back.

Marka led Kade down a long hallway, drawing him into a room at the end, which was just as sparsely furnished as the foyer. Kade dropped his bag by the door, did the lock, and turned his attention to Marka, who sat patiently on the edge of the bed.

"Off with it," he said, undoing his belt.

While he pulled off his own clothing, Marka let her dress drop to the floor. She stepped out of it, and he stopped to look at her, shirt in hand. There was a calmness in her dark eyes and her head was held high. Her breasts were hardly wanting, and a flat stomach gave way to rounded hips. He couldn't complain.

Marka came forward and began to kiss along the side of his neck. Feeling her teeth pulling at his skin, Kade pushed her back onto the bed. He started slowly, wanting to enjoy this; who knew when he'd get the chance again. Wanting to get his money's worth, he reached to grope her breasts, which were soft underneath his calloused hands.

Beneath him, Marka feigned pleasure and he felt a twinge in his ego. As he changed his strokes, her tone changed, too, and he grinned. Being one to make a point, he rolled over onto the bed, sitting Marka atop of himself and watched her face contort into one of pure ecstasy.

Sweat covered their bodies and in the final throes of passion, he let out a grunt of euphoria as his muscles relaxed. With a heavy breath, Marka rolled over onto the bed beside him.

Without so much as a glance towards her, Kade pushed off the bed and dressed. He made for the door, shouldering the pack.

"Aren't you forgetting something?" Marka said, sitting up on the bed, still baring all.

He callously flipped her a silver coin, which landed beside her, and strode from the room.

✝✝✝

Someone was kicking her leg.

I swear, Keegan thought sleepily, *I'm gonna kill him.*

"What?" she growled, opening her eyes, expecting to see Kade. Instead, she as looking up at a steely-eyed man who had a sword pointed at her chest.

Keegan scrambled to her feet. Seeing the other soldier with a blade at Jared's throat across the clearing, she asked, "What do you want?"

The man just grinned and pulled her away from the tree.

Noticing a branch on the ground, Keegan feigned tripping to land beside it. Her hand closed around the branch, and she swung it, rolling onto her back. It caught the man in the face, and she brought a foot up between his legs. As he groaned and dropped to his knees, she took his sword, placing it against his collarbone.

"Let Jared go," she told the other soldier.

A large part of her suddenly wished her elemental training had included weapons. And another part wished she'd properly learned to use her newfound magic as a weapon. But that could be remedied later… hopefully.

The second man laughed, digging the point of the blade into Jared's neck, drawing a ruby droplet of blood. "I think not."

"I'll kill him."

"I don't think you will."

"Let him go. And tell me what you want with us?"

"I want to take you to Caius."

Shit, shit, shit, she thought. "Well, you're not gonna."

He threw his head back and roared with laughter.

"You should listen to her, Cralter," Kade said, riding into the clearing.

"It's Finlay, you bwint, and we were wondering where you got to," he said. Turning to look at his companion, he asked, "Thahan, how long do you think it'll take me to run my sword through the boy?"

"About as long as it'll take me to do this," Thahan responded, springing forward, and throwing Keegan to the ground. He sat on her chest, wrapping one hand around her neck, the other pinning her hand that no longer held the sword.

If she survived this, there was no more just dicking around with magic training. This world was very willing to kill her if she allowed it.

As she struggled against Thahan, he glanced at her wrist. It was an impulsive action and she watched confusion knit his eyebrows together. His hand covered most of the markings, but the edge of the earth symbol was visible.

"You almost fooled us with those false trails," Thahan said, looking up at Kade.

"If that were true, there'd be more of you here," Keegan challenged, her mouth acting before her brain could think.

She gasped as Thahan's hand tightened around her throat. Knowing she only had one chance, she brought her free arm inside his elbow, loosening his grip, and punched him in the throat. His hand released her instantly and she grabbed the neck of his shirt. Flinging him aside, she reversed their positions. She quickly punched him in the throat a few times to make sure he stayed down. Better him struggling to breathe than her.

When she looked up, Kade had the point of his sword against Cralter's neck.

"Go help Keegan," he told Jared.

"Are you alright?" Jared asked, kneeling beside her. He tried to wipe away the blood on his neck, only succeeding in smearing it across his skin.

She nodded and, though Thahan was unconscious, kept her attention on him. When Jared remained silent, she looked up and stared at Kade in shock. His sword was bathed in red and Cralter lay on the ground, throat slit.

Jumping to her feet, she yelled, "Why'd you do that?"

Kade wiped his blade on Cralter's shirt. "He would've told the others where we are."

"There must've been another way."

"There wasn't. And we need to leave, now. Before the rest of them realize these two are missing."

"Oh my god," Keegan muttered, face paling as she ran her hands through her hair. "You killed him."

"If you're going to be sick, do it quickly."

"What the hell is wrong with you? You just killed someone!"

Kade made his way over. "And you killed Thahan."

"What? Keegan knelt beside Thahan, "No, I didn't!" She sighed with relief when she found him breathing.

Glancing back at Kade, she noticed he was gripping his sword tightly and advancing towards them.

She asked, "What're you doing?" When he didn't respond, she asked again, "What are you doing?" Realizing his intentions, she stood between him and Thahan. "I won't let you."

Kade's voice was unnaturally even, "Move."

"No."

"Let him do it," Jared said, trying to pull her out of Kade's path.

"No."

"Do you really want to do this?" Kade asked warningly.

"Yes," Keegan gulped. "It's what's right."

Kade stared at her for a second longer, then shoved her aside.

Stumbling, she watched as the sword neared Thahan's chest.

Keegan cried, "No!" subconsciously reaching for the energy that would allow her to move mountains.

A rock pulled itself from the ground and hit Kade in the head and, rather than the sword going through Thahan's chest, its point went harmlessly into soil.

Kade stared at the ground, stunned, before toppling over.

"What did you do?" Jared yelled.

"I- I don't know," Keegan said in as much shock as Jared. Her eyes darted between Kade and Thahan. "What... what do we do now?"

"Leave. Grab his sword."

✝✝✝

At sunrise, the Vosjnik packed up camp and crossed the river. The water was cold and chilled Nico to the core. Around mid-evening they arrived in a clearing to find Cralter with his throat slit and Thahan lying on the ground; Nico couldn't tell if he was alive.

Vitia slid from her horse and began working her magic. Thahan awoke shortly, coughing and sputtering curses.

"What happened?" Connery asked grimly.

"Kade," Thahan bit. "Royiken Kade Tavin happened."

Dax cursed under his breath. "This entire mission has gone to the dogs."

"How exactly did you and Cralter get yourselves in this situation?" Connery pressed.

"We found Keegan and Jared," Thahan started. "Cralter dealt with the boy while I grabbed the girl. The insolent little opida fought back and managed to get my sword, but not for long. Then Kade showed up and that's when this happened," he said, gesturing to his fallen comrade. "I assume. The girl knocked me out."

Vitia roared with laughter. "You let that weak, little opida get the best of you?"

Thahan got to his feet unsteadily. "She's not as weak as she appears. She's an elemental."

"That cannot be," Connery said. "The king himself confirmed she was not."

"I saw the mark."

"I told you!" Brennian exclaimed. "I wasn't imagining I saw her practicing magic."

Connery was silent, his face hard, eyes filled with fury and a flicker of worry.

Nico had no doubt that if he couldn't salvage the situation he wouldn't have his head much longer.

"Burn the body," Connery said rigidly. "Then we move out."

CHAPTER 13

Lucas's foot fell on a branch, snapping it in two. The sound was like thunder compared to the silence he'd grown accustomed to. It was their third day walking, though it felt like a lifetime; from experience, he estimated they'd reach Tratoleck before nightfall.

Though they'd planned to head east, to find Jared and Nico, they'd decided to first go to Tratoleck, as they had friends there and needed horses, food, and other necessities for a long journey.

While Jude did his best to not show it, Lucas could see how much their mother's death was hurting him. Jude was normally quiet, but he'd become despondent. Lucas understood—they were all aching in the worst way.

As the sun made its descent, they came upon the gates of Tratoleck, the guards ignoring them as they entered. They would go to Virgil and Laiyla Fulpe first, who had been family friends of theirs for years. Laiyla had grown up in Suilenroc and was—*had been*—Alessandra's closest friend.

Lucas led the way, and they soon reached the Fulpe house in the inner quarter of the city. Their home was tall, reaching three stories, its surface made of dark brick with a few windows overlooking the street.

Alivia, the Fulpes' daughter, opened the door when they knocked. Her face lit up upon seeing Lucas, then turned to worry when she noticed Jude and Carter.

"Mama, Papa," she called into the house before inviting them in.

As she closed the door behind them, Virgil descended the stairs.

"Jude," he said cheerfully. "It has been quite some time since I last saw you. And this must be Carter; my, what a handsome young man you are turning into. Where is the rest of that motley crew of yours?"

"We've had a bit of… misfortune," Jude told him.

Virgil's face fell. "You need a place to stay; of course, you will stay here."

"Thank you. You don't know what that means to us."

Virgil turned to his daughter. "Get Carter and Lucas settled in. I believe I have some things to discuss with Jude."

Lucas and Carter followed Alivia upstairs, the faint smell of honey wafting from her.

The upstairs hallway was lined with doors and, opening one, Alivia said, "Carter, this will be your room."

Alivia continued down the hallway before saying, "Lucas, this is yours."

As he entered, he mumbled a thank you.

"If you need anything at all," Alivia told him, gently placing a hand on his shoulder, "my room is right across the hall."

Lucas gave her a small smile, though it must've looked more like a grimace, and shut the door. She was still enamored with him, regardless of the fact he'd turned her down on multiple occasions. Her constant attention was the primary reason he'd made Jared take his place on errand runs.

The room was simple to those who'd grown up in the upper echelons of society, but for him it was luxurious. A large bed covered in colorful pillows was set against the wall. There was a writing desk pushed into one corner and opposite the bed was a full-length mirror.

The reflection staring back from the mirror seemed empty. There was no life in the blue eyes, only sorrow and anger. A knock at the door pulled him away and, before he could reach the door, Carter burst in.

"What do you think of this place?" Carter asked, quickly shutting the door.

"It's exceedingly temporary."

"Are you sure?"

"What do you know?" Lucas asked, anger rising; he clenched his fists, daring the wounds to reopen; daring the world to steal revenge from him.

"I overheard Father and Virgil; we might be staying longer than we thought."

"How much longer?"

"Indefinitely."

There was another knock and Jude entered. He took one look at Lucas. "Carter already told you what little he heard."

"Yes," Lucas said sourly.

Jude sighed. "Boys, we're in a very difficult situation and there's little we can do."

"The—"

"Let me finish. There's little we can do, but we'll make it count. Lucas, I know you want to go after the Vosjnik, but that's suicide. Our best course of action is going to the Lazado. Now, I've talked with Virgil and they're planning to flee too. When they leave, we're going with them."

"When will that be?" Carter questioned.

"Soon, hopefully. Until then, Virgil recommends we find work to occupy our time. Distract us from…" he choked and couldn't finish. "Lucas, he's going to introduce you to one of his friends in need of an assistant. Carter, you and I will go out tomorrow and see what we can find."

✠✠✠

Jared took a bite of half-stale bread; since the Vosjnik were still on their trail, Kade refused to let them make a fire large enough to cook over. Kade had regained consciousness relatively soon after they took off, a dark bruise marring his face. He was rightly mad, but Jared knew Keegan had never intended to hurt him. The magic had come from instinct, as, at its core, magic was a tool of survival.

"Hey… uhh…" Keegan mumbled awkwardly, "you've got some dirt on your neck."

Kade glared at her but reached up regardless.

"Other side."

He rubbed his neck. "Did I get it?"

"No. It looks like it may be a bruise." She eyed him for a second. "If I didn't know better, I'd say it was a hickey."

"A what?" Jared asked.

"A hickey. You get them when someone sucks or bites your neck when things get… passionate."

Jared stared at her at a loss for words and Kade matched his silence.

Keegan raised an eyebrow. "You gonna say something, Kade?"

"No," he growled

They stared each other down, fire dancing in both their eyes.

"How many of you were in the Vosjnik?" Jared said, aiming to break the tension.

Kade was slow to answer. "Including me? Eight. Seven now." A log popped. "It should've been six."

"I can make it six," Keegan muttered.

"Keegan," Jared snapped.

Rolling her eyes, she asked with a sigh, "Anything we should know about them?"

"Avoid them at all costs; they're monsters," Kade said.

"What's that tell us about you?"

"The lengths I'm willing to go to to deliver you to the Lazado."

"Is there anything *else* we should know if, God forbid, we get caught?"

"No. If you're caught, nothing but death will help you."

"We're screwed," Keegan said bluntly.

Jared pressed, "What can you tell us about them in general?"

"There's a life, water, fire, earth, and air elemental, a telepath, an archer, and a swordsman."

"What was Cralter?"

"Fire."

"Thahan?"

"Archer. How do you know their names?"

"They were said earlier."

"Were they?" Kade asked Jared.

Jared rubbed his nose. "Maybe."

Kade turned to Keegan. "Hmmm."

"I don't know what you're thinking," Keegan started, "well, I have an idea, and you're wrong. I'm just really good with names, faces, and weird facts."

"I find that hard to believe."

"The only thing hard around here is your head." There was a moment's pause before she burst into laughter.

"What's so funny?"

Her laugh dwindled to a chuckle. "Nothing you'd understand."

Jared steered the conversation away from an argument. "Who's the leader?"

"Commander," Kade corrected. "Connery Sray."

"Which one's he?" she enquired.

"Telepath."

"Ah, that's so cool! Man, I wish I could read minds."

"I'm not sure it's what you think it is," Jared disputed. "And it'd be annoying, always hearing everyone's thoughts."

"I'm sure there's a way to block it out and stuff. Any light you can shed on the matter?" she asked Kade.

"Not at the moment."

"We'll just have to ask a telepath when we see one."

"No," Jared bit.

"Why?"

"Avoid telepaths; they're snakes."

"Okay…" She turned to Kade. "Did you get what we needed?"

"Yes." He stood and removed several rolled items from his saddlebag, handing half of them to Jared, throwing the rest at Keegan; she caught the bundle with her face.

Jared opened his and found there was a bedroll, a cloak, and an empty water-skin.

"Why do I need this?" Keegan asked, holding up a dress.

Kade sat down again. "Women don't wear trousers."

"I do."

"You shouldn't; it looks peculiar."

"I'm a peculiar person."

"Keegan," Kade said sternly, "just wear the royiken dress."

Jared could tell she was momentarily confused by Kade's vernacular.

Surprising them, she stood, sighing, and said, "Fine."

"What, no further arguing?"

She turned her back to them, grabbing the bottom of her shirt. "Honestly, I'm too damn tired to."

"Whoa!" Kade and Jared yelled, causing her to stop.

She turned back to face them, the bottom of her stomach showing. "What?"

"You should… uh… be more modest," Jared stuttered.

"Oh, chill," Keegan chided, turning again, and pulling her shirt off.

Jared looked away quickly, cheeks reddening.

Keegan laughed when she noticed his flushed face. "I'll assume you don't have much experience with women."

"No," he admitted self-consciously.

"Talk to Kade. He can probably give you some tips on how to get laid."

"Get what?"

"Laid—have sex."

Jared stared at her mortified. "Why would you even say something like that?"

"It's a joke, calm down." Giving a shrug, she added, "Though, there's probably some truth to it."

"How could there possibly be *any* truth in that?"

"I'm willing to bet Kade's been to a few brothels."

"More than a few," Kade commented casually.

She motioned at him. "There ya go."

"You forgot to remove your trousers," Kade pointed out.

"Yeah, those ain't coming off."

"The whole point of wearing a dress is so you don't need to wear trousers."

"You can't see them, and I've already done as much compromising as I'm gonna do."

Jared attempted to stifle a yawn.

"Get some sleep," Kade said. "Keegan, you have watch."

✠✠✠

The air was pleasant now that it was late spring, and a light breeze sent Aron's hair skittering. In the winter, the winds were biting, keeping their meetings short. But it was a clear night with a new moon forcing the stars to illuminate the gable. The torches below stood out like candles in a dark room.

He heard Shiloh making her way up the last few steps and turned to greet her. Her long, blonde tresses were piled in a loose coil on top of her head.

Meeting her with a passionate kiss, he announced, "We will leave on the next new moon."

Shiloh leaned forward and gently kissed his lips. "I can't wait."

Hand in hand they made their way to the edge of the gable and stood staring out over the darkness. The breeze sent wisps of golden hair dancing about Shiloh's face.

"Where shall we go?" she asked, voice floating in the draft.

"Anywhere we like," Aron said, wrapping his arm around her shoulders, "as long as we are together."

She rested her head against him. "I've always wanted to see the Merfolk."

"Then that is where we shall go."

"Have you thought about how we're going to get out of the castle?"

"Not extensively. But I am thinking we can stow away on a wagon at the end of the day."

"I love you," Shiloh whispered after a moment.

"And I you." Aron looked up at the sky and, for the first time, felt as if the misery of his family was lifting. But Alyck's words replayed in his head: 'there will be no happy ending'.

Yes, there will, he told himself.

‡‡‡

It would have been great if the book gave a direct translation of the prophecy, but Braxton was not that lucky. The book was a dictionary of sorts, giving translations of words from the Old Language. Thus far, he had managed to translate most of the first line: 'While you have slaughtered — children of the dragon, she will rise again from the ashes by your own...'

He flipped through the pages looking for *þen*. It translated to 'doing'.

Braxton leaned back in the chair and was suprised to find darkness had fallen. He stood, streching his muscles, and considered pushing through the night. Eventually, he decided against it.

Blowing out the candle and yawning, he pulled off his clothes and crawled into bed, the blankets enveloping him in a welcoming embrace.

His night visions were filled with slick, purple blood covering the ground. His sword was similarly coated. Painful screams assaulted his ears.

"Haxnug," he cried to his mind's foe.

A voice shrieked in, "Betrayer!"

Wind buffeted him, throwing his sword from his grasp as long talons reached towards his chest. As they were about to touch him, he bolted upright, heart beating against his breastbone.

The room was only half-lit by the rising sun.

Taking a deep breath, he lay back down and returned to sleep, muttering, "Only a dream."

CHAPTER 14

The clang of metal on metal rang throughout the shop as Lucas stood beside Virgil. They'd been in the city for five days, giving him all too much time to ruminate on their circumstances; Virgil was just now finding the time to take him to the blacksmith, who would hopefully become his new employer.

"Waylan," Virgil called out.

No response.

"Waylan," Virgil called louder.

The noise stopped and a surly, dark-skinned man came from the back. He was taller than Lucas by several inches—something he was unaccustomed to from anyone aside from his father. A wiry black beard covered the smith's jaw and in his hand was a large hammer.

The blacksmith greeted Virgil with a hardy handshake. "Virgil, how's that chandelier holding up?"

"Quite well. Laiyla loves the noxþ thing."

"Well, what can I do for you?"

"You still in need of an assistant?"

"I am. Ya got one for me?"

Placing a hand on Lucas's shoulder, Virgil said, "I do, if you are willing to give him a chance."

The smith introduced himself. "Waylan Piscol."

"Lucas Sieme," he reciprocated.

"Have you ever apprenticed for a blacksmith, boy?"

"No, sir."

"Then I doubt you'll be of use."

Virgil stopped the smith as he made to return to the back of the shop. "The boy may not have experience, but he is strong and willing to learn. At least give him a chance; it cannot hurt."

Sighing, Waylan answered, "Fine. Your wage'll be a copper a day until you can prove your worth, at which time we'll renegotiate. Be here an hour after dawn the day after tomorrow."

"That went better than expected," Virgil said once they'd left the shop.

"Is there something you haven't told me about my employer?"

"Waylan can be a *tad* prickly and hard-headed. But he means well," Virgil promised.

✠✠✠

The last four days of travel had been grueling. Though they were certain the Vosjnik were still trailing them, Kade felt there was enough distance between them to stop for a few hours every night. Continued lack of sleep made them short-tempered and the littlest things were certain to spark a fight between Keegan and Kade; Jared did his best to not get involved. He couldn't muster the energy—not when his whole world had fallen apart, and the last remains were even now crumbling away.

"Put your cloak on," Kade instructed on the fifth morning.

As Keegan pulled the cloak from her saddlebag, she asked, "Why?"

"It'll help conceal your face."

"Oooh, are we gonna reach Suttan today?"

"Yes. And whatever you do, say *nothing*."

"Why?"

"Is that your favorite question?"

"No... Yes... I don't know. Why?"

"Just, do as I say."

"Sir, yes, sir," Keegan said, feigning indignation, doing the cloak's clasp.

They rode for a little longer before emerging onto a wide dirt road. A few weary travelers walked along the sides. In the distance, the high walls surrounding Suttan could be seen silhouetted against the hazy, mid-morning sky. Behind the city rose tall mountains.

"I didn't know there were mountains nearby," Keegan commented.

"Those are the Westerlies," Jared told her.

"Wow, such a creative name. What's on the other side?"

"Nothing," Kade answered. "This kingdom ends where they begin."

"There has to be something, the world doesn't just drop off like a cliff."

"I didn't say that. I said we don't know what's on the other side."

"No, you didn't," Keegan argued, "you said 'nothing' which isn't the same thing as 'we don't know'."

"Th—" Kade started, then shook his head and became quiet; apparently, this wasn't worth fighting over.

"Why doesn't anyone explore?" Keegan queried. "It might be a way to get away from Caius."

"People have," Jared provided, "but it's said few came back and those who did vowed to never cross the mountains again."

There was a gleam of curiosity in her eyes. "Why?"

"Something about giant, horned men—if I remember the story correctly."

As the walls grew closer, more travelers appeared on the road. Nearing the gates, Jared eyed the sentries nervously. Neither paid them much attention, but as they started through, there was a clang and his heart dropped.

"Halt," one of the guards called.

Jared turned to see one of Kade's saddlebags had worked itself loose and was now lying on the ground.

Kade pulled Aros around, hissing in passing, "Keep going."

Keegan gave Jared an uneasy look and pulled Bastille to a stop.

As Kade slid from Aros, one of the guards was already picking up the bag and opening it.

"What are you doing with a set of the king's armor?"

"I'm one of the king's men," Kade returned, reaching for the bag.

The guard pulled it away. "A slack jaw like you would never be allowed t' serve in the king's army. You stole this."

Kade grabbed at the bag, placing his hand so his brand faced upwards.

The guard glanced down and his face paled. "M-my deepe-est ap-pologies… sir. I-I didn't know."

"Obviously," Kade snarled.

The guard continued, "If you don' mind me asking, what 're you doing with these villeins?"

"That's none of your concern. Oh, and should you tell anyone we're in the city, I can assure you, you won't live to see the new week."

The guard ashamedly retook his post with a pale face.

After re-securing the bag to Aros's saddle, Kade led the way into Suttan. Thankfully there was no mention of how they'd ignored his command to continue on without him.

Once out of earshot from the guards, Jared asked, "Was it a good idea to show your brand? The Vosjnik will know we're here."

Kade didn't visibly react. "Probably not. But it stopped a scene. I'm not really worried about the Vosjnik knowing where we are. It wouldn't take an alchemist to figure out we're heading to Suttan."

Within the walls, the buildings grew steadily in size as they converged at the city's castle in the center.

"Where do we go?" Keegan asked.

"To see a friend," Kade said, leading them through the gate's square.

"How do you know where you're going?" Jared asked.

"I used to live here."

Both Jared and Kade paused, waiting for Keegan to say something. When she didn't, they turned to look at her. She seemed distracted, eyes darting about, following random pedestrians.

"Keegan," Jared said to get her attention.

"Yeah," she responded, still looking around absentmindedly.

"You alright?"

"Mhmm," she nodded airily.

✠✠✠

Keegan was sweating in the midday sun; however, it wasn't the heat causing her to perspire. Since they'd begun encountering people on the road, she'd started hearing voices. At first, they were faint, barely whispers, but as they neared the city and the number of people increased, so did the babble.

Now, inside Suttan, it was like a concert in her head. Voices of men, women, and children flooded her mind. She looked around, trying to discern to whom they belonged, but they were never present long enough for her to pinpoint.

I need to buy—

Hmm, he's quite—

—stay away from that.

Pass—

—not to him.

Jared noticed her discomfort and she stopped looking around, instead focusing on Bastille's neck.

Left up ahead, then—

Kade took the next left, leading them towards the inner section of the city. The central streets weren't as crowded and they were able to move faster, but the voices didn't lessen.

—can't be preg—

Keegan had underestimated how large Suttan was, expecting it to be something even she could easily navigate; instead, it was a maze. Without Kade, she and Jared would've been hopelessly lost.

—late. I must be getting home.

Kade stopped outside a haggard-looking building and dismounted. A crooked sign above the door read 'Gydrick's Inn and Tavern'.

I cannot stand h—

"Are you sure we should stay here?" Jared asked.

"Yes," Kade answered, almost happily. "Gydrick's has the best ale in the city."

Keegan rolled her eyes.

—needs a bath.

They dismounted, handing their reins to a stable boy, and followed Kade into Gydrick's. Inside, tables crowded the room, at which a few patrons sat, some already evidently drunk.

Anuhher rund!

Kade headed to the bar, telling them, "Wait here."

Jared pointedly watched him while Keegan leaned against the wall.

The voices were constant. It wasn't as if they were simply one after the other, but all at the same time. It made focusing on any one voice, or anything, really difficult. Her head was beginning to hurt from being pulled in so many directions.

Where's my ale?

Jared leaned over and whispered, "Are you sure you're alright?"

She realized she'd been scowling. "Yeah."

Kade approached, a key in hand. "Room eight."

The stairs to the second floor were narrow, forcing them to walk single file and to hug the wall when another patron came down. The landing was only slightly wider. Doors lined the hall with numbers in their centers.

Kade unlocked the door to reveal a small room. There was only one bed pushed against the wall and a small, grimy window to filter the sunlight.

Tentatively, Keegan entered and made her way to the bed.

La ladi da di di da—

The lumps in the mattress were large, but after a week of sleeping on the ground, it felt like a cloud. She swung her feet up and lay back.

Look at the p—

When Kade shut the door, the voices became muffled. While she didn't understand why, she was glad. Keegan took a breath, feeling like a weight had been lifted.

"Who gets the bed?" she asked.

"You," Kade answered, dropping his bag.

Don't touch—

"You sure?" Keegan asked, closing her eyes. "We can rock, paper, scissors for it."

"Pardon?"

"Never mind." Given the chance, sleep would come quickly.

AAAHHHH!

Keegan jolted up in a state of panic and tumbled to the floor. As she lay there, it felt as if someone was taking a hammer to the inside of her head. Whatever was happening was going to relieve her of her sanity—what little of it was left.

Jared rushed over. "What happened?"

She pushed herself up, eyes glazed over, and was barely aware of him kneeling beside her. *Breathe. In, out. In, out,* Keegan told herself.

Jared called her name.

"Yeah, what?"

"What's wrong?"

"Nothing."

Across the room, a frown graced Kade's already naturally harsh features. "Jared, go check the horses."

Jared turned to him, confused. "The horses are fine."

"Go check."

Quietly, Keegan told him, "Just go. I'll be fine."

Kade shut the door behind Jared and there was the faint click of the lock.

Something wasn't right; all the voices had vanished. "Why'd you lock the door?"

"I don't want to be interrupted," Kade said darkly.

She regretted having told Jared to go. "What are you planning?"

"You tell me."

She got to her feet. "I don't know; I can't read minds."

Or can you?

"I can't."

"You just did."

"Huh?"

Watch my lips; they don't move, yet you hear me speaking.

Keegan stared at him blank-faced. "You've gotta be freakin' kidding me."

"How long have you been hearing voices?"

"How do you know I've been hearing voices?"

"I'm a telepath, too."

"So, every telepath goes through this?"

Kade nodded.

"Why didn't you tell us you're a telepath?"

"There was no need to."

"I beg to differ."

"Would it have changed anything?"

"I don't know—it could've. We're gonna have to tell Jared."

"No," Kade growled.

"He's gotta deal with us, he has a right to know."

"No."

She crossed her arms stubbornly. "I'm telling him."

Anger crossed Kade's face. "I don't recommend that."

"What're you gonna do? Jack shit."

"Haven't you learned anything?"

"I've learned you're an asshole. You don't scare me." That was a lie; he did scare her sometimes.

Kade started towards her when the door handle turned and there was a thump.

Jared called, "Why's the door locked?"

"Say nothing," Kade ordered, unlocking the door.

"The horses are fine," Jared told him, walking in.

"Jared, Kade's a tele—" Keegan started. It suddenly felt like a million white-hot nails were digging into her head. Screaming, she dropped to her knees, hunched over.

Jared rushed to her side, frantically asking what the source of her agony was.

She took gulping breaths and managed to steal a glance at Kade through watery eyes. He had a face like thunder, and she realized this was his doing.

"He's a telepath," she managed in a voice that felt incredibly small. The nails dug in deeper, and she compressed her body even more.

Jared turned on Kade, drawing the knife he kept in his boot. "Stay away from us."

Kade laughed and with a flick of the wrist sent Jared's knife flying. It embedded itself into one of the wooden panels of the wall.

"No," Keegan said as Jared advanced towards Kade, "we need him."

Jared shook his head. "We don't need this manipulative bwint."

"Yes, we do. I'm a telepath too."

Jared crouched before her. "Then give me one good reason why I shouldn't wash my hands of you—*both* of you."

She raised her eyes to look at him pleadingly. "I just found out. And, really, what's so bad about telepaths?"

"I'll let Kade explain."

"Telepaths are notorious for being informants for Caius," Kade said.

"So?" Keegan shakily got to her feet. "That doesn't mean we are."

"Maybe not you, but Kade's already confirmed the stereotype that they're all snakes," Jared snapped.

"Does the good not outweigh the bad here?" she argued in Kade's defense, pausing in surprise that those words had come from her.

"I don't believe so."

"So, what're you gonna do; leave?"

"Yes. Grab your things, *we* are going."

Kade drew his sword. "You're welcome to go, but she stays."

"What kind of person would I be to leave her with a monster like you?"

Kade placed the point of the sword against Jared's sternum. "She stays."

Keegan looked helplessly between them. "Kade, would you go downstairs so I can talk to Jared?"

"How do I know you won't run?" Kade countered, eyes locked with Jared's.

"I have nowhere to run to, nor do I even know *where* to go."

Kade's gaze fixed on her for a moment. Pulling his sword away, he sheathed it, and slammed the door behind himself.

Chapter 15

Kade stomped down the stairs, muttering curses under his breath. Reaching the tavern, he wished someone would pick a fight because he *really* wanted to hit something.

Approaching the bar, he barked, "A pint."

"Comin' up," the barman said cheerfully, grabbing a glass and filling it from the tap.

Kade slid him a copper coin. He thought about listening in on the conversation upstairs but doing so would only further the stigma surrounding telepaths and it wouldn't change the outcome; Keegan was coming with him. He took a long gulp.

A woman sidled up next to him. "Is there anything I can help you with?"

He ignored her.

She ran a hand down his back. "A big strong man like you must need something."

"There are many things I need," he began without looking at her, assuming a smirk had crossed her face, "but I don't need a filthy hynak like you."

Turning to face her, he saw the woman staring at him open-mouthed, revealing the few yellow teeth stuck in her gums. She looked like she'd been dragged behind a horse through the city.

He added, "Nor would I want to associate with an old hag like—."

She quickly lashed out to slap him.

Kade sat calmly for a moment, before rising to tower above her. "Never touch me again," he growled, "you filthy, sti—"

"Leave it, Kade," came Keegan, who had appeared out of nowhere. To the woman, she said, "Get outta here."

The woman pushed past them hurriedly.

Keegan leaned against the bar. "Now, Jared has agreed to stay under the stipulation you answer *all* of our questions. Understood?"

He glared at her.

Taking his silence for agreement, Keegan said, "Come on then. Oh, if you ever do that mental torture shit again, I'll listen to Jared."

He followed her to the table where Jared sat scowling and nursing a tankard.

As Keegan sat, she asked, "Do we wanna get some food?"

Jared's stomach grumbled as he downed the rest of his ale.

"I'll take that as a yes. Mr. Money Man, would you care to order?" When no one moved, she fixed her gaze on Kade. "That's you."

He was quick in ordering with the barman.

"First and foremost," Keegan said, rubbing her temples once he returned, "how do I block out the voices?"

"Put up a wall," he answered.

She looked at him, unamused. "And how, pray tell, do I do that?"

"I can't explain the minutia of it. It's a skill I picked up as a child."

She dropped her head onto the table. "So *fucking* helpful."

Kade slowly expanded his own wall to encompass her mind.

It took her a few seconds to realize the thoughts were being blocked. "Why can't I hear voices anymore?"

"I'm shielding you," Kade said as the barmaid brought them food and drink. "I remember going through the same thing." He took a gulp of ale. "Except no one was there to help me."

Keegan stared at him, shocked. "Are you actually being decent? Holy crap. Where's the real Kade?"

"This is a one-time thing."

"And there's the Kade we know and tolerate."

"What's your motivation?" Jared finally asked.

Kade bit into a piece of bread. "To kill those who wronged me."

Jared scowled and downed half his pint.

"Slow down," Keegan told him. "That's your third one; I don't wanna be lookin' after your drunk ass."

Jared glared at her and, spitefully, emptied the tankard, slamming it onto the table in a show of bravado.

"Another," he yelled to the barmaid.

Keegan turned to Kade. "How exactly do you make a shield for someone else?"

"Again, it's not something I can explain."

"You h'd better start giving us some real answers," Jared snapped as the barmaid returned with his drink.

"Then ask questions I can capably answer," he seethed.

"Why was it when you shut the door, the voices… thoughts, became muffled?" Keegan enquired.

"Solid objects interfere with reception. Being underground will completely block thoughts from the surface. Though, anyone underground can be heard just fine."

Keegan knitted her brows together. "What?"

Kade sighed and clarified, "If you're underground, you can't hear someone who's on the surface nor can they hear you. Anyone who's underground with you can be heard just fine."

"Okay, so it's like an internal walkie-talkie."

Kade and Jared looked at her perplexed.

She shook her head. "I'll explain that once I've explained the three billion other things y'all need to understand to get what the hell a walkie-talkie is. So, I know that not all elementals are telepaths by the fact that Jared isn't one. But why are you a telepath?"

Kade paused thinking of how best to explain. "I just am. I don't understand how all… *that* works. Though, twins, especially those that are elementals, are more likely to be telepaths as well."

He knew his answer wasn't exactly elucidating, but he'd never really questioned his abilities. Maybe one day Keegan would meet someone who could properly answer that question—but it wasn't him.

Jared downed the ale and slammed the tankard down on the table again. "How 'id you find us?"

"The Blind Prophet."

"How did you know to look for us at the forest's edge?" Keegan pressed.

The barmaid collected Jared's tankard once more.

"You," Kade lied. Even if Jared wasn't well on his way to getting drunk, Kade would never tell them what had occurred. "Your thoughts are unusually loud." While that wasn't how he'd found them, it was a true statement.

"How? Wouldn't all thoughts be at the same volume?"

"No. Some tend to be louder than others."

"How does that make it easier to find a person?"

"It's the same as if someone's actually speaking. The louder someone speaks, the easier it is to find them in a crowd."

Keegan nodded. "Okay. Wait, wouldn't you have to know what my… Do voices and thoughts sound the same?"

The barmaid set another mug in front of Jared.

"I don't understand your question."

Jared reached for the tankard's handle.

Keegan slapped his hand away and pulled the drink to their side of the table. "You've had enough."

Jared frowned, then took her cup and downed it.

She sighed, clenching her fists, and continued with the conversation. "Does a person's voice and thoughts have the same voice, I guess is the way to put it."

"Yes."

The barmaid made her way back to their table. As she reached for Jared's tankard, Keegan told her, "He's cut off." Then, once more, she jumped back into the conversation. "Huh… interesting. Okay, so how did you know whose voice to follow when you were looking for us?"

"Again, I don't understand."

"When you were looking for me in… wherever the place Jared lived—"

"Suilenroc," Jared slurred, grabbing the drink Keegan had taken from him and swallowing it before she could scold him.

"Yeah, Suilenroc," she continued. "How did you know which voice was mine?"

Kade finished his drink. "The Vosjnik almost captured you a couple of weeks prior."

"That was y'all? No wonder Cralter and Thahan looked familiar. Damn, I'm losing my touch."

"How d' you do that? Remember things?" Jared said, his slur worse.

"I'm good with names, faces, birthdays, things like that; I told y'all this before." Keegan sighed, "I'm gonna take him upstairs; he's gone."

"He's right there," Kade said.

"No, I mean he's drunk." Once she got Jared to his feet, she asked, "You comin' or stayin'?"

"Staying."

Steering Jared towards the stairs, she added, "Oh, and don't think we're done asking questions."

Kade ignored her and called out to the barmaid, "Another ale."

‡‡‡

Keegan pushed Jared forward. "Come on."

They made it up the stairs without too much difficulty and moved towards the room. Jared took the door handle, turned it, and found it locked.

"Stay here, I'll get the key," Keegan told him.

Downstairs, she had to push through the crowd to get to Kade. He was still sitting at the table, gulping down ale like water.

"I need the key."

He pulled it from his pocket and placed it on the table without breaking from the tankard.

Hurrying back upstairs, she found Jared sitting on the floor, arms crossed and scowling. "Up ya get," she told him.

"I ca n't," Jared hiccupped. "My 'ead feels funny."

She offered him a hand. "Yeah, that happens when you get drunk."

Taking her hand, instead of her pulling him up, he pulled her down.

Keegan's knee drove into the floor and her forehead went into the wall. She knelt back, groaning and rubbing her head.

"I um surry," Jared slurred, placing his hands on her cheeks. He gave her a wet kiss on the forehead. "To make better."

Grabbing his forearm and elbow, she helped him to his feet and, after unlocking the door, led him inside.

"Can you stand on your own?"

"Sur'."

Almost instantly his hands were grabbing the back of her dress and pulling her to the floor again.

She got him on his feet again and half-dragged him to the bed.

"You 're supposed to be in the bed," Jared said.

"I know." Kneeling, she undid the laces of his boots and pulled them off. Looking up, she saw he'd removed his shirt.

He undid his belt and handed it to her.

She placed it on the floor. "You good?"

Jared nodded.

"Then get some sleep."

As he lay down, he asked, "How 're are you s' gentle now, yet always fighting with Kade?"

Once Jared had succumbed to sleep, she responded, "Where to even begin?" Keegan took the bedroll from her pack, setting it beside the bed. "For starters, I don't really mean to fight with him. He just gets under my skin and my mouth has a mind of its own. It's a habit I really gotta break. As for being 'gentle' with you, it's 'cause I care about you."

She was quiet for a second and a tear rolled down her cheek

"I don't know if you know this, but…" she whispered, wiping her eyes, "I'm scared shitless. But what worries me most is that you might get hurt. I know I'm a goner—I've kinda come to grips with that, also kinda haven't—but I can't stand the thought of something happening to you. I can't protect myself, so how the hell am I supposed to protect the people I care about? I can't, and that terrifies me."

CHAPTER 16

Connery led the way towards Suttan slowly, no longer finding need for haste. Nico knew that if they hadn't caught up to the Vosjnik's quarry yet, it was because they were likely safe within the city. People on the road saw them and scurried away. Under most circumstances, the only way to discern a member of the Vosjnik was to see the star branded on their thumb, but the griffin emblem on their armor identified them as king's men, ensuring people steered clear. Nico hated to be associated with them.

They were stopped at the gates. "What be yer business?"

"We are chasing fugitives," Connery announced. "Have you seen two men traveling with an odd-looking woman?"

"We see many people passin' through 'ere 'eryday," the other guard sniped, "most of 'em strange lookin'. What makes ya think these three would stand out? And even if someone 'ad seen 'em, it'd be neither o' us; we were up on the wall 'esterday."

"Who was here yesterday?"

"No idea. You 'ill have ta ask the Captain," the first man said.

"Where can I find him?"

"In the castle wi'h the lord."

"Send a runner to inform them we are coming."

The second man guffawed, "Who 're you ta give us orders?"

"Commander of the Vosjnik."

Both of their faces paled.

"We 'ill get right on that… sir," the first soldier said, scrambling away.

Inside, the city bustled, and the horses made their way through the crowd slowly. As they traveled farther from the wall, the crowds lessened. High above them, the castle loomed over the smaller houses and soon its shadow engulfed them.

The gates were open, and four guards stood at attention. Upon seeing them, one man rushed inside. The courtyard was cobbled and on the steps stood several men.

Connery dismounted, handing his reins to a frightened-looking stable boy.

"Welcome to Suttan, Commander," a man in dark blue silks said. Nico presumed this was a lord or some such.

"I need to speak to the Captain," Connery said coarsely.

"Present," another man said, stepping forward. Two swords were belted around his waist, one on each hip, and the point of a dagger's sheath protruded from the back of his belt. "How can I be of service?"

"I need to speak with anyone who was on duty at the North gate yesterday and the day before."

"Of course." The Captain gave a slight bow then turned on his heels and walked across the courtyard.

The other men were silent.

Taking charge, the lord said, "Is there any other way I may be of service?"

"Yes," Connery stated, "my men need room and food, and see to it their horses are fed and stabled. I need a hall in which to conduct interviews and the men guarding the gates are to account for *everyone* entering and exiting. I also need access to your Looking Glass."

The lord seemed taken aback by Connery's brusqueness. "For how long?"

"Until we find who we are looking for."

Nodding, the lord snapped his fingers and a page scrambled forward. "Tell the servants to prepare… one, two…" he mumbled a bit, "seven rooms."

"Six. The boy will be staying in a cell."

Seeing they were growing restless, the lord invited them in. "Let us continue talking inside, Commander. I am sure your men are weary, and some matters are best discussed behind closed doors."

Connery motioned for him to lead the way.

To the Vosjnik the lord said, "Stefan here will show you to your rooms. If you have any wants, let him know. I ask only one favor, leave the lad his life; it is ever so hard to find a decent page."

Dax handed Nico over to two guards in breastplates and leather armor. He strained against them, but they yanked hard and dug their fingers into his arms. In the depths of the castle, the cells were mostly empty, but a few housed grungy-looking men with scraggly beards.

Coming to the end of a row, the guards threw him in a cell, his hands still bound. He turned to ask them to release his hands but found they were already walking away.

Surveying the cell, he found it was small, maybe ten feet in width and length. A pile of hay was pushed into a back corner and a chamber pot sat in the other.

He plopped down onto the hay and began undoing his bonds. It took some time, but they finally came loose. Slowly, the reality of the situation and all that had ensued sunk in as he was given time to think. His surroundings' bleakness only strengthened his dark feelings, caused by loss and distress, and, finally, anguish broke forth as he buried his head in the straw to hide his tears.

✠✠✠

Jared woke with a pounding headache and found most of the previous night was a hazy memory. What he did remember was sitting at the table, drinking, and Keegan telling him not to. And waking up in the middle of the night and starting to cry. He'd dreamt his family was whole. Upon waking up and realizing they weren't, he'd begun to sob quietly.

He opened his eyes blearily, the light pouring through the window hurting them. Groaning, he attempted to sit up. His head felt light, and he slowly lowered himself again, sinking into the pillow. It was then he realized he was in the bed. Turning his head, he saw Keegan curled up on the floor. Kade was nowhere to be seen.

Son of a— he thought, as he forced himself upright, stomach twisting as he swung his legs over the side of the bed. Berating himself, he held his head in his hands.

The door opened and he looked up. Kade held a water-skin and half a loaf of bread.

As the door shut, it sounded like a painfully loud clap of thunder. "Quietly."

Kade threw the water-skin on the bed. "Drink up."

Jared tentatively took a sip. The water was cool as it ran down his parched throat.

"Why's Keegan on the floor?" he asked.

"You'll have to ask her that yourself." Kade handed him the bread. "I would've left you downstairs."

Jared ate quietly until Kade finally said, "Get dressed, we have business to attend to."

Looking down, he realized he was in only his trousers. "Where's my shirt?"

Locating it at the foot of the bed, Kade picked it up and threw it at him.

He pulled the coarse woolen garment over his head, then found his belt at the head of the bed. The world swam and he had to steady himself against the wall.

As he pulled on his boots, he asked, "Do you want to wake Keegan?"

"No, she had a rough night."

"And whose fault is that?"

"Yours actually."

"How—"

"Both of you, shut up," Keegan mumbled. "Jared, you made last night difficult, Kade, you're making today difficult. If y'all're gonna fight, do it elsewhere." She pulled the blanket tighter around her shoulders. "Jared, Kade still owes you answers, so do that while y'all're out."

"I will." Jared knelt beside her. There was an obvious knot on her forehead, and he wondered about its origin. "How are you feeling?"

"Like shit," she answered. "The voices kept me up most of the night."

"Try to get some sleep."

"No, I'm gonna stay up and throw a rager."

"A rager?"

"Big ass party."

Kade stood impatiently by the door. "Let's go, we have much to do."

Jared looked over his shoulder at him, then back at Keegan. He scooped her up in his arms but, halfway up, collapsed onto his knees, making her gasp in surprise.

Squirming out of his hold, she muttered, "I got it," and shuffled over to the bed, blanket draped around her like a cloak.

Kade waited impatiently for him with crossed arms. Once out in the hallway, he asked, "Was that necessary?"

"Yes."

Kade locked the door.

"Is *that* necessary?"

"Yes."

Making their way down the hall, Jared steadied himself against the wall, his legs still weak at the knees. Halfway down the stairs, another patron stumbled upon them; he was an older man with graying hair, lips pulled back into a sloppy, drunken smile, and mumbling to himself.

Kade and Jared hugged the wall to let him by.

Unsteadily, the man lurched into Kade, apologizing profusely in slurred speech.

The smell of alcohol emanating from his breath made Jared's stomach churn.

Pushing past the man, they descended into the tavern, which was mostly empty. Kade strolled casually out onto the street, but Jared stopped on the doorstep, hiding in the inn's shadowy innards.

"I don't have all day," Kade called.

Taking a deep breath, he stepped over the threshold. The light was blinding, causing his pupils to dilate painfully. Squinting and gritting his teeth, he followed Kade.

"Where are we going?"

"To see a friend."

"Why?"

"To save Keegan."

He grabbed Kade's arm. "I told you to stop giving us vite answers."

Kade jerked away. "Learn to ask better questions if you don't like my answers."

"That's exactly what a telepath would say."

"That's exactly what an idiot would say."

Rage welled up, but, before he had time to react, Kade's countenance turned to worry.

Kade patted his pockets and, when he couldn't find what he was looking for, sprinted towards the inn.

✚✚✚

It felt like only a few minutes had passed when Keegan heard the door open and close again. She heard the padding of leather boots on the wooden floor, then nothing. As she was beginning to question the silence, someone grabbed her wrist.

Her eyes snapped open and looked straight at Kade. "What're you doing?" she asked, pulling her hand away.

"I, uh, forgot somethin'," Kade stammered.

"Yeah, your head. Where's Jared?" she asked, noticing his absence.

"Hmm? Oh, he 's runnin' a few errands."

Keegan eyed him suspiciously. His manner of speaking was drastically different from normal. "Did you find us a boat?"

"Yes."

"Great, when can we leave?"

"In a week."

She nodded, smiling lightly, before letting her face became flat. "Who are you?"

"Pardon?"

"Who are you?" she growled, getting to her feet. "You're not Kade."

The impersonator could see the ruse was up. "I 'm a thief."

She crossed her arms. "We don't have anything valuable, so save yourself some time and *leave*."

The man began circling her. "Now that can n't be true. I wonder 'ow much the king would pay for you. Maybe 'e would make me a lord."

"Why would Caius want me?" she asked uneasily.

The man tucked a strand of her auburn hair behind an ear. "I 'ave never seen a quintuple elemental 'fore; I do n't believe anyone 'as."

The door burst open and Kade—the real, very angry Kade—stormed in. Seeing the imposter, he hesitated for a moment before flinging himself at him.

In the time it took for them to fall, the imposter transformed. He now had stark black curls and his skin was sun-kissed. His eyes turned to a stormy gray and running diagonally from the top of his forehead across his face was a thin white scar.

Jared joined them, standing in the doorway out of breath.

"Raven?" Kade said, stopping his fist mid-punch.

"*Reven*," the man responded. "You always did love that pet name."

Kade's face remained blank, then slowly pulled into a smile reserved for old friends as he helped Reven to his feet.

"Have n't seen your face 'round these parts for a while," Reven commented, brushing himself off. "It 's made the whole city all the more pretty. Though, I 'ave to say, your mug 'as gotten much uglier, with that nasty bruise an' all. Or maybe that 's an addition."

Kade was smiling all the while.

"Where 'ave you been?"

"Here and there," Kade answered nonchalantly.

"Doin' this an' that an' the occasional hynak." Reven embraced Kade, clapping him on the back.

Kade reciprocated the gesture. "More than the occasional hynak."

Keegan looked to Jared, who was as confused as her, then back to Reven and Kade. "Y'all know each other?"

They laughed. "Yeah."

"What the hell is wrong with you?" Keegan barked at Reven.

He shrugged. "Man 's got to get his kicks somehow."

She clenched her fists.

Seeing her anger, Reven sought to placate her. "Calm, little lady, I jest. There 'ave been rumors 'bout an elemental the king 'as been searching for. As I was enjoying a fine pint o' ale last night, I sensed you. Your being was strange an' foreign t' me an' I wished t' find out more."

Keegan crossed her arms. "So, you break into our room and threaten to hand me over to Caius?"

"No, I find out what kind o' person you and your companions 're. And they 're good ones at that."

"What do you mean by sensed her?" Jared asked, finally shutting the door.

"I 'm a life elemental," Reven said, pulling back his shirtsleeve to reveal the mark denoting his magic.

"How does that work exactly?" Keegan questioned, suddenly intrigued.

"You'll have to ask a Silver Tongue. I can n't explain it."

The four of them stared at each other silently.

"So…" she encouraged.

Reven turned to Kade, "I s'ppose you need t' see Thaddeus."

"Yes," Kade said in a low voice.

"Who's that?" Jared asked.

"The man who raised me after my parents died," Kade answered.

"Well, have fun." Keegan sat back on the bed and swung the covers over her legs.

"You're coming, too," Kade said.

She pursed her lips. "Why?"

"I don't trust you alone. And no number of dirty looks is going to change anything." Kade handed her shoes to her. "Now, be a good girl and do as you're told."

✞✞✞

Keegan had been reluctant to go to Thaddeus's but was smart enough to realize arguing wouldn't change Kade's mind. As for Reven's actions… she'd some choice words for him, but smartly kept them to herself.

"How'd you know I was in trouble?" she asked Kade as they walked down the street.

"I felt you getting nervous," Kade answered.

"How?"

"What do you mean *how*?"

"Feeling nervous is an emotion, not a thought."

"Emotions are thoughts."

Keegan paused. With a slight sideways nod of the head, she said, "Okay, I can roll with that; emotions are thoughts on a basal level." She peered over at Reven. "How did you not recognize Kade?"

"I 'ave n't seen 'im in almost five years."

"Still, wouldn't you recognize him? From what I've gathered, y'all were pretty good friends."

"People change quite a bit in five years," Kade commented.

"An' with my bad eye, you 're lucky if I can tell a man from a dog," Reven added.

"Is it really that bad?" she asked suspiciously.

"No. I 'm only half blind in tha' eye. Still, makes seein' a bit diff'cult."

"Speaking of which," Kade said, "how'd you get that lovely addition?"

"Disgruntled fighter. Thought I cheated, so 'e swung a knife at me. Last time he 'ill do that," Reven promised.

"…you killed him?" Keegan said with a half-cocked eyebrow.

Reven feigned offence. "D' you really think I could kill a man?"

Bluntly, Keegan said, "Wouldn't put it past you."

Reven elbowed Kade. "This one 'as fire in more than just 'er hair."

"Don't remind me," he muttered.

"Keegan, where 're ya' from? I do n't think I 've heard an accent like yours 'fore."

"Uh…" Keegan fumbled, "The South. I'll explain later."

"I 'll hold you to it. Well, we 're here."

"Where's *here* exactly?" Keegan asked, looking skeptically at the two-story, brick building.

"Come inside an' see."

The interior was exactly as Kade remembered—a warren of bookshelves. Dust hung suspended in the air, making Jared sneeze. Keegan bore a childlike grin as she beheld the seemingly endless number of books.

"D' ya' remember the way?" Reven jibbed.

Kade gave him a sideways glance, before starting through the store. Every so often, he took a wrong turn, making Reven snicker. At one point, they had to backtrack to find Keegan. When he found her, she held a book open in her hands.

"Stay with us," he scolded, grabbing the book, and shoving it onto the shelf.

After a few more turns, the shelves gave way to a cleared space where the counter was. Behind it stood Thaddeus. His brown hair had turned gray, but the same kindness and warmth Kade had known as a child exuded from his eyes.

"Kade, my boy," Thaddeus said with a wide smile. "Too much time has passed since we last saw each other." He came from behind the counter and embraced him in a one-sided hug.

"I need to know how to get to the Lazado," Kade said abruptly.

"What, no pleasantries for an old man?"

"No time."

"Is he an elemental?" Thaddeus asked, nodding to the person behind Kade.

"Yes, he's a… *He*?" Kade spun. "Where's Keegan?"

Jared shrugged. "I don't know; she *was* behind me."

"Keegan," Kade yelled. Nothing. "KEEGAN!"

"Whaaat?" came a faint reply.

Kade started to make his way back into the store.

"It is fine," Thaddeus said with a small smile. "Leave her be, I can meet her later. But you, you must tell me all that has transpired in these last five years."

"I don't have time."

"Of course, you do."

Kade frowned as he was propelled into the back room.

CHAPTER 17

Keegan had meant to follow, but the temptation of the books was overpowering. First, she'd stopped to look at a title, then, before she knew it, was sitting on the floor enthralled by its pages. The book in her lap was entitled *The Peoples of Arciol*; the first chapter gave a brief history of this world.

The origins of most of the races can be attributed to the Merfolk. They are humanoid creatures with certain fish-like attributes, such as webbed fingers and toes and dorsal and pectoral fins. No one is certain how long they called the seabed of the Eastern Ocean home before taking their first steps onto land. The Merfolk are the first of the humanoid elementals and most notably known for their control of water.

The first Merfolk to emerge from the sea stayed for only short periods, never venturing far from the waves. Over time, they grew accustomed to the land and began wandering farther, at which time they came upon the Illeria Mountains. A few took residence within, beginning their excavation. After several generations, the Merfolk lost the ability to live on land and in sea. They lost the webbing between their fingers and toes, and their fins. They also became much larger, towering over their oceanic brethren. Small horns sprouted from their skulls and their skin turned to a dull gray. In time, what was once control over water, became control over earth. This new race was deemed the Torrpeki.

Over the next century, the Torrpeki excavated a series of cities and tunnels through the mountains, preferring subterranean dwellings. After several centuries of underground living, the desire to explore arose once more. Exploration parties left the mountains, heading west into the Yarav Forest, where they discovered an untouched woodland with trees larger than twelve Torrpeki in circumference.

Some fought to preserve the forest while others began to tear it down to make way for great cities. A rift formed between the two sides and eventually those who wished to tear it down were driven further west, where they have disappeared from our history. Those who remained worked to create a harmonious existence between wild and tame. Over generations, their physiques and magic evolved once more, as did their name. The Alvor lost the immense girths they had possessed as Torrpeki and became graceful beings. They also gained navels and their tongues took on a silvery hue. The small Torrpeki horns morphed into large curling ram's horns that grow with the Alvor throughout their life.

Their magic became what is now classified as the element of life. Some Alvor sought to fuse themselves with nature and began changing themselves into beasts; some permanently so, while others could transform between forms at will. Those who did these transformations were seen as abominations and were driven east into the Glensung Plains. Some retained the abi—

Someone was calling her. She looked up and yelled, "Whaaat?" Hearing nothing more she continued reading.

Some retained the ability to shift, while others permanently reverted to their Alvor shapes. Those who continued life as shifters were dubbed Werewolves, as their preferred shape was that of a wolf. Now, a wolf is the only thing they can shift into. These two, now very different races, continued to travel together and made their way across the Glensung Plains. Though these peoples would eventually split into different tribes, they have all remained nomadic.

Gradually, the Werewolves lost the ability to be elementals while the non-shifting Alvor gained the ability to control air. With this new evolution, they became the Buluo. These people's physiques also changed, becoming rugged and stout, their skin darkening until it was a rich red-brown. With continued movement north, the Buluo discovered the dragons, who resided in the Averit Volcanoes. The dragons refused to communicate with the Buluo, despite being sentient, and fighting between them ensued.

It was here the world discovered dragons could breathe fire, which led to their classification as fire elementals. The Buluo were pushed south, though they continued to seek a way north. This war was not over land but principles and respect. Returning to their roots, the Buluo requested the help of the Alvor, Torrpeki, and Merfolk. At first, all refused, but as the dragons pushed further south and discovered the other races, they began ravaging the Yarav Forest and Illeria Mountains. The Merfolk still refused to join, safe in their watery domain. Fighting continued for near a century.

Finally, after so many years of bloodshed, the Merfolk could take it no longer and called a meeting between the leaders of every race. This meeting was deemed the Council of Elders. A treaty was drawn up and stipulated that while any person of any race could walk through the lands unhindered, as a people each race would not seek to push the boundaries of their territories. Each race was given no more and no less than what had been their original territory. The Alvor were given the forest, the Torrpeki the mountains, the Buluo the plains, the dragons the volcanoes, and the Merfolk the oceans. To further unify these newly formed "nations", the Council of Elders combined the existing five elements and created humans.

Due to them being a combination of the existing races and their elemental abilities, there is no one element that presents itself more often than another in the human race overall—although, there can appear to be oversaturation of one element.

The Council of Elders was set to meet once a year or when needed to settle a dispute. The members were to consist of the single strongest elemental from each race, regardless of the type of magic they wielded.

For a brief time, humans were subservient to the other races which was eventually ended by The Dragon King. Humans were given the lands west of the Yarav Forest and a seat on the Council of Elders. Progressively, many humans lost the ability to control an element, thus, only a small proportion of the current population are elementals. For the other races, the majority of their numbers are elementals. While each race is known for controlling a certain element, it must be noted that there are exceptions to this rule in abundance.

The text then went into further detail about each race's history, cities, and abilities. Keegan might have continued reading had Reven not appeared.

"Kade wants you."

She got to her feet. "I'd've thought y'all'd've sent Jared to get me."

Reven stared at her for a second before managing to parse her words. "Kade wanted t', but then we would 'ave had to find two people instead o' one."

"I told you to stay with us," Kade said crossly as she entered the back room.

He and Jared sat at a square table and across from them was a man with dark gray hair and deep brown eyes, his skin a series of mountains and valleys. She presumed him to be Thaddeus.

As the man scrutinized her, she saw surprise, confusion, and worry blemish his features.

Kade made introductions, the irritation in his voice noticeable.

"Hi," she acknowledged Thaddeus with a rigid wave. "Whatcha want, Kade?"

"Thaddeus wishes to speak with you."

She crossed her arms. "Okay…"

"Tell him about… yourself," Kade instructed, waving a hand towards her.

"I thought *he* wanted to talk to me."

"He does."

"Then why hasn't he said a word to me?"

Kade was about to respond when Thaddeus said, "You must stay with us while in Suttan."

"No, we—" Kade started quickly.

"I insist. Reven, take them back to Gydrick's to retrieve their belongings while I talk to Keegan."

Kade yielded with a scowl, his chair scraping against the floor. He stomped from the room, pulling Reven and Jared out by the fronts of their shirts.

Thaddeus motioned to the now empty chair.

Guardedly, Keegan took the seat. "I've never seen him listen to anyone."

"Neither have I," Thaddeus revealed lightheartedly. "May I see your hands?"

She set them on the table, palms down.

Thaddeus gently picked up her left hand, turning it over and running a finger over the marks on her wrist.

A shiver coursed down her spine.

"Kade was not lying."

She pulled her hand away. "About what?"

"You, possessing all five elements."

"Why is everyone so shocked by that?"

"Do you know why a soul can only innately control one element?"

"No."

"When two elements are selected by a body—"

"Wait, you can pick what element you want?"

"No, it is randomized. When I say selected, I mean the specific element that will present itself. When two manifest, they battle each other, tearing apart the person from the inside. Yet, inexplicably, they are in perfect harmony within you."

She shrugged, "I don't know what to tell you." They were silent for a moment. "Why do they react like that?"

"The elements counter each other like water and oil."

"Why?"

Thaddeus's eyes twinkled as his lips pulled back into a small smile. "You will have to ask someone more knowledgeable than I."

"If people can't have two elements, how do you know having two will kill you?"

"On very rare occasions, a child is born with two elements. None of them have lived longer than a few months."

"I haven't been an elemental that long, it's possible this could still kill me."

"I doubt it."

"Why?"

"Have your organs begun to fail?"

"No."

"Then you shall live."

With a grimace, she commented, "I wouldn't bet money on that."

"You underestimate yourself."

"No, I'm realistic."

Thaddeus leaned back in the chair. "You seem—" he broke off.

"I'm what?"

Thaddeus rose to his feet and headed towards the stairs in the back corner of the room. "All in good time."

‡‡‡

Aron stood in the chamber housing the Looking Glass. The surface of the full-length mirror rippled, and Connery's image replaced Caius's. Aron and his brothers stood behind their father, half listening to what was being said—feigning in his case.

"We followed them to Suttan, but have not found them yet," Connery reported. "I have enlisted the help of the city guard. So, while they made it into the city, they will not make it out."

"Who is 'they'?" Caius growled.

Connery paused. "Kade and another man identified as Jared Sieme."

Rage contorted Caius's face. "I sent you on a simple mission! How hard is it to capture one girl?"

"We might have succeeded had we known she was an earth elemental."

Caius froze. "She is not an elemental; I checked myself."

"Brennian saw her practicing magic and Thahan confirmed the mark when he and Cralter caught up with them outside Drath."

"If they found them, why are they not in custody?"

"Kade killed Cralter, and the girl was able to disarm Thahan."

"When you return, you will answer for your incompetence."

"We did manage to capture an elemental, a boy by the name of Nico Sieme, who was able to stand against Kade for a time; he will make a wonderful addition to your army."

"I do not want him; I want the girl. Find her!" Caius roared, storming out.

‡‡‡

With the horses boarded in a communal stable, they headed back. Reven led the way through the shop, lest Kade, who'd never understood why Thaddeus made it so difficult to get through the place, got them lost again.

Thaddeus was waiting for them behind the counter. As Kade walked by, Thaddeus grabbed his arm. "There is something you need to know."

Kade rounded the counter and waited patiently, finally blurting, "Well? Say it already."

Reaching into his vest, Thaddeus produced a yellowed envelope, which he sat on the counter. "Do what you will, but you impart this upon… others when the time is right."

"What does that mean?"

"You will understand once you have read it." Thaddeus patted him on the back before walking away.

Kade stared after him, then returned his attention to the letter. The parchment was browned from age and worn where it had been unfolded and refolded countless times.

Dearest Father,

If you are reading this then I have likely perished at the hands of those I called comrades for the past six years. Granted, in their eyes, it is justified as I have deceived them. But do not think less of me; I have betrayed no one, only ever stood against. These six years you have seen me not I have been a member of the Vosjnik as a spy for the Lazado.

For the most part, my time with them yielded standard information that I passed on, but recently I had to act. The Blind Prophet, Alyck, for the first time, made a voluntary prophecy to Caius on the twentieth of April. 'A child is about to be born who shall play a part in your demise. Search high, search low, but look no further than Suttan. Find it if you can, but know this, as long as it remains in this world, your tale is drawing to a close.'

Caius immediately ordered the Vosjnik to find the child. Before we left, Alyck found me, strange in itself because

Caius keeps him locked away in the castle's belly. He implored me to find the child before the others. When I asked why, he said, 'Because this is the one who begins and ends it all, the center upon which the revolution will circle, the conduit of our freedom. I know who you are, Rosh Broyker; I know you yearn to change our fate. This is the chance for you to do so, but only if you are quick. Caius has chosen the path the prophecy will take so do as he says and travel to Suttan. The child will be fathered by Kagen and mothered by Korissa. Bring it to the center of the Mountain of Marble. But remember this, you can only save one.'

Kade paused; Kagen and Korissa were his parents' names. He leaned against the wall, letting himself slide down until he sat on the floor.

He was right; I do want to change our future. We arrived in Suttan on the fifth of May and the Vosjnik wasted no time beginning their search. Any infant found to be less than thirty-five days of age was killed, no exceptions. Any child older than thirty-five days and not an elemental was spared. Any elemental found, regardless of age, was to be escorted to the city's castle to be dealt with later. After we cleared a house, we chalked an 'x' above the doorframe.

It took me over a month to find them and when I did, Korissa had just given birth. At first, Kagen and Korissa resisted relinquishing the babe to me, as they assumed I was working for the king.

His heart pounded against his breastbone. He'd grown up with his parents; how was this possible?

After explaining the situation and with much persuading, they agreed with heavy hearts to relinquish their daughter to me.

His head reeled.

Before I left, Kagen scrawled a few words onto a piece of parchment. 'Give her this,' he said, 'Let her know we love her.' He had written four words: Her name is Keegan.

Kade's breath caught in his throat. Could it be… was Keegan his sibling?

With the child, I fled. We are currently halfway to our destination, the Mountain of Marble—the castle of Agrielha. For a babe, Keegan is remarkably well behaved. Seldom does she cry, preferring to stare at me inquisitively. I regret taking her, as she needs a mother's milk, but it could not be avoided. As a life elemental, I have found a way around this by transferring energy to her whenever she screams for food, but I fear it may stunt her growth.
By now, you must be wondering why I am telling you this. First and foremost, you are my father and deserve to know what happened to your only son. Second, because you are one of the last Keepers of Prophecy. Third, because I request you help my wife and unborn child with whatever they need. Finally, because I must ask another favor. Korissa gave birth to a second child, a boy they named Kade. I ask you to look after him. I would do it myself, but I suspect my time in this world is about to end.
Forever and always your son,
Rosh

Kade reread the last few lines again, then shakily lowered the letter, understanding at last; he and Keegan were twins. Jumping up, he stalked into the warren of shelves, his fury growing with each step until he could contain it no more.

The muscles in his arm tensed and his fist met the hard wood of a shelf. There was a splintering crack and he stared at the end of the shelf; there was barely a dent. Looked at his fist, blood dripped from his broken hand.

Raven, he thought.

Yes?

I need you.

Where 're you?

Figure it out.

A sudden realization struck him, and he wasn't sure whether it made him want to laugh or cry. He could answer the question of why he was both an elemental and a telepath. He had a twin, and they were both elementals. While it wasn't the only way to have dual powers, it was the most common one. And it applied to him. *Them.*

He leaned against the wall and thankfully Reven wasn't long. Too much time with his thoughts was not going to do him any favors. "Heal this," he said angrily.

Reven examined the hand. "What did ya get int' a fight with?"

"Bookshelf."

"Can I ask why?"

"No."

As Reven healed him, Kade's hand tingled as the splintered bones fused together and the skin stitched itself shut.

"What d' you 'ave there?" Reven asked, noticing the letter.

Kade tucked the parchment into his tunic. "Nothing."

"He gave it to you," Reven said quietly.

"Pardon?"

"Father's letter."

Kade eyed him. "How do you know about that?"

"I 'm a Keeper o' Prophecy, too; it 's my job to know 'bout that."

Kade gritted his teeth.

"Do n't worry, I 'ill not tell Keegan. Come on now, Grandfather wants us in the backroom."

"For what?"
"He did n't say."

✠✠✠

Braxton exited the darkness, entering the anterior room. From the clinking of metal, he knew the griffins were awake. Taking a torch off the wall, he headed into the stable.

The twelve griffins stared at him, hardly balking at the sudden brightness.

Any word? Crowlin asked.

"The girl continues to evade the Vosjnik."

A sense of ease overcame the griffins.

Braxton made his way to Iwin. "You speak the Old Language." It was said as a statement but possessed the elements of a question.

I do, Iwin answered, his glossy eyes giving no hint of what he was thinking.

"Will you help me translate something?"

No. I would sooner break my wings than give you information to further enslave the world.

The silence from the other griffins told Braxton that while they agreed, they believed the malice behind the words was unfounded. Having to swallow the hurt, he made his way back to the hidden passage.

Just as the door was closing, Myrish spoke to him, *Alyck knows the Old Language.*

He paused. Why would Alyck make him work for the translation when he could do it himself?

Braxton headed back to his room to retrieve the key to the Blind Prophet's chambers and made his way over, running his thumb over the key's bit absentmindedly. Inside, he found Alyck waiting for him.

"Why?" he asked.

"Why what?" Alyck parroted.

"Why make me work when you know the Old Language?"

"Why not? It will not harm you to learn it."

"Tell me what it says."

"Oh, come now, you are over halfway done, finish it yourself."

"Translate it."

"No."

He eyed his uncle angrily and turned to leave.

"Oh, just as a reference, it is plural."

"What?"

"Finish translating and you will understand."

Braxton let the door slam behind him and stomped to his room in a foul mood.

At his desk, he pulled out the *Evolution of Languages* and began working to parse the prophecy again. 'While you have slaughtered — child of the dragon, she will rise again from the ashes by your own doing. Rule while you can, false lord, for it will only be for the moment. A child will come who can challenge you. From the fire, from the earth, from adversity, from the…'

It was mostly complete, but, after what Alyck said, he knew there was something he was mistranslating. He let the book fall open heavily and rested his head on a hand. Angrily, he turned the pages, struggling to find the translation for *payn.* Eventually finding it to mean 'path'.

He moved on to '*ri luxyen*'. It meant 'of exile'. By the time he finished the fourth line, the sky was pastel colored with the sun halfway below the horizon.

✠✠✠

In the back room, Reven took the last empty seat, forcing Kade to stand against the wall.

"I suppose it is time I tell what I know," Thaddeus said, more to Reven and Kade than the others.

176

Keegan had a pained look upon her face. "Why do I get the feeling I'm not gonna like what you're about to say?"

Thaddeus ignored her comment. "A few days before Seleena Vælar was dethroned, a prophecy was made."

"How does this have anything to do with us?" Keegan asked. "From what I understand that was like two hundred years ago."

"Two hundred, thirty-seven," Jared corrected.

Thaddeus looked at her knowingly. "It has everything to do with you."

"Okay…" Keegan said, "I'll play along. Who made this prophecy?"

"The Blind Prophet, Angela Alaga."

Keegan stared at him confused.

"With each ruling bloodline, a prophet is designated. So long as someone of immediate relation to that bloodline remains on the throne, that prophet will live indefinitely. In exchange for their sight, the prophet gains the power of foresight. The pro—"

She interrupted again, "How could *you* know about this prophecy? Cause again, hasn't Caius ruled for like, two hundred years?"

"Two hundred, thirty-seven," Jared corrected.

"Thank you, Jared," she said through gritted teeth.

Thaddeus continued, "With each Blind Prophet, comes a Keeper of Prophecy, though we have a normal lifespan. My ancestor was training to become the next Keeper when the prophecy was made, and we have passed it down through the generations."

Kade stared blankly at the wall, only half listening.

Thaddeus began to recite, "Four children shall defeat the despot. To rouse, drive, intercede, and assuage his companions is one's self-given duty. A life of displacement one must lead. To right the wrong is one's ambition. To sit upon the throne is one's right by ancient blood. Black and white yet compelled to stand in spite. To each their own misfortune; forbidden love shall be the ruin of the first, the light before the thunder shall be the second's demise, the steel of the blade shall cast down the third, the lies of the mother shall condemn the fourth. Twenty fingers from their birth must we count until revolution is sparked by the one of all elements."

Keegan rested her head against her hands. "Great. Anything else I should know?" When the room remained silent, her frown deepened and she stood, the chair scraping against the floor. "Well then."

"Where 're you going?" Reven asked.

"Anywhere that isn't here," she flared, storming away. "I can't deal with this right now."

"What 's there to deal with?" Reven questioned.

"The fact there's a damn good chance I'm gonna die—painfully. I'm involved in some century-long war. And let's not forget, a bat-shit crazy king wants me dead!" When nothing more was said, she made her exit.

Chapter 18

Keegan tore through the bookshop, barely paying attention to where she was going, her mind lurching. Finally, completely lost, she stopped and sank down against the end of a bookshelf, her breaths ragged as she cursed the maze of shelves.

Her thoughts didn't know where to start. Until now she'd been able to convince herself things would turn out fine. It was hard to hold onto that sliver of hope now. Saving herself was going to be impossible since the universe seemed to have other plans.

She tried to cry quietly, not thinking Kade or Jared would understand. And because, for once, she wanted to not hold back the fear, anger, and pain. Slowly, the tears stopped coming. Keegan by no means felt better, but at least physically, crying had been somewhat cathartic.

It was then she noticed the way out. Keegan stood and made her way to the door. With a deep breath, she turned the handle. If the world couldn't find her, neither could death.

Keegan stepped into the street and surveyed the open door for a moment before taking off. She had no idea where she was going, but it felt good to be moving away from the problem. Lanterns on posts lit the streets and no one was about. It felt like she'd been running for no time at all, but a stitch was forming in her side, and she slowed to a walk.

Yes, if the world couldn't find her, neither could death. A small part of her knew that wasn't true, but logic wasn't guiding her at the moment.

Turning down a side alley, she found a stoop to sit on. She let her breathing return to normal and her heart rate slow. There wasn't much light, but the lanterns from the street provided just enough to make the night a deep twilight.

She took a deep breath, *I'm gonna make it.* There really wasn't another option. It was survive or die. And she wasn't prepared to let the latter be a reality. Another breath, *I'm not alone, I'm gonna make it.* She had friends. Ones that had proven they wanted to keep her alive. Keegan began to wipe away the tear streaks running over her cheeks, *I'm gonn—*

A voice in the darkness called out, "Well, what do we have here?"

Keegan bolted to her feet, muscles tense and her heart picking up its pace.

From the gloom, three figures emerged. "What are you doing out here all alone?" the same voice, which came from the middle figure, asked.

She only needed to eye the men for a second to know they were nothing but trouble. There was nothing to visually say they were up to no good, but Keegan knew deep in her bones she needed to get as far away from them as possible. She had just started to move to flee when an arm wrapped around her, pinning her arms to her side, and a hand was placed over her mouth.

"We should offer to walk her home, Evan," one of the men in front of her said mockingly.

"We should," the middle guy, Evan, said.

Keegan struggled against the man holding her, but it did little good. Even when she stomped on the arch of his foot, his hold didn't slacken.

"We insist," Evan said, keeping up the pretense that she was responding. He gave a slight nod of his head towards the building.

Shit, shit, shit, Keegan thought.

"Save your energy," Evan said, giving a rancid smile, as she continued fighting her captor's vice-like grip, "you'll need it later."

✝✝✝

Long after Keegan had left them, Jared's mind was still processing things. She was right; their lives were about to become filled with even more difficulties and hardships. As if losing his entire family wasn't enough pain for one life. He took a deep breath, letting it out slowly.

"Take a seat," Reven said to Kade.

"Thaddeus spoke of four children, yet there are only three of us," Jared stated.

"Right you 're," Reven said, "there's a fourth who 'ill join you, though I do n't know who he 's."

"Some forgotten, bastard royal by the sounds of it," Kade answered sourly.

"Where's Keegan?" For once, Jared found it useful to know a telepath.

"Front door."

They sat in silence.

Out in the body of the shop, they could hear Thaddeus shuffling about. With his work done, he bid them goodnight. "Do not stay up too late and do *try* to keep out of trouble."

"Yes, Grandda," Reven said.

Silence once more.

Trying not to let his mind wander, Jared glanced at Kade, who was sitting as stiff as a board, a worried, unsure look on his face.

"Is everything fine?"

Kade's eyebrows creased further, and scowling he muttered, "Noxþilk, Keegan! Just couldn't stay out of trouble."

"What are you talking about?"

"She got herself kidnapped," Kade griped.

Jared was on his feet in an instant. "By who?"

"No idea; her thoughts are too muffled to tell."

"Muffled by what?" Reven asked.

"Walls I presume," Kade answered crassly. "Vitt, I can't sense her at all now."

"What does that mean?" Jared pressed.

"She must've been taken underground. That door still in Downey's Alley?" Kade asked Reven.

"Yeah. Why?"

"That's where she was. You two stay here, I'll go *retrieve* her."

Reven laughed, "Good luck getting int' the underworld. It 's been five years since anyone 'as seen your face; they 'ill not rem'ber you."

Kade gave a sly grin. "Just don't get in my way."

"I won't," Jared said, rising.

Kade and Reven shared a look before bursting into laughter.

"You won't last five minutes in the underworld," Kade said. "Stay here."

"No," Jared said. "She's my friend, too."

"You'll only get in the way," Kade told him.

"I will not," Jared argued.

"Ye—" he made to argue.

"Enough," Reven said loudly. "You can both come, as long as you let me do the talking."

Kade glanced to Jared, who nodded. Taking this as a sign of compliance, Reven headed for the door.

✣✣✣

The man that had grabbed Keegan pulled her into the building. She kicked at her captor's shins and squirmed, trying to elbow him in the stomach. Once Evan and his two lackeys were inside, the man holding Keegan threw her to the floor. Scrambling to her feet, she prepared herself to fight; Evan seemed amused by this, given the snide way in which he smiled. The other three men flanked her, backing her into a corner.

Keegan studied the men, trying to decide who was the weak link. The man who'd grabbed her was strong and had already proven she was no match for him. The one to her left had an unnerving smile and bulging arms. The man on her right looked about as strong as a three-year-old; he was stick thin and his expression made it clear he'd rather be anywhere else.

Making her choice, Keegan rushed at the lanky goon. She intended to take him down with a kick to the knee, but instead found herself flat on her back, winded, the man sitting on her hips and pinning her hands.

Evan chuckled. "You made the wrong choice going after Rory."

Though still dazed, Keegan struggled underneath Rory's weight.

"Daytahn," Evan instructed his second lackey, "grab her."

Daytahn did as commanded, grabbing Keegan's arm and pulling her to her feet as soon as Rory had removed himself. Evan and the man who'd grabbed her opened a trapdoor in the floor. With her free arm, Keegan attempted to strike at Daytahn, but Rory grabbed her wrist, stopping her.

"Let go of me," she growled, pulling against them.

They pushed her towards the trapdoor and rightly assumed she'd never climb through on her own, for they lowered her into the opening then dropped her. Evan was ready to catch her.

She'd assumed the door led to a cellar but discovered it was actually a tunnel.

"Where are you taking me?" Keegan asked Evan once Rory and Daytahn had joined them.

"Quiet," he said.

"Where are you taking me?" she demanded.

"I said quiet."

"And I asked you a question."

Evan spun around, grabbing her jaw. "Feisty one you are." Keegan stared at him taken aback, reminded of a similar situation. One involving Caius and a time she'd rather forget. "Men will pay greatly for that."

Keegan's eyebrows knitted together in confusion. "The hell—"

Evan slapped her. "Do not speak."

She shied away as memories flooded back en masse. Evan snickered and she looked definitely into his green eyes.

He had a use for her. She could afford to fight back. "Make me."

Evan punched her in the gut and Keegan could do nothing but wheeze.

She didn't fight as she was pushed down the tunnel, but Rory felt the need to take precautions and held onto a handful of her hair. As they walked, she noticed the number of invasive thoughts wasn't nearly as great as on the street. Small tributaries joined the larger tunnel and, while part of her wanted to see if they led to freedom, she knew better than to try anything. She might be kept alive, but Evan and his crew would only do so as long as she could benefit them. Keegan couldn't tell how long they'd been walking when her ears began to pick up sounds aside from the scrap of feet on dirt.

They rounded a corner and were suddenly engulfed by a screaming crowd. Keegan cringed as the noise assaulted her ears while thoughts flooded her brain. No one in the crowd paid them any attention as they pushed through. On the opposite side, they came upon a door set within the earthen wall. Evan opened it and Keegan was shoved through.

The room was dark and dingy, lit by a few candles in brackets. Groups of dirt-covered women huddled along the back wall. A tall woman with messily plaited brown hair stood and approached her.

"I would tell you to not be afraid," the woman began, "but I can't even follow my own advice."

Taken aback and even more worried than before, Keegan brusquely asked, "Where the hell am I?"

"To put it eloquently," the woman began, "this is a bordello."

"A what?"

"A brothel," a woman in the back snapped.

With pursed lips and tears threatening to spill, Keegan muttered, "Fucking great."

"What's your name?" the woman asked her.

"Keegan."

"I am Adria."

She gave a small nod, then began to pace.

"What are you doing?" Adria asked softly.

"Thinking."

"About what?"

"A way to get out of here."

"Do you think none of us have tried?"

Keegan gulped. "I'm someone new." She couldn't consign herself to the fate Evan wanted for her. Not without at least trying to escape. And, who knew, maybe she would find the answer they all so desperately needed.

"Why should that matter?"

"I can—" Keegan was cut off by the sound of the lock being undone.

Adria pulled her to where the other women were huddled, making her sit. "Stay quiet."

The door opened and Evan and a man stood in the doorway. Keegan couldn't make out any features of the new man, as the light was coming from behind him.

"Which one?" Evan asked.

"That one," the man said, pointing to a blonde woman across the room from Keegan and Adria.

Evan's henchmen entered and pulled the blonde from the room.

Keegan started to go to the woman's aid, but Adria held her back.

"Let go," Keegan demanded, pulling away from Adria. She chased after the woman, but the door closed before she could reach them. There was a collective sigh of relief from the other women.

Angrily, Keegan turned to Adria. "Why didn't any of you speak up?"

"Better her than us," a brunette sitting next to Adria said.

"And I'm sure she says that when you get dragged out," Keegan spat back, effectively quieting the woman. "Why don't you guys fight back?"

"We're weak," the brunette asserted. "And we've tried. It didn't end well."

And just like that, what little hope Keegan had shattered. Hope had been fleeting for a long time, but true helplessness… that was a new low. Part of her wanted to sob and scream. Another part wanted to be stubborn. But she was tired and afraid.

This would be like her time with Caius. Except so much worse. She hadn't imagined that was possible, but, clearly, she was wrong. She would be violated in the worst way possible. And no one cared. No one but her.

Keegan covered her face with her hands to hold back a choked sob that would start a flood. She was exhausted from constantly fighting, from constantly having to be strong. She didn't want to be anyone's chosen one. She wanted to be back home. But deep down she knew what she had to do. And she knew it'd bring nothing but more pain. Yet she had to try for the alternative was worse.

There was the sound of a key being inserted into a lock. Keegan eyed Adria for a moment before she started towards the door. She would die trying to escape before she ever let a man rape her.

Adria fumbled to pull Keegan back, "No!" But her fear wasn't enough to make her do more than that.

Keegan stood before the doorway, surprising Evan and the man with him.

"Sit down," Evan growled.

"No," Keegan said defiantly.

She turned her attention to the man with Evan. He was in his late thirties with a receding hairline, overweight, and wore a wedding band. From the way he was nervously avoiding her gaze, Keegan figured this was probably his first time there.

"Why're you here?" Keegan asked him, hoping there was a way of talking herself out of this situation.

"P-pardon?" the man stammered.

Evan pushed her back.

Keegan stepped forward and continued, "Why are you here? Why are you paying for sex?"

The man began to stammer, and Evan started towards Keegan again. She brought her foot up between his legs and he fell back against the doorframe in pain.

"You have a wife, yes?" Keegan said.

The man nodded in shock.

"Then why aren't you having sex with her? I'm sure she'd enjoy it a hell of a lot more than any of us would."

The man continued blubbering.

"What would she think of you? What would your *children* think of you? Shameful man whore, that's what they'd think."

Evan began to regain his composure while the man just stood there, mouth agape. Keegan watched as the cogs began turning and his face fell.

"You're right," the man said, turning and walking away. It seemed like he couldn't flee fast enough.

Keegan allowed herself a smile. While she wouldn't be able to talk every man off, it was nice to know the tactic could work.

Having watched a customer all but flee, Rory and Daytahn were now standing in the doorway, waiting for a command from Evan.

"You opida," Evan said, striking out.

Keegan dodged by stepping back. She wanted to call out insults but knew she could only push her luck so far.

Enraged, Evan responded with a volley of attacks which Keegan managed to evade or block. When he faltered, Keegan reciprocated with a kick to the abdomen. She hadn't meant to, but her mind had switched to defense mode.

The moment her attack landed, Evan's lackeys jumped forward. Before Daytahn and Rory managed to restrain her, she landed another kick on Evan's jaw. She was already screwed, why not do what damage she could.

Evan started towards her, a hand raised. Keegan flinched and waited for what felt like ages. Slowly, she looked up; Evan's hand was still raised, but he bore a malevolent smirk.

"You want to fight," Evan said intimidatingly. "That can be arranged."

He strode from the room, Rory and Emery dragging Keegan behind him.

Chapter 19

Kade and Jared followed Reven down the street in silence. Reven turned down Downey's Alley and knocked on a door.

A man in his late thirties answered the door. "Reven, my boy."

"I 'm not your boy," Reven responded light-heartedly, "but it 's good t' see you, Porter."

Porter stepped aside, allowing Reven past. "I didn't know you were scheduled for a fight tonight."

"I 'm not." With an impish smile Reven said, "We want to have a little fun."

Porter eyed Jared and Kade for a moment, then let them through. Inside, Reven was already pulling up the trapdoor. Kade lowered himself through and waited below for Reven and Jared. Once they were underneath the floor, Porter closed the door, sending them into twilight.

Reven began leading the way through the gloomy tunnel, the silence amongst them awkward. In the five years since Kade had walked these tunnels, nothing had changed: the stone was still the same dull brown, the same sense of excitement still hung in the air, and there was still that familiar stone of fear in his belly.

After a few minutes, when shouting and yelling could be heard, Reven asked, "Can you hear her?"

Kade sent out a tendril of thought. "Yes."

"Say nothing," Reven reminded them.

They rounded a corner and found a crowd standing about. Reven pushed through the mass to the opposite side. He approached two men who were guarding a door. The first one was muscular with a slight barrel chest and a mop of brown hair. The second had blond hair and looked as though the slightest gust of wind would blow him over.

"Daytahn, tell Evan I 'm lookin' for 'im," Reven said casually.

The muscular one nodded and walked away. Kade and Jared stood around waiting while Reven talked with the lanky one, whom he called Rory. Daytahn came back with a blond-haired man, whom Kade took to be Evan. Something about him seemed familiar.

"Reven Broyker," Evan said, giving a smile that revealed large canines, "what can I help you with tonight?"

"My friends and I 're lookin' for a girl," Reven said with a fake smile.

"Women are my specialty," Evan said, laughing. He then looked over at Kade. "Tavin, right?"

Flatly, Kade said, "Do I know you?"

"I was your first fight," Evan said, clapping Kade on the shoulder with a laugh. "I beat you to a pulp."

Kade scowled at Evan, aggressively removing his hand from his shoulder.

"He repaid the favor later," Reven said before Kade could respond.

Evan chuckled. "Right he did. Let's see what we can do about that girl." He opened the door and Reven stood in the doorway with him.

They stood there for a few minutes before turning back to Kade and Jared. Reven shook his head slightly, signifying Keegan wasn't there.

"I'm sorry you didn't see any that interested you," Evan said.

"Ah, us too," Reven sighed. "We 're looking for someone who 's... a bit more spirited," he finished.

"Actually, we have a new girl like that," Evan said.

"Where is she?" Reven asked.

"In the ring," Evan said with a nod of the head towards the middle of the crowd.

"You sent her to the ring?" Reven said, worry in his voice.

"Yes, needed to break that one's spirit. She had the audacity to send a customer away."

With a nervous laugh, Reven said, "Well, she got you three more."

Kade noticed the crowd behind them had become deathly quiet. Everyone stood staring at the center of the room.

Noticing the silence too, Evan cursed under his breath. "What did the opida do now?"

Kade followed Evan as he pushed to the front of the crowd, which stood around a fighters' ring enclosed with wooden boards. In the center, Keegan stood overtop a man, her hands clutching her side.

✣✣✣

Daytahn and Rory dragged her to the center of the room, whereupon Keegan discovered a ring enclosed with wooden boards. At the moment, a brutish man was wailing on a stick of a kid. The boy was doing his best to put up a fight, but his opponent had too much on him. One hit to the side of the face and the kid was down for the count. Keegan was pretty sure she saw one of his teeth dislodge and fly across the ring.

The crowd erupted and the kid was hauled out. Evan entered the ring, Daytahn and Rory dragging Keegan in behind him.

"We have a special treat tonight," Evan announced to the men surrounding the ring. "The new girl," he reached over and grabbed a handful of Keegan's hair, forcing her to look at the crowd, "has decided she wants to fight. And Payden, well, he loves to fight."

Cheering assaulted Keegan's ears. The thoughts from the men filling the room washed over her, calling for bloodshed.

Rory and Daytahn released her arms, leaving her standing in the center of the ring wide-eyed and anxious. Evan disentangled his fingers from her hair and approached Payden to whisper something to him.

As Evan exited the ring, he called, "Let's have a fair fight."

Laughter rang out from the crowd.

Keegan gulped. *I've got this, no problem. I know how to fight.*

But she wasn't delusional. She could fight—people her own size, not this giant mass of muscle. There was no doubt she was fucked. And, not knowing what Evan had told Payden, either this was to teach her a lesson or to kill her. She had to act as if it was the latter.

Payden took a step towards her, cracking his knuckles. Attempting to make Payden uneasy, Keegan rolled her eyes and responded in kind.

This elicited a few chuckles from the crowd.

Payden's lips pulled back into a small smile, and Keegan realized he saw her action as a challenge. She brought her hands up and put her left foot back as Payden edged forward and threw his first attack.

Keegan went to swat his jab away like she would any other punch but found she could barely move his fist off course. The strike glanced the left side of her face and the realization of just how outmatched she was sank in.

Payden could see she knew she was beat, and probably saw absolute terror in her eyes too, and his lips pulled back to reveal a mouth filled with crooked and overlapping teeth. Keegan began backing away, frantically trying to think of an escape option. None came to mind. Without realizing it,

Keegan backed herself against the boards surrounding the ring, and hands began pushing her forward. As Payden closed the distance, she pushed harder against the hands.

Payden was easily within striking distance, but he kept coming forward. His chest was almost pushed up against Keegan's body, as if he planned to flatten her beneath his bulk. Keegan put her hands up and felt a tightness in her throat. Suddenly, the hands pushing her froze, and she watched as Payden sailed through the air to land on the other side of the ring with a painful thud.

She looked down at her hands. *Magic! How the hell did I forget about magic?* Keegan smiled, realizing she'd found her hidden ace. And that she might actually survive the night.

The crowd was quiet for all of a few seconds, but resumed yelling as Payden got to his feet, fury in his eyes.

Keegan looked around for anything that was earth and her gaze settled on the floor. She concentrated and caused a block of earth to shoot up between Payden's legs. His eyes widened in pain, and he fell to the floor clutching his groin. The crowd was now bellowing angrily at her.

"I don't want to fight," Keegan announced.

"Should've thought of that sooner," a man yelled.

"I wasn't given a choice, jackass!"

If anything was said in return, it was lost amongst the other voices screaming at her.

Payden was slow to rise to his feet. "Had enough, big boy?" Keegan teased, hoping her voice exuded confidence. She really needed him to believe fighting her wasn't worth it.

Payden roared and charged at her. Fear momentarily paralyzed her, allowing Payden to catch her and throw her to the ground. Her head struck the earth and bright blues and yellows swam before her eyes.

Before Keegan could react, Payden was sitting on her chest. She struggled to breathe underneath his weight.

Bucking her hips, she tried to unseat him and when that fail, punched at his stomach.

Catching her hands, Payden gripped both her wrists in one hand, then reached forward and grabbed her jaw, turning her head to the side. "Evan asked me not to mess up that pretty little face of yours."

With his hand so close to her mouth, Keegan quickly turned her head and bit down. She tasted blood and Payden released her hands in surprise. She pushed against his knees and managed to partially slip out from under him. While she had yet to free her legs, Payden slammed his fist down on her side.

Keegan gasped as she felt her ribs crack. Payden moved forward and sat himself on top her chest once more, his hands wrapping around her throat.

Gagging for air, she reached towards his face hoping she'd be able to claw at him, but found her arms barely made it to his shoulders.

Desperately, she felt around his elbow for the radial nerve. When she applied pressure, Payden winced, but it wasn't enough to make him let go. Payden's face was beginning to blur and, succumbing to asphyxiation, Keegan closed her eyes and pushed her arms against his elbow in a last-ditch effort. There was a sickening crack, a scream, and Payden pulled away.

Keegan sucked in air and curled up on her side. She glanced up at Payden and saw his radius sticking out the side of his elbow.

"What did you do, you little opida?" Payden cried as he cradled his arm.

She could only stare in disbelief. She'd barely touched him. There's no way she'd been able to do that. Not while half asphyxiated. And not with her only knowing the basics of earth magic.

Keegan pushed to her feet, wincing and wobbling, and began to edge around Payden.

With his good arm, Payden grabbed her around the waist and pulled her close. "Where do you think you're going?"

Keegan gasped as pressure was applied to her ribs. "Away from you," she said, jabbing her thumbs into his eyes.

Payden yelled and released Keegan. She took the opportunity to launch a rock at his head and she watched as he was felled.

Keegan barely had a moment to breathe before Evan was hurdling over the boards, yelling, "What did you do?"

Holding a hand over her side, she weakly said, "I fought."

As soon as Evan was close enough, he punched her, sending her sprawling. Before she could react, he landed another punch, then another, and another. Keegan expected more to come, but none did.

Looking up, she saw Kade had pulled Evan away. He struck him in the face. Never had she been so happy to see Kade.

Suddenly, Reven was beside her. "Are you alright?" he asked.

"Yeah," Keegan groaned. Reven helped her to her feet and began walking her to the edge of the ring.

"What are you doing?" Evan yelled. "She doesn't belong to you."

"She does not belong to anyone," Kade snarled. "Least of all a bwint like you." To Jared and Reven, he said, "Take her home."

"Wh—" Keegan started.

"Go home," Kade barked.

"But—"

"Go home!" growled Kade.

"But what about the other women?" she said weakly to Reven

Pulling her along, Reven said, "I 'ill deal with 'em."

From the other side of the ring, Jared helped her climb over the boards. Reven pushed through the crowd and was subsequently swallowed.

"He can manage," Jared reassured her. He wrapped Keegan's arm around his hip, doing the same to her and led her away.

✠✠✠

Kade made sure the others were at the entrance of the tunnel before turning his full attention back to Evan.

"You son of a bwint," Evan snarled.

Kade lashed out and punched him in the face. There was the sweet sound of crackling cartilage as his nose broke.

Evan yelled and held his hand against his face, blood trickling between his fingers. "You will pay for that hynak!"

Kade said nothing and simply stared at him with a look of contempt.

"Did you hear me?" Evan yelled.

"I heard you," Kade growled. "That doesn't mean I'm going to though."

"You'll never make it out of here until you do."

"Who's going to stop me? You?" Kade chortled.

Evan roared and rushed at him.

He sidestepped and brought his elbow up against Evan's jaw. Evan staggered back, spitting blood. He reached into his mouth and pulled out a tooth. Tossing it aside, he came at Kade again.

Kade waited until Evan was close, then delivered a strike to the bottom of his jaw and kicked Evan's legs out from underneath him. "I'm not the scrawny boy I was eight years ago," Kade said, looking down at Evan.

"No," Evan said looking up at him, "you're a weak little man now."

Fury welled inside Kade, and he kneeled beside Evan. Grabbing the collar of his shirt, he made sure he could see the star branded on the side of his thumb. "I have *never* been weak."

Kade saw fear flash across Evan's eyes, but, as soon as it was there, it was gone.

"I'll just find the little opida again," Evan said with a bloody grin. "I have men all over the city. There's nowhere you will be able to hide her."

Kade pulled out his knife and pressed it against Evan's neck. "If you *ever* lay a finger on my sister again…" Kade realized his mistake and trailed off.

"Your sister, eh?" Evan said with a conniving grin.

Kade sighed. "Yes, my sister." He pulled the knife across Evan's throat; blood splattered up, landing on his face and arms.

He stood and left Evan, blood trickling from the tear in this neck. Kade wiped his blade on his pants and sheathed it. As he neared the boards, the crowd pushed against each other to get out of his way. He vaulted over the boards and began the walk down the tunnel.

CHAPTER 20

L et 's get you cleaned up," Reven said, gently but sternly ushering Keegan into one of the wooden seats at the table.

Having supported her most of the way back to the bookshop, Jared knew there was more than the obvious injuries. Reven, after having released the rest of the women, had joined them at the trap door. As they walked through Suttan, he'd acted as a scout, making sure they didn't cross paths with any guards. It was only once back in the shop that Reven took Keegan from him.

"I'm fine," Keegan asserted.

Reven gently placed a hand on her side, making her wince. "You sure 'bout that?"

"Where's our stuff?"

"Upstairs. What d' you need?"

"My black shirt."

"What were you thinking?" Jared asked, sitting in the chair beside her as Reven headed upstairs, presumably to retrieve Keegan's shirt. When she didn't respond, he snapped his fingers to get her attention.

"What?"

"What were you thinking?"

"Wha'do you mean?"

"Why'd you leave?"

She avoided his gaze, mumbling, "I dunno."

"Keegan."

"I wanted out."

"Why?" Jared asked, wiping away some of the dried blood from her face.

"I- I just don't- I don't wanna be here. I don't wanna deal with any of this." She flinched and took the rag from him.

"And Kade and I do?"

"No, but you're used to this world."

"What are we going to do with you?"

She gave him a depressed look and shrugged.

Reven returned and tossed her the shirt. "That's very revealing."

"Not really," Keegan said, catching it and resting her head against the back of the chair.

Reven squatted in front of her. "Are you alright?"

"Tired, sore, beat to hell, and sick of y'all asking me if I'm okay when you know I'm not," she answered grumpily.

Reven turned to Jared. "Why do you n't head up t' bed; I 'm just going t' tend to her bruises."

"No more running away," Jared said, heading towards the stairs.

"Hardy har har," was Keegan's response.

✚✚✚

Reven stared at her for a moment before situating himself in the chair next to her. He reached forward and placed his hand on her cheek.

"Wha—" Keegan started.

"Hush."

Unsure of what to do, Keegan sat still, even as a tingling in her cheek began—it wasn't a painful feeling, but it made staying stationary difficult. Reven pulled his hand away and the sensation disappeared.

She ran a hand over her skin. "What'd you do?"

"Healed you."

"How'd you do that?"

"I 'm a life elemental, remember?" He extended a hand towards her face again, placing it over her eye this time.

She felt the same sensation as before and, when he removed his hand, asked, "So that's what life elementals do, heal?"

Reven placed a hand on her collarbone and the side of her neck. "'Mongst other things."

"What else can y'all do?" she asked, rolling her shoulders.

"Sit still. Healing, obviously, make things grow, control living things, and change our 'ppearance. There 's much more you can do, but those 're the big things."

"That's how you were able to look like Kade."

"Yes."

As his hand fell away, Kade came through the doorway, and she mumbled, "Speak of the devil."

Kade glared at her, arms folded across his chest, blood splattered across his torso and face. "Can you not stay out of trouble?"

"It's not like I went looking for it," she responded defensively.

"I swear, you—"

"Not now," Reven said, standing. "We 'ave all had a long day; this can wait till the mornin'."

"Normally, I'd agree," Kade opened, "but I don't know what asinine things she'll do overnight."

"It 's fairly hard t' get into trouble while sleeping."

Kade stared blankly at his friend. "With her, you'd be amazed."

"It can wait," Reven repeated, placing a hand on Kade's shoulder. He returned his attention to Keegan, "It 'ill take me a while to heal your ribs; can I do it in the mornin'?"

"Sure," she groaned, pushing herself from the chair and beginning to make her way to the stairs.

"Where are you going?" Kade demanded.

"To bed. I'm tired and I don't feel like getting bitched at."

"Bitched at?" Reven asked.

"Yelled at," Keegan explained. Over her shoulder, she said to Kade, "You coming or not?"

"It doesn't appear I have a choice."

"You don't *have to*," she pointed out. "You could go do something else. Or someone else." Halfway up, she turned and headed back down.

"Where are you going?" Kade demanded, blocking her way.

She pointed to the table. "To get my t-shirt."

Kade eyed her for a second, then let her by.

"Y'all head up," she said, noticing neither he nor Reven had moved.

"What are you planning on doing?"

"Changing." With a small smile she added, "I mean, y'all're more than welcome to watch, but then I'll have to kill you."

Reven stared at her, obviously surprised by her brass.

Kade began pushing him up the stairs.

"Stop that."

"Trust me, not worth it," Kade said as the second floor swallowed them.

✝✝✝

Wind buffeted him, making it hard to stay on his feet, and the sword in his hand was bathed in purple blood.

An angry voice from seemingly nowhere screamed, "Betrayer! Marmarda! Soucer!"

"Az ryla sarig," he cried back. "Plazde, haxnug!"

The voices repeated those three words relentlessly. "Betrayer! Marmarda! Soucer!"

Talons reached towards him, scraping at his flesh, making pain radiate across his body. The world turned black, darkness coating him like a blanket while voices began to call out from afar.

Three men emerged from the gloom, and he recognized two of them: Aron and Kade. The third was a stranger.

"Jyken eya meki lunviyda zæ psodæ ri ayþ drackyn, æay woth viæn nuþ qalx ayþ æyscs fayo eyar oywn þen," Aron said.

"Nackh jyken eya casne, fackyon ictotm, iruh du woth unla ryo iruh ayþ adæmno," Kade added.

Braxton tried to speak, but no words came forth. He had no choice but to listen.

Together the three said, "Psodæ woth yarv rhæpn casne jappec eya."

The man he did not recognize said, "Qalx ayþ buna, qalx ayþ waysne, qalx okæpyio, qalx ayþ payn ri luxyen, zæ psodæ woth viæn."

Suddenly, he was awake. Confused, he tried to stand and realized he had become tangled in his sheets. Once he extricated himself, he paused to think. The dream's details were fuzzy, but there was one thing he recalled perfectly—pain.

CHAPTER 21

Keegan yawned, groaning as she stretched, feeling the tight soreness in her side. Sitting up, she carefully got to her feet.

On her way downstairs, she noticed a mirror and lifted her shirt to look at the bruising on her side. The area around her ribs was dark and sickly. She was no stranger to bruises, but this one was unsettling. Running her fingers lightly over the edge of the contusion, she clenched her jaw in discomfort.

Letting the shirt fall, she looked at her reflection in its entirety. Even though her borrowed pants were black, she could still see patches of dirt. Her face seemed to have aged, and she hated that. Running a hand through her hair, she found it was slick with grease. Quickly, she pulled it into a bun and began to slowly make her way downstairs.

Kade and Reven were talking at the table while Jared read from a thick, leather-bound book. Descending, she noticed voices beginning to mingle with her thoughts. It wasn't that they hadn't been present upstairs, but up there they were soft, and she'd barely noticed them.

"So nice of you to join us," Kade said, hearing her groan with each step.

"Yeah, yeah, yeah."

"What were you thinking?"

"Oh god, we're starting with this already?"

"Yes, because apparently it's something we need to talk about."

She made her way to the table. "What is?"

"You shouldn't run off."

"I goofed," she shrugged. "Sorry, I shoulda known some asshats would try to sell me as a hooker."

"Yes, you should have."

"I can heal your ribs now," Reven interjected.

"Yes, please." Sitting next to Reven, she pulled up her shirt, exposing her ribs.

Kade said snidely, "Seems you'll lift your shirt for any man."

"At least I won't drop my pants for any man like you," she retorted. She could only hold her tongue for so long and it seemed the dan had finally burst with Kade.

Reven snickered, placing his hands on her side and she leaned against the back of the chair, letting him work his magic.

"What time is it?" she asked.

"Midafternoon," Jared answered without looking up from his book.

She looked to Kade. "So… can you explain how to put up that, wall thingamajig?"

Under no circumstances could she afford to not learn how to protect her mind. Not if she wanted to retain her sanity.

"I told you, it's just something I picked up."

"Well, help me pick it up."

"Practice," Kade said bluntly.

She glared at him. "No shit, Sherlock. But I kinda have to understand what I'm doing before I can practice said thing."

Reven gave her a baffled look, trying to work out her first phrase.

"Fine," Kade said gruffly. "Keep me out."

All voices but her own were gone. "Wait, what're—" It was then she noticed another entity in her head. The feeling was strange, like ice water rushing through her mind.

Push me out, Kade told her.

Closing her eyes, she gathered her thoughts and pushed back against him. It was like running into a brick wall. The next time she threw herself at him, he moved slightly. Repeating the action, she slowly pushed Kade out. Once he was removed, she opened her eyes, surprised at how much energy it'd taken.

Kade sat in his chair like nothing had happened. Clearly, he'd let her remove him.

"It's a start. Again."

She jolted, feeling the icy tendril. Over the initial shock, Keegan sent her consciousness at his like a battering ram and slowly pushed him towards the edge of her mind. As he neared it, he slipped back into her mind. Keegan gritted her teeth and started over. Again, once she had Kade on the outskirts of her mind, he slipped back in.

"Stop doing that," she snapped.

"Make me," Kade said snarkily.

"That's my line."

She closed her eyes and tried to force him out again, but several more times he played a game of cat and mouse. Finally, her frustration boiled over and her consciousness grabbed the tail of Kade's tendril and dragged him out. Once he was removed, Keegan retreated to the innards of her mind. Though she could still feel him testing her, her frustration acted like a barrier to keep him out.

"You managed to put up a wall," Kade said.

She smiled. "Really?"

Her guard lowered and he slipped back in.

"Goddamn it."

"Sit still," Reven chided, as she squirmed in the chair.

"Sorry. How much longer is this gonna take?"

"A while," Reven answered unenthusiastically.

"Ugh." Keegan let her head drop forward. "Can I get a book or something?"

"No."

"You'd best let her," Kade spoke up.

Grumbling, Reven leaned back in the chair. "Fine."

"Back in a jiffy. Erff," she complained, popping out of the chair.

Excitedly, she walked into the bookshop. Striding past the counter, she overlooked Thaddeus and another man with him.

Thaddeus called her back. "How are you feeling? I heard about last night."

She bit the inside of her cheek. "I'm fine."

"Ah, where are my manners? Taite, this is Keegan Digore. Keegan, Taite Ault."

She glanced at the man beside her, who was barely taller than she, and gave him a once over. He was stocky, with slightly greasy brown hair and jade green eyes. Based on appearances, he seemed like he'd be a somewhat decent person, but something was off.

"Uh, nice to meet you," she said, holding out a hand.

Taite looked at her blankly, then turned back to Thaddeus. "I'll need a week. There are some matters I must attend to before I take them."

"Thank you," Thaddeus said, smiling.

"By *them*," Keegan remarked, "I hope you're not referring to Jared, Kade, and I."

Taite ignored her and continued his conversation with Thaddeus. "Not a problem, old friend. I'll see you in a week."

Aggravated that she was being ignored, Keegan snapped, "Are you deaf or just stupid?"

Taite started towards the door, "Women should be seen, not heard."

Open-mouthed, she stared after him. "You son of a—"

"Keegan," Thaddeus cut her off.

‡‡‡

Kade stormed into the body of the bookshop and slammed his hands on the counter. "No," he said furiously. "Absolutely not."

"No?" Thaddeus repeated.

"Taite is *not* taking us to the Lazado." Keegan had just told him about the supposed plan, and he was not happy about it.

Thaddeus came from behind the counter and, taking a stack of books, headed towards the warren of shelves.

"And why is that?" Thaddeus questioned.

"I don't trust that rat." Seeing him struggle with the weight of the books, Kade took them.

Thaddeus began placing books on a shelf. "I am sorry you feel that way."

"W—"

"You need Taite. Do you think it is easy to get to Edreba?"

"Yes," Kade answered exasperated. "People do it all the time."

Thaddeus grinned. "I assure you it is not. There is a reason Kjotes exist."

"We don't need him."

Placing the last volume on the shelf, Thaddeus said, "You do. There is much about reaching the Lazado you have not accounted for."

"Such as?"

"Do you know how to get there?"

"That's why we came to you."

"Getting there is only half the battle. They do not readily accept strangers into their stronghold."

"You can vouch for us."

Thaddeus placed his hands on his shoulders. "These old bones of mine cannot make that long journey."

"We will—"

"For once in your life, trust me. Taite will not lead you astray. Now, end of conversation."

✝✝✝

Reven spent a large part of the afternoon healing Keegan's ribs, often yelling at her to sit still. When he was finally done, he seemed relieved and exhausted.

"Try not to' break any more bones," he told her, devouring a loaf of bread.

She nodded. "Thanks."

"D' you want t' get Kade? Grandda should 'ave dinner ready shortly."

On the second floor, she found Kade sitting on one of the beds looking at something.

"Whatcha got there?" she asked, surprising him.

"A portrait of my parents," he answered.

She took a seat beside him. The portrait was no more than a few inches long, small enough to fit in a pocket. The couple in the painting looked strikingly like Kade or, rather, he looked very much like them.

The woman had rich brown hair that fell in gentle waves over her shoulders. Her nose was small, giving it a button-like appearance. Pale, sea green eyes gave Keegan a yearning for the ocean.

The man stood above the woman, a hand on her shoulder. He bore a cheeky smile and his red hair stood out in relief like a spark. Light freckles dotted his features and matched the hue of his brown eyes. She had to stop herself from laughing at his large forehead.

"Your dad looks like a real character."

"A what?" Kade questioned.

"Like he was a fun person."

Kade smiled sadly. "He was. He always found something to get into. Mostly trouble."

"What were their names?"

"Kagen and Korissa."

"They really liked 'k' names, didn't they?"

"It was a tradition on Father's side. Mother just happened to fit the pattern." Kade looked back at the portrait longingly.

"Were they elementals?"

"Yes. Father was an earth elemental and Mother was water."

From downstairs, Thaddeus called, "Dinner."

Keegan laughed. "That's what I came up to tell you."

✝✝✝

Kade reflected on the earlier moment with Keegan; it felt strange to show her a side of his life few had seen. It was even stranger to think she should've been part of it.

Dinner passed quickly and afterwards Thaddeus retired for the night.

"Can we practice earth magic?" Keegan asked.

"Absolutely not," Kade said.

"Goddamnit. Jared said the same thing."

"As he should."

"Ugh, do y'all not trust me?"

"No."

She looked offended. "Why not?"

Kade gave her a look. "Really? After last night, you shouldn't need to ask."

"But you'll be with me."

"*No.*"

"Then what am I gonna do for a week?"

"Train."

"You just said I couldn't."

"I said you couldn't practice earth magic," Kade explained. "Nothing was said about telepathy and life magic."

Keegan pursed her lips. "I'm not gonna get to see the sun this week, am I?"

"With any luck, no."

She gave him an annoyed glare before stalking upstairs.

"Do you really intend to keep her inside all week?" Jared asked.

"Yes. The Vosjnik are probably in the city and there's no need to increase the chances of them finding us. You might be able to get away with a little training at night. But I wouldn't do so without a lookout. And even then…"

Jared nodded. "I'll be careful." Looking to Reven he asked, "You up for being a lookout tonight?"

"As long as it 's a short session," he answered tiredly.

Going upstairs to deal with Keegan, Kade found her lying on a bed, staring at the ceiling. "Are you going to be bitter all week?"

She sighed, "No. I just wish y'all wouldn't treat me like a kid."

"Then stop acting like one."

Her fists clenched and she rolled over to face the wall. "It's not like I'm doing it on purpose."

He crossed his arms, hearing her thoughts, which contained many harsh words directed at him. "Say that to my face."

"Get out of my head."

"Make me."

She turned to scowl at him. "I'm *really* not in the mood."

He extended his thoughts and was met with a thick wall of anger. "We'll begin in the morning."

Knowing it was best to leave her be for now, he made his way downstairs. To help her keep up a wall, he was going to have to keep her angry. Anger and fear made even the person who was worst at guarding their mind a master. And while anger was the best learning tool, he didn't want to deal with Keegan's moodiness—even if he caused it—all week. *Someone help us all*, he thought.

We could use your help, came Reven.

Be there in a moment, he answered.

‡‡‡

Jared sat on the stoop with Reven. Behind the shop was a small walled-in garden, enclosed on three sides by buildings and a tall wooden fence on the fourth. They were lucky no windows looked out onto the courtyard.

When Kade arrived, he asked, "What do you need me for?"

"We need you as a target," Reven answered. "Well… not so much a target as a victim."

Kade looked highly unamused. "Let's get this over with. What move are you trying?"

"The Rimor," Jared told him.

While browsing the shop shelves, he hadn't expected to find anything, yet he had. He hadn't even known there were specific techniques to magic. And if he could figure out the Rimor, he knew exactly what he wanted to do with it. *Who* he wanted to use it on.

Kade stood across the way from him, arms folded.

Jared took a breath and reached for his magic. With a movement of his hands, he made the earth rise around Kade's feet. Instead of it rising to Kade's knees on both legs, it shot up to his hip, encasing only one leg.

Kade's eyes widened drastically. "Careful there."

"'Sorry," Jared said, lowering the earth.

"Start slowly. This is just practice."

He gave a curt nod and tried again. The earth still only rose on one leg. Seeing this, he directed more magic to the other leg. Now it went up too high on the other side. Several times he tried to correct the imbalance, but it just shifted from side to side.

"You don't do many precise techniques," Kade asserted.

"No."

He tried again and had Kade's leg encased up to the middle of a shin when he shook the dirt off and started towards him.

"Best thing to do is work on controlling two very different pieces of earth that require precise dimensions. I would start with a block and an orb."

"Why not continue practicing this?"

"The concept spans many techniques. While you might master this eventually, you'll still struggle with the others. Get the building blocks and the rest comes easy." Kade said with a yawn before heading inside.

Jared crossed his arms, not finding verity in the philosophy.

"I 'd give his way a chance," Reven spoke up. "Kade may be a bit of an arse, but 'e knows what 'e 's doing."

CHAPTER 22

"R eady?" Kade asked from across the table. His arms were loosely crossed over his chest and he was leaned back lazily.

"I guess," Keegan replied.

While she was still annoyed about last night, she was managing to keep it from being overly apparent. And Kade only knew her true feelings because he was already in her head.

Keegan constructed her wall under the belief he had yet to attack. It was flimsy but was a good start.

"You gonna attack or just sit there?" she asked, bouncing her knee.

I already have.

Damn it, she snapped, more at herself than him. *How long've you been in here?*

Not long, Kade said, removing himself.

"Why didn't I feel you chillin' inside my head?"

"If you're not being actively invasive, it's easy to go unnoticed. You'll have to learn to pick up on the subtle cues of someone being passively intrusive."

Sighing, she said, "Let's try again."

He gave her a moment to put up a wall. Placing a hand on it, it crumbled; it was weaker than the first one. "Are you even trying?"

"Yes," she answered in what might have been described as a half-whine.

"You need to learn this. Your life could depend upon it."

"How 's it goin'?" Reven asked, strolling into the back room.

Keegan slouched. "Lousy."

Knowing he might regret it, Kade revealed one of her thoughts. "Did you know Keegan thinks you're… cute." He didn't need to look at her face to know how she felt; her emotions came rolling off her like storm waves.

"Cute?" Reven questioned.

"Oh, you know…" Kade started. Glancing at Keegan, the muscles in her jaw were tight. "Help me here, what's the word I'm looking for?" Her eyes shot daggers at him. "Ah, yes, handsome."

Reven gave a small, cocky smile. "Why, thank you."

Examining her wall, Kade found it much sturdier, actually having to push and batter before it gave. "Better, but you still need work."

Keegan silently glared at him.

"Are you going to say anything?" He wanted to smile but knew it might push her over the edge.

"You can't do shit like that," she growled.

"Until you can stop me, I can. And I will."

✜✜✜

The falcon sat heavily on Braxton's arm and the sun was warm on his face. While he had not been fortunate in the hunt, he still found it liberating to be outside the castle walls; it was not often Caius allowed him to leave the grounds. While Kolt had a little more leeway, it was still not much. However, it was far better than what Aron got; Braxton was fairly certain his youngest brother had never left the castle.

The resident falconer reached to take the bird from him and, with it gone, he dismounted. Sighing, he made his way across the grass, the men who had gone hawking with him following, grumbling about the day's failure. Aden Kota was the most open about his disappointment—and the most annoying.

He considered going to the bathhouse, but decided against it, ready for time alone after spending the day with superficial nobles. When he reached his chambers, a servant was still in the process of changing the sheets.

"I apologize, sir," she said, flustered. "I'll be done momentarily."

"Take your time, Shiloh," Braxton said with an easy smile.

She gave him a nervous grin, returning to her work. In an attempt to make idle talk, she asked, "How was your day of hawking?"

"Wonderful."

"I take it you caught quite a bit then."

"No," he said with a light laugh, "nothing at all."

She seemed confused by his answer, but, her work completed, took her leave.

As she left, he told her, "Tell your father I enjoyed his stuffed quail last night."

"Of course, sir," she answered, closing the door.

Alone again, he found the sun seemed to shine less brightly and colors became drearier. This was one of the times he wished he had a friend—a true friend, not one of the nobles' sons he was forced to interact with. Of the three siblings, Aron was the only one who had managed the feat.

About a decade ago, Aron had befriended one of the cook's daughters. Braxton was almost certain he was the only person who knew of the girl, which had occurred by pure happenstance one night when he saw them coming from the secret passage leading to the roof. He smiled to himself; just knowing Aron had someone with whom he willingly spent time made the day regain some of its brightness.

Going to his desk, he pulled out a sheet of paper. It had taken time, but he had finished translating the prophecy. It read, '*While you have slaughtered — child of the dragon, she will rise again from the ashes by your own doing. Rule while you can, false lord, for it shall only be for the moment. A child will come who can defeat you. From the fire, from the earth, from adversity, from the path of exile, this child will rise. But know it will be your own foolishness that will seal your fate, oh wicked king.'*

He had been able to fill in most of the gaps where inkblots had obscured the words, however, he still felt he had mistranslated something.

Kicking off his boots, he pulled out a leather notebook. He had spent enough time worrying about the things others wanted him to do. Taking a stick of graphite, he opened the cover of his sketchbook to a blank page.

‡‡‡

Earlier in passing, Shiloh had requested they meet. It was unusual for her to set up a meeting in such a manner, but something in her voice implied importance. Now, Aron stood on the roof as the sun set, casting oranges and pinks into the sky.

When Shiloh arrived, she rushed into his arms, pressing her head against his shoulder.

"What is troubling you?" he inquired, stroking her hair.

"Braxton," she told him. "He knows something."

"How could he possibly know anything?"

"I… I'm not sure. He told me to tell my father he enjoyed the stuffed quail."

"So?"

"Braxton's never set foot in the kitchens. How does he know my father's a cook? And he knew my name."

"None of that is cause for concern," Aron reassured her, tucking a strand of golden hair behind her ears.

"Aron, something's not right."

There will be no happy ending.

He pulled her close. "We are leaving soon. Neither Braxton, nor anyone else will be able to hurt us. *Ever.*"

Shiloh remained silent, then after a moment pushed away. "I should be going. Father will start worrying soon."

Aron let her take a few steps before pulling her back and into a kiss. "I am not going to let anything happen to you."

"I know." There was something sad about the way she said it, almost as if she did not believe him.

He let her go and was alone on the gable as the stars awoke. Looking up, he muttered to the heavens, "There will be a happy ending." By Sola and Lunos, he swore it.

CHAPTER 23

The floor was hard, but, compared to the snow and forests Kade was accustomed to on missions, it was considerably better. He'd been training Keegan for four days now and, while she still had a long way to go, was making good progress. The mental wall she could construct was much sturdier, although she still had trouble maintaining it. To help her do so, he would divulge some of her inner thoughts. It was a tricky proposition as he had to choose thoughts that did little harm besides embarrassing her.

Beside him, he could hear Keegan breathing softly. Dreams were one of his favorite things to observe; they revealed much about how a person rationalized the world. Kade slipped into her mind and watched as she reached into a cabinet.

He looked around the room; it was large and airy, and he sat on a high countertop made of dark black-blue granite. Cabinets lined the walls and made up the base of the counters. There was a large sink set within the countertop, halfway filled with dishes. Large items he couldn't name interrupted the cabinets. One was quite tall and made of metal; two handles divided it and there was a quiet whirring coming from it.

Keegan turned and froze upon seeing him. "What're you doing here?" she asked uncharacteristically pleasantly.

"Observing." He pointed to the structure behind her, "What's that tall thing?"

"A fridge." She began to scrutinize him.

"What does it do?"

"It keeps food cold…"

He watched as the pieces fell into place.

"*Son of a bitch.* You're invading my dreams now? Seriously, Kade, what the fuck?"

"What a useful device. How does it work?"

"I- I don't know the mechanics of it," she said, giving him a puzzled look. "Why are you in my dreams?"

He looked around. "I'm not sure this is a dream; the details are too crisp. I'd say this is a memory."

She crossed her arms. "Whatever. Either way, you're not supposed to be here."

"I know."

"Then get out."

"Make me and put up a wall."

"Dude, I'm asleep; I can't even control what I'm dreaming about. Or remembering…"

"It's something you'll have to work on." He could feel her anger solidifying into a wall. It was weaker than anything she'd created while awake but was a fair start.

Kegan reached out and slapped him.

There was a sudden pressure on his throat and Kade pulled himself from her mind. In the dark, he lay on the floor coughing and spluttering curses. In her sleep, Keegan had managed to hit him in the throat.

From the bed, she mumbled, "Serves you right."

‡‡‡

Keegan awoke with the feeling that something was amiss but couldn't pinpoint what. Downstairs, Jared sat at the table, his nose in a book. Having only spent a few weeks with Jared before… everything, Keegan couldn't say if this was normal for him, or if he was just doing his best to keep it all together and under wraps. Reven chatted with Kade, who nursed what appeared to be a cup of tea.

"I didn't take you as a tea person," she commented, taking a seat.

Kade gave her a harsh glare.

"Jeez, what crawled up your butt and died?"

Reven laughed unabashedly.

"Don't you remember?" Kade asked, voice slightly hoarse.

She shook her head.

"You hit him in the throat," Reven said. "Actually, I 'm impressed 'cause it 'ppears you did it in your sleep."

"She wasn't aiming for my throat though," Kade snapped.

"Or was I," she teased.

Kade's scowl deepened.

"If I wasn't aiming for your throat, where was I aiming for?"

"My face."

"What'd you do to warrant that?"

"I was in your dream," he told her with little remorse.

Her smile faded. "Serves you damn right."

Kade gritted his teeth, clearly doing his best to not give a snide retort. "Work with Reven today; I'm done with you."

"Gladly. At least Reven isn't a blabbermouth."

The boys looked at her blankly.

She elaborated, "Someone who can't keep a secret."

Kade rolled his eyes dramatically.

Turning to Reven, she said, "So, where do we start?"

"Healing," he answered. "Cuts and bruises for now, maybe major injuries later, depending on how you do."

‡‡‡

Jared watched as Reven endeavored to teach Keegan life magic. The lesson had started as mundane, but as Keegan continued to struggle, he found her to be comical. And it was nice to feel something other than fear or sadness. Even if only for a moment.

Keegan and Reven had been working for a few hours now and she had yet to perform any life magic. He could see how frustrated she was becoming after earth magic had come seemingly naturally to her.

Keegan leaned back in the chair, crossing her arms with a huff. "Ugh! Why can't I get this? I break the gem, then focus on the bruise, but nothing happens."

Something dawned on Jared. "Are you accessing earth or life magic?"

Her head bobbed back. "There's a difference?"

"I s'ppose this 's my blunder. For each magic there's a different paika," Reven said.

"A what?" Keegan and Jared questioned at the same time.

"A paika. It 's the source of your magic."

"Ohhhh, you mean the gem thingy," Keegan said.

Reven chuckled. "Yes, the gem thingy."

"So I've been breaking the wrong one for, like, three hours?"

"It 'ppears so. The life paika 's at the base of your neck."

"Where are the other ones?"

"Fire 's in the heart, air in the throat, an' water in the right eye."

"Why are they there?"

"I 'm not sure. Now, get t' it."

Keegan gave a sarcastic salute, saying, "Sir, yes, sir!" She closed her eyes, and, after a moment, commented, "It's purple, like an amethyst."

"Now that you 've found it, try healing me."

She placed her hands over the bruise on Reven's arm and Jared found himself leaning forward expectantly. When Keegan removed her hands, there was still a bruise, though it was now more of a greenish tint now.

Continuing to work, it was two hours before she completely healed the bruise.

"It looks like we need t' get you more injuries t' heal," Reven said.

"Yeah," Keegan agreed enthusiastically.

Jared immediately noticed Reven tensing.

Keegan too saw the change in his demeanor. "Wait, no."

"What do you want?" Kade said from the doorway.

Slowly, Reven got to his feet. "I need you t' hit me."

Without so much as blinking an eye, Kade punched Reven in the face.

Keegan grimaced sympathetically and began to chastise Kade. She was ignored.

"Again." Reven staggered back slightly but retook his place in front of Kade. "Once more."

Jared grimaced; Kade took a cheap shot and punched Reven in the stomach.

Hunched over, Reven huffed, catching his breath. "Thank you."

"My pleasure," Kade responded, walking back into the shop.

"Why'd you do that?" Keegan questioned angrily, making Reven sit.

"You needed somethin' t' practice with."

She gave him an annoyed look, setting to work. It took her several hours, and a few instances of making things worse, but she eventually managed to remove the new bruising.

"Don't do that again or I'll be the one beating you," Keegan reprimanded.

"Yes, ma'am."

"Kade's already on his way, isn't he?"

"Unfortunately."

‡‡‡

One more day, Keegan told herself, trudging down the stairs; they'd finally leave Suttan soon. While she wasn't looking forward to meager meals and sleeping on the ground, being stuck inside with Kade made leaving seem all the better.

Downstairs, Reven was waiting for her, a knife on the table.

"Where's Jared?" she asked.

"He went t' market with Kade."

"What've you got me doing today?"

While she'd by no means mastered bruises, she could heal them—given enough time. And maybe some help. More or less, in a pinch, she'd do the trick. Outside of that… maybe not the best idea.

Reven took the knife and placed the blade against his palm. He pulled it along and a line of red pooled in the concave of his hand.

"Cuts. Now this gets a little trickier," Reven started. "You 'll need t' make sure the muscles, skin, and nerves reconnect correctly. Work from the inside out. That way, if you make a mistake, we do n't have t' reopen the wound."

Without responding, Keegan reached for her magic. The life paika was a fragile thing that she simply had to touch to gain access to. Purple light filled her vision and energy flowed through her into Reven. Though she couldn't see on a microscopic level, she could feel cells moving and shifting at her will. Opening her eyes, his skin was healed, but she'd failed ultimately.

The blood vessels and muscles underneath hadn't been repaired and a bloom of red was growing in Reven's palm. He carefully sliced the skin of his palm again, a gush of blood spurting out. After repeating his warning of needing to deal with the underlying tissues first, Reven held his hand out for her to try again.

Closing her eyes and concentrating, in what felt like no time, all that remained of the rift was a thin scar. It wasn't entirely her doing as Reven had been more or less guiding her by the hand through the process. But at least there wasn't a pool of blood bubbling beneath his skin this time.

Reven examined his hand. "People tend to' have difficulties with reconstructing the tissue." He closed his fist and when he reopened it, the scar was gone. "But you 'll learn."

"It's like putting paste in a crack You've got the base and you're just filling it in," Keegan rationalized, hoping it'd help her do better in the future.

Reven nodded, rolling up his sleeve and picking up the knife again. "Let 's see how you do with somethin' deeper. And on your own." He hesitated, readjusting his grip on the handle before cutting along the middle of his forearm.

Alarmed by the heavy flow of blood, she reached for his arm, magic already at her fingertips. Though he hadn't entirely severed it, Keegan found the blade had gone about halfway through the radial artery. She worked quickly, regenerating the wall of the blood vessel, and proceeding outwards. Unfortunately, Reven was left to mend the muscle and skin as she had trouble with it on her own.

"Don't do that again!" she yelled when the damage was reversed.

"I 'm fine, 'm I not?"

"That's not the point. If we hadn't been able to fix at least your radial artery, you might not've been doing so hot."

"How d' you know it was the radial artery?" he questioned sardonically.

"I took human anatomy last semester. Don't do that again."

"I 'm teaching you. I could 'ave fixed myself. And, for the most part, I did."

"Still. You've bled and been hit enough to give me something to practice with; no sense in doing more than necessary."

"I find it completely necessary, otherwise I would n't be doing it."

CHAPTER 24

It was late when Kade and Jared returned laden with supplies. Though they weren't leaving for another day, Kade had needed to do something besides sit. They'd also managed to get Jared a sword—even if it was a well-used one.

Entering the back room, Kade dropped his bag. A pool of blood covered the floorboards. Behind the table, Reven lay on the floor, Keegan crouched beside him.

"Thaddeus," he yelled. "What happened?" he questioned Keegan, rushing over. To Jared, he said, "Get some bandages."

Shakily, Keegan answered, "We were practicing, and he kept cutting himself. I- I was able to close the artery be-before, but something went wrong this time."

Thaddeus joined them and calmly instructed, "Keegan, step away, we will take care of this." When she didn't move, he pried her hands off the wound. "He is going to be fine; I promise."

Thaddeus took a bandage and, wadding it up, placed it over the wound. "I need your belt," he said to Kade. "Wrap it around his bicep and cinch it as tight as you can." Looking to Keegan, he asked, "How long has Reven been like this?"

"I don't know."

"How many times did he cut?"

"I don't remember." From the way she spoke, she was on the verge of breaking down.

Kade whispered to Thaddeus, "We need a healer. Now."

"None will make it here in time." Thaddeus glanced at Keegan. "She is our only option."

"Do you think she can do it?"

"We do not have a choice." Thaddeus motioned for Keegan come go forward.

"I need you to heal Reven."

She gave him a dumbfounded look. "I- I tried," she choked, kneeling between them.

"Keegan," Thaddeus said, making her look at him, "you can do this. Take a deep breath. Try again."

"But if I can't…"

"If you don't try, he *will* die," Kade told her.

Thaddeus took her hands and placed them over the wound. "It is going to be all right, just do your best."

She still didn't move.

Steeling himself, Kade dove into her mind, prepared to implant the idea that she should begin healing, but found it was unnecessary. Trying to remove himself, he found he couldn't. A purple light overtook his vision, and a sense of tranquility sang in his ears. Through Keegan, he felt Reven's artery rejoining. There was an attempt to make his muscles reconnect, his nerves rewire, and his skin seamless, but it was all very fragile. He was just thankful she'd gotten the artery closed; the rest Reven could deal with later.

Thaddeus placed a hand on Keegan's arm, leaving a bloody print on her skin. "Jared, take her outside and get her cleaned up. You can fill the tub using the spigot." To Kade, he said, "Help me get him upstairs."

Slinging one of Reven's arms across his shoulders, being careful of his freshly healed wound, Kade helped Thaddeus carefully maneuver him up the stairs and into a bed.

Placing a hand on Kade's shoulder, Thaddeus thanked him wordlessly.

‡‡‡

The wooden tub filled quickly, and Jared closed the spigot. Beside him, Keegan stood silently, arms pulled close across her chest, dark blood staining her clothes and skin.

She stood frozen, eyes glazed over, and he gently nudged her.

"Turn around," she told him.

Jared faced the wall and waited until he heard the water settle. The water came up to Keegan's collarbone and was already beginning to turn a pale red. He'd never met a woman who would've done anything like this, but he supposed necessity demanded it. And a small part of him wanted to believe Keegan knew he'd never do anything to her.

As he handed Keegan a bar of soap, he heard Kade say, "He's going to be fine. I would wash your clothes, too."

Relief crossed Keegan's face and even Jared felt the tension in his shoulders dissipating.

"Jared, can you hand them to me?" Keegan asked, reaching towards the pile of her clothing.

He handed the clothes to her over his shoulder without turning around. Siting and resting his back against the tub, he asked, "What happened? I've never seen you react like that."

"I panicked."

Sensing it was a sore topic, he was content to sit in silence until Keegan requested a towel. He kept his back turned until he heard the water settle.

Wrapped in the towel, water dripped heavily down Keegan's legs and arms. "I need dry clothes."

"Uh…"

She raised her eyebrows and gave a tight smile before heading into the shop. Inside, Kade and Thaddeus were scrubbing the floor. So far, it looked like they'd diluted the blood and spread it around more than anything.

"Do we have any clean clothes for me?" Keegan asked shyly.

"Oh, goodness," Thaddeus said, standing, quite at ease regardless of Keegan's state of undress. "Just a moment."

Keegan stood awkwardly until Thaddeus returned with a set of pants and a shirt.

After thanking him, she went upstairs to change. Dressed, she returned, the pants too long, completely covering her feet with a few inches to spare. As her stomach released an unearthly growl, she asked, "Can I get something to eat?"

"I do not have anything prepared yet," Thaddeus said. "Will bread suffice for now?"

"Absolutely."

✠✠✠

"How's he doing?" Kade asked from the doorway to the bedroom.

"Fine; the moment of danger has passed," Thaddeus responded.

"Go eat."

"I am fine for now. For a life elemental, Reven is something of an exception. His gift would imply he would know much about the body, but days like this prove otherwise."

Kade laughed lightly. "He's always been more likely to rely on his brawn than his wits."

"I find that quite offensive," Reven said weakly.

"Good," Kade said, squatting beside the bed. "How are you feeling?"

"A bit drowsy. What happened?"

"You went unconscious from blood loss," Thaddeus said. "Gave us all quite a scare."

"I 'pologize, Grandda."

"I am just glad you are all right. If you can manage, let us put some food in you."

Reven gave him a small smile.

Thaddeus stood and went to get a bowl of soup.

Kade took the chair and turned to his friend. "Sometimes I wonder if you have a brain at all. *You*, of all people, should've known better. It's almost as if you intended to pull something like that."

"I knew what I was doing," Reven claimed. "And she coped."

"She almost wasn't able to. When you became unconscious, she panicked. We don't know how long you were bleeding before we managed to calm her down and she was able to partially heal you."

Reven seemed surprised. He then looked to the bandages wrapped around his arm.

Quietly, Kade added, "I thought you were past this."

"I am. But I still 'ave bad days."

"You should tell Thaddeus. He can help you."

"No," Reven said forcefully. "He 'as enough t' worry 'bout without adding a depressed grandson."

"You're not depressed. You moved past that years ago."

"Like I said, I still 'ave bad days."

"We all do," Kade said, placing a hand on Reven's shoulder. "No more hurting yourself. To give Keegan something to practice with or otherwise."

"For now, at least."

"Reven," Kade snapped angrily, the usage of his friend's actual name signifying how serious he was.

"Oh, do n't get your britches in a bunch. I can work with 'er on manipulation."

"That'll suffice."

‡‡‡

Reven sat in bed, propped up against several pillows. While appearing fine, Thaddeus insisted he remain in bed for the day; Keegan agreed.

"So, what're we doing today?" she asked. If it required him hurting himself, she was going to have some strong words.

"Manipulation."

She breathed a sigh of relief. "Okay. How does that work?"

"Like this."

Keegan felt a force present itself throughout her mind. It was similar to when Kade got inside her head, but on a different level. She might as well have become a marionette.

"That was awful."

"I 'm glad you feel that way. Manipulation should only be used when absolutely necessary; you 're taking control o' someone's entire body."

"Sounds a lot like mind control."

"No. Mind control takes over the thoughts and implants ideas, but a person still retains control o' their body. I could tell you t' stand on one leg forever, but at some point, you simply will n't be able t' any longer. Someone could force your leg down or the implanted idea could be broken, freeing you. With manipulation, I take control of the function in the brain that tells the muscles in your leg t' rise and stay there. The only way t' break free from that is t' kill me or if I decide t' release you. However, the downfall t' manipulation 's that you must actively retain control. Do you understand the difference?"

"I think so. Mind control's psychological, manipulation's physiological."

"Yes… I think. So, now t' begin. I want you to' start by imposing your conscious on mine. Once you 've done that, impose your will, which, if you can manage, I want you to make me stand."

Keegan closed her eyes. She was easily able to encompass his brain with her consciousness but enforcing her will was a harder task. She found that once she gave the command to stand, the impulse was swept away and diffused. Frustrated, she pulled away.

"I can't get it."

"You can; it 's just going to take practice," Reven corrected. "I 'm going to manipulate you again. Pay attention."

Keegan felt him encompass her brain and he worked slowly to give her a better context of the process. She noticed he wasn't cordoning her entire brain, just the portion above her vertebrae.

"Did that help?" Reven asked.

"Maybe."

"Give it a go."

Keegan closed her eyes and made her way into Reven's mind. Once she'd blanketed herself over the small portion at the top of his vertebrae, she started trying to make him stand.

There was a crunch and grunt.

Opening her eyes, she saw him rubbing his jaw. "What happened?"

"You made me knee myself in the face."

Grimacing, she apologized profusely.

"At least it 's a step in the right direction."

CHAPTER 25

Everyone stood in the backroom. Three packs sat on the table, stuffed with provisions. Keegan had reluctantly donned her dress once more.

"We should head outside," Thaddeus said with a somber expression.

Kade nodded, shouldering his pack. Behind him, Keegan grumbled about the early departure time. Once on the street, he stopped, breathing in the fresh morning air. The sun had yet to rise, but the predawn light was enough to see by.

Keegan dumped her pack on the ground and sat next to it, resting her head on it. "Why do we have to leave so early?"

"To put distance behind us," Kade said.

The clop of horses' hooves echoed off the cobblestones and Reven rounded the corner with their horses. From the other end of the street rode Taite, with him another rider.

"It's not too late for us to make our own way," Kade said.

"No," Thaddeus said definitively.

Kade crossed his arms and turned to Keegan. "Stand up, you're not a child." She didn't respond and he realized she'd fallen asleep. He prodded her with his boot and her head popped up with a dazed expression. "Get up."

"No need to be cranky," she griped, stretching, and releasing a wide-mouthed yawn as he took Aros's reins from Reven.

"Taite," Thaddeus said as there came the sound of a creaking saddle.

"Is everyone ready to go?" Taite questioned.

"Almost," Kade said.

"Be quick about it, boy." He could hear the scorn in Taite's voice.

Gritting his teeth, he secured his pack to Aros's saddle.

"I did not know you were taking another person," Thaddeus commented.

"Ah, yes," responded Taite, "it was a last-minute decision."

"Of what element?"

"Air."

"Not too many of those in the city."

After that, Kade paid little attention to the conversation. He finished tying his pack down and went to help Keegan. "Can you do anything yourself?"

"It's not like I didn't try," she answered. "I'm just short… and weak-ish."

Jared snickered at her response and even Kade couldn't help but smile.

Thaddeus beckoned him away from the group and said in a low voice, "Look after them; especially Keegan, she is the only family you have. And be careful; no doubt Caius has men everywhere."

"Yes, sir," he said in a serious tone.

Thaddeus pulled him into an embrace. "I just got you back, I am not ready to say goodbye again."

Kade wrapped his arms around the man who had become a father to him. "At least there is a goodbye this time."

As he pulled away, Thaddeus slipped something into his pocket and whispered, "Open that only in imminent danger. Destroy it once you have read it or reached the Lazado. I pray it will be the latter. Let *no one* know you have it."

"We need to leave before the guards are too alert," Taite said.

Kade looked into Thaddeus's eyes; the corners glistened with tears and shone with pride.

"You have become a man any father would be proud of. I am blessed to have been able to call you my own, even if only for a short time. Now, go, shape the world, and take my blessing."

"Thank you," he said, for the first time in a long while feeling a pull on his heartstrings.

As he was about to pull himself into the saddle, Reven stopped him. "You 're forgetting someone."

"Am I?" Kade asked with a grin, turning back to embrace his friend. "Look after the old man."

"What else 'm I goin' t' do? Go on, get out o' here. I 'ill see you again."

‡‡‡

Jared was surprised another elemental was going with them but supposed she had as much right to leave as they. Keegan eyed her questioningly but remained silent; he'd learned it took some time after waking before she became talkative—and coherent.

Their new companion was stunning, having lustrous black locks reaching the small of her back in loose spirals. Her eyes were a deep blue that seemed violet in most lights. She sat atop her appaloosa with an air of elegance, skin soft as honeyed milk.

By the time they reached the east gate, the sun was halfway above the horizon and the Suttanese were beginning to rouse. At the gates, many people milled about, most looking like travelers trying to leave. The gates were open, but no one seemed to be passing through.

"What's going on?" Jared asked.

"Wait here," Taite instructed, riding forward.

They waited tentatively, glancing awkwardly at each other.

It was then Kade seemed to notice their new companion. He maneuvered his horse over to the girl. "I'm Kade Tavin."

She brushed her hair behind an ear nervously. "Cassidy Wungim." There was a hint of fear in her eyes; clearly she was acquainted with his name.

Taite returned. "The guards are questioning everyone who's coming or going. We're going to split into two groups: Cassidy, Jared, and myself, and Kade and Keegan. My group will go first. Keegan say nothing; Kade, I trust you can handle this. We'll wait for you a mile down the road."

Jared followed and at the gate, uninterested and weary guards stopped them.

"Where are you going?" one asked.

"I'm taking my niece and nephew to Whendell to see their grandparents," Taite answered.

They were motioned through the gate, and they casually made their way along the east road. As they neared the rendezvous point, a horn blew.

Jared spun around. From the gate, he could see two blurry figures racing towards them.

Keegan, what did you do? he thought.

✝✝✝

Keegan watched Jared, Taite, and Cassidy make their way through the gate. They talked to the guards for scarcely a moment before being waved through. Hopefully, she and Kade would have the same luck.

After several minutes Kade started towards the gate.

As expected, the guards stopped them. "Where are you going?"

"Móverth," Kade told them.

"For what purpose?"

"To, uh, visit our parents' graves."

"Be on your—"

The second guard interrupted, "Do I know you, girl?"

Keegan shook her head.

"Can you speak?"

She nodded.

"Can you speak?" the guard snarled.

"Yeah, I can speak," she snapped.

"Then answer when we ask ya' a question."

"Didn't I just do that?"

"You will show us some respect," the first man said angrily.

Keegan refrained from rolling her eyes, and kept her mouth shut, sighing through her nose as Kade made to placate them. "Forgive my sister's crass behavior."

"After she apologizes."

"Do it," Kade commanded with a stern look.

"Sorry," she said, glaring at them.

The first guard nodded for them to be on their way, but the second stopped them again. His eyes scrunched together, scrutinizing Keegan. "I do know you."

"I've never seen you." She could see the gears turning as he made his way to a bulletin board covered in posters.

He pulled one off the board and she could just make it out; it was a wanted poster in her liking.

"Shit," she muttered, jabbing her heels into Bastille.

Kade chased after her, the guards calling after them to stop. *Why'd you take off?*

That was a wanted poster of me, she explained.

Behind them, a horn blared.

✞✞✞

Jared shifted agitatedly, urging Kade and Keegan to reach them faster. Behind them, blurs of browns and blacks shadowed by a cloud of dust chased them.

As Keegan and Kade neared, Taite yelled, "What the royik happened?"

"They made us," Keegan told him, reining Bastille in.

Taite looked at her blankly.

"They recognized her," Kade clarified.

237

"Where did you tell them you were going?" Taite demanded.

"Móverth. But if they're not as dull as they appear, or tell the Vosjnik, they'll know it was a lie."

Taite steered his horse into the woods. "Follow me."

Cassidy was the first to follow, with Kade coming last and looking like he would've preferred to stay and fight. They rode at a near breakneck speed, low lying branches threatening to unseat them. After almost an hour, Taite had them slow down.

"Why are we stopping?" Keegan asked.

Taite disregarded her. "Nothing you need to worry about."

Keegan went to retort, but Kade responded before she could. "She may be rude and annoying and stubborn," he started.

"Thanks for the support," Keegan said indignantly.

"But you have no right to ignore her; she poses a relevant question. I suggest you answer her."

"And if I don't?" Taite sneered.

"You don't want to know."

Slowly, Taite said, "We're not stopping; we're slowing down."

"Why?" Keegan pressed.

"It wouldn't look good to go flying past the south gate."

Jared asked, "Wouldn't it have made more sense to continue east?"

"That's exactly what they expect us to do," Kade countered.

Taite explained further, "By going south through Aylentowne, rather than east through Bouyne—"

"They lose our trail," Jared finished.

Taite nodded, urging his horse through the undergrowth.

They emerged back onto the road, Suttan's south gate behind them. A few people walked along the road, while most were gathered outside the gate waiting to enter.

Silently Taite led the way from the city.

‡‡‡

Nico stared at the ceiling, his eyes tracing the maze-like edges of the stones from one side to the other. There was the sound of scurrying and he flinched. He'd come to fear the rats. More than once, he'd woken to them nibbling on his fingers or to see them staring at him with their beady eyes.

From the hallway came the jangling of keys and the scraping of cell doors against the floor. The guards were coming to collect the bowls and water pitchers from the morning meal, though it barely qualified as such. All his food and drink had been infused with ether and, thankfully, he couldn't taste it that way.

"On your feet, boy," came a gruff voice as the door opened; it was Dax.

Slowly, Nico stood.

Grabbing his arm, Dax pulled him into the corridor.

Futile as it was, Nico resisted, yielding after receiving a backhand to the side of the head. In the courtyard, the Vosjnik waited.

He was forced to mount a horse and his hands were bound to the saddle horn; the reins were tied to Dax's steed.

Connery led the way through the portcullis and a sinking feeling hit Nico's stomach. The Vosjnik appeared to be in high spirits—especially Vitia; they were on the hunt again. He had no idea if his brother would be able to stay one step ahead again, but he prayed to Sola and Lunos he could.

CHAPTER 26

Come on, boy, put some back into it," Waylan barked. Lucas pushed on the bellow, sending a puff of air into the flames. The metal in the embers glowed bright red.

Waylan pulled the metal from the fire and sat it on the anvil. "Quickly. I don't want to have to reheat this. *Again.*"

His words died as the hammer in Lucas's hands came down. Waylan pulled the rod back slowly, allowing Lucas to flatten it along its entire length. Once the whole piece was flat, it was placed back into the fire until it glowed. This time, the metal was rounded until it made a perfect circle—a band for a small wine barrel. It was then dipped into a vat for quenching, steam rising in a quickly dissipating cloud.

"Good work, boy," Waylan told him as Lucas wiped the sweat from his forehead. "You're done for the day."

Lucas gave a curt nod and made his way from the shop. While Waylan had finally started having him work in the forge, they were limited to simple jobs because of his inexperience. The smith sent him home early so he could complete the more difficult pieces without having to yell instructions and Lucas wasn't about to complain.

Back at the Fulpe house, he made his way upstairs quietly. In his room, he found it was peacefully quiet after the din of the smithy. While he enjoyed the silence, he also dreaded it. It was times like these when anger bubbled in his stomach.

Looking at the crescent shaped scars on his palms, he was reminded he still had a debt to pay.

‡‡‡

His heart was heavy with loss, but Thaddeus knew he could no more keep Kade here now than he could five years before. Kade was destined to walk a dangerous path. Yet, he had the mettle to make it through.

There was another pang in his chest, this one not from sadness. This was his Calling. He belonged with the Blind Prophet, yet he had denied that fate for decades, but the call was becoming harder to ignore.

A cough pulled him from his thoughts. Looking up, he saw several soldiers emerging from between the bookshelves.

"Can I help you, gentlemen?" he asked, an unsettled feeling replacing the Calling.

"You can come with us quietly," one man said.

"Whatever for?" Thaddeus asked, glad Reven was not present.

"For questioning about several elementals who were, until today, refuging here."

"I would like to say I have no clue what you are talking about."

"Are you telling me you had no knowledge of elementals staying here?"

"No, I was fully aware of them." He stepped forward and the soldiers reached for their weapons. "I am not going to fight, do as you must."

The men relaxed, circling around him, and allowed him to calmly walk with them from the shop. Outside, it did not take long for people to notice.

Thaddeus spied Reven across the street and gave him a subtle shake of the head in warning.

Reven followed along at the edge of the crowd. And Thaddeus though, *Get away from here, you fool,* wishing, not for the first time, his grandson was a telepath.

"Your grandson's a fool," the man next to him said. "He should've run when he 'ad the chance."

Realizing there were more soldiers ahead to apprehend Reven, he yelled, "Run!"

Their eyes locked and Thaddeus saw the spark in Reven's eyes. He shook his head, knowing what he wanted to do. Little good it did though, as the soldiers around him toppled to the ground, their eyes glassy and lifeless.

Someone screamed and others joined the hysterical call. Thaddeus watched as people fled in the face of an unknown assailant.

It took him a moment to register what Reven was saying. "We 'ave t' go!"

Reven pulled him down the street and towards the stables. By luck, two horses were picketed outside, and his grandson did not hesitate as he pulled their reins free and swung up.

Thaddeus paused; he could not explain it, but his Calling was encouraging him to flee.

"Grandda," Reven said frantically. He was probably sensing more soldiers.

Swinging into the saddle with more agility than he thought he possessed, he followed Reven as they began a frantic dash towards the gates. With each hooffall, his Calling sang; he was headed where he was needed—somehow.

Ahead, he could see the wide-open gates. People rushed to get out of the way and soon they were through. His horse gave a shrill cry and the world tumbled around him. His head struck the ground and for a moment everything was silent.

As his woes flooded back, a stirring he had not felt in years—not since Rosh's death—reappeared. His magic was rearing its head.

Reven pulled his horse around to come to his rescue.

"This is not your path," Thaddeus mumbled, calling upon his magic and releasing a shockwave.

Reven slowed and Thaddeus knew the message had been heard. But he also knew how stubborn his grandson was—a family trait.

"Caxone proytyct," he muttered.

It took Reven a moment to understand Thaddeus had erected a barrier between the soldiers and him.

Knowing he could only maintain the barrier for so long, Thaddeus instructed, "Go. I promise this is not where I meet death."

"I wouldn't be so sure about that, old man," a soldier said, pulling him to his feet.

Thaddeus gave him a small smile. "You would be surprised what I know." Looking over his shoulder, he was heartened to see Reven was already a small figure in the distance.

✠✠✠

Jared was glad when they stopped in the afternoon for a lunch of bread and cheese. Afterwards, they continued until the sun was touching the treetops. Camp was set up in a clearing not far off the road.

Cassidy appeared unaccustomed to the forest and simply sat and watched the rest of them work. Keegan clearly wanted to protest, but kept her mouth shut.

As they waited for Taite to finish cooking dinner, Keegan broke the tension. "Cassidy, tell us about yourself."

Her voice came softly. "What would you like to know?"

Keegan shrugged. "I dunno; whatever you want to tell us."

Cassidy looked at her with searching eyes.

Seeing they wouldn't get anything freely, Keegan asked, "How old are you?"

"Sixteen."

"I presume you are an elemental," Jared stated.

Cassidy nodded.

"What element?"

The word came like a whisper in the wind. "Air."

"Cool," Keegan said. "We'll have to spar some time."

An overwhelmed expression crossed Cassidy's countenance, "I… uh…"

"It's okay if you don't want to," Keegan reassured her.

Silence resumed as Taite handed out food and they all readily dug in.

When everything had been cleaned and put away, Taite said, "Everyone to sleep."

Keegan raised an eyebrow. "It's not even late."

"Everyone to sleep," reiterated Taite.

Jared heard the words, but it seemed as if remnants lingered in his mind. Like there was a thought that wasn't his own.

Keegan started to lie down then shook her head, eyes narrowed as if trying to solve some conundrum. "What did you just do?" she questioned Taite.

Taite looked at her, aggravated. "Nothing."

"That wasn't—"

"Leave it," Kade cut her off. "Go to sleep."

As Jared lay watching the smoke from the campfire drift into the treetops, he heard Kade, *Careful, Taite's a telepath.*

Easy enough, was Keegan's response. *We'll just keep a wall up.* She said it like it was simple. Even for her—which he knew it wasn't.

Easier said than done, Jared told her. *I still have to concentrate hard to even form a weak wall, let alone keep it standing.*

Though some time had been afforded to training him in the mental arts while in Sutton, most of Kade's time had been dedicated to Keegan. And it showed. He hadn't progressed nearly as much, or as quickly, as Keegan had and his wall, at best, been described as a paper partition. He shivered remembering the icy sensation of Kade in his mind. And how removing him had been like trying to bathe a cat.

You'll have to work on it, Kade told them, *Taite's very good at planting thoughts.*

That's what happened! Keegan exclaimed.

How do we counteract it? Jared asked.

Keeping a wall up is the best way, Kade explained. *But, since neither of you is particularly good at it, just be aware of when he's doing it and keep your resolve to do the opposite strong. It doesn't work as well, but, given your competencies, it'll have to do for now. We'll keep working on your walls as we ride.*

Sounds good, Keegan said, turning her back to the fire.

✠✠✠

The pain ripping through Braxton's chest was iron hot.

A voice yelled at him, "Betrayer! Marmarda! Soucer!"

He shouted into the darkness, "Az ryla sarig. Plazde, haxnug!"

Slowly, the pain made him fade into a darkness that he was sure was death. Voices he had heard before began to rise from the gloom and the three men came forward: Kade, Aron, and the stranger. They stepped aside, letting Keegan through, fire flickering openly in her hair. She gave him a sly grin before Aron began to speak.

Braxton blinked and found himself in the throne room, six people knelt before him.

Someone behind him said, "Woth eya sesuna eyar kunyi?"

He tried to turn to see who had spoken but discovered he could only observe those directly in front of him. Studying their features, he did not recognize any of them and the more he focused the fuzzier the details became.

"Naya," the first man responded. There was a metallic flash and the man disappeared.

A wailing filled the air, and he pressed his hands against his ears, the action doing little to block the sound.

The question was repeated to the next person. This time the answer was, "Avu." Four more times that answer was given.

When the voice questioned the last man, no answer came. The question was repeated impatiently. Though the man looked at the floor, Braxton could tell he was smiling.

Slowly, the man lifted his head, his brown eyes holding a twinge of contempt.

"Naya." Again, there was a flash, above his head. "Astæm az woth sesuna ayþ—"

Something tore across Braxton's chest, and he awoke violently, tumbling over the side of the bed. He groaned, the floor cold beneath his body. Running a hand over his chest, he knew he had been dreaming, but it all felt too real.

CHAPTER 27

They rose just after sunrise and had a modest breakfast before setting out. They proceeded in pairs—Jared and Keegan, Kade and Cassidy, with Taite leading the way.

Kade found himself captivated by Cassidy, her beauty truly enchanting. "Uh…" he began, trying to strike up a conversation.

"You were one of the Vosjnik," she said softly.

He was surprised by her directness. "Yes."

"Why would you join them only to turn against them years later?"

"Revenge."

Keegan twisted in the saddle. "Ooh, are we finally gonna get your backstory?"

"I suppose," Kade said, feeling uncharacteristically self-conscious. "Both of my parents were elementals. My father, Kagen, was an earth elemental, and my mother, Korissa, was a water elemental. Both were Lazado agents, but their roles were primarily to keep a watch on the elementals in the city and soldiers' movements. When I was ten, the city guards did a round up and the Vosjnik were with them. My parents got caught up in it and resisted. I'd been out playing with Reven, and Thaddeus was taking me home. We arrived just as the soldiers were swinging their swords. I'll never forget the faces of the men who killed my parents; they belonged to Connery Sray and the previous earth elemental, Noriss Ett.

"I don't recall much of what happened after that. Thaddeus took me in and treated me like his own. I vowed to kill the men who'd murdered my parents. A couple of years passed and Reven and I found ourselves in the underground world one night. We watched a fight, and a man approached us with the offer to join, which we accepted. Neither of us was very good, but our capabilities grew and soon no one dared fight me. I was fifteen then. Knowing I had a chance, I slipped away one night, made my way to Agrielha, and sought an audience with Caius. When I requested a place in the Vosjnik, he laughed saying I had to earn the position.

"I killed Noriss and joined the Vosjnik. During the next five years, I grew close to Connery and Caius. I wanted to kill Caius too, but quickly realized I had no hope of doing so. That is until you appeared, Keegan. From there, it was a matter of finding a way to get ahold of you and take you to the Lazado. You haven't made my job easy. And here we are."

"Damn…" Keegan said. "I honestly don't know if I should hug you or slap you."

This elicited a chuckle from Taite.

With his story bared, Kade found Cassidy began to open up to him. He learned her parents were wealthy merchants who'd kept her safe by concealing her existence from all but a few family friends and paying off the city guards whenever they did round ups. But with rumors of Caius madly searching for a powerful entity, they'd finally decided to send her to the Lazado.

Once more, they stopped at sunset, the Westerlies glowing blue in the darkening sky. Dinner consisted of bird stew, thanks to Kade.

"Hey, Kade," Keegan began once they'd finished their meal.

He groaned; this could lead to nothing good.

"Wanna teach me how to use a sword?"

Taite, who was drinking from his water-skin, nearly choked. "Women do not use swords!"

Keegan looked at him, a mischievous gleam in her eyes. "Screw the system. Kade?"

Taite's disapproval made him want to train her out of spite. But after the debacle with Cralter and Thahan, he'd been meaning to teach both her and Jared how to properly use a sword anyway. He looked to Jared and shrugged. "It can't hurt to teach you. Both of you."

Keegan's lips pulled back into a smile and she held an open hand out towards him.

He looked at her, confused.

She sighed and grabbed his hand, making it meet hers. "We're gonna have to teach y'all how to high five."

"Jared, get your sword," Kade said.

Returning with his sword in hand, Jared noticed Keegan's impish grin and how she was drumming her fingers together. "Should we be worried?"

"Not sure," Kade answered. To Keegan he said, "This isn't a toy."

"I know."

He offered her the hilt and as she pulled the sword from its sheath, her arm dropped instantly.

"Damn, this is a lot heavier than I thought it'd be." As Kade unsheathed his weapon, she looked at him startled. "Dude, you're gonna cut me to pieces!"

He smirked. "Not if you block. And seeing as I don't actually want you dead, I was planning on blocking the edge." Kade let the tip of his sword touch the ground and earth rose to cover the edge. "Happy?"

"Yes," Keegan said with a sharp nod.

Kade did the same to her sword and they began.

Keegan struggled with the weight and needed both hands to keep the blade elevated. In the long term, if he was going to train her, she'd probably need something better suited for her short stature—maybe an estoc or a rapier. But tonight, Jared's sword would suffice.

Kade lunged and slashed at her shoulders. She jumped away, managing to only just block his attack, the sword instantly falling afterwards. His next strike came down; she was slow to react, and the blade made heavy contact with her.

Keegan yelped, the sword dropping from her hands. "Son of a…" she grumbled, rubbing her shoulder.

Her stubborn nature presented itself as she picked up the sword again.

He attacked again, this time with a slash to the hip. Keegan stepped back, avoiding the hit, and tried to counterattack with a jab. She over-extended and he grabbed her wrist, pulling her forward and sending her tumbling to the ground as he placed the sword against her neck.

As he pulled away, she grabbed the sword again. Her stubbornness continued for a while, keeping her coming back for more, but before long she was moving slower. And even tenacity had a limit.

Getting to her feet after a heavy fall onto her backside, Keegan announced her defeated handed the sword back to Jared. Nestling into her bedroll, she promptly fell asleep.

"We should follow her example," Kade said, returning his sword to its sheath and placing it beside his bedroll.

Tomorrow would be Jared's turn to learn.

✚✚✚

Keegan awoke to the sound of flint on knife. Rolling onto her side, she stifled a groan as her body protested.

"Up," Taite instructed, rousing Kade with a halfhearted kick to the shoulder. "Wake everyone else."

Blinking the sleep from his eyes, Kade sat up.

Pushing herself upright, Keegan watched Kade wake Cassidy gently with a few soft words.

Noticing she was up, he told her, "Wake Jared."

Looking to where Jared lay, it seemed *so* far away. She found a stick and tried to jab him, but it fell short. *Yo, get up,* she thought to him, grinning at her ingenuity.

Jared turned over and mumbled something but remained steadfastly in sleep's grip.

Come on, up and at 'em.

He turned onto his side.

Up, she said forcefully.

Jared bolted upright with a yelp of surprise. He looked at her blearily and confused.

"Mornin'."

"*Never* do that again," Jared growled once he understood what she'd done. "And are you really that lazy?"

"Yeah." She'd sooner let him think that before allowing him to know how sore and bruised she was.

"Liar," Kade blurted.

She realized he'd been in her mind and fortified her wall, giving him a mental finger.

"Didn't Reven teach you how to heal?" Jared asked, getting up.

"He did, but I've never tried it on myself. And I still struggle to finish the job. And start it. But it's worth a try I guess."

Keegan found a bruise on her forearm and reached for her life magic. It flowed forth and she felt her skin tingle. After a few seconds, she pulled away; the bruise appeared no different.

Before she could pout, Kade told her, "It's hardest to perform magic on yourself. Something about the energy being in a loop."

She sighed. "I think you're talking about the first law of thermodynamics, but at least I'll get plenty of practice."

Once breakfast was eaten and the fire put out, they left the campsite at a walk.

The day was long, and Keegan spent the ride flitting between letting her mind wander and trying to heal herself. Dinner consisted of bread and a rabbit, kindly provided by Jared. Afterwards, she waited anxiously for Kade to begin the night's training.

Grabbing two sticks, Kade tossed one to Jared. "Ready?"

"For what?" was Jared's response.

"To train."

"Why are we doing it with sticks?"

"Do you want to end up like Keegan?"

Keegan frowned. "You couldn't've done that last night?"

"No," Kade said.

Jared mirrored Kade, raising his weapon. He had one foot back, but it looked like he was trying to balance on a tightrope.

"Feet shoulder-width apart," Keegan commented. "You'll have better balance and movement."

Jared looked to Kade, unsure if he should listen.

Kade nodded. "That's correct. I'm surprised you know that."

"I've actually done something similar to sword fighting with my martial arts training; I'm not *entirely* incompetent."

"If that's so, then why are you covered in bruises?"

"Cause that sword weighs a crap ton," she answered. "Kali sticks are a light and short weapon. And I actually won state champ for combat sparring with it in high school. Which is more or less sword fighting with ouchy noodles."

Kade's eyebrows scrunched together not understanding completely. "Well, when I'm done here, you can prove you know something."

"Gladly."

Returning his attention to Jared, Kade said, "Keep the weapon in front of your body. You need to be able to block and attack." Taking a step with his front leg, Kade cut at Jared's side.

Jared brought his stick down, attempting to block, but just caused the attack to hit him on the upper thigh.

"Don't block down," Keegan said, "unless you're moving back at the same time or it's an uppercut. Otherwise, the hit's still going to land, it just might not be on target."

Jared nodded, keeping his eyes on Kade, who had taken a step back and started to move around. He followed Kade's movements with his eyes, feet remaining rooted in place.

"Move with me," Kade said calmly. "Never give your back to an opponent."

Jared nodded and moved his back foot, crossing it behind his other leg.

"Don't cross your legs," Keegan said. "It'll put you off balance. Lead with your front leg."

Jared stopped, letting his arm fall, the stick slapping his leg. "Can you just let me fight without critiquing?"

"I'm not critiquing, I'm helping. Well… both."

"How is this helping me?"

Keegan got to her feet. "Stand like you were before." Jared did so and she pushed his shoulder, sending him stumbling back. "Stand like I told you to." He did and when she pushed him again, he didn't give. "Get it now?"

As Kade continued the lesson, Jared struggled to fend off his attacks, but that was expected. Every so often, Keegan or Kade gave some advice or correction. When they were through, red welts marked where bruises would form.

Jared handed the stick to Keegan, and she took his spot. While her muscles were sore from several weeks of disuse and last night's heavy sword, she could still move—albeit slower. And she fully intended to give Kade a run for his money—if she could. Compared to Kade and even in the eyes of an untried swordsman she looked inexperienced. But that was not the case. She knew enough and, sometimes, that was all you needed. And luck.

"Ready?" Kade asked as they crossed their makeshift weapons.

She nodded and quickly pulled back to give room for movement.

Kade circled and she followed his movements nimbly. As he lunged, she stepped to the side and, brought the stick down on his knuckles, catching him off guard. Taking advantage of this, she whopped him across the ear and side of the face.

Keegan gave a waggish smile; it faded quickly as she saw the storm brewing in Kade's eyes. The next set of attacks came in a furious flurry. A blocked slash across the chest, a whack to the leg, a dodged sweeping strike at the neck, a jab to the shoulder, and finally a down strike that she caught on her own weapon, the force splintering and snapping the stick.

Eyes widening, Keegan did the only thing that came to mind, throwing the smaller piece, hitting Kade in the face. It was enough to make his next attack falter. She rushed in, placed both hands along the length of the weapon, and wrenched it from his grasp. She then delivered a kick to his stomach.

Kade grabbed her leg and pulled it out from under her. He would have followed her to the ground but was restrained by Taite and Jared and they struggled to pull him across the campsite.

Keegan scrambled back, suddenly finding Cassidy beside her, saying something that was drowned out by the blood pounding through her ears.

Kade shoved Jared off and made to punch at Taite.

"Kade!" Cassidy yelled, panic in her voice.

He froze.

"Stop."

Slowly, he relaxed and Taite and Jared stopped trying to restrain him.

Jared came to Keegan. "Are you alright?"

"Yeah." She brushed him off. Getting to her feet, she yelled at Kade, "What the hell is wrong with you?"

Without a word, he turned and stormed into the woods.

Cassidy glanced back at Jared and Keegan, before chasing after him.

‡‡‡

As Kade pushed through the undergrowth, anger leading him, Cassidy followed, calling, "Wait. Kade, wait!"

He ignored her until she grabbed his arm.

"What?" he snarled, rounding on her.

Cassidy shrank back. "What happened back there?"

He continued walking. "Nothing."

"That was not nothing. You… seemed so full of hatred."

"I was."

She was shocked by his answer. "Why?"

"It's nothing I can discuss with you."

"I am sure you can if you try."

His eyes were steely. "No."

Finding a moss-covered log, she sat and reluctantly Kade sat beside her. Together they listened to the music of the night for what seemed half a lifetime.

"It made me angry," Kade began.

"What did?"

"Keegan. She…" he paused to think. "She can fight."

"I cannot see why that would anger you. She told you as much, I believe."

"It's the fact that she was able to strike me." He seethed, "*Me*!"

"So, she wounded your pride."

He stared into the dark forest.

Noticing a scrape along his cheek where blood sat in droplets, Cassidy placed a hand on his face, running her thumb along his skin.

"Does it hurt?"

Kade ran a hand across his face, seeming mildly surprised to see blood on his palm. "Only now that you mention it. Is it bad?"

"Barely a scratch."

"Maybe you should kiss it."

"Maybe." She hesitated before leaning forward and gently kissing his cheek.

Pulling away, she stared into his eyes, becoming mesmerized by greens and browns dancing around his pupils. Kade began to lean forward and she reciprocated the movement.

They were close, so close she could feel his breath on her lips when Kade jerked back. "We should head back."

She nodded and stood, brushing the moss from the seat of her dress.

The walk back to camp was silent and, when they returned, they found Jared and Keegan asleep.

They separated, each going to their own bedrolls on opposite sides of the fire. Cassidy had just gotten inside hers when she found Kade beside her; she fell asleep smiling that night.

CHAPTER 28

Waking up, Jared noticed Kade was across the campsite next to Cassidy. He had nothing against the girl, but the two together didn't seem right. Not at the moment anyway. Not while it felt like at any moment something could go terribly awry. Not when so many moments already had.

Taite soon had breakfast cooked, and everyone sat around the fire eating quietly. Keegan stole subtle glances at Kade, while he looked apathetically at the food before him. Neither said a word.

Just before they left, Jared overheard Kade half-heartedly apologizing; he was impressed Kade had swallowed his pride. Keegan readily accepted the apology but couldn't resist making a less-than-witty comment.

They stopped once more just before nightfall, repeating the process of pitching camp and eating. They sat silently for a while, stealing awkward glances at each other, or staring at the fire.

Finally, Kade began the night's events.

Jared looked to Keegan for a cue as to whether or not he should spar, and she gave him a blank stare. He decided to take his chances.

Kade's movements were slow and his blows light, though that didn't mean they wouldn't cause injury. He was holding back, and Jared presumed it was in light of last night. He didn't complain; he had no wish to suffer the consequences of that kind of anger.

When they finished, he made to hand the match over to Keegan. She made no motion to take the stick, so he tossed it into the woods, sitting next to her.

Kade gave her a blank stare, before dropping his stick into the fire and sitting beside Cassidy. They began to talk and laugh.

Jared nudged Keegan; she'd been uncharacteristically quiet all day.

"Are you alright?"

"Yeah."

"You don't seem to be."

"What makes you say that?"

"You've been quiet."

"Is that a crime?"

"Well… no. It's just unusual for you."

"I'm an unusual person."

✢✢✢

The days were long and hard and the nights short. A week ago, the Vosjnik had left Suttan at a breakneck pace, dragging Nico along. The guards at the gate swore Keegan and Kade had headed east towards Bouyne. There was no mention of Jared, and Nico wondered about the fate of his brother.

Everyone's fuses had worn down—sleep was a sought-after commodity and anger was the currency of exchanges. Though they were sure they were close behind Kade and company, they'd seen no signs of them.

The Vosjnik had stopped securing Nico to a tree at night, but still bound his hands. He often contemplated making another bid for freedom, but Vitia's glares chilled him to the core. He hoped to never see her wrath, for, on a good day, she was prickly.

Midday was drawing to a close and in the distance, Bouyne appeared. The river city was a brown mole on the horizon, the Tatat River winding behind it like a wound on the earth. The mud walls around the city were painted in faded murals depicting the rise and fall of the Dragon King. Though Nico could only see the beginning and end of the story, every man, woman, and child knew the tale.

Centuries ago, a warrior had come from a far, foreign land. He'd had a name once, but it had long been forgotten and a new one, the Dragon King, was given to him. When the Dragon King arrived, humans were slaves. Wanting peace rather than war, the Dragon King held council with the other races, imploring them to release the humans. Slavery had been on its deathbed for near a century, but only the dragons were willing to grant them freedom. The only reason they sided with the Dragon King was due to his being bonded to a beast of flame. After much time, the other races agreed to free their slaves, under the stipulation homage was paid to them. The deal having been struck, humans were granted the lands west of the Yarav Forest to plant crops; a third of whatever grew was to be given as tribute each year.

The newly freed humans spread across Arciol in a state of disarray, fighting amongst themselves. The Dragon King hoped to let humans rule themselves, but soon realized it was an impossible dream. With a sword red as blood and a dragon of the same color, he conquered the lands given to humans, uniting them. He raised great cities and ensued peace. As his reign neared a century, people began to question his long life. He shared a bond with his dragon, which allowed his life to be prolonged for as long as the beast lived. A few tried to kill the creature, but failed, for no one could withstand the fire from the dragon's maw.

As he continued to rule, humans lost their boorish ways. The Dragon King brought learning, religion, culture, and crafts that benefited all. Never did he kill without a reason, and he did his best to help all in any way he could, regardless of how small the act.

With no rebellions to take care of, the Dragon King set to building the home from which he would rule. It wasn't long before the castle of Agrielha was raised on the plains between two rivers. A city thrived nearby, but the castle was away from it to give room for his ever-growing dragon.

Near the end of his fifth century of rule, he took a wife, a maiden by the name of Suki Vælar. Together, they ruled Arciol with kindness and the world prospered. Years passed and the queen suddenly grew sick. The Dragon King took her south into lands unknown to the people of Arciol. When they returned, the queen was in radiant health, bearing a child and an emerald dragon. She too had become bonded with a beast of flame.

Soon, it was not only that child's tiny feet that pitter-pattered in the halls of the castle; the king and queen were blessed with eight beautiful children: Seleena, Fraisher, Ocea, Uri, Caldon, Bevel, Esen, and Aræhgan. They grew quickly and followed in their parents' footsteps as defenders of peace, which lasted for a number of years before rebellion sparked.

Some had grown tired of the Dragon King in his long rule. To placate them and avoid war, he granted Suttan as a free city, but soon they came back demanding more. He acquiesced, but when even this didn't result in peace, he was forced to take up his bloody sword once more.

Many humans stood with the king, as did the dragons, Merfolk, Torrpeki, Buluo, and Alvor. In the final battle of the rebellion, the queen's dragon took a poisoned arrow to the eye. The emerald beast died in screams of agony, but somehow, the Queen lived. She wasn't the same though; her mind was lost, and she begged for death. The Dragon King, with sad eyes, granted her wish and the red of her blood mixed with the red of his sword.

In his sorrow and grief, he and his dragon bathed the battlefield in fire and the rebellion was no more. The realm wept along with him at the outcome. While others were sad for a time, the seasons turned and they forgot their sorrows, but not the Dragon King. As time went on, nothing lessened his grief.

Finally, he decided his rule would end after nearly six and a half centuries. No dangers threatened the realm, and it was time he grieved for his beloved in earnest. He gave the throne to his eldest, Seleena. To ensure no such hardships as he'd faced would befall her, he created the Blind Prophet. While someone of Seleena's immediate blood line should rule, the Prophet would remain. As a final parting gift to all his children, he endowed them with long lives. He then mounted his dragon and became nothing more than a part of the red sunset.

Now that they were closer to the wall, Nico could see the finer details of the pictorial. Given the chance, he would've marveled at it all day.

The Vosjnik rode through the earthen wall, the guards letting them through without so much as a word. Once again, they made their way to the city's castle. Words were exchanged with the lord of the city and Nico was escorted to the dungeon.

‡‡‡

The door to the cell swung open. When the guard entered, Thaddeus was waiting patiently for him.

"Make no trouble, old man."

"Never," Thaddeus said, pushing off the wall. "I take it my journey to Agrielha is about to begin."

"How d' you know that?" the man asked, a frown marking his suspicion.

Thaddeus held his arms out to be shackled. "Lucky guess."

He was brusquely pushed from the cell, and, from the man's tense nature, Thaddeus knew to expect the worst. He might be well-numbered in years, but the fight had yet to

261

leave him, and, with the reawakening of his spell-casting abilities, there was much he could do to escape the current and impending situations. But he had no such intentions. His Calling, for the first time in years, was calm, as if it knew he was headed in the right direction.

When they emerged under the sun's rays, Thaddeus shielded his eyes, the daylight blinding after a week of gloom.

A wagon waited in the courtyard, the faint sounds of sobbing coming from within. The door was yanked open, causing the inhabitants to hiccup and shy away. Thaddeus climbed into the cart and allowed himself to be chained to its wall. The door was shut, and a padlock clipped into place. He heard orders being called to the guards outside and they lurched forward.

A woman beside him buried her face in her hands, tears rolling down her cheeks. He wished he could offer words of comfort, but they all knew where they were headed. And no words but one would save them.

CHAPTER 29

The next few days found Keegan abnormally quiet. Kade and Cassidy were too enraptured in each other to notice and Taite preferred her silence. Jared was the only one concerned, even if Keegan found no reason for it.

Despite Kade's apology, Keegan remained wary of him during sparring. His movements were slow and deliberate, but when she landed an attack, he struggled furiously to swallow his pride.

The days of riding were long and, after eight of them, they reached the next large city, Aylentowne.

The inn they stayed at, The Magnenpie, wasn't Keegan's first choice in accommodation; the folk in the tavern eyed her unscrupulously. Kade linked his arm with Cassidy's when he saw her discomfort. Over the last week, Keegan had watched them become close and was skeptical of Kade's intentions.

Taite led the way to their room, where there were two beds waiting for them.

"How long are we staying?" Keegan asked.

"Couple of days," Taite answered.

"Why so long?" Kade questioned.

"We're in no particular rush," Taite continued. "We can afford to spend a few days recuperating and resupplying."

"Who gets the beds?" Keegan asked.

"I get one. The rest of you can fight for the other," Taite said.

"And they say chivalry's dead," she scoffed.

✢✢✢

The tavern was still packed when they returned, only now the men were more content with harassing the barmaids. Taite ordered food and they attempted to find seats together, giving up when a barmaid approached with their drinks. They split into a group of two and three, Kade and Cassidy, and Jared, Keegan, and Taite.

As Jared brought his tankard to his lips, Keegan said, "That'd better be water."

"Pardon?"

"That'd better be water," she repeated

"Who are you to stop a man from drinking?" Taite griped. To make a point, he downed his pint.

"The person who looked after his drunk ass last time," she said coolly.

Taite muttered something under his breath and Jared felt his cheeks flush.

"It's not shameful," Keegan defended. "It happens; lord knows I've spent a night or two bent over a toilet."

"Why would you be bent over that?" Jared questioned.

Keegan gave him a funny look. "Oh. My toilet and your toilet probably don't mean the same thing. Mine's a big porcelain bowl that you piss and shit in."

"That's a chamber pot," Taite said, finishing his drink.

"No, it's bigger and it's got plumbing."

"Plumbing?"

"Uhh… drainage pipes."

Taite looked at her incredulously. "What a strange thing you talk of."

"It's less strange than this world."

"How so?"

"In every way."

"That doesn't prove anything," Jared told her.

Keegan gave him an annoyed glance. "Well, the things I consider normal would be like magic to y'all."

"I'm not understanding the analogy."

"What I consider normal would make you react the same way I did when I found out magic was real."

Taking a drink, Jared said, "Out of curiosity, what kinds of things are you referring to?"

"We have these metal contraptions that go faster than a horse, and some can fly, and some can let people survive underwater."

Taite looked at her unfazed, though disbelief pulled at the corners of his expression.

"We've been on the moon."

"Impossible," Taite balked.

"Nope and that's barely scraping the surface. We have these little rectangles that let us talk to anyone on the planet, give us access to just about any piece of information, no matter how mundane or obscure, and you know what we use them for? To watch videos of cats and porn."

"What's porn?" Jared asked.

Keegan leaned close and whispered in his ear the answer.

Heat flooded his cheeks. "That's not a normal world."

Keegan took a bite of her food and retracted her previous argument, "Normal's relative."

"I'll agree with that," Taite said.

She commented, "Wow, a first."

"And a last."

After that, they were content to eat their meal in silence. Keegan kept stealing glances down the table towards Kade and Cassidy, her eyes always returning to her plate with a roll.

Jared understood Kade's romanticisms but took Keegan's stance that this was neither the time nor place.

Her plate cleared, Keegan stifled a yawn. "I'm headin' to bed."

"I'll join you," Jared said.

She snickered, "Not in the same bed."

Taite, who was taking a drink, nearly choked. "You should never make jokes about that. You're a lady; act like it!"

Keegan looked at him blankly and snorted. "I'm not a lady and good luck making me act like one." She made her way along the tables and, coming across Kade and Cassidy, stopped to talk to them.

"You need to control that girl," Taite said.

Jared smiled. "Kade's tried and I like her the way she is."

✝✝✝

Aron watched the castle gate from his room. A few straggling carts were pulled through the portcullis before it closed for the night. He had considered bribing one of the merchants to give him and Shiloh passage out, but with her being wary of Braxton, he knew they would have to carry themselves out on their own two feet.

They needed some diversion, but what would be enough to let them go unnoticed? Aron pushed himself away from the window and started making his way to Alyck. Halfway there, he turned around; he was not ready to say goodbye to Shiloh, and until he did Alyck would refuse him.

Walking back through the halls, he became lost in his own thoughts, finding himself where the hidden passage was. He pressed the stone and stepped into the darkness. At the end of the corridor, a crescent moon illuminated the gable. He sat in the middle of the rooftop and looked up at the stars.

He thought a fire might be a good distraction. But there was no way to create a large enough blaze and fires rarely spread because almost everything in the castle was stone.

Aron toyed with other ideas, ranging from ridiculous ones like killing Kolt, to potential ones, like killing a guard to insinuate an attack. None would work though, and he still had no plan as the moon neared its peak.

From the plains surrounding the castle came a deep screech. He strained his eyes, but for all his worth could not spot the night eagle. The bird called again, and it reminded him of another sound. Aron smiled as the night eagle flew overhead, soaring on a light wind. He had an idea.

‡‡‡

His hair whipped around his face and his clothes pulled against his body. A shrieking was added to the wind. Braxton looked at the sword in his hand, which was covered in purple blood.

A voice screamed violently, "Betrayer! Marmarda! Soucer!"

Braxton cried in return, "Az ryla sarig. Plazde, haxnug!"

His chest was ripped open, forcing a wild yell from his throat. Darkness surrounded him and whispers danced in the air.

His chest seamlessly repaired itself and he saw four figures across the void from him.

He already knew what they were going to say and, one at a time, all repeated the lines he had heard so many times before. Then together they said, "Psodæ woth yarv." Slowly, their voices jumbled and faded to whispers as their forms melted into the darkness.

He repeated their words, hoping to be able to recall them when he awoke.

The world began to brighten, and he stood in the throne room, six individuals kneeling before him.

A voice asked, "Woth eya sesuna eyar kunyi?"

"Naya," the first man responded. There was a flash and his body fell forward, truncated.

Sobs filled the air as the same question was repeated to the five-remaining people. Four responded "Avu."

When it came to the sixth man, he raised his head and smiled. "Naya." A streak of gray appeared over his body. "Astæm az woth sesuna ayþ bindiar darvesen."

Then, the world was nothing but gray.

Momentarily confused, Braxton realized he was awake and staring at the ceiling. Sitting up, he was relieved to not be in pain. Outside his window, the sun shone brightly—he had slept through the night.

Throwing back the covers, he went to his desk and began trying to recall the prophecy as it had been told in his dream. Only one fragment seemed to have stuck: psodæ woth yarv.

CHAPTER 30

Cassidy was the first to greet the day. Rolling onto her side, she saw Keegan slept diagonally between Jared, who had his back to her, and Kade, who was within arms reach.

Reaching over, she ran her fingers through Kade's auburn hair.

A small smile graced his lips. *Good morning.*

It still felt strange to communicate telepathically, but she responded in kind. *Good morning. How did you sleep?*

Well. When Keegan wasn't kicking me, that is.

Soon the others roused, and they breakfasted in the tavern.

"So, what's on the agenda?" Keegan questioned when they returned to the room.

Tying a purse to his belt, Taite answered, "I need to go to the market."

"Okay. What're the rest of us supposed to do?"

"Stay here."

"Ugh, that's so boring," Keegan said dramatically.

"That's not my—"

"I could go for a bath," Cassidy commented.

"Abs—" Taite started.

Keegan cut him off. "I like the sound of that."

Pinching the bridge of his nose, Taite growled, "Fine." Digging through his purse, he pulled out a few bronze coins, and handed them to Kade. "For the bathhouse."

Kade passed the coins along to Jared. "I'm going with you. I don't trust you."

Realizing Kade was not going to be swayed, Taite snarled, "Suit yourself."

"So…" Keegan began as soon as they had left, "how does this work exactly?"

Cassidy giggled. "First, we find a bathhouse."

"The innkeepers should know of one," Jared said.

Downstairs, the tavern was mostly empty, a few people still eating, and one man was hunched over a table, drool pooled on the side of his face.

Jared was brief in talking to the inn keeper. "He said there's one not too far from here."

Out on the streets, people went about their daily lives. Women carried empty baskets to market and others carried them piled high with fruits and vegetables as they made their way home. Children wove between the crowds, their giggles floating above everyone's heads.

The buildings of Aylentowne were mostly made of a mixture of stone foundations with plaster uppers imbedded with wooden timbers for support. Windowpanes were crisscrossed with veins of gray metal and the streets were cobbled with worn stones cemented together with dirt.

Jared stopped outside a wide building that took up what should have been several house fronts. Walking through the doorway, Cassidy instantly felt the difference in humidity weighing down on her.

A fat woman sat behind a table. "Three coppers," she said lazily.

Jared fished the money from his pocket, and she gave them three folded linens to serve as towels.

"Will you be needing an attendant?"

Jared looked to Cassidy. She gave him a slight nod and he answered, "Yes."

"Phinne," she yelled.

A young man came forward. He was handsome, but Cassidy could immediately tell why he had such a lowly job—a rich fire-mark starting under his right eye that made its way across his nose and down the side of his face.

"If you'll follow," Phinne said, starting through a doorway.

They were hit with a wall of steam and, pushing through, came into a wide, open area. There was a large pool in the center with tubs of varying sizes surrounding it. Small groups of people sat in larger tubs, letting attendants wash their hair or rub soap across their backs. In the pool, people lounged, happily talking to one another or swimming across the clear water.

Phinne led them a to a large tub. "If you will disrobe."

Jared had few qualms about doing so. Keegan, on the other hand, was less enthusiastic and stood awkwardly.

"It is not so bad, especially once you are in the water. Would you undo the lacing?" Cassidy asked, turning her back to Keegan.

With nimble fingers, Keegan pulled away the ties of her dress. Gritting her teeth, Keegan began to undress and, as the last piece of clothing fell away, quickly got into the water. She pulled her knees up, folding her arms across her chest, though it concealed little, as her bosom was more than ample.

"Relax, sweetheart," Phinne said. "Here, we're all as Sola and Lunos made us."

Keegan eyed him for a moment before saying to Jared, "This is the first time I've heard any mention of religion."

Phinne poured water from a pitcher over Jared's head. "Really? How strange. If you don't pray to Sola and Lunos, then who do you pray to?"

"No one really."

"Who do you look to when seeking guidance or help?"

"People and science. Honestly, I feel the existence of gods can neither be proven nor disproven and, until such time, I choose to remain neutral on the matter."

"Are all people like this where you're from?"

"Nope. There are a lot of religions and just as many gods to go with 'em."

"Impossibly impressive; I do wonder how you all live in harmony."

Keegan gave a snort of laughter as Phinne moved to Cassidy. "We don't, not by a long shot."

"A strange place to live in."

"You don't know the half of it," she muttered under her breath.

"Where was it you said you're from again?"

"I didn't."

Phinne had the sense to not press further. The water he poured over Cassidy's head was warm and had the faint smell of violets. His fingers worked gently through the knots in her dark hair. Once he had washed Keegan's hair, he told them, "Feel free to lounge in the central pool for as long as you like."

"Thank you," Cassidy said. "You may excuse yourself until further notice."

Phinne bowed his head, "As you wish."

When they clambered from the water, Phinne offered them towels and they dressed quickly. Back at the inn, they found Kade and Taite had yet to return.

✠✠✠

"Hurry up with that barrel band," Waylan chided.

Lucas brought the hammer down on the metal a few more times before stepping away from the anvil.

He'd been working under Waylan for the better part of a month now. While his skills still needed honing, they were well on their way and today the master had decided it was time for a test.

As he looked over the band, Waylan gave a few grunts. "Not half bad. May make a smith out of you yet."

Lucas felt the corners of his lips begin to pull up.

"I need nine more. I trust you can manage by yourself."

"Yes, sir."

"Hop to it."

Lucas gave the fire a few puffs from the bellow before sticking nine rods of steel into the flames. Once they glowed red, he removed one and set to forming it, the hammer in his hand setting a steady rhythm. In the background, he could hear Waylan working on a project of his own.

Slowly, he made his way through the steel rods. When he reached number seven, he heard the smith curse. He turned to see what had made the usually austere man react. In his hands, Waylan held the pieces of a cold chisel.

Not long after, Waylan cursed again. "Finish those bands and watch the shop," he instructed, walking by. "If a customer comes in, tell 'em I'm out and they'll need to come back tomorrow."

Lucas called after him, "Where are you going?"

"To Arkav's to see if he'll lend me a chisel."

"Just make a new one."

"That crest goes out tomorrow; I don't have time."

Lucas returned to the bands and finished with them quickly. As he was cleaning up, he heard the bell on the front door chime. Peeking into the front room, he saw four soldiers, all roughly his age.

"The smith's not here, you'll need to come back tomorrow," he told them.

"Who are you then, boy?" one asked. The man had long, greasy brown hair and wide-set eyes, giving him a dull appearance.

"His apprentice."

"Then you'll take my order. I, Maryn Arst, squad three of the inner quarter's corps newest second lieutenant, need a helmet in the form of a dragon's head."

The ego on this fool, Lucas thought.

"No," he said, repeating himself, "orders will be received tomorrow when the smith returns."

"You'll take it now."

"I've been instructed not to and for an order like that, measurements and preferences will need to be taken."

"Boy, we are soldiers! You will do as—"

Lucas laughed. "Unless you'd like to craft it yourself, you'll have to wait."

"You dare deny us?" one of the other soldiers spoke up, his voice high-pitched.

"Quiet, Elza," Maryn snapped.

"I'm not refusing you," Lucas bit. "The smith's just asked you return tomorrow to place the order when he's here."

"Piece of vite. How dare you refuse me, squad three of the—"

"No one cares," Lucas cut him off. With a wave of the hand, he told them, "Now leave, I have no time for idiots."

As he turned, a force struck him in the back of the head, sending him careening into one of the posts bearing the upper level. His head struck the corner of the wood and his vision faded momentarily. He could feel blood trickling down his forehead.

"Graw, Hynde, grab his arms," Maryn ordered.

Still dazed, Lucas was unable to react before the soldiers latched onto his arms and Maryn punched him in the face. "Son of a bw—" he began as he was struck in the stomach.

"Be quie—" Maryn ordered.

"Is that all you've got? I know women who hit harder."

Flying into a rage, Maryn continued to strike. Not being one to back down, Lucas took each hit and returned it with an insult.

Seeing hitting him wasn't having the desired effect, Maryn paused, breathing heavily. After a moment, he asked, "What do we do to dogs that enjoy being hit?"

"We brand them," Elza answered, taking a handful of Lucas's hair.

With a nasty smile, Maryn took a rod of metal and shoved it into the fire.

Lucas began to tug against Graw and Hynde in earnest.

"Oh look, the dog fears fire," Elza sneered.

When the rod was cerise red, Maryn pulled it from the flames and neared Lucas's bare neck. "Hold him still."

He could feel the driving heat when the soldier was yanked away.

"What the fuck do you think you're doing?" roared Waylan. He grabbed Graw and threw him on top of Maryn.

Hynde released Lucas and tried to draw his sword. Waylan placed an open hand over his face and shoved him backwards. His head struck Elza's and the two fell to the floor, dazed.

"My commander will hear about this," Maryn threatened.

"And he'll beat your ass for it," Waylan yelled. "Every commander knows who I am, knows the value of my work. Get the fuck out of my shop. And don't come back."

The men scrambled out, holding their injuries.

Lucas lay on the floor, thankful for Waylan's impeccable timing.

The smith offered him a hand. "What were you doing to piss them off?"

"They wouldn't leave when asked nicely."

Waylan shook his head. "Clean yourself up and go home." He walked away muttering under his breath, though Lucas did hear one thing: "Idiot."

✠✠✠

Caius stood before the Looking Glass. "Where is Connery?"

"He's… preoccupied," Vitia answered slyly.

Something about the way she said it did not sit right with Braxton.

"Have you found the girl?"

"No, sir," Vitia answered with a hint of shame.

"And why is that?"

"Uh… we…"

"Out with it."

"They seem to have vanished. We thought they were headed to Bouyne, bu—"

"You thought?" Caius cut her off.

Vitia declined to respond.

"You imbeciles!" Caius stormed towards the door.

"What about the boy?" Braxton asked.

His father paused.

"What boy?" Vitia asked, feigning ignorance.

"Yes, the boy?" Caius said, returning. "Do you still have him?"

Vitia was slow in answering. "Yes."

"What was his name again?"

"Nico Sieme," Vitia answered. Clearly, she was not making the connections his father was.

"I want him brought here. Unharmed."

"But he's just a stup—" Vitia started.

"Unharmed."

Finding she had no other choice, Vitia responded, "Yes, sir."

A shrewd smile played across Caius's lips as he left the room.

Braxton chased after him. "Why did you ask for only me today?"

"You are the one poised to take the throne. There is no need to involve your brothers in such mundane things. But you must learn to handle any situation. And, unfortunately, I must thank you for reminding me of the boy."

"Why the sudden interest in him?"

"He will be of use," was all Caius would say.

‡‡‡

Kade crossed his arms, leaning against the pole of the stall and let Taite talk to the merchant. Thankfully, this was the last item on his list. The transaction finished, they headed back to the inn, and he was more than happy to let Taite struggle to carry everything.

Back in the room, they found Jared and Cassidy lounging and Keegan asleep on the floor.

Taite grunted in greeting, then mumbled something about going to the bar.

Sitting on the bed next to Cassidy, Kade wrapped an arm around her. "I presume your day was better than mine."

"I would hope so," Cassidy said with a smile.

She'd held Taite in high regard in the beginning, as one normally would a Kjote. But as they traveled, she too had begun to dislike him, noticing he never had a kind word for anyone and that he treated them with undue disdain.

Kade let out a sigh and pulled her closer.

Opening her eyes, Keegan mocked, "Daw, look at the lovebirds."

Kade quickly retracted his arm. *Must you always do that,* he snapped at Keegan.

Yeah, she said with a small snigger. *It's hella funny. Plus, you don't need to be hooking up with Cassidy.*

Hooking up?

Doing anything sexual. It's not the time or place, and Cassidy doesn't need to be hurt by your lack of restraint.

Kade stared at her angrily.

"I really dislike it when you two do that," Jared commented.

"Do what?" Keegan asked.

"Have your own private conversations."

"I can understand wanting to hear me chew Kade out, but it's best not to air one's dirty laundry."

"Air dirty laundry?"

"Make yourself look like an ass."

"You do that just fine on your own," Kade said, pushing off the bed and storming across the room, making sure to slam the door behind him. He stomped down the stairs and made his way to the bar. "Give me a pint."

The barman looked at him doubtfully. "Bronze coin."

He pulled a coin from his pocket, slamming it on the counter.

"That didn't take long," Taite said.

Kade gritted his teeth, turning to see the Kjote nursing a pint. The barman placed a tankard before him, which he took and sculled.

"Another," he snapped, throwing down a second coin.

"She put you in a state," Taite commented.

He returned, "She's put you in plenty, too."

"That she has."

Kade felt a gentle tap on his shoulder. Turning, he barked, "What?"

Cassidy pulled away at his aggressive response.

"I'm sorry; I thought you were... anyone else."

"May I talk to you?" she said softly.

"Of course."

Taking his hand, she led him across the bar, out the back door, and into the stables.

"Couldn't we have talked inside?"

"I didn't want Taite overhearing us. Keegan told me what she said."

Kade gritted his teeth.

"I think she is wrong."

"In what way?"

"You do not sully me. I find you bring out parts of me even I have not yet discovered." Her dazzling eyes looked up at him. "Like the parts of me that are not afraid of the world. The part that is not afraid of my magic, the part that has learned to trust another."

He was drawn in by her gaze, the sincerity in her irises mesmerizing. Suddenly, their lips were touching, hers soft and gentle against his.

He broke away. "We shouldn't."

"Why?"

"I don't want to hurt you. You know my reputation."

Cassidy placed a warm hand on his cheek. "I do not believe you will hurt me."

"I wish that were true, but I'm a killer and have little capacity to change."

"Everyone is capable of change, even you."

"Doubtful," Kade said, holding her hand against his face.

"No," Cassidy said definitively, kissing him again. "I have seen it. You can be kind and gentle when you want."

Giving into his temptation, he told her, "With you, I want to. But I'm not sure that's enough."

✝✝✝

Bouyne's dungeon was hardly better than Suttan's. Instead of a pile of hay for a bed, there was a platform bracketed to the wall. While the board was hard, Nico found it preferable to being on the floor with the rats.

Mostly, he slept. There was little else to do, and it was the only time he wasn't hungry. And the only time he wasn't thinking about his mother. Sometimes, he almost wished the Vosjnik would catch their quarry so he wouldn't be alone.

It seemed like months before Dax came to collect him, but he knew it'd only been a few days. When he was led outside, the sky was dark, clouds obscuring the moon and stars. Six horses stood saddled in the courtyard. Only four had riders. In the gloom, it was hard to make out who was missing.

"Where's Connery?" Nico asked, dread in his heart.

"Dead," Vitia answered, smiling cruelly. "He tried to flee."

"More like gutted in his sleep," Dax muttered under his breath.

"He was a dead man," Vitia sneered. "He was charged with capturing the girl and failed. He knew if he rode to Agrielha, it was to his death. So, like a coward, he tried to flee, but didn't get far before I drove my sword through his belly."

"Didn't get anywhere at all; sleeping men don't run."

Nico felt his heart pounding away in his chest; Connery had been the only one keeping him alive.

"Don't fret," Dax said, helping him onto a horse, "the king's commanded you be brought to him unharmed."

Nico cursed to himself; it'd be better to die now than face Caius's torments.

CHAPTER 31

Aron rounded the corner in the dark passageway, the knot in his stomach weighing heavily. That morning, he had found a note from Shiloh requesting they meet on the rooftop at midday. While they had used notes to set up rendezvous in the past, it had only been in dire emergencies. And to be meeting in the middle of the day was unusual.

Reaching the second doorway, he stopped, his heart beating quickly. Stepping onto the gable, he found the sun was blinding and shielded his eyes. As his sight adjusted, he saw Shiloh, tears streaming down her face. Kolt held her arm.

His stomach dropped and he rushed forward, barely making it a few feet before two guards grabbed his arms.

Aron strained against the men, bellowing. "Kolt!"

Pleasantly, Kolt said, "Why, hello."

"Let her go!"

"Oh, come. I am offended you have not introduced me to Shiloh. She is quite beautiful."

Kolt reached towards her face and Shiloh gave an anxious hiccup. Jerking her by her arm, Kolt forced her closer to him and brushed away the tears.

"Please, let her go," Aron said. "I will give you whatever you want."

Kolt laughed. "You cannot give me what I want." Drawing his knife, he watched the sunlight catch its edge.

"Your quarrel is with me. *Please*, let her go."

"That is true. However, the issue is, Shiloh makes you happy and that makes me very *un*happy. See the dilemma? You took someone I loved away from me."

"It was not my fault," Aron said, finally understanding.

Kolt's calm and cool demeanor disappeared, replaced instead by one of pure hatred. "You killed her." Taking a deep breath, he collected himself. "And now I am going to kill her."

Aron wanted to cry out, but it was too late.

Helplessly, he watched Kolt jam the knife into Shiloh's stomach. A sickening crimson instantly stained the cloth around the wound.

The guards released Aron and he started towards her.

Kolt scoffed, "You think I would allow you any chance to save her?" With that, he pushed Shiloh back and over the edge of the wall.

Aron knew he was screaming but could not hear himself.

Kolt pulled him back from the edge. "Cannot have you following her, *dear* brother. Father would have my head. But do look."

Far below, he could see the mark that was once Shiloh.

"Take him to his chambers," Kolt said, passing him off to the guards.

The men propelled him along, his body uncooperative, and he took no comfort in knowing they were injured at every pitfall of the secret passage. His mind entered a blank state, and his body went numb.

Suddenly, he found himself sitting on his bed. No one was around, the sky was dark, and a single candle by the door lit the room. Exhaustion hit him like a brick, and he knew he should blow the candle out, but his body refused to respond.

At some point, he fell back onto the mattress and his eyelids closed, sending him into yet another nightmare.

All he could think was: *There will be no happy ending.*

✝✝✝

Kade and Cassidy explored the streets of Aylentowne, or so they claimed, and didn't return until well after Jared and Keegan had finished dinner.

Looking at Keegan, Jared could tell something was bothering her, but didn't know how to ask her how she felt. Sure, he'd done it before, but he somehow felt that if he asked today she'd break. And he wasn't sure he'd be able to put the pieces back together. Not when he was still broken.

The next morning, they quickly breakfasted before leaving. Luckily, exiting wasn't as much of a trial as it had been in Suttan. Taite was in a foul temperament from a hangover, his eyes bloodshot and wild, and his mood seemed to transfer to Keegan. Jared wanted to be mad at her, but… figured it was part of whatever had been affecting her of late. And didn't they all deserve bad days?

When they stopped for the night, most everything was done in silence including eating.

Away from prying eyes once more, Kade resumed their training and, as always, made his movements seem easy and fluid. Jared wasn't as graceful, finding his hands and feet faltering as his brain struggled to direct them. Keegan often yelled at him for telegraphing, though he had no idea what that was. Yet, while it was still no contest, there was no doubt he was getting better. Slowly but surely.

Kade ended another bout and let Jared rest. Keegan took his spot with none of her usual energy.

They began edging around each other. Keegan lifted her front foot and stomped, faking an intention to lunge. Instinctively, Kade's arm twitched. When still unaccustomed to the other's fighting style, her tricks had worked and she'd easily landed blows; now that Kade had learned the praxes, it took a bit more before she was successful. Jared watched patiently, knowing Keegan would soon actually attack.

Kade made the first attack with a slash.

Keegan parried, retaliating by rolling in against his arms, making her way to his back. Before Kade could launch another attack, she had her weapon against his neck.

Without warning, Kade spun, swinging his weapon.

She dropped and brought the stick across his shins, then jabbed it up into his ribcage. "Step it up."

"Remember, you asked f—" Kade started as she kicked the side of his knee.

Kade's leg buckle and Jared knew she'd hit the nerves. Struggling to put weight on the leg, Kade swung, but they both knew it'd do no good.

Keegan easily evaded the strike and placed the end of the stick against his chest. "You're losing it."

"No," Kade said, tossing his stick aside, "I just don't want to hurt you."

"Letting me win teaches me nothing."

"Let's be honest, it's not because I'm going easy that you're mad."

Keegan threw her stick into the fire. "Not entirely, but it's not helping."

"What have I done to anger you?"

"Nothing."

"Then what's upsetting you?"

"Nothing," she answered, making her way to her bedroll.

"Bulla vite. I'm getting really ti—" He cut himself off and glanced at Cassidy.

Noxþ telepathy, Jared thought.

Now that Keegan faced away from everyone, her anger dissipated to be replaced by gloom; Jared couldn't explain how he knew how she felt. The air in the camp was awkward and, with nothing better to do, he followed Keegan's example.

CHAPTER 32

While Keegan, like everyone, had days where she was more introspective, Jared was beginning to worry—she seemed downcast and fragile. When they stopped the next night he pulled Kade aside. "I think something's bothering Keegan."

"She seemed fine when I talked to her earlier," he said, stealing a glance at her.

"When did you talk to her?"

"Before the rest of you were awake."

Jared crossed his arms. "What did you talk about?"

"She apologized for being a bwint last night."

"She *apologized*?"

"Yes. I was just as surprised as you."

"That's very out of character for her."

"Oh no, something may actually be wrong," Kade said sarcastically. He was quiet for a moment. "She didn't eat breakfast and barely touched lunch. I'll talk to her."

Jared stopped him. "Are you sure that's the best idea? You'll just end up fighting."

"Fine," Kade snapped, "you talk to her."

Jared nodded and turned to find both Keegan and Cassidy were gone. "Where are they?"

"How should I know! I was talking to you."

"Where are Keegan and Cassidy?" Jared questioned Taite, who was tending the fire.

"Wandered off," he answered apathetically.

"Did you not think to ask where they were going?" Kade said angrily.

"No. They can only get so far."

Kade clenched his fists. "We'll split up and look for them," he told Jared.

‡‡‡

As soon as they stopped to set up camp, Jared pulled Kade aside and spoke to him in hushed tones.

Cassidy presumed it had something to do with Keegan.

"Would you come get firewood with me?" she asked Keegan.

"Doesn't Kade usually go with you?" she said, unfurling her bedroll.

"Yes, but he is preoccupied."

"Uh… fine."

Heading into the forest, Keegan began picking up fodder at the tree line.

"Not those."

"Why?"

"Just not those," Cassidy insisted, continuing to walk.

Keegan hesitated but followed all the same.

They walked silently for several more minutes before Cassidy stopped. "This should be far enough."

Quietly, Keegan started collecting sticks again.

Cassidy placed a hand on her arm. "Leave those, I want to talk to you."

"About what?" Keegan questioned defensively.

"Something is weighing on you; do you want to talk?"

"Not really. And even if I did, why would I talk to you?"

"I just figured you would be more open with me— considering how you are around the boys."

"And how is that?"

"You try to act like them and make it appear as if nothing bothers you."

"That's not acting."

Softly, Cassidy said, "You and I both know that is not true."

Keegan declined to respond.

She sensed the emotions radiating from Keegan and recalled Kade explaining that when telepaths experienced strong emotions, they could inadvertently broadcast them. Waves of anger and misery emanated from Keegan, and it was then Cassidy realized what she needed.

Gently, she wrapped her arms around Keegan. "It is going to be alright."

Keegan remained still for a moment, surprised, then slowly reciprocated. It was not long before Cassidy felt hot tears on her shoulder.

"I can't do this," Keegan broke out, pulling away to sit against a tree, tears flowing freely.

Cassidy knelt beside her. "What can you not do?"

"Anything," Keegan cried. "I can't save y'all; I can't even save myself. I can't be this person everyone wants me to be. All I want is to go home."

Keegan buried her face in her hands, crying in earnest with sobs that shook her body.

Jared materialized from the woods like a spirit. Placing a hand on Keegan's shoulder, he pulled her close as her head jerked up.

As the sobs subsided, Keegan pulled away with a broken laugh. "God, I'm such a mess."

Jared wiped away her tears. "No more than the rest of us. Do you want to talk?"

"There's not much to talk about; I'm just really homesick. Yesterday was my birthday and it's the first time since I was adopted that I haven't spent it with my family."

Jared took her hand. "We are always here for you."

Keegan smiled weakly. "I know. Thank you."

✝✝✝

Kade tramped through the trees, calling, "Keegan! Cassidy!"

He'd been searching for what felt like hours. Frustrated, he gave up and stormed back to camp to find everyone sitting around the fire.

"Where have you been?" he asked furiously.

"Around," was Keegan's answer.

He made to retort but stopped; she'd answered in a way that didn't convey anger or attitude and seemed calm—which was a welcome change.

He took a seat next to Cassidy. *What happened?*

She is not as strong as the façade she puts up.

What's that supposed to mean?

Cassidy smiled sweetly, *I have faith you will understand in time.*

"We practicing tonight?" Keegan asked quietly.

"No," Kade answered. On a normal night, he would've made them, but there was something brittle about Keegan.

They were silent, the only sounds coming from the forest and the fire. Keegan wiped her eyes with the back of her hand and moved closer to Jared. At first, he didn't seem to notice, but, when he did, wrapped his arm around her shoulders and let her rest against his chest.

Taking note, Kade questioned, *Did I miss something?*

Oh yes, Cassidy responded, *but it is not what you think.*

Are you ever going to tell me what happened?

It is not my place.

Kade got to his feet and offered Cassidy a hand. *Walk with me.*

"Where are you going?" Taite questioned.

"To get firewood," Kade lied.

A laugh came from Cassidy, *We used that excuse earlier.*

Taite glared at him. "Don't lie to me, boy."

For a moment Kade worried Taite had gotten through his wall, then realized he was bluffing.

"Prove it," he said, pulling Cassidy from the campsite.

Once out of earshot, she asked, "Where are we going?"

"A place I found earlier."

She let him lead her along and, after a time, they emerged from the forest at the base of a small hill. They climbed to its crest, a breeze pulling at them gently.

"What is so special?" Cassidy asked, looping her arm through his.

"You can see the sky here. Tell me, what do you see that's different from what you saw in Suttan?"

"I never studied astronomy."

"You don't have to have studied the stars before."

Scrutinizing the sky, she said, "I cannot discern a difference."

"Exactly."

"What is your point?"

"No matter where you are, we all see the same sky. The only thing that changes it is time."

"How do you know that?" Cassidy asked, looking back up.

"I've traveled across Arciol," he said. "Over all that time, the sky was the only constant."

Cassidy leaned against him. "Do you ever miss it?"

"Miss what?"

"Your life before the Vosjnik."

He enveloped her in his arms and kissed the top of her raven curls. "Every day. But the past is said and done. The only thing to do is move forward."

✠✠✠

"Tomorrow?" Virgil exclaimed. A few people in the tavern turned to look at his outburst. "That gives me no time to put my affairs in order."

"That's when I leave," the Kjote said. The man had his hood pulled low, making it hard to discern his features and his voice was gruff, only adding to the mystery of his persona.

"When will your next trip be?" Virgil pressed.

"This is my last one. The state's become increasingly dangerous for elementals and the like."

"We can always talk to another Kjote," Jude said quietly to Virgil.

"No," Virgil responded, "he is the only one I trust."

"Then there's no other choice."

"When do you leave?" Virgil asked.

"Dawn. Meet me at the north gate." The Kjote stood and made his way from the tavern without looking back.

"Why did you need us here?" Carter asked.

"Safety in numbers, my boy," Virgil answered. "The country is uneasy, and soldiers have become quick to draw their swords."

"We should return home. I'm sure Laiyla and Alivia have much to prepare for," Jude pointed out.

They quietly made their way from the tavern and into the humid night air. Across the street, the door to another tavern opened, spilling light and four stumbling soldiers.

The soldiers were making their way behind them, and, after some time, Lucas stole a glance back. It was Maryn and his crew of idiots. He turned around quickly, hoping he hadn't been recognized.

Maryn called out drunkenly, "Boy!"

"Keep walking," Lucas hissed.

"Boy, I um talkin' to ya," Maryn yelled.

A hand grabbed his arm. "'id yu not hear 'im?" Graw asked.

"Leave him alone," Carter said.

Elza pushed Carter. "Mind ye own business."

Carter stumbled into Jude, who had to stop him from rushing forward.

Virgil stepped in. "Gentlemen, what is the problem here?"

"'oy here insulted meh," Maryn said, punching at Lucas.

He was too far away for Lucas to need to dodge. Yet, recalling the heat from the iron, he lunged.

Virgil stepped between them. "Let us be civil."

"I um always 'ivil," Maryn said, puffing out his chest, "but dogs j'st d' n't know h' to do wha—"

His words were cut off as Lucas pushed past Virgil and shoved Maryn to the ground. The other soldiers stared and unsteadily drew their swords.

"N', this 's ma fight," Maryn yelled at them.

Glancing down, Lucas saw Maryn had drawn a dagger, which he threw. It went wide.

"Fool," he chuckled.

There came a gasp from behind Lucas. Turning he saw the knife protruding from his father's chest. Jude gagged, staggered, and fell to his knees.

Fury rose in Lucas's chest, and he began to strike Maryn. The drunken man didn't fight back, and his head smashed into the ground with each punch. Soon, his face was distorted, and life had left him.

"Lucas!" Virgil roared, finally getting his attention. "We need to leave."

He stared at the other soldiers, who seemed dazed, as if waking from a dream. He begrudgingly followed Virgil, Jude stumbling along as Carter supported him.

After a few minutes, Jude forced them to stop.

"I can't," he said, leaning against a wall. Coughing, droplets of blood coated his lips.

"No, we can't lose you, too," pleaded Carter.

"Lucas, look after your bother. Find Jared and Nico," Jude instructed. "Go with Virgil and *listen* to him. Don't be a fool."

"You're coming with us," Carter protested.

Jude coughed again, spurting red onto his son.

"Carter, keep Lucas levelheaded. I love you boys. Pass it along." He gave a final wheeze before his eyes glazed over.

Tears fell down Carter's cheeks and Lucas knew his brother would've remained there had Virgil not pulled them along.

"Nothing we could do," Virgil said in a pathetic attempt to console them. Once inside the house, he began scrambling to prepare Laiyla and Alivia to flee.

Lucas and Carter sat on the steps, their lives crumbling about them. Again.

"Pack, boys," Virgil said in passing.

"No, we're staying," Lucas said.

"Your fath—"

"I know what he said and we're staying!"

"I know you are upset," Virgil said softly, "but trust me, it is in your best interest to come with us."

"We're staying."

Seeing there was no use in arguing, Virgil shook his head. "You are grown men and I cannot force you to do anything. Just know you will not be able to stay here forever."

"I don't care." Lucas yelled, "I don't care about anything but revenge!"

"We should go with them," Carter said feebly.

"No, we're going to stay here and kill the men who murdered our father. Then we're going to kill the Vosjnik."

CHAPTER 33

With no one to chase after, travel slowed to a comfortable pace, but each passing day filled Nico with dread. When they came across Lake Romann, they were waylaid by a passing storm. In the morn, they boarded a boat with the horses and crossed. Nico spent the whole time hunched over the railing divulging the contents of his stomach. Dax was beside him, his face green.

Since morning, the castle of Agrielha had been visible, sitting on its lonely hill, as was the city itself was up against the winding river. When the castle was no more than a few miles before them, the brickwork became visible as a dark color, contrasting against the lush grass around it. By afternoon, they were in its shadow.

Since Connery's death, Vitia had stepped in as Commander and Dax had become her lieutenant. She left the rest of her comrades in the stables while Dax towed Nico towards the castle.

He desperately thought of escape, but to run meant death. Yet to be taken to Caius also meant death. Since the Vosjnik had captured him, he knew it was simply a matter of when.

The inside of the castle was cool, and Nico stumbled as his eyes adjusted to the dimness. Dax marched him up flights of stairs and, by the time they reached the upper levels, his heart was pounding.

They came upon black oak doors with rearing griffins carved into each side. The room was cavernous, their steps echoing off the walls. Ash sat between the stones like blood and a throne inlaid with copious amounts of gold sat near the far wall. The man sitting on it bore a deep scowl that was darkened by the scruff on his jaw. Two young men stood next to the king, one on either side of him.

Just before they reached the steps leading to the throne, Vitia stopped.

"Kneel before your king," she commanded. When Nico remained standing, she pushed him forward. "I said kneel!"

Vitia went to smack him, but the king stopped her. "Where is Connery?"

Hand still raised, Vitia answered, "Dead."

"By whose hand?"

She looked the king in the eye. "Mine, sir."

"Why?"

"Coward tried to run."

Dax's jaw tightened as he restrained himself from divulging the truth.

Satisfied, Caius told her, "You are the new Commander. I take it you have chosen Dax as your lieutenant?"

"Yes, sir."

"Good. Replace the members you lost, then report back to me."

As Vitia and Dax turned to leave, Nico could feel his body quivering. Gritting his teeth, he dared to look at the king.

Caius studied him, his brown eyes boring into him and Nico lowered his gaze.

"Nico," the king began, "you will enter under the tutelage of Braxton."

His head snapped up in surprise.

"Now, there are a few ways in which we can proceed; you can do as told, and all will be well, or you can resist, and my son will break you."

"I w—" Braxton started to butt in.

"Silence," Caius snapped before returning his attention to Nico. "What will it be?"

Nico mustered all his courage. "I will never serve you."

The king waved his hand and two guards led Nico from the room. "Never say never, boy."

‡‡‡

"I will not—" Braxton started as he chased after his father.

Caius cut him off nonchalantly, "You can, and you will."

"He is just a child."

"That means nothing."

Braxton blocked his path. "I will not do it."

Darkness overcame his vision and a voice cried, "Betrayer! Marmarda! Soucer!"

He could feel something sharp ripping across his chest as the world came to light again.

A sneer crossed Caius's face. "You do it or I will. Which would you prefer?"

Braxton stared angrily and, thinking he had won, Caius pushed past him.

"I *will not* do it."

"Fine, be stubborn. I will start the process. Just let me know when you wish to take over."

Voices whispered the words he had heard in his dreams in his ear. Braxton shook his head and returned to the present, then berated himself; he had just condemned the poor boy. Few grown men lasted long under his father's thumb—a child would fall even quicker. He turned to walk in the other direction and knocked into Kolt.

Kolt shoved him. "Watch where you are going."

Angry at the cards life had dealt, Braxton pushed Kolt back, sending him into the wall.

"You may be father's favorite, but do not forget who I am," he snarled, clutching his brother's collar.

Six people knelt before him, and a question was asked. A man disappeared. The question was repeated, and the answer changed.

"And who would that be?" Kolt tested with a sneer.

He cleared his thoughts before answering. "The heir." Then, tightening his grip on Kolt's shirt, he snarled, "I should rid myself of you now, little monster. The only thing you do is take up space."

"But you will not," Kolt said dismissively, loosening Braxton's grip and walking away. "Run along now, we all know you will never lay a hand on me. Oh, you might want to check on the youngest." With a laugh he added, "Something seems to be upsetting the poor bastard. I wonder what it could be?"

Braxton immediately started making his way towards Aron's room, but, before going to see his brother, went to his own chambers. As soon as his altercation with Kolt had diffused, he had begun repeating what he had heard in his vision. But with each reiteration, he recalled less and less. When he reached his room, he could only recall 'psodæ woth yarv'.

✟✟✟

Aron lay beneath the covers, staring at the opposite wall— the same one he had been staring at for so many days he had lost count. On the bedside table sat a tray of untouched food. His stomach gave a soft gurgle, but he ignored it, knowing he would not be able to keep it down.

Closing his eyes, he saw Shiloh's face and her look of terror as she fell over the edge of the castle. He opened his eyes, unable to stand her frightened expression anymore. Sadness welled and he buried his face into the pillow.

There was a knock, but he made no motion to answer it. The knock came again. He hoped they would go away, wanting nothing more than to be left to wallow in his misery. In time, he would fade from memory and this world.

The knock became more persistence.

"Aron, open up," Braxton called. "I know you are in there."

He wanted to yell, tell him to leave, but could not muster the energy.

"Open the noxþox door," Braxton shouted. Finally, in frustration, he barged in. His face was hard and angry, but, when he saw Aron, it softened. He poked his head into the hall and instructed a servant to draw a bath.

"You cannot hide in here forever," his brother said, approaching.

Aron remained silent.

"Kolt has done some vicious things to torment you over the years, but I have never seen you react like this; what did he do?"

"He killed her," he whispered.

Braxton paused. "Who?"

Aron choked on her name. "Shiloh."

"The girl who fell off the roof last week?"

"She did not fall, she was pushed."

Braxton sighed. "By Kolt."

"After he stuck a knife in her belly."

There was a knock and a servant entered carrying a tub. Others followed with buckets to fill it. Once the tub was full, a fire elemental heated it until a light steam rose off the surface.

"You stink," Braxton told him.

Aron looked away.

Braxton took this to be his argument against bathing and pulled back the covers. "You cannot sit in your own filth forever. People die, it happens. Celebrate the life they had instead of mourning their death."

"I loved her," Aron said.

Braxton grabbed his arm and pulled him upright. "And that is why Kolt killed her. If you want to get back at him, do not let him know it hurts you this badly."

"Easier said."

Getting him to his feet, Braxton pulled him towards the tub. "At least try. Undress." When Aron did not, he continued, "Please do not make me do that for you."

Aron gave his brother a hard stare before slowly disrobing and climbing in. The water was warm and soothing, and he slipped in until his nose was just above the waterline. Braxton dumped a pitcher of water over his head, making his hair plaster over his eyes, and handed him a bar of soap.

As Aron scrubbed, he wished he could wash away the sorrow.

"Father requested your presence earlier," Braxton said casually.

"What for?"

Braxton gritted his teeth, looking away. "The Vosjnik returned."

His stomach sank. "Did they have the girl?"

"No. Worse." He mumbled, "For me at least. They had an elemental father has given to me to train."

"How is that so bad?"

"He is still resilient." Braxton made his way to the window. "Father wants me to break him."

Pulling himself from the water, Aron wrapped a towel around his waist. "What are you going to do?"

"I do not know." Braxton turned back to face him, and, for the first time, Aron could see the toll life had taken on his brother. His face was covered in small scars, and he was perpetually tense. There was no happiness in any of his mannerisms—there never had been.

Staring out the window, Braxton repeated, "I do not know."

✠✠✠

The house was eerily quiet.

Lucas had considered making Carter go with the Fulpes, but his brother had as much right to revenge as anyone. He'd considered continuing working with Waylan but didn't see the point. Carter still worked at the carpenter's and each night came back with a loaf of bread, cheese, a small portion of meat, and a few worthless coins.

Vengeance kept them in the city, though Lucas had no idea whom to exact it upon. He'd considered going after the men who'd been with Maryn, but knew it'd be hard to find a few rats in a city full of them. The other path was to go after the Vosjnik, which required time and funding.

Waiting for Carter to return, he heard a knock on the front door. He thought nothing of it until he realized his brother wouldn't knock. Pulling the knife from his boot, he crept through the foyer. Holding the knife against his leg, he opened the door.

"You," he snarled, raising the knife to drive it into Elza's chest.

"I came to apologize," Elza said quickly, making him pause. "for what happened. And to let you know it wasn't my fault."

"You did the deeds; how can they *not* be your fault?" Lucas snarled.

"Maryn is—was a life elemental. He forced us to do those things. May I come in?"

"No. How'd you find us?"

"I followed your friend home yesterday. There's something I want to do… it's hard to explain without going into the entirety of it."

"I don't trust you."

Elza unbuckled his belt and handed Lucas his sword. "Do you trust me now?"

"No." Nevertheless, he let the soldier in.

Carter was just reaching the bottom of the stairs on the street. "What—"

"Just go with it," Lucas told him.

In the kitchen, Elza sat at the table, looking at them tentatively.

"Speak," Lucas barked.

"All right, here's the thing," Elza began, "I'm not happy. When I told the higher-ups what Maryn did, they laughed and said they would've done the same."

"How's that our problem?" Carter asked.

"I want to get back at them," Elza said with a sly grin. "I want to start doing right."

"Why should we help you?" Lucas growled.

"Well, you'll get to knock a few heads together, create some chaos."

Lucas considered the offer. As much as he'd like to, it'd unnecessarily endanger Carter, and he wasn't willing to risk his brother's life for Elza's petty payback. He couldn't risk that kind of loss over something so little. If he was going to do something, he was going after the men at the top.

"We'll do it," Carter said in a low tone.

Lucas turned to him, surprised. "No!"

"Look around you," Carter said angrily. "The world has taken a giant vite on us. It's time we gave some of it back."

"It's not worth it." Lucas paused; it was unusual for him to be the levelheaded one. "Why attack lowly peons?"

Elza chimed in, "You have to make enough of a nuisance before anyone of worth will look at you."

"Why do you even want to get back at them?" Lucas snapped. "You call those bastards comrades."

"I became a soldier to protect the people of this city," Elza said, standing. "Instead, I've been told I'm of no importance and the people don't matter. You don't have to help me, I just thought you might like the opportunity. But seeing as you'd rather wallow, I'll show myself out."

"Wait," Lucas said. "What *exactly* do you have in mind?"

"How big a risk you willing to take?"

‡‡‡

In the last week, Keegan seemed to have changed. She was no longer hostile towards everyone and had begun to genuinely laugh more. Kade also noticed she and Jared were becoming increasingly familiar. Often, he wondered if it was more than platonic, but that was none of his business.

He and Cassidy had openly become close, and it still elicited commentary from Keegan. Some nights they slipped away for a quiet walk—this was one of them.

Looking over his shoulder, Kade made sure they were far enough from camp before gently pushing Cassidy against a tree. She wrapped her arms around his neck, pulling him close. As their lips met, he let himself fall into the moment. The rush was euphoric—nothing he'd felt before compared. Each touch warmed his body and sent shivers down his spine.

Cassidy began fumbling with his belt buckle and he pulled away, "You don't have to do that; I'll never force you to."

"I know," she said. "I… want to."

Kade kissed her again. The buckle came undone, and his pants worked their way down his legs. Placing his hands on the small of Cassidy's back, he pulled her away from the tree.

Your ass is showing.

Startled, his teeth knocked into Cassidy's. Pulling away he spun around, expecting to find Keegan behind him. *Where are you?* he asked angrily.

Camp, she answered.

How do you know my ass is showing then?

Your wall came a-tumblin' down. Taite and I know exactly what kinda hanky-panky shit y'all're doing.

Kade grimaced, knowing he'd never hear the end of it.

"What happened?" Cassidy asked.

He turned to face her, and she stifled a giggle.

Looking down, he realized his pants were still around his ankles. He fumbled to pull them up, muttering, "My royiken sister, that's what."

He'd been working on reconciling himself to the knowledge that Keegan was his twin, but, until that moment, had been failing miserably.

A hush fell over them.

"Your sister?"

He took a deep breath. "Yes, Keegan's my sister. Twin, to be precise."

"Oh… my…"

"You can't tell her."

"She does not know?"

"No… and I only just found out myself." He told her about the letter.

"I cannot believe it," Cassidy said. "That is all so inconceivable. Is she really the Child of Prophecy?"

"Yes."

"And is she really from another…" she trailed off as he nodded. "I knew she was from… somewhere far off, but to be from another world entirely… It makes it much more understandable for her to be so homesick."

"Homesick?"

"Yes," Cassidy said sheepishly. "That is why she was upset last week. But you are not supposed to know that."

"Hmm…" Kade said, giving her a quick peck on the lips, "I won't tell if you won't."

Cassidy pulled him close. "It is a deal."

‡‡‡

With a devilish grin, Keegan asked, "If you had to guess, what'do you think they're up to?"

Jared looked at her. "I really don't want to know."

"You're the lucky one."

"How so?"

"Kade's wall faltered and let's just say he and Cassidy are having… a bit of fun."

"That's what you were laughing at?"

She nodded. Kade and Cassidy decided to walk back into camp at that moment.

"Speak of the devil," she said, sitting up.

Kade glared. "I don't know what you find so funny."

"Dude, your dumb ass got caught with your pants around your ankles and it's your fault. Everything about that is hilarious."

"How would you like it if you were I?"

"I wouldn't be in your situation 'cause I'm not dumb enough to do that in the woods. And I really hope y'all don't have splinters in your asses."

"You are never going to let that one go, are you?" Cassidy stated.

"Nope," Keegan said. "And if I do anything as stupid, I'd expect nothing less from y'all."

To change the subject, Jared asked, "When will we reach the next city?"

"Early tomorrow," Taite answered.

"Are we going to stay in the city again?" Cassidy asked hopefully.

"Most likely."

"I don't see why we should," Kade argued. "We'll have all day to get supplies and it'll save money."

"Come on," Keegan groaned, "don't you want to sleep in a bed?"

"I won't get to either way," Kade pointed out. "Besides, the sooner we get to the Lazado, the better."

Keegan rolled her eyes. "One night won't kill us."

"I don't know why you're trying to convince him," Taite said. "He has no power here."

"Are we staying in the city or not?" Cassidy asked.

Simultaneously, Kade answered, "No," while Taite said, "Yes."

"Okay, since you two will never agree, let's take a vote," Keegan suggested. "I vote we stay in the city. Cassidy?"

She remained quiet for a moment. "I agree with Kade."

Keegan sighed. "Jared?"

"I agree with Kade, too."

Keegan looked to Taite disappointed. "Sorry, seems we'll be camping again."

Taite looked like he wanted to argue, but gritting his teeth, said, "Get some sleep. *Apparently,* we have a long day ahead."

✝✝✝

Nico stretched out on the cot; after sleeping on the ground for weeks, it was a welcome change. He bolted upright as the cell door scraped open.

Caius entered. Braxton followed with a tray of food and stood behind the king sullenly avoiding Nico's gaze.

"Will you serve me?" Caius asked.

"No," Nico spat.

Lazily, Caius said, "Fine. Braxton."

Nico was handed the tray and he accepted it warily.

"Go ahead, eat," Caius said with a wry smile.

Cautiously, Nico picked up the chicken leg, turning it over. Finding nothing visibly wrong, he decided to take his chances. The meat was dry, but he wasn't about to complain.

Caius's grin grew. "Tell me, boy, where are you from?"

"Don't you already know?" Nico snapped.

"Ah, yes, Suilenroc. I am aware the Vosjnik killed your mother, but I presume you have other family still living."

Nico looked at him blankly, taking another large bite.

"Of course; three brothers and your father. I need to have a word with Vitia about her thoroughness."

Nico froze; there was no way he could've known that.

"And now you are curious as to how I knew that."

His eyebrows furrowed in confusion.

"Serve me and I shall tell you."

"No."

"Tell me about your brothers. How many of them are elementals?" Before Nico could even formulate his thoughts, Caius said, "Ah, just the one: Jared."

What is going on? Nico wondered.

"Keep eating. We cannot have you starving. Tell me about Jared."

"Why—"

"Another earth elemental."

"How are you doing that?" Nico questioned, aggravated he could keep nothing from this man.

"Serve me and I will tell you, but your answer is still no." Caius continued, "Jared befriended that lovely girl, Keegan. He will be an easy convert; I have the perfect weapon to use against him: you."

As anger welled, Nico threw down the tray and jumped to his feet. Something in his stomach dropped and a shooting pain spread fast. He clutched his abdomen, sucking in a ragged breath.

"I see it has taken effect," Caius said, motioning for Braxton to collect the tray.

Nico grimaced as another bolt of pain ran through his stomach. "What are you talking about?"

"Will you serve me?"

"No," he snarled.

Caius walked away. "Then there is nothing to tell."

As they neared the door, Nico cried out, sinking to his knees, the pain burgeoning as if thousands of knives were driving into him. Soon the only thing he could do was lie on the cold stone floor and pray it would end.

CHAPTER 34

Ohvenail was nothing like Suttan or Aylentowne. There was no castle, no large buildings, no wall for protection. The city was built on both banks of the Tatat River with a few homes even floating on the slow waters. The buildings were mostly made of mud bricks and clay mortar with grasses and reeds pressed into the roofs and sides.

The roads leading to the city were dirt that slowly became littered with cobbled stones. People milled about as Taite led them to a stable and the residents seemed lively comparatively.

"So, what're we doing while you shop?" Keegan questioned.

"Staying here," Taite said.

"That doesn't make a lot of sense," Jared commented. "Why don't we split up and each buy a few things?"

"I don't trust any of you to not get into trouble," Taite countered.

"We did just fine in Aylentowne," Keegan remarked.

"No."

"Keegan, you and Jared go with Taite," Kade said.

"What did I just say?" Taite snapped.

"It'll save time and I don't trust them or *you* wandering off alone."

Taite insisted, "That's not what we're doing!"

"It is now." Kade took Cassidy's hand, walking away before Taite could get another word in.

"Stay here," Taite instructed.

"Uh, no," Keegan said blatantly.

"That wasn't a request," the Kjote barked.

Keegan shrugged.

"Stay here."

"Try and make me."

Taite's face was red with fury and with clenched fists, he stormed from the stable.

Keegan gave Jared a small smirk before ambling after him.

The market was a hectic place. Vendors sold an immense number of items, ranging from food to jewels, and Jared was even surprised to find a section dedicated to spices. Once they entered the bustle, they fell away from Taite, though still kept him in sight.

Keegan walked from stall to stall, taking it all in, gravitating towards stands selling trinkets. When vendors asked if she wanted to buy anything, she'd give a small, sad smile and walk away. Although she kept to herself, Jared could tell she was savoring the experience. He, on the other hand, disliked being surrounded by so many people; it reminded him too much of Tratoleck.

"What's Taite doing?" Keegan asked, not bothering to look for him as she was too short to see over the crowd.

Jared searched the throng. "I don't know."

She caught the uncertainty in his voice. "What's happening?"

"He's talking to a soldier."

"Why?"

"How should I know?" Jared bit.

Taite and the soldier talked for only a few minutes before going their separate ways.

"He's coming over."

"We have everything. Time to go," Taite told them.

"Why were you talking to that soldier?" Keegan asked innocently.

"We grew up together; I was just saying hello."

"Oh." She let Taite lead the way from the market, then leaned over to Jared and whispered, "Is he telling the truth?"

"No idea." Jared was disinclined to believe Taite, but it was possible; rarely did people travel too far from their hometowns—unless they were elementals, Kjotes, or forced to become soldiers for the king.

✠✠✠

Cassidy and Kade strolled through the market, vendors calling for them to come look at their wares. She hugged Kade's arm, a smile on her face. A table of trinkets caught her attention and she dragged him over.

"Ho' are 'he lady and 'he gentleman?" the vendor asked in a thick Northron accent.

"Wonderful," Cassidy answered.

"Wha' a beautiful voice tha' sends sweet 'isses t' 'he ear," the man commented flirtatiously. "Befitting o' such a stunning lady."

Color rushed to her cheeks and Kade wrapped an arm around her waist.

The vendor gave a hearty laugh. "No need t' worry, son, ol' Dunkan 's not on 'he market."

Kade did not remove his arm.

"D' you see anything you like, m' dear?"

"They are all so beautiful," Cassidy commented, eyeing the necklaces displayed.

"Sha' I surprise you 'hen?"

She looked to Kade, and he gave a small nod.

Dunkan surveyed his wares and after a moment, reached forward to pick up a simple piece. The stone was a pale blue larimar encased in an intricate wire setting on a thin silver chain.

She marveled at it. "Oh, it is gorgeous."

"How much?" Kade asked.

"For you, ah silver coin," Dunkan said with a charming grin.

Kade fished a coin from his purse.

"Help me put it on?" Cassidy asked.

Taking the necklace, he set the pendant on her chest and did the clasp.

Turning to face him, she stood on her toes to kiss his cheek.

A perturbed look crossed his face.

"What is wrong?"

"Taite," Kade answered. "It's time to leave."

"Then we should go meet him."

"Do we have to?"

Cassidy gave a little laugh. "Unfortunately."

✟✟✟

There was a knock at the door, followed by, "The king demands your presence in the Glass Chamber."

Aron had no desire to get up but decided to take Braxton's advice. Kolt was aware of how he felt, so even just seeing him out of his room would put a damper on his smugness.

As he was about to leave, he went to his bedside table, placing the only key he possessed in his pocket.

Contrary to popular belief, the Glass Chamber was not made of glass—it simply housed the Looking Glass. The walk there seemed gloomy despite the warm sunshine streaming through the windows. His father and brothers were already inside.

Seeing him, Kolt sneered, "Aron, how—"

"Be quiet," Braxton snapped.

Kolt was about to retort when the surface of the mirror rippled, and a man's image appeared.

"Sir," the man said, bowing.

"What is so pressing it could not wait for your monthly report?" questioned Caius.

The man stepped aside and was replaced by a low-ranking soldier. "Sir," he said nervously.

"Out with it, I do not have all day."

"The girl you've been looking for, Keegan Digore, will be in Revod in a week."

"How do you know this?"

"A Kjote approached me in the market and said he has this girl, as well as three other elementals."

"What is the name of this Kjote?"

"Taite Ault."

"He usually delivers elementals in Bouyne. Why the change of location?"

"He was apparently forced to take them along a southern route to dispel suspicion. One of the Vosjnik, Kade Tavin, is with him and doesn't trust him. He had enough of a hard time telling me this without them being any the wiser."

"Dismissed." Caius waved a hand over the surface of the mirror and the image went blank. With another wave, the Glass Chamber in Revod appeared. "Get your Captain," he ordered the timid-looking guard who sat in the room.

The man rushed away, time slipping by slowly before he returned. Breathlessly, he informed them the Captain was on his way and gave a bow before being replaced.

"I want every guard on high alert." Caius announced. "The girl I have been looking for, as well as three others, will reportedly be passing through Revod in a week. Your guards should engage only if absolutely necessary, otherwise, leave them to the Vosjnik."

The Captain bowed. "Yes, sir."

As the man turned to walk away, Caius added, "They are to be taken alive and I want the girl unharmed."

"Of course."

The mirror's surface rippled and Caius's reflection stared back.

"Get the Vosjnik," he told the guard waiting outside the room, walking away with an unsettling grin.

As Kolt and Braxton headed towards the throne room, Aron stood in the hallway, unsure of where he should go. Braxton turned to look at him and Aron took off, running in the opposite direction.

✝✝✝

Lying on the cold stone floor, Nico had no idea how long it'd been since he'd been poisoned. His clothes were damp with sweat and his hair was plastered to his face. As he tried to move onto the cot, a jolt lanced through his stomach and he fell to his knees, crying out. The pain waned slowly, and he struggled onto the cot before the next pang came.

Shadowed light came from the window. Had it really been only a day?

Mercifully, the ache subsided completely, and he began to relax. His eyelids were heavy, and he knew it wouldn't be long before he drifted off. The door scraped open, and he turned to see his visitor.

Instead of Caius, a man entered, followed by a servant carrying a tray. They stood across from the cot and he had trouble focusing on them.

"Will you serve your king?" the man asked.

"No," Nico managed.

"Give the boy his dinner."

The servant approached and Nico desperately slapped the tray from his hand, sending its contents tumbling.

"Hold him down."

Nico struggled under the weight of the servant but couldn't get free. The man pulled a bottle from his pocket and poured a few drops into Nico's mouth. After instructing the servant to clean up the food, he walked away.

Thankfully, there was no immediate pain. After the servant left, Nico relaxed and closed his eyes, exhaustion overcoming him. He bolted up as he saw his mother's final minutes.

Taking a deep breath, he lay down again, warily closing his eyes. The moment he entered darkness, the vision replayed, and his eyes snapped open. In the light, he watched it happen again and as soon as his mother died the scene began anew.

He let out an anguished scream at the image of Connery pulling the knife across her throat. Nico raced forward to try to stop him, but simply passed through the mirage. Confused, he looked about the cell, only to watch it all over again.

He sank onto the floor, tears rolling down his face. His nightmare had come to haunt him during his waking hours.

✝✝✝

The Vosjnik filed into the throne room, Vitia leading the way with an arrogant swagger.

Braxton was surprised to see she had managed to fill the three open positions already.

Mara Foxire, the new telepath, was a mousy girl of fifteen—barely more than a child really. It had taken Caius over a year to break her, proving her strength and mettle. He was also surprised to see his own tutor, Evard Poukyn, had filled the earth elemental position. The man was brutish and had often intentionally inflicted pain; Braxton could not say he was unhappy the man had made himself a target for Lunos. The fire elemental, Nicandro Quolt, was much older than the other members, being at least sixty. What little hair he had was stark white and he stood hunched over.

"I see you had no trouble finding replacements," Caius said with a pleased grin.

"Would you like to test them?" Vitia asked.

"I would, but a more pressing matter has arisen. In a week, the girl will be in Revod."

A vicious smile crossed Vitia's face. "We'll depart immediately."

"I want the girl brought back alive *and* unharmed."

Vitia made to leave.

Caius stayed her, continuing, "I have been informed three other elementals are traveling with her. I take two of these to be Kade and Nico's brother. I want them brought back alive and in decent health as well. As for the fourth, I would prefer alive… but the other three are priority."

Braxton could see Vitia was displeased at the prospect of having to leave Kade alive, yet, nonetheless, she bowed, answering, "Yes, sir."

‡‡‡

Aron made his way through the castle, the path ahead lit sparsely, his heavy footfalls echoing off the stones. Coming to a door, he rammed the key into the lock.

Inside, Alyck sat in his usual chair, a look of sadness upon his face. "I am sorry for your loss, Little King; I did try to warn you." A wave of guilt washed over Aron. "But that is not why you are here."

"Father knows where Keegan is going to be. What should I do?"

"What you were going to do originally." Alyck leaned forward and whispered, "Run." When Aron did not move, he repeated, "Run, Little King, you do not have much time."

He backed slowly towards the door, eyes still on Alyck.

Impatiently, the Blind Prophet yelled, "Go!"

Aron turned and ran, only stopping when he came to the hidden door. He hesitated, then pressed the stone and easily made his way through the dark passage.

On the rooftop, the air was warm, the sky a clear blue tinged with orange as the sun set. A light northward wind gently pulled at him and something about it felt familiar. To the south, a line of horses galloped away, and he figured they must belong to the Vosjnik. And here was his choice; run towards nothing and save himself or follow the Vosjnik and save Keegan.

There was a shift in the wind, and it began to blow in a southerly direction.

Aloud, he said, "It seems you have made the decision for me. I know I could not save you, Shiloh, but I will save her. It does not make up for my failure, but it is what you would have wanted me to do—the right thing."

CHAPTER 35

Aron peered around the corner; a single torch at the end of the corridor lit the way, which was guarded by two men. Taking a breath and gripping his bow tighter, he stepped into the middle of the hall. As the men spotted him, he released two arrows in quick succession, which pierced flesh with ease.

Taking the keys from the belt of one of the men, he opened the door. The inside of the room was dark, and he returned to the hall for a torch; the griffins shied away from the sudden brightness. Legends spoke of noble creatures to be reckoned with, but the griffin he beheld were forlorn and dejected.

He cautiously approached one with bronze feathers.

"I know how you feel," he whispered.

It stared back at him with glossy black eyes.

Reaching forward, he unlocked the bond around its neck. As soon as the iron was removed, it pounced, sending him sprawling, his bow clattering away and the torch landing out of reach.

The beast pinned him, and it lowered its head, its beak coming within inches of his exposed throat. It sent a puff of warm breath over his face and turned its head to look at him. Then, it took off, leaving him unharmed. With mighty swings of its taloned paw, it broke the chains holding its brethren.

Frozen, Aron watched as the eleven other griffins were released. Where he assumed a wall existed, they ran through, dropping into the night, leaving a lingering thought that filled him with a sense of freedom and gratitude.

Shakily, he got to his feet, retrieving the torch. Looking out from the open wall, he watched as twelve shadows ambushed the men along the battlements. He raced back to the door, retrieving his bow along the way.

Now, he needed to get to the stables without being seen by guards or attacked by a griffin. Inconspicuously, he made his way to the door that led to the plains. While he could not see the griffins above, he could hear them—and the cries of the men they assailed.

Inhaling deeply, he gathered himself and sprinted across the grass. Once safely inside the stables, he saddled Kolt's sabino palfrey. He could take any horse he wanted, but this was meant to be a final affront.

Under the stars once more, he turned back to look at the castle, the screams of men and griffins breaking the night. He was finally free.

✠✠✠

Braxton slashed at a griffin as it dove at him, feeling his blade dig into flesh. As the griffin pulled away, it left his sword bathed in dark purple blood.

There was a lull in the attacks, giving him time to think.

"Grab those chains," he yelled at the soldiers nearby. "Hurry, we do not have much time!"

Kolt clutched a wound on his arm. "What are you planning?"

"We can throw the chains at them. They will wrap around their wings and ground them."

"That is a stupid idea."

Braxton turned on him. "I do not see you coming up with anything better. So, until such time, shut the royik up. And do as I say!" To the men, he yelled, "Here they come!"

The griffins dropped out of the night and once more yells surrounded him. He heard chains clinking together, a loud *thunk,* and the cry of a griffin.

He rushed over. "Keep it down!"

It was Myrish, his wings and legs entangled in the chains.

Please, stop! Braxton begged, struggling to make his thoughts heard.

Myrish thrashed, screaming, *Betrayer!*

Myrish, I do not want to kill you. Please do not make me.

Murderer! Finding he could not stand, Myrish thrust out his head, snapping at the men. He seized one by the leg, pulling him to the ground.

His companions grabbed ahold of his arms and there was a sickening snap and a blood-curdling scream as his leg was severed.

Braxton looked around. Finding a long, leather cord, he jumped onto Myrish's back, and quickly wound it around his beak. As he worked, he yelled, "I need a life elemental."

A soldier stepped forward. "What do you need?"

"Take the griffin's energy."

"We tried that before; there's too much."

"Distribute it amongst us," Braxton said while Myrish struggled under him. "Quickly!"

The man held his hand out toward the griffin and began to concentrate. After a moment, Braxton felt his fatigue melting away and the beast beneath him settle. Soon, Myrish could do little more than breathe.

I am sorry, he told the griffin. Turning to the man, he said, "Good work. Come with me, we are going to need you." To the others, he ordered, "Two of you take that man to Rohan; the rest of you, get the griffin back to the stable."

"Yes, sir."

A screech came from the sky, and he looked up. Time stood still and he recognized the scene of chaos from his nightmares.

The descending griffin shrieked, *Betrayer! Murderer! Coward!*

Talons reached for his chest and pierced his skin, burning as they cut through him. He was thrown sideways as the beast landed atop him and he could just make out the spear protruding from its neck.

Betrayer, murderer, coward.

Stay with me, Braxton murmured.

Betrayer, murderer, coward.

Iwin, do not go dying on me. Please, the others need you.

The griffin's words were scarcely more than a whisper, *Betrayer, murderer, coward. Hero.*

As life left the old beast, Braxton's world sank into darkness.

"Jyken eya meki lunviyda zæ psodæ ri ayþ drackyn, æay woth viæn nuþ qalx ayþ æyscs fayo eyar oywn þen," Aron said harshly, suddenly materializing and placing a hand over his ravaged chest.

"Nackh jyken eya casne, fackyon ictotm, iruh du woth unla ryo iruh ayþ adæmno," Kade added, putting a hand on his forehead.

Heat seared across his body, and he tried to call out.

Kade and Aron smiled cruelly before continuing, "Psodæ woth yarv rhæpn casne jappec eya."

A third man behind Braxton said, "Qalx ayþ buna, qalx ayþ waysne, qalx okæpyio, qalx ayþ payn ri luxyen, zæ psodæ woth viæn," placing his hands on his shoulders, pushing him down.

Keegan appeared before him and paused before speaking. "Astæm egreþer du woth ryo eyar oywn foylisha ghæ woth solcan eyar hayclen oh kævoka kunyi." She leaned over and gently kissed him, sucking the breath from his lungs as a pressure squeezed his body. "Eya wye rimbor."

His eyes snapped open and found his father crouched over him.

"Calm," Caius said. "You are not fully healed yet."

He had a moment to take in the people holding him down before he was sent back into darkness.

✠✠✠

Over and over Nico watched his mother's death. At first, a flurry of emotions had raged inside. Now, as the image blurred and faded, he could barely feel anything—except exhaustion.

With the mirage finally gone, he lay on the cot, letting his weary eyes close. As soon as they did, the cell door opened.

"How are you today?" the king questioned, pulling a small vial from his pocket. "Will you serve me?"

Naturally, there would be some form of torment inside and Nico knew he couldn't keep doing this.

"Excellent," Caius said, putting the vial away. "I was almost hoping you would be more tenacious. Oh, you are going to *love* this; in a week, I will have possession of Jared"

Jared, Nico thought; there was no way *he* would've given in already.

"It will be brilliant watching you break him."

Furiously, he yelled, "I will never hurt my brother. And I will never serve you!"

"H-ho," Caius grinned, taking out the vial again. "There is still some fight in you yet."

Nico wanted to resist, but some unseen force prevented him from doing so as Caius forced a few drops into his mouth.

Sitting on the edge of the cot, Nico wondered what distress this new poison would bring. A fly buzzed by his ear, and he swatted it away. It soon returned and refused to leave him alone. He gritted his teeth, doing his best to ignore it. He could feel something crawling on his leg and, looking down, saw ants scuttling up.

Jumping to his feet, he frantically brushed them off. The fly was back, buzzing loudly, but now it was more than one. Bugs were everywhere, crawling, buzzing, biting… No matter how many he brushed away, more always came.

✠✠✠

Exhausted, Braxton trudged to the griffin stable. He placed a hand against his chest, feeling the tattered remains of his shirt—underneath, his skin was unmarked. He stood outside the door a moment, knowing many of the griffins had been slain. Inside, stood only five: Myrish, Niyth, Crowlin, Phynex, and Oxren. His heart grieved for the other seven.

The griffins pulled against their chains, emitting low growls.

Jyken eya meki lunviyda zæ psodæ ri ayþ drackyn, æay woth viæn nuþ qalx ayþ æyscs fayo eyar oywn þen, he repeated to himself. "How did they get loose?" he asked the stable master.

"Someone released them."

"Why would anyone do that?"

"To create confusion."

Braxton sighed. "Attend to their injuries."

Making his way from the stable, he did his best to keep tears from sliding down his cheeks.

Nackh jyken eya casne, fackyon ictotm, iruh du woth unla ryo iruh ayþ adæmno.

His body felt heavy, and his clothes were soaked in blood. Some was his, but most belonged to the griffins.

As he neared his chambers, he was approached by a guard. "Your father requests your presence."

Sighing, Braxton made his way to the throne room. It was strange to be standing before his father rather than beside him.

Psodæ woth yarv rhæpn casne jappec eya.

"How many griffins still live?" Caius asked.

"Five."

"I suppose you saved as many as you could."

Tiredly, he nodded. "And we still have the hatchlings. Whoever released the griffins did not know about them."

"Someone freed the griffins?"

Qalx ayþ buna, qalx ayþ waysne, qalx okæpyio, qalx ayþ payn ri luxyen, zæ psodæ woth viæn.

"It appears so."

"While I am not pleased with the outcome," Caius began, "you did well. Rest. And once you have, find the culprit."

Braxton bowed and made his exit.

Astæm egreþer du woth ryo eyar oywn foylisha ghæ woth solcan eyar hayclen oh kævoka kunyi.

It took an eternity to reach his chambers and, once there, he locked the door, not wanting anyone to disturb him. He stripped from his soiled clothes, leaving them scattered about the floor. With a wet rag, he wiped away the blood from his body. What he could not wipe away was the contrition.

Tears began to slide down his face and he did nothing to stop them. Going to his desk, he pulled out a fresh sheet of parchment and slowly transcribed the prophecy. Something had changed after Iwin died; he could remember every detail now.

✠✠✠

Aron had not gone far before stopping for the night. He awoke when the sun was high in the sky and his body protested against rising and pressing on. Mounting the palfrey, he spurred it away from the wooded area.

In the daylight and out on the grasslands, he felt exposed. He scanned the skies and horizon for any evidence of pursuers; none materialized, no matter how much he strained his eyes.

321

With any luck, it would be several days before anyone noticed his absence. He wondered who would discover it. While Kolt enjoyed tormenting him, he usually did not go out of his way to do so. His father would call upon him and while he customarily made an appearance, he was free to decline without consequence. He had barely interacted with any of the castle's servants—aside from Shiloh; the thought of her made his heart hurt. That left Braxton, who, when permitted, chose to spend time with him.

He hoped releasing the griffins would prevent Braxton from doing so for quite some time. A feeling of guilt struck him as he realized he had abandoned the one person who cared about him. He pushed the thought aside; there was no going back now.

CHAPTER 36

Braxton opened his eyes groggily and groaned, his muscles tense and sore. As he pushed himself into a sitting position, a servant shuffled in with a tray of food. She placed it before him, then stood against the wall passively.

As he ate, a thought struck him. "I take it you needed an elemental to open the door."

"It wasn't locked, sir," she stated.

"If you did not unlock my door, then who did?"

"I don't know."

"Leave."

Once the woman was gone, he rose and dressed quickly in a fresh pair of pants and a rich, red silk shirt. He quickly traded it for dark green; the red reminded him too much of blood. As he buckled his sword around his waist, a slip of paper on his desk caught his attention.

It appears you have made progress. Do not leave it too long.

"Alyck," he muttered.

He pulled out the pages with relevant information from his desk drawer but paused. Now was not the time to be doing this. However, there was something he needed to discuss with Alyck.

Walking through the halls, he couldn't help but notice the diminished number of guards; the griffins had dealt a heavy blow. When he stood outside Alyck's door, he paused, formulating his thoughts. Entering, he found his uncle waiting—like always.

"I- I have been having these dreams… but now I do not think they are dreams," Braxton began.

"What do you think they are?" Alyck asked, genuinely curious.

"I am not sure. That is why I came to see you."

"I wish I had answers for you."

Braxton creased his eyebrows. "How is it you know nothing about this? You know everything."

Alyck sighed. "I know everything, except when it pertains to you. And I cannot answer why, as I do not know."

"Then how have you been able to tell me… things?"

"Through some very creative means. Since I cannot see your path, I look at how you affect the people and objects around you. From that, I can paint a picture."

"You must know what these dreams mean," Braxton said, almost pleading. "They are driving me mad. I wake up almost every night in a panic, feeling like someone has tried to kill me. I kept dreaming about talons ripping me apart and—" he broke off, the cobwebs beginning to fall away.

"You dreamt the future?"

He hesitated. "I think so."

✟✟✟

Lucas crept forward, using the shadows to hide. His foot struck a loose rock, sending it skittering. Cursing, he froze, but the guards he was tailing didn't seem to hear. He gave it a few moments before slinking forward again, Carter trailing him.

The soldiers stopped outside a house; inside lived a family of elementals. While Lucas didn't see the point in freeing them, Elza assured him it was part of the master plan.

The men traded words with a third at the door, then continued down the street. They would walk to the next alley, about face, and make their way back.

Making sure Carter was concealed behind some barrels, Lucas picked up a few stones and joined him. Every noise seemed incredibly loud, even his heartbeat. Soon, they heard the soldiers' footsteps.

"Ready?" he asked.

"Yeah," Carter returned in a low tone.

As the men passed the alleyway, Lucas threw a pebble.

One of the men called, "Who's there?"

"Just a rat," the other jibed.

Seeing they were about to continue on, Lucas threw another rock, hitting the first soldier in the head.

"Can a rat do that?" the man exclaimed, drawing his sword.

Coming into the alley, the men searched the gloom.

Using their daggers' hilts, Lucas and Carter struck them on the back of the heads. Lucas's victim fell forward like a tree while Carter's man stumbled but remained standing. He began to turn, and Lucas hit him in the temple.

"Hit harder next time," Lucas advised as they dragged the guards to the end of the alley.

"Two down, one to go," Carter said, taking the men's weapons.

Peering around the corner, Lucas saw the guard at the doorway craning his neck to see where his counterparts had gone, shifting from foot to foot. Curiosity overpowered duty and he abandoned his post, looking over his shoulder to check the street was empty. Warily, he came towards the alley, but wasn't smart enough to draw his weapon.

As soon as he was within reach, Lucas jumped from behind the wall and punched him in the face. The soldier held his face as tears welled in his eyes. Taking a handful of hair, Lucas rammed his head into the wall and the guard slumped over.

They quickly made their way towards the house.

Trying the door, Carter found it locked and cursed.

"I don't have time for this," Lucas said, kicking down the door.

It swung open with a heavy boom and there were shrieks from the inhabitants within. Entering, Lucas found a man standing protectively in front of his wife and two daughters. At first, the man looked alarmed, but soon relief crossed his face.

"Go, quickly," Lucas told them.

"Are you with the Lazado?" the man asked.

"No," Carter said.

"Then who are you?" the woman questioned.

"Doesn't matter," Lucas said. "But you'd best leave before the soldiers wake up."

The man turned to his children, trying to soothe them. "No need to be afraid; everything's going to be just fine."

"Thank you," the woman said, harrying her family past.

As the man pushed by, Lucas shoved a sword into his hand. "You might want this."

Carter crossed his arms, watching the family take off down the street. "That was easy."

"Humph," was Lucas's response. "Let's get out of here."

✠✠✠

"Where is he?" Kolt yelled, crashing through the door.

"Wha—" Braxton started groggily.

"Where is he? Our royiken bastard of a brother!"

Braxton rubbed the sleep from his eyes. "How the royik should I know?"

"You—" Kolt stammered furiously, "You are the one who likes the bastard."

He got to his feet. "That does not mean I know where he is at all hours. Now, get out."

Anger contorted Kolt's face as he struck out.

Braxton stopped his fist mid-punch and wrenched his arm aside. "Do not take your anger out on me. What did he do anyway?"

"Stole my horse," Kolt grunted.

Braxton released Kolt's hand and snorted. "Why would he do that? He is not allowed to leave the castle grounds."

"That makes no difference. He stole my horse!"

"I find that hard to believe."

"I do not care what you believe. He stole it, hid it, whatever!"

Braxton crossed his arms. "What do you want me to do about it?"

His brother was red in the face. "Fix it!"

"Get out."

Kolt gave him a final glare before storming out.

Braxton rubbed his eyes; it was always something with his brothers. Dressing, he went to Aron's room.

Knocking on the door, he called, "Aron, we need to talk." There was no answer. He knocked again. "Aron?" Growing impatient, he pushed the door open.

The room was dark and eerily still, the bed appearing as if it had not been slept in for days. He cursed as he stormed off; it was *always* something.

"Aron is to be brought back unharmed," Braxton told the assembled soldiers. "You will ride for a day; if you find no sign of him, return to the castle. Norm, Orville, Jai, and—"

"And I," Kolt cut him off, "will be leading the teams."

Braxton grabbed his arm. "What do you think you are doing?"

"Finding my bastard of a brother."

"No."

"Try and stop me. And you had better hope I do not find him." Turning to the men, Kolt barked, "Move out."

The groups mounted, each choosing a direction. A dozen men remained to be split between Braxton and Kolt.

With a sneer, Braxton said, "Hammond, you are taking over Kolt's squad."

Kolt started, "What do you think—"

"You have no horse; how do you expect to ride along?" He did not give his brother time to respond before yelling at the men to depart.

✠✠✠

Someone was shaking his shoulder and Nico awoke, startled. The man looked familiar, and Nico recalled seeing him with Caius that day in the throne room. The man was a few inches shorter than Braxton and his fine, ash blond hair was cut short. His dark brown eyes scowled menacingly.

"What's going on?" Nico questioned, blinking the sleep from his eyes as he was pulled to his feet.

He expected to be dragged away, but instead was thrown into the corner of the cell. Something was wrong.

"I am teaching my brother a lesson," the man growled, punching him in the stomach.

Nico coughed, hunching over. The next strike landed on the side of his head, flinging him into the wall. A strike to the back of his head sent him to the floor. He brought his hands up to shield himself, which only seemed to anger the man more. Nico lost his breath as a boot connected with his chest.

It seemed an eternity before the man grew bored and left, leaving him on the floor, his body numb, throbbing, and beaten.

Gingerly, Nico pushed himself up and stumbled back to the cot.

Blood came from his mouth, and he choked on the iron taste of it. Already, one of his eyes was swelling shut. The ringing in his ears was beginning to fade, leaving him with a pounding headache.

Groaning, he hoped the next person to visit would take him to the infirmary and that this was not to become the norm.

✛✛✛

"Did you see the look on their faces?" Carter said, laughing excitedly.

Out of breath, Lucas slowed to a walk. "I did."

Over the last three days, they'd been causing disorder. They'd knocked soldiers out and stripped them of their armor and weapons, freed elementals under house arrest, taken cartloads of food headed to the barracks, and even liberated some tax money. No one had been seriously injured, but they were causing enough trouble that there were whispers about who might be committing the deeds.

Lucas had already heard several theories. Most believed it was Lazado agents, others thought it was youngsters, and some thought it was rogue citizens. *If only they knew it was two shepherds.*

Climbing the steps to the house, they were joined by Elza.

"Seems you two have been keeping busy," the soldier commented.

Carter led the way inside. "Can't say otherwise."

"What're you doing here?" Lucas asked. While he went along with Elza's plans, something was off-putting about the man, and he didn't entirely trust him.

"It's time to step up our game," Elza said.

"There isn't much else we can do just the two of us," Carter pointed out.

"I'd say otherwise."

"What scheme do you have this time?" Lucas asked.

"I was thinking we could release everyone from the dungeon."

"Are you insane?" Lucas barked. "That's a great way to get us killed."

"It won't be hard," Elza said, playing it off.

"Oh, really?"

"Yeah. If you look like you belong there, no one will bother you. After that, it's pretty simple."

"How do you propose we look like we belong?"

"Well, there are two options: you look like a soldier or a prisoner."

"You're going to get us killed."

"I think it'll work," Carter contradicted.

"Then do it yourselves," Lucas told them. "Count me out."

"Really? After all you've done these past few days, you balk now?"

"To dress like a soldier means our heads if we're caught. And I'll never allow myself to become a prisoner willingly."

"Elza, come back tomorrow. Give me some time to work on him," Carter said.

Giving a wave, Elza said, "Let your answer be the right one, Lucas."

CHAPTER 37

ngrily, Braxton slammed the door to the stable. Two days of searching and no one had found a trace of Aron. He had not expected much, but, regardless, was still frustrated.

He stormed across the grass and found a soldier waiting for him on the lower levels of the castle.

"Your father requested you cater to the boy tonight," the man said as he breezed past.

Braxton gave a lazy wave to show he had heard, muttering under his breath, "Of course he has me acting like a servant. Of course he has me doing this the moment I get back." He wanted to punch something. "Of course, of course, of course!"

Unhappily, he made his way to the kitchens. There, a small tray of food and a vial with a thick, red liquid awaited him.

Taking the tray, he made his way through the halls. Kolt passed him and gave an intentionally audible snigger. Heat rose to his ears, and he had to refrain from bashing Kolt's head in with the tray.

Outside the cell, he paused. Nico lay on the cot, staring up at the ceiling. Having no desire to do this, Braxton took a deep breath before opening the door.

Nico sat up warily, dark bruises covering his face.

Setting the tray down, Braxton made his way to the boy, kneeling by the cot. He took Nico's head and turned it to the side. "Who did this?"

Nico avoided his gaze.

"Who did this?" he demanded.

"I don't know," the boy said submissively.

"What did he look like?"

Nico rubbed his jaw. "Average, had a big ring…"

Braxton turned his head again to look at the bruise; it had an impression. The form was misshapen, but he would know that symbol anywhere.

He removed the ring from his right hand. "Did it look like this?"

"I think so."

Without another word, Braxton slipped his ring back on and stalked out. He was going to kill him; Kolt had no right… and how could he do that to a child?

Storming through the halls, his anger grew. His brother had gone too far. When he reached Kolt's room, he did not bother knocking and kicked the door in.

Two women were kneeling on the bed, enraptured in each other, both wearing nothing. Another, clothed in only a skirt, was leaning over Kolt, who sat in a chair, a smug smile on his vile face. The three women shrieked and made pathetic attempts to cover themselves as Braxton entered the room.

He pulled Kolt from the chair, punching him in the face. "Do not ever touch that boy again!" Kolt tried to retaliate and Braxton kneed him in the groin. "Do you hear me?"

Kolt feigned ignorance. "What are you talking about?"

"NICO!" Braxton kicked him in the stomach. "You beat the boy because I did not allow you on the search for Aron."

"What if I did?"

"You little vitot," Braxton bellowed, striking him in the mouth.

Kolt gave him a bloody grin. "What are you going to do about it?"

"What the nastor do you think?" There was a satisfying crack with Braxton's next strike and Kolt dropped to the floor, clutching his side and what were likely broken ribs. "Do not touch the boy again."

"You are not his tutor; you have no say."

"I am now. Touch him again and I will leave you with little more than your life."

‡‡‡

"Hey, we've made pretty good time," Keegan commented as they emerged from the forest. "You said it'd take a week and we made it in six days."

"Yes," Taite said absentmindedly, mumbling something she didn't catch.

"You gonna let us stay in the city tonight?" Keegan questioned Kade.

"I don—" he started.

"We'll see how we feel later," Taite interrupted.

Turning her attention to the city before them, Keegan could tell they were approaching from the southwest, the sun casting long shadows of the city's profile. Tall walls rose well into the sky and only a few roofs peeked their heads over the battlements. The stones constructing the ramparts were a dark, somber gray and flags flew from the top of the wall, gently waving in the breeze.

Inside, Revod seemed as grim as the outside looked. The buildings were all made of dark stone and the inhabitants dressed in drab colors. No one smiled.

They stabled the horses and Taite released them on the city, knowing they'd do what they wanted anyway. Kade and Cassidy eagerly went their own way, but Keegan and Jared, not knowing what to do, did as before, and followed Taite to the market.

"Ten bucks says Kade and Cassidy go to the closest inn," Keegan remarked.

"Ten bucks?" Jared questioned. "I'm impressed you can carry that many deer."

333

"Hey," Keegan said happily, playfully hitting Jared's arm, "you're picking up sarcasm!"

He smirked. "I'm not sure that's a good thing."

Keegan waved her hand. "Psh. And I didn't mean literal deer. 'Bucks' is another word for money where I'm from. Here, I guess it'd be like betting ten coins."

"I see. And why would you bet they're going to an inn?"

"I wasn't literally betting money, it's kind of a figure of speech. And they would go to an inn to… well, to do the thing Kade *really* likes."

Jared gave an unamused look. "I can't believe you say things like that."

Once they reached the market, they left Taite's side, though kept him in sight. Wandering through the market, Keegan was happy to look through everything and just forget the world for a moment.

"Taite seems to know many people," Jared noted, pulling her from her mind.

"Huh?"

Jared pointed through the crowd. "There."

The Kjote was deep in conversation with a soldier, and it looked like he was trying to convince him of something. Taite motioned in their direction and her heart beat faster as more soldiers gathered around. She locked eyes with Taite, and he started pointing furiously and yelling. Frustrated, Taite started exuding his feelings and she felt the bottled-up emotions spilling forth. There was excitement—no, anticipation and it had something to do with them.

She began pushing Jared. "Run. The cunt sold us out."

Jared led the way as they shoved through the market, soldiers yelling for them to stop. Keegan started to lose him in the crowd, and she called out, but her words were lost, and Jared was swallowed up.

The soldiers were getting closer and, knowing there was nothing else to do, she took off. For once, she was glad to be short; it made getting through the throng easier than it was for her bulky pursuers. As she darted along, she realized she needed to warn Kade and Cassidy.

Kade, she yelled, praying he hadn't set up an impenetrable wall.

What's wrong?

Taite sold us out.

Get somewhere safe, Kade instructed.

And where would that be? she snapped.

Just get somewhere; I'll find you.

Okay. You'll need to find Jared too.

Anger bubbled in his next question. *Why isn't he with you?*

We got separated. It's not his fault.

Just get somewhere safe, he said, breaking contact.

Keegan stopped, a stitch in her side. Looking behind, she noticed a mass of men further up the street.

"Goddamnit."

Within minutes, she had to stop again. Breathing heavily, she looked around for some place to duck into, but there was no time. Cursing, she took flight again.

Rounding a corner, she nearly tripped over a few children huddled against the wall. A thought struck her, and she took a seat beside them.

"Shh," she whispered, pressing a finger to her lips, and pulling the smallest child onto her lap.

None protested, though they did give her looks of wild confusion.

As the soldiers rounded the corner and sprinted past, she kept her head down, heart hammering as she waited for someone to grab her. When the soldiers had cleared the street, she slid the child from her lap.

Please tell me you're close, she said to Kade, walking in the opposite direction of the soldiers.

I'd be closer if you'd stop moving.

I was being chased; what was I supposed to do?

Just stay where you are.

Spotting a side alley, she made her way to it, *Hurry.*

As she saw the lane came to a dead end, Keegan heard a man behind her yell, "Over here."

She turned to see two soldiers standing at the top of the alley.

"We found her," a second man exclaimed as they came towards her.

Both men were overweight, their enlarged bellies hanging from under their leather armor. One was stout, with the beginnings of a waddle, while the other looked like he belonged on a football team.

"Shit," Keegan groaned. "Look, just let me go and… just let me go."

"Why would we do that?" the first man questioned.

She gave a nervous smile. "Please?"

Neither responded, inching towards her.

Looking around, she saw nothing to use as a weapon and reached for her magic. As one of the men lunged, she sent a column of earth into his stomach, stopping him in his tracks.

The other came at her with a punch, which she ducked under, retaliating with an uppercut to his ribcage. She kept the first at bay with a well-placed sidekick. With her distracted, the second soldier landed a hook punch to her jaw, making her stumble.

Regaining her composure, she realized her back foot was against the wall. The soldiers stood awkwardly in front of her, as if unsure of how to proceed. She lunged at one then attacked the other, punching him in the jaw and pulling him into his comrade.

While the two men disentangled themselves, she ran up the alley, and was halfway to the street when one of them grabbed her hair.

She winced and swung an arm wildly.

The man caught her arm, twisting it behind her back. "Quickly," he called.

Not knowing what the man was waiting for and not wanting to find out, she strained against her captor.

Twisting his fist into her hair, he snarled, "You're not going anywhere."

She kicked back, aiming for the man's knee. Her foot found its mark and there was a crunch as the force broke his patella. The man fell to the ground, screaming in pain, pulling her with him.

As Keegan scrambled to her feet, the other man grabbed her and slammed her into the wall, blurring her vision. Her eyes watered, making it even harder to see straight.

The man placed a hand over her throat to keep her in place while he endeavored to pull something from his pocket, which turned out to be a rag. With her vision beginning to clear, Keegan struggled against him, and he had difficulty holding her in place with one hand.

Just as the rag touched her face, someone pulled the soldier away. Whatever the cloth was soaked in made her throat sting, making her cough and gag. There was the sickening crack and the man fell to the ground, neck broken.

Keegan coughed violently as she stared at Kade, her mind fuzzy.

"Bloody good timing you've got," she managed.

‡‡‡

"Where are we going?" Cassidy asked as Kade pulled her through the streets of Revod.

With a smile, he answered, "I don't know yet."

They walked hand in hand, eventually finding themselves on the outskirts of a square. Street performers pranced about; some juggled, while a few danced to merry jigs, and others were telling stories with the aid of puppets.

Approaching the puppeteers, they watched the story unfold. From what Cassidy could tell, it was the fable of the cat and the dragon.

Kade was relaxed, something rare, and wrapped an arm around her. She smiled as they watched the show, gently leaning against him, wishing the moment would never end. Feeling Kade tense, she looked up to find a worrisome expression on his face.

"Is everything okay?"

"No." He dragged her away from the crowd. "Taite betrayed us."

She covered her mouth in shock. "What are we going to do?"

"You're going to stay here while I look for Keegan and Jared."

"I want to go with you."

"No," he told her, placing a hand on her cheek. "I'll be faster on my own and it'll be safer for you here."

"Fine, but hurry."

He gave her a quick kiss on the cheek before starting away, not making it far before Jared ran headlong into him.

"Oh, thank Sola and Lunos. Taite—"

"I know."

"Good, but I lost Keegan."

"I know that, too; I was just going to get her. Go get the horses and meet us at the north gate," Kade said, not giving them time to respond before he was gone.

"Well, what are we doing just standing here?" Cassidy said, taking charge.

CHAPTER 38

Kade turned down a street and was faced a dead-end—another one. He cursed under his breath, having no idea how to reach Keegan.

Please tell me you're close, she said.

I'd be closer if you'd stop moving, he responded.

I was being chased; what was I supposed to do?

Just stay where you are.

There was a slight pause. *Hurry.*

He took another turn and found another dead-end. Backtracking, he thought, *If I can't even find Keegan, how the nastor are we going to find the Lazado?*

The Lazado… In the chaos, he'd forgotten they no longer had a Kjote. Cursing under his breath, he stopped in an alley.

Kade ran a hand over his jaw, thinking, *Why couldn't Thaddeus just give us directions?* Then he remembered the letter. This certainly qualified as an emergency.

Kade,

If you are reading this, then some calamity has happened. Or you just could not listen—if that is the case, shame on you.

The Lazado are in Edreba, as everyone knows. They do not keep themselves hidden for several reasons, the main one being no man ordered by Caius can cross the boundary separating our kingdom from the other races. However, they are still cautious about allowing outsiders in.

To gain entrance, you need to answer their questions correctly. You will be asked the following:

    1. *Who are you? Kade Tavin, son of Kagen Tavin, ward of Thaddeus Broyker, subject of none.*

    2. *Where do you come from? A land of subjugation and hate.*

    3. *Why should we admit you? War cannot be fought only in the minds of men. It must be fought on the field, with payment of blood, in the hopes Sola and Lunos will see us through.*

After you give these answers, you should be welcomed with open arms. Memorize these responses and destroy this letter. Be safe and look after your family.

Thaddeus

He reread the missive before tearing the paper to ribbons, throwing a handful in a puddle, and shoving the rest into his pocket to discard later. Reaching out, he found Keegan's consciousness shrouded by adrenaline-addled thoughts and could sense she was close.

About to run past an alley, he saw her held against the wall by a man with a rag, which was no doubt soaked in ether.

He raced towards them and pulled the soldier away. Giving a sharp tug, he broke the man's neck.

Keegan bent over coughing. "Bloody good timing you've got."

"Come on."

"Where are Jared and Cassidy?"

"Waiting for us at the north gate."

She took the fallen soldier's sword and followed him. "What was on that rag?"

"Ether." He peered around the corner of the wall. There were a few people talking in the street.

"What does it do?"

"Inhibits magic."

"Should I be worried?"

"No, it'll fade in a bit. Follow me and do *exactly* as I say." Pointing to the sword, he said, "Hide that."

She fumbled to conceal the weapon in the folds of her dress as they left the cover of the alley.

They quickly made their way through Revod, doing their best to not look questionable. It was slow going, but they eventually reached the north gate.

"I don't see them," Keegan said worriedly, as they searched for Jared and Cassidy from behind some barrels in an alley.

Kade pointed across the way. "There."

✝✝✝

As Cassidy and Jared walked down the street, they tried to appear casual. It seemed to take an eternity to reach the stable and the whole time she was sure soldiers would stop them.

Thankfully, their horses were handed over without questions and they led them towards the north gate. After a while, they found it and ducked into a lane to wait for Kade and Keegan.

As they waited, an unpleasant feeling sat in Cassidy's stomach. "I think something is wrong. We should look for them."

"No," Jared said calmly. "Kade can manage. And if we leave it could create complications."

"How long can we wait?"

"I see them," Jared said in a hushed voice, pointing across the square.

Spotting them, Cassidy was about to make her way over.

No. Stay there, Kade said.

But—

It'll look suspicious.

What're we doing? Keegan questioned, forcing herself into the exchange.

When I say, meet in the middle, Kade instructed.

Cassidy looked towards the gate; they were wide open, people bustling through like nothing was amiss. She watched a man approach the guards. After a moment, the guard called to the men on top of the gate. Knowing they were about to close the portcullis, she grabbed two of the horses and ran into the square.

The others were caught off guard, but followed, realizing there was nothing else to do. They converged in the middle, mounted, and raced towards the gates as they began to close, soldiers yelling for them to halt. Cassidy rode through first, followed by Keegan and Kade. Jared was the last through and only just made it.

✝✝✝

Keegan yelled to be heard, "We need to stop."

"Why?" Kade snapped, reining in his horse.

"We need to figure out where we're going."

"I know where we're going."

"Are you sure? We've been heading north."

"No, we haven't."

"What makes you think we're heading north?" Jared questioned.

"The moon's rising on our right," Keegan explained.

Kade countered, "It's cloudy and we've barely seen the moon."

"Stop for a minute and prove me wrong."

"Fine."

From the way he answered, she could tell he felt unsure.

Coming upon a clearing, they dismounted. Kade looked up at the dark sky, watching for a break in the clouds. About to give up, a cloud shifted, letting pale moonlight shine through. His countenance shifted from one of annoyance to one of concern and frustration.

"We've been heading north," he mumbled.

"So glad I made us stop," Keegan said.

"Be quiet."

She was about to pull herself up into the saddle when there was a sound from within the forest. "Did you hear that?"

"Hear what?" Kade questioned, placing a hand on the hilt of his sword.

As soon as he said that eight figures emerged from the trees. A man tried to grab Keegan and she swung her ill-begotten sword, catching him with a slash to the arm; he stepped away cursing. The figure closest to Cassidy seized her and pulled her away.

Keegan recognized a few of the attackers and backed into the middle of the clearing, as did Kade and Jared, their swords drawn.

"Let her go, Vitia," Kade snarled.

"Why would I do that?" Vitia asked with a smug look.

"I'll kill you."

Vitia laughed. "I doubt that. Drop your weapons or the girl won't be doing so well."

Kade gritted his teeth but made no move to surrender.

Sighing theatrically, Vitia continued, "I'm not patient like Connery. I gave you a chance." She placed her hands on the sides of Cassidy's head and gave a quick jerk.

There was a sickening snap and Cassidy fell to the ground, her beautiful bright eyes no longer reflecting life and light.

Kade only remained rooted in place long enough for the blood to drain from his face. He gave a ferocious yell, charging at Vitia.

Keegan could feel anger and anguish roiling from him and would've followed had Jared not held her back.

As Kade neared Vitia, he slowed, face contorting in pain. He dropped to his knees, clutching his head.

Keegan watched as Vitia's malicious grin grew and Kade cried out. Within a moment, he became silent, collapsing beside Cassidy's body.

Vitia started towards them, clearly proud of what she'd done.

A piercing pain began in Keegan's head, the sensation increasing with each passing second. Dropping the sword, she clutched at her temples as it felt like shards of glass ground into her skull. Automatically, she reached for her life magic, focusing its power on herself. It didn't completely alleviate the pain but did make it more bearable. Jared wasn't as lucky, screaming helplessly until he became deathly still.

Dropping to her knees, Keegan hunched over. Hands wrapped around her arms and pulled her to her feet. It was only once she was standing that she realized how drained she felt; it was almost too much of an effort to stand. Looking up, she saw Vitia approaching, a deep scowl on her face.

"Now, how is that possible?" Vitia drawled, stepping over Jared. "You're just a little earth elemental."

Keegan pulled against the men; they didn't know.

Taking her arm, Vitia forced her wrist up. She stared at the marks in disbelief.

"That can't be." There was a pause. "How can this be? Get the ether!"

One of the men holding Keegan grabbed the back of her neck, anticipating resistance.

She wasn't completely prepared for the reaction the ether caused. Her throat burned and it felt as if someone was searing the inside of her lungs. The more she breathed, the fuzzier her mind became.

When Vitia pulled the rag away, she was left doing her best to simply breathe. Sagging, the men holding her let her drop to the ground. Slowly, Keegan managed to stop coughing, containing it to a wheeze. As she attempted to stand, a blinding pain radiated across the back of her head.

CHAPTER 39

Jared tasted dirt and his throat stung. He coughed and a wave of dizziness washed over him. Hands clutched his arms and pulled him up. Looking around, he became acutely aware of his predicament. He was dragged to a tree to have his hands bound and forced above his head.

Vitia approached and he tensed, expecting pain, but the only thing he felt was a gentle scrape against his inner forearms. Looking up, he saw she'd made a branch grow from the tree behind him, which went between his arms, keeping them raised. He glanced at Keegan, who was still unconscious, dried blood staining her hair.

Vitia snapped her fingers to get his attention. "You're going to want to focus on me."

"What do you want with us?"

"Absolutely nothing. However, the king wants something."

"What does *he* want?"

"You can ask him yourself when you see him."

Jared shifted uncomfortably as his arms began to lose feeling.

"Anyway, let's get to business. How do you get to the Lazado?"

"I don't know."

"Evard." A pale-skinned man stepped forward; the scowl he bore sent a chill down Jared's spine. "Would you like the honors?"

Evard's lips pulled into a malicious smile as he cracked his knuckles and rolled his shoulders. Jared was struck mid-abdomen and, had his hands not been restrained, he would've doubled over.

"Tell me how to reach the Lazado," Vitia demanded.

"I don't know."

"Tch, Kade must've told you."

"Kade doesn't know either. None of us do. The only person who knew was Taite."

"Ah, Taite Ault." Vitia reached over to the girl standing in the circle around him, pulling her over. "You remember Taite, Mara?"

The girl had dark red hair that fell gently over her shoulders, and she could be no older than fifteen. His gut wrenched as he was reminded of Nico.

"I asked a question," Vitia growled when the girl didn't respond.

"Yes, ma'am, I remember," Mara answered quietly.

Vitia released Mara and she backed away, eyes never leaving the ground.

"Tell me how to reach the Lazado."

"I don't know."

Evard delivered a blow to his side.

"T—" Vitia started again.

"I can't tell you something I don't know!"

"You have to know."

"He doesn't," Mara said quietly.

"What was that?" Vitia snapped.

"He- he doesn't know," she repeated, trembling.

Vitia pulled out a knife. "Hmm. Regardless, I still haven't had any fun yet."

Jared strained against his bonds, causing many of the Vosjnik to chuckle.

With a smile that revealed pointed canines, Vitia placed the knife against his neck. "As much as I'd like to see you bleed," she whispered, "I've been instructed otherwise." She dropped the knife to the neckline of his shirt and ran it through the cloth, pulling apart the seam to reveal his naked chest. She gave a disappointed sigh, running her fingers down his stomach. His skin burned where she touched and he grimaced, inadvertently giving a pained grunt. She let her palm rest on his collarbone. His skin began to sizzle, and he shook, refusing to cry out.

Finally, Vitia pulled away, leaving him with a burn that would scar. "So docile. Nothing like Nico."

He felt a constriction in his chest, his heart felt in a fiery grasp. "You opida."

"I see where he gets his mouth from."

Jared started, "Murderer! Roy—" He was cut off by a strike to the jaw.

"Murderer? Didn't Kade tell you?" she questioned with an air of arrogance. "Nico's alive and well. Maybe not well, but alive."

"He's alive?"

"Isn't that what I just said?"

Jared merely stared at her.

Vitia waved a hand. "Get him down. And take his shirt."

The branch between his arms receded and he groaned as needles shot through his limbs.

Two men hauled him to the middle of the clearing, stripping his shirt before rebinding his hands behind his back, and shoving him into the dirt.

His mind was racing; Nico was alive.

✠✠✠

Kade felt fingers running gently through his hair. Smiling, he opened his eyes and looked straight at Vitia. He scrambled away, quickly rising to his feet; it took him a moment to recall what had transpired. As he remembered, he threw himself at the Alvor and was within inches of her when he was dragged away.

"I'm going to kill you," he screamed. "I royiken swear it!"

Vitia gave a cold-hearted laugh. "I await the day you try so I can run you through."

He strained against those holding him, almost pulling free. Vitia caused his vision to darken and, while he still fought, was no match blind. His hands were bound and forced against a tree, and he felt the rough bark of a branch between his arms.

Slowly, his vision returned. Around him stood the Vosjnik, staring murderously, the new members mimicking the others' looks.

"Your new recruits are an old man and a bwint," he goaded. "You must've been desperate."

Realizing the insult was directed at him, Evard stormed forward and punched Kade in the face.

Kade tasted blood and spat to alleviate the tang. "Losing your touch there."

Evard's face reddened and he brought back his fist again.

"Leave it," Vitia barked. He looked at her furiously and she gave him an unwavering stare until he pulled away.

"Who put you in charge?" Kade said in a belittling tone.

"Caius," Vitia answered coolly.

It was then he noticed Mara. He'd heard the stories of when she'd been handed over to Caius. She'd been a child, eight, and for one so young, had resisted the king longer than most adults, lasting over a year. Her presence could only mean Connery was dead.

Vitia said, "Formalities over, let's begin. Who's first?"

"I am," Thahan said. He took a few quick steps to reach Kade and violently brought his knee up between his legs.

Kade groaned as a fist connected with his nose. He could feel blood trickling out of his nostrils and tasted it on his lips. Thahan delivered several heavy blows before Vitia called him away.

Dax pulled the stopper off a water-skin and jerked its contents towards Kade. It wasn't a lot of water, but it had the desired effect as it painfully forced its way through the nose and mouth. Kade gasped, but all he got was more pain; his body stung as it pleaded for air. Dax removed the water just long enough for Kade to take a breath before forcing it back. And so it went until he was left feeling dizzy and light-headed.

Nicandro went next, holding balls of flames to the exposed underside of his arms. Guthrie was content to send a biting stream of wind that caused his neck to snap painfully. Evard shot rocks at his stomach, and he was certain a few ribs had been cracked. Brennian chose to carve a griffin into his lower back and while the blade didn't cut deep, it was still agonizing, especially when he rubbed salt in the wound.

There was a lull after Brennian stepped away.

"Mara," Vitia snapped.

The girl shook her head.

"Do it!" Vitia screamed, making Mara flinched.

"I can't," the girl mumbled, "he's done nothing to me."

Vitia struck her. "You will do as you're instructed!"

Picking herself up, Mara approached slowly, and entered his mind, gently pushing through his consciousness. After a moment, he realized her ploy and scrunched up his face, hoping Vitia believed the horrible acting.

When Mara quickly retreated to the shadows, Vitia stared at him with a virulent smile.

"I think I'll do this the hard way," she said, lashing out to catching him in his already tender ribs.

He gave an involuntary wheeze.

She paused. "What have you got in your pocket?"

He reacted quickly, pulling his legs up and planting his feet against Vitia's chest. She rolled backwards and he would've continued fighting had she not annihilated the feeling in his legs making him hang painfully, the rope cutting into his wrists.

Vitia dusted herself off casually. "It must be good!"

He cursed at her as she rifled through his pockets, producing Rosh's letter.

"What do we have here?" She didn't have time to read it as she confusedly watched Thahan walked away.

Kade looked to see where the archer was going and saw Keegan standing across the clearing, dazed and disorientated.

‡‡‡

Rocks dug into Keegan, telling her the world was solid, but it felt like everything was spinning, turning, and tumbling. There was a throbbing in her head, and she reached up to touch it; a clump of dried blood crumbled between her fingers.

Groggily, Keegan opened her eyes and was assaulted by many brown colored shapes. As her vision became clearer, she could distinguish individual trees. Jared was kneeling in the center of her vision and, for reasons she couldn't understand, was shirtless.

He was mouthing something, and his eyes begged her to understand. She pushed herself up, body crying in pain, beseeching her to stay down. Agonizingly, she made it to her feet while Jared continued mouthing frantically.

She mimicked him. R, r, ru, ru, ru, run. Run. *Run.* Finally, she understood, but it was too late; Keegan had failed to notice the man walking towards her.

He took her arm, setting her off balance. As she steadied herself, she was surprised to be looking up at Thahan.

He shook her again. As she slammed into something solid, another set of hands wrapped around her other arm. This man looked familiar too, but she couldn't recall his name.

Keegan was pulled to where Jared knelt, and a group from across the clearing came to meet them. As they approached, she saw Kade in the background, dark splotches on his face, blood trickling across his skin. He pulled at the branch that kept his hands raised, but the limb remained steadfast.

Though unsure of what had happened, what *was* happening, she still knew something was amiss. As she pulled against the men holding her, she saw something, and her heart stopped… there lay Cassidy. Her mind was instantly clear.

"Get away from me," she screamed, resisting in earnest. As she continued to give screams of frustration, the Vosjnik froze.

"Get the ether," Vitia said, her tone conveying disbelief and fear.

A man pressed a rag against her face and Keegan broke into a fit of coughing, her throat burning as if the air had turned to acid. None too soon, the rag was removed, and she sagged between her captors, gasping for air.

"How did you manage that?" Vitia asked.

Her throat still reacting to the irritation, she gave Vitia a confused look.

"Show her."

The men turned her; the ground where they'd stood was raised in spikey waves.

"Did I…" Keegan muttered.

"Yes, while still under the effects of ether. How did you come by your powers?" Vitia said almost fearfully.

"Hell, if I know."

Vitia laughed and pinched Keegan's cheek. "You're the only one I believe when they say that."

"Don't touch her," Jared yelled, awkwardly rising to his feet.

"Bring them over here," Vitia instructed. "Kade needs to be able to see."

While being pushed towards Kade, Keegan caught her foot on the hem of her dress and the fabric ripped.

"What's this?" Vitia questioned, returning her attention to her. "Are you wearing trousers?" The corners of Vitia's lips turned up. "No use having so many layers." She widened the tear, leaving only the bodice behind; Keegan assumed it was a play to embarrass her.

"What do you want with us?" she asked.

"They're here to take us to Caius," Kade said weakly.

A chill raced down her spine.

"Oh, that's not all we're going to do," Vitia said, running a finger along Kade's jaw. "We're going to make you *suffer*."

"Opida," Kade spat.

Vitia lingered for a moment, giving him a pompous smile, then quickly turned on Keegan. "How do we get to the Lazado?"

"I don't know," she answered.

Vitia slapped her and she felt blood rushing to her cheek.

"I wasn't asking you," Vitia snapped. "I'm already aware you and pretty boy over there," she said, motioning towards Jared, "know nothing."

"Kade doesn't know either."

Vitia delivered a backhanded blow. "The only thing I want to hear from you are screams."

"No," she snarled, driving her heel into Thahan's foot.

He released her and she clawed at the other man, her nails digging deep into the flesh of his face. He yelled but didn't let go. Before she could do any further damage, Thahan grabbed her arm and a fistful of hair, pulling hard, making her yelp.

"Evard, take Guthrie's place," Vitia commanded.

Guthrie, the blond-haired man, stepped away, blood running down his cheek.

Vitia came within inches of Keegan's face. "How dare you attack my men."

Keegan's eyebrows furrowed and she conveyed as much hate as she could in one look.

Vitia stood still for a moment before placing a foot on Keegan's left calf. "Wipe that look off your face." She applied pressure and, with a crack, the bone broke under the stress.

For a moment Keegan felt no discomfort, then she looked at her leg. There was an explosion of pain, and she gave a shrill cry, sucking in deep breaths as hot tears came forth.

Jared pulled against the men holding him, only yielding when struck in the stomach.

Vitia turned back to Kade. "How do we get to the Lazado?"

He stayed quiet.

"Fine." Vitia turned on Keegan and violently attacked her.

When Vitia was done, Keegan could barely breathe, and a good portion of her face had gone numb.

The men holding Jared were beginning to struggle to restrain him as he twisted and screamed endless curses.

Several times Vitia asked Kade the same question and, every time, he remained silent. In retaliation, she struck Keegan.

In her half-conscious state, Keegan was barely aware of Jared repeatedly saying, "We don't know."

Slowly, she raised her head, knowing Vitia thought she was bested. While it was true, Keegan refused to give her the satisfaction. Placing her weight on her right leg, she rose to her full height—what little of it there was.

"Clearly, this isn't working," Vitia said, unsheathing a knife belted to her thigh.

"You wouldn't," Kade said, visibly agitated.

"Oh, I would." Vitia let the blade rest against Keegan's chest. "That is, unless you tell me what I want to know."

Kade gulped. "I don't know."

"Wrong answer." Vitia drove the knife into Keegan's shoulder just below the clavicle.

She gave a shattering scream and hell broke loose.

CHAPTER 40

Aron crouched in the bushes, having a perfect view through the foliage. Evard and Thahan held Keegan while Vitia beat her. Slowly he notched an arrow and drew his bow.

The man restrained by Dax and Brennian yelled profanities; this only made Vitia smile. Kade stared silently from his dangling position while Keegan sagged, barely keeping herself standing. She weakly raised her head and Aron saw a spark in her eyes as she lifted herself, putting all the weight on her right leg. He noticed the slight deformation in her left calf and grimaced.

Vitia unsheathed a knife and, before he knew it, drove it deep into Keegan's shoulder.

Keegan released a wounded cry, which rang in his ears, and a force seemed to take control of his body. He sprang to his feet, shooting an arrow, which buried itself deep in Evard's jugular. The man dropped to the ground, pulling Keegan with him. Thahan, caught off guard, failed to release Keegan and tripped over her. She gave another cry as he scrambled back to his feet and the rest of the Vosjnik looked for the source of the arrow.

Redrawing his bow, Aron pushed through the bushes, letting an arrow fly towards Vitia.

She moved at the last moment, and it grazed her arm.

"Who are you?" she spat, a hand covering her arm, unable to recognize him with his hood drawn low.

He sent an arrow towards Kade; it sunk through the rope and into the branch, allowing a strand to snap and Kade dropped to his knees. Notching another arrow and aiming it at Vitia, he carefully stepped towards Kade, letting him take the sword belted around his waist.

Making his voice deeper than normal, he said, "Leave. I have twenty soldiers in the forest."

"You lie," Vitia scoffed.

"Are you sure?"

"He's lying," Mara said.

The Alvor laughed. "Fool. You thought—"

"He has forty men."

"Walk away now and my men will not pursue," Aron said.

Vitia scowled but gestured for the Vosjnik to slowly advance towards their horses. Though cruel to extremes, Vitia knew how to lose gracefully. He would not call it caring for her comrades, more a way to make sure she lived to fight another day.

"I said walk," he snarled.

Glaring, the Vosjnik complied, retreating one step at a time.

As the Vosjnik reached the tree line, Aron stopped them. "Leave your weapons."

"No," Vitia said coldly.

He released an arrow, and it found its mark in Brennian's hip, who fell to a knee with a strangled yelp.

"Leave, your, weapons."

"You'll never be safe, not even in the Lazado."

Aron pulled the bowstring back further.

The Vosjnik gave Vitia worried looks, shifting uncomfortably. With a deep scowl, she unbuckled her belt, letting its weight pull it to the ground. The others followed suit quickly, then backed into the forest.

Aron waited several minutes before relaxing and rushing to Keegan, throwing back his hood. He gently turned her over and she gave a choked groan, dirt sticking to her face where tears wetted her skin.

"Aron?" she said in a whisper only he heard.

Having freed Jared and recognizing Aron, Kade shoved him away from Keegan. "What are you doing here?"

Aron wished he had held onto his bow. "Saving you."

"She's not doing well," Jared said from his position next to Keegan.

Aron pushed past Kade to return to Keegan. Her eyes were closed, and he wished she were awake to speak on his behalf.

"Don't touch her," Kade snarled.

Jared gave Kade a confused look. "What's the matter with you? He just saved us."

Kade tried to speak, but found no words formed and cursed to himself. For once, Aron was glad his father spelled his men so none could speak of his sons' existence in the presence of those who did not already know.

"He can't be trusted," Kade said finally.

"Why not?" Jared probed.

"I can't say, you just have to trust me."

"We need to leave," Aron said. "We are vulnerable here."

"What about the men with you, won't they protect us?" Jared asked.

"I was bluffing."

Jared mounted his large Clydesdale, cradling Keegan in his arms. To Aron he said, "Thank you for your help."

He nodded, cutting the Vosjnik's horses free and sending them trotting. Mounting his own horse, Aron figured Kade would refuse his addition, but he seemed preoccupied by something else. With interest, he watched Kade cross the clearing to where someone lay, sadness overtaking him.

Gently, Kade lifted the body and carried it over to Aros, struggling to get it onto the horse's back. Giving Jared a small nod, Aron galloped from the clearing.

✝✝✝

Kade and the mysterious archer raced alongside Jared, and he swallowed his anger. He was furious; how could Kade have kept the fact Nico was alive secret? But that was a matter for later.

Keegan's head lay on his shoulder. As her head started to loll, her eyes fluttered open, and she gasped in pain.

As Jared reigned in Brewer, Kade called, "Why are you stopping?"

"Keegan's awake."

"It's not safe to stop yet."

"Can you make it a little further?" he whispered to Keegan.

Giving a dazed moan, she nodded.

There was no need to say anything else and he jabbed his heels into Brewer. With each footfall, Keegan gave a pained look. They covered a few more miles before he pulled to a stop; enough was enough. She was in agony—as was he. He expected a rebuke from Kade, which didn't come. Instead, Jared noticed him grimacing and he wondered about the condition of his injuries.

"What are you doing here?" Keegan questioned as the archer approached to help her from the horse.

"Rescuing you," he answered softly.

"You know him?" Jared asked.

"Yeah," Keegan groaned uncomfortably. "He's the one who helped me escape from Caius."

Kade looked genuinely surprised. "We need to set a few things and bandage others."

"Unh," she groaned, shifting slightly, face crinkling in pain. "Jared, I have an extra shirt in my saddlebag."

He knelt beside her. "I can wait."

Kade turned to the archer. "Take a blanket and rip it into as many strips as you can. Then I need two sturdy sticks at least two feet long." He then asked Keegan, "What hurts most?"

"All of it."

Kade instructed Jared, "Get her on her left side; I'll start with her shoulder."

Jared glanced at Keegan's shoulder, noticing the distortion, and wondered when she'd dislocated it. He turned Keegan onto her side as gently as he could, but she still let out a stifled scream.

Kade took her arm, raising it as she sucked in shallow breaths.

"Hold her still. On the count of three. One. Two." There was a loud pop as he pushed her shoulder back into place

"What happened to three?" Keegan panted.

Kade gave no answer, ripping her left sleeve off, intending to deal with the stab wound.

"What's your issue with Aron?" she asked, and Jared was surprised she could think past the pain.

"Can't say," Kade muttered.

"Bullshit."

Blood from the wound held the fabric to her skin and Kade had to pry it away. More began to flow as the wound reopened.

"I'd tell you if I could," he promised.

A yelp escaped her lips as he dabbed the gash with a cloth.

"I have to clean it," he chastised.

"I know, I know."

"Is there anything you can do to heal her magically?" Aron asked.

"Ether's still affecting us," Kade answered, "and Jared and I are earth elementals. Keegan might be able to do something, but she's not particularly good at healing herself."

"She is an elemental?" Aron enquired.

"I'll explain later," Jared promised.

Once Kade finished flushing the wound, he wrapped Keegan's shoulder in one of the blanket strips and secured her right arm across her chest in a sling.

"I'm going to set your leg now," Kade told Keegan.

"Do it quickly." She half-watched as Kade went about it. After several minutes, with tears welling in her eyes, she asked, "Have you ever set a bone before?"

Kade glanced at Jared to avoid her gaze. "Um… no. This was Vitia's domain."

"Archer," Jared said, "h—"

"Aron."

"Aron," he amended, "help Kade hold her still."

Aron did as told, cradling Keegan's head in his lap.

With a knife, Jared sliced through her trousers, stopping at the knee to tear away the loose fabric.

It was fortunate the bone hadn't pierced the skin, though there was a large section of swelling. But it was better than it could've been, and all the bone likely needed was a splint and time to heal.

"I think it's a clean break," Jared said, splinting the leg.

"Are we good to keep going?" Aron questioned. "Or do you need to attend to your own injuries?"

Keegan spoke before either he or Kade could respond, "Don't try to be macho. Sort yourselves out. Jared, there's that extra shirt in my saddlebag."

"Get some sleep," Kade told her.

She nodded, eyelids already heavy.

‡‡‡

Kade's ribs protested as he rose to his feet. Taking a damp cloth, he wiped his lower back where a griffin was now etched into his skin. Once clean, he wound a cloth around his abdomen. He would've liked to bind his ribs, but it would require help. And he could not afford to look weak in front of Aron.

Injuries dealt with—in a manner—he walked to the horses. Seeing Cassidy's lifeless body lying across Aros's back, he found a lump rose in his throat, and he fought to maintain his composure.

"Do you want help?" Aron asked.

Voice catching, he shook his head. Heading into the forest, he searched for logs. The task didn't take long, at least he didn't think it did—time had little meaning right then.

After wrapping Cassidy in a blanket, he placed her on the pyre he'd built. Seeing the larimar necklace, he gently removed it, clenching it tightly in his fist.

Aron placed a hand on his shoulder in condolence.

"Don't touch me," he said coldly, covering Cassidy's face. His body ached as if a part of him were missing.

His hands trembled as he endeavored to light the pyre and he caught himself beginning to cry. He wiped his eyes, reminding himself he couldn't appear weak. The pyre was slow to catch, but once it did, it raged wildly.

"Time to go," he said lowly.

"How do we get to the Lazado?" Jared asked.

"Don't worry about it."

"We're not going with you. Nico's alive."

Kade cursed under his breath. "Yes, he is. And the only way to help him is through the Lazado."

"I know. But we won't be arriving together."

"I'll do the same thing to you I did to Keegan when she didn't want to go."

Jared drew his dagger. "I'm not Keegan."

"No, you're more sensible. We need to leave; the Vosjnik won't be waylaid for long."

Jared turned to Aron. "I say we leave him. They'll be too preoccupied dealing with him to chase us."

The prince looked uncomfortable to be suddenly dragged into their quarrel. "I think he may have a use yet."

"Of course, I do," Kade said, "but you don't. Leave."

"I set out to help Keegan."

"And you've done that," Kade snapped, picking Keegan up. Her head lolled and he felt a pit in his stomach. He knew all Vitia's evil tricks, and this had the trademark of her poisoned blade.

"I intend to see her through until the end," Aron persisted.

"We don't need you. I'd tell you to go home, but no one there wants you either."

"I want him here," Jared said.

"We don't have time for this," Kade snarled. "So, either fight me and die, or be quiet and come with me."

Jared seemed conflicted, then stormed to Brewer and swung into the saddle. "This isn't over."

"Of course not," Kade said sarcastically, handing Keegan to him. "Leave," he told Aron.

Aron gritted his teeth. "You want me gone, make me."

Kade began to draw his sword.

"He comes," Jared blurted, "or I ride off with Keegan."

Glancing at him, Kade knew Jared would deliver on his threat. The entire thing had gone to vito, the secrets he'd kept to make Jared compliant no longer holding sway—*he* had to bend or break now.

CHAPTER 41

Nico had expected anyone but the person who walked into his cell that morning.

Braxton gave him a stare that had a mixture of sympathy, guilt, and—oddly enough—warmth. "Come with me."

"Where are we going?"

"See for yourself."

Nico hesitated before chasing after him.

"How old are you?" Braxton asked eventually when they were well clear of the dungeon.

Nico repeated his question, "How old are you?"

"Twenty-four."

"Fourteen." Nico looked around, wondering why there were no guards. He was tempted to run, but imagined it wasn't in his best interest. "Where are we going?" he repeated.

"Almost there."

They made their way up another long, winding set of stairs and along a landing.

Braxton pushed open a door open, "This is my room. You will be sleeping on the cot over there."

"Wh—"

"I am your tutor. You will follow my orders without question, understood?"

"I didn't agree to this."

Braxton shut the door. "I know but trust me when I say this is for your benefit."

A chill ran down his spine. "What do—"

"My father is not a kind man. Neither is Kolt. This is the only way I can protect you. Please do not make this harder than necessary."

Nico scowled.

"Of course, you will not take my word for it. Not you, not my own brother, not even Keegan."

"You know Keegan?"

"I would have to use *know* loosely, but yes."

"Did she trust you?"

"I do not think so, but she must have realized I only did what I had to."

"Why should I trust you?"

"You should not." There was a pause. "I am just trying to minimize the pain you must endure."

Nico searched Braxton's face for any sign he spoke false and found none. "What happens if I don't cooperate?"

"You have already experienced it. Worse is to come though, much worse."

"I'll make you a deal."

Braxton's eyebrows raised, the hint of a smile appearing on his lips.

"I'll let you tutor me if you promise nothing bad will happen to my family."

"I cannot promise that. There are many things outside of my control and my father does not have your family imprisoned."

Nico thought for a moment. "Then promise if my family does gets caught, nothing bad will happen to them."

"I cannot do that either, but I will do what is within my power."

Nico understood nothing more could be asked. "Then I'm your student."

‡‡‡

The sun shone through the branches of the trees ahead, blinding Jared every so often. Keegan was still in a dream state, and he supposed that was best. She didn't have to endure the discomfort of her injuries this way—nor Kade's lies.

By the time they stopped, for it was too dark to continue on, the horses were grateful that their burdens dismounted.

Setting Keegan near to where they'd build a fire, Jared watched Aron and Kade set up camp, an icy silence between them. Studying Keegan, he saw her cheeks were heavily flushed and she appeared to shiver.

"Kade," he said.

"What?"

"I think something's wrong."

Without walking over, Kade answered, "I *know* something's wrong. She's been poisoned."

"And you didn't think to mention this sooner?" he barked.

"How could you keep that to yourself?" Aron chimed in.

"There's nothing we can do about it. And *you*," Kade said to Aron, "won't be with us much longer anyway."

"Like nastor I will not," Aron said angrily.

Kade placed a hand on the pommel of his sword. "You're not coming with us."

"I am."

Not interested in their quarrel, Jared interjected, "Enough; I already said he's coming. Now we have more pressing matters. Tell us about the poison."

"What's there to say, it's a poison."

"How was it introduced? What does it do?" Jared paused. "How long does she have?"

"It happened when Vitia stabbed her in the shoulder. It's called Ramilla; it's made from the dogwood nectar and octopus venom. It puts the victim into a deep sleep and slowly eats at their muscle. As for time, with a grown man, three weeks, four if they're lucky. With her, maybe two."

"Is there an antidote?"

"Yes, but it's hard to come by." There was silence. "The Lazado might have some, but there's no telling for sure."

"How long will it take us to reach them?" Aron asked.

"It will take Jared and me—" Kade started.

"Us," Aron snarled.

"Why are you so desperate to come?"

"I promised someone I would look after her."

"Who?"

"It does not matter," Aron answered. "How long will it take us to reach the Lazado?"

"Three weeks. If we push, we can make it in two."

"We have to," Jared said. "There's no other choice."

"There is *one* other choice. But I'll only consider it if all else fails."

Jared sensed he wasn't going to like the answer. "What is it?"

"We turn ourselves over to the Vosjnik."

✝✝✝

"Remember the plan?" Carter whispered.

Lucas gave him a flat look. "Yes, I remember the royiken plan."

He had no idea how Carter had managed it, but he'd talked Lucas into going along with Elza's idea.

They hid in the darkness of an alleyway, waiting for Elza to deal with the sentries at the door. There was a sudden shift in one of the men and he fell forward. The other, caught unawares, quickly followed.

They snuck forward and as he neared the downed guards Lucas could see the bloodstains creeping across their backs.

"Here," Elza murmured, thrusting a handful of keys into Carter's hand. "Dungeon's down those steps. The guards shouldn't be making rounds for another hour."

"Got it," Carter said eagerly.

Lucas pulled a torch from its bracket and led the way down the stairs. Soon, they leveled out, giving way to a long hallway.

Stopping at the first cell, Carter began to fumble with the keys. The man inside seemed surprised and leaned against the back wall patiently. There was a click of the lock and the door swung inwards. Carter gave a curt nod and moved to the next cell.

"You're free to go," Lucas whispered.

"What's goin' on?" the man questioned.

"We're breaking everyone out."

"I don't know I'd do that now." The man stepped into the torch's light. The rough, scraggly beard that reached his collarbone was run with through by thick shocks of gray which also peppered his hair. Tired blue eyes gave him a questioning look.

"Why not?" Lucas asked.

"Most of the men in here are murderers and thieves."

"Which one are you?" Lucas asked, placing a hand on the door, ready to slam it shut.

"Both. But with good reason; I work with the Lazado."

"Can you prove that?"

"I can't."

"Hold on," Lucas told Carter, who was still working on the second door.

"The name's Felix Isaacs," the man said. There was the sound of footsteps from the stairs. "I'd suggest runnin', lest the guards find us."

Nodding, he pushed Carter down the hall.

They were a good distance from the open cell when they heard a voice ask, "Where are they?"

"I swear I saw them come down here," Elza responded.

Lucas cursed quietly.

"Check the rest of the cells," the voice ordered.

Ahead, they reached a set of stairs and quickly climbed them.

"You can hear them," Elza called.

"Faster," Lucas urged.

"Sorry," Felix wheezed. "Sittin' in a cell's made me a tad unfit, lad."

"If you can talk, you can move faster."

They stumbled into an empty corridor and followed Felix as he veered left. It wasn't long before a gang of guards appeared at the top of the stairs.

"Either ye lads got a weapon I can borrow?" Felix asked, halting.

Carter glanced at Lucas then tossed his sword to Felix.

"Go ahead, lads," Felix said with a devilish grin, "I can handle this." When they hesitated, he turned to them. "Seriously, go."

Not in the mood or position to argue, Lucas pulled Carter down the hall. Soon the clanging of swords chased after them.

"You know where we're going?" Carter questioned.

"No," Lucas snapped, taking a sharp left. They were rewarded with a locked door. When they turned back, they faced Elza.

"You son of a bwint," Carter growled.

Elza shrugged. "You morons played straight into my hand. Thanks to you two, I should be getting a promotion."

"We won't go down without a fight."

"Only Lucas has a sword, so I don't expect this to be a very long one."

Lucas's heart pounded furiously, instinct telling him to rush Elza and surprise him. The soldier was caught off-guard, and his sword dropped with a clang.

Unaccustomed to handling a weapon, Lucas's sword followed suit. His fist connected with flesh, sending Elza into the wall.

"Don't ever threaten my brother," he roared.

Lucas relented as the man began to slump—a mistake. There was a sharp pain in his side, and he looked down to see the handle of a knife protruding from his abdomen.

Elza savagely withdrew the blood-soaked blade.

"I was prepared to let you live, but not anymore," he snarled. "I'll make sure Carter suffers."

Lucas staggered and fell, clutching his side, then closed his eyes, waiting for pain to pierce him. Instead, he felt a warm liquid splash across his face. Opening his eyes, he saw Elza's gaping mouth and a sword protruding through his chest. As the iron was removed, he fell forward.

Felix replaced him above Lucas. "Pig," was all the man muttered, spitting on the body. "Help him up," he told Carter.

Carter wrapped an arm under Lucas's shoulder and heaved him to his feet. "We can't go that way; door's locked."

Felix took in a deep breath and kicked it down. "That door?"

"Do you know where you're going?"

"I think so," Felix said, checking the way was clear. "Do ye have somewhere we can go?"

"The house," Carter suggested.

"No," Lucas wheezed, "Waylan's. Go to Waylan's."

"You know the way?" Felix questioned.

Carter nodded.

"Quickly now, 'fore your friend bleeds out."

✜✜✜

Braxton found Nico's snoring atrociously loud. Finally realizing he was not going to sleep, he rose and went to his desk. Lighting a candle, he checked to make sure the boy did not wake.

He read the completed translation. 'While you have slaughtered — child of the dragon, she will rise again from the ashes by your own doing. Rule while you can, false lord, for it shall only be for the moment. A child will come who can defeat you. From the fire, from the earth, from adversity, from the path of exile this child will rise. But know it will be your own foolishness that will seal your fate, oh wicked king.'

He pulled out the page with the version he had been dreaming about and compared it to the version he had found in the library. It was instantly clear where he had gone wrong. The addition of *zæ* in the original prophecy after *lunviyda* changed the meaning of *psodæ* in the first line from child to children. In the second part of the first line, he had assumed *æa*— was *æayu*, meaning her. Now, he realized it was *æay*, meaning they. Originally, in the fourth line he had used *dæ* instead of *zæ*, which again, changed child to children.

He looked at the properly translated prophecy, 'While you have slaughtered these children of the dragon, they will rise again from the ashes by your own doing. Rule while you can, false lord, for it shall only be for the moment. Children will come who can defeat you. From the fire, from the earth, from adversity, from the path of exile, these children will rise. But know it will be your own foolishness that will seal your fate, oh wicked king.'

Alyck's words became clear: there was not *one* child of prophecy, but multiple—and he knew exactly who they were.

CHAPTER 42

The sun was just beginning to light the city streets. Lucas teetered beside Carter, his wound sending painful flashes across his torso.

"Not much further, yeah?" Felix asked.

"It's that shop there," Lucas managed, nodding towards the shop.

Felix followed his line of sight. "The blacksmith?"

"Yes."

Checking the area was clear, Felix bolted across and began hammering on the door while Carter half-dragged Lucas over.

By the time they reached the shop, Waylan was opening the door.

"The hell yo—" When he saw Lucas, he grew silent and ushered them in. "What the hell happened?"

"Later," Felix told the smith. "We need to stitch this up before he bleeds out. Get him on the table."

None too gently, Carter deposited Lucas on the tabletop after Waylan cleared it.

"Right," Felix started, "I need a needle, thread, a rag, water, a knife, and a lit candle." He turned his attention to Lucas. "How ya doing, lad?"

"Who knew getting stabbed hurt so noxþ much," he groaned.

"I did. It's about to get worse now."

"What do you mean?"

Felix grimaced, taking the knife and running it over the candle flame.

"This is goin' to… burn. Try not to scream. Don't need to bring more attention to ourselves at all." He pressed the hot metal against the wound before Lucas could respond.

To Lucas, the sound of his sizzling skin was deafening. He clenched his teeth to keep from yelling and it felt like an eternity before the searing blade was removed. He sucked in deep breaths, blinking hard as darkness encroached on his vision.

Taking the rag, Felix dabbed at the cauterized cut then took the needle and held it over the flame, watching the shiny metal turn red.

Lucas let his head fall back on the table, trying to mentally prepare himself. When the needle touched his skin, he flinched; when it pierced him, he bit down on the inside of his cheek. He tasted blood and for a moment forgot to breathe.

"Let go of your cheek, boy," Waylan snapped.

Lucas unclenched his jaw and took a gasping breath. Slowly, he counted each time the needle passed through his skin—nine in total.

Felix leaned back. "All better. For now."

"Take him upstairs," Waylan told Carter. "I need to have a talk with your… *friend*."

Braxton stared at the canopy of his bed tiredly. Across the room, Nico snored to the point that he questioned how such a small person could make so much noise. Light morning sunshine peaked through the window, and he was thankful for the few hours of sleep he had managed.

Rubbing his eyes, he threw back the covers, shivering as his feet touched the cool stone floor.

He shook Nico awake then went to dress. Pulling on a dark silk shirt he asked, "Hungry?"

Nico said nothing.

"I am not going to hurt you." He gave what he hoped was a reassuring smile.

"Yes," Nico said. "Starving."

"Come on then."

Nico slipped on his boots and followed timidly. As they walked through the halls, the servants eyed Braxton scornfully, their looks turning to pity as their gazes shifted to Nico.

Reaching an empty section of hallway, Braxton turned to the boy, "Do not let them dismay you; I have no intention of doing you harm."

"Caius may have other ideas," Nico pointed out.

He sighed. "Yes, he may. So, let me amend my statement; I will not do you any more harm than necessary to keep."

Nico nodded in understanding.

As they neared the dining hall, Braxton felt a knot in his stomach and prayed Kolt would behave. Inside, his father sat at the head of the table, hands folded beneath his chin smugly. Avoiding his father's gaze, Braxton took a seat.

Food was brought and placed before him, though none was given to Nico.

"Bring him a plate," Braxton ordered.

"Yes, s—" the man started.

"A student only eats after his master has finished," Caius commented.

Braxton looked his father in the eye. "Bring him a plate."

Caius raised an eyebrow.

"He is my student; I shall treat him how I see fit."

The boy looked at him warily when a plate was set before him.

"Eat," Braxton commanded.

Nico needed no further coaxing.

"Bring him more," Braxton ordered when his plate was cleared in what might have been seconds.

"You do not want him getting fat," Kolt said, joining them. The dark bruises on his skin only seemed to enhance his brutal nature. "Have you beaten him yet?"

"No."

A malicious grin ran across Kolt's countenance. "I will do it for you. I do owe you… something of that nature."

Caius spoke up and Kolt's grin faltered. "His student, his way." Continuing on, Caius said, "I take it you remember where the training fields are."

"Yes, sir," Braxton answered.

"I expect to see results, mind you, or I will give him over to Eamon." As a second plate of food was set before Nico, he added slyly, "Get to it."

‡‡‡

His body felt hot and sticky, like he was in the center of a bonfire. Opening his eyes, Lucas found himself in a small room where random smithy tools rested just about everywhere. A candle on the table just barely illuminated the area. He shifted slightly and pain lanced up his side. Lucas tried to sit up, only making it a few inches before falling back with a pained groan. Spots of fuzziness confused his vision as he heard footsteps approaching.

"Up already?" he heard Felix say.

"What—" he began, a displaced anxiety rising in his chest.

As if sensing his angst, Felix told him, "Relax, you've only been asleep. You suffered a trauma; your body needed time to rest and begin healing. Speaking of which, we should change your bandages."

Lucas gave him what must have been a baffled look.

"Do you remember what happened?"

"Yes," he croaked.

Felix took a glass that sat on the bedside table. "Here."

Gingerly, Lucas lifted his head and took a small sip. As the cool water raced down his throat, he realized just how thirsty he was. Bit by bit, he drained the glass.

"There's a good lad." Felix pulled a chair next to the bed. "Have you ever had an injury like this before?"

"No. But I've seen them. Caused them." He didn't mention it was mostly on animals.

"It's not the same. To see this kind of damage on one's own body, makes it seem more… potent. I'd advise you not to look." Pulling back the blanket, he muttered, "Good timin',"

Going slightly crossed-eyed, Lucas looked down at his chest. His torso was wrapped in white linen bandages, a small red spot beginning to peek through.

"Sit up," Felix instructed, placing a hand in the crook of Lucas's shoulder to help him upright.

Lucas winced as Felix neared the inner layers of the wrapping where blood and skin clawed to keep the cloth in place. When the last piece was pulled away, he looked down. He was never one to feel queasy at the sight of blood or open wounds but felt his face draining of color.

"I told you not to look," Felix chastised.

The words hurt his pride, and, despite himself, he returned his attention to the wound. He could see clearly where the knife had penetrated; it was a clean, straight-edged cut, about three inches in length. The area around the wound was red and taking on a bluish tinge from inflammation. Black thread spiraled through the wound, binding the rift together.

Felix wetted a rag and gently dabbed the wound. Each time it touched him, Lucas gave an involuntary hiss. Felix placed gauze atop the cut before winding clean bandages around him and pinning the end neatly in place.

Lucas's stomach gave a low growl and Felix gave him the loaf of bread that sat on the table. After a few bites, he asked, "Where's Carter?"

"Downstairs."

"Can I speak with him?"

"I'd advise against it."

Lucas made to protest.

"It's the middle of the night. Let him rest, he'll still be here in the mornin'."

"I slept all day?"

"Sure did. And I expected you not to wake til tomorrow. Full of surprises you are." Felix gave a yawn. "Get some sleep."

He didn't give Lucas the chance to respond before blowing out the candle, casting them into darkness.

CHAPTER 43

Lucas awoke to daylight. Woozily looking around, he saw Carter crouched at the top of the stairs.

"What's happening?" he asked.

"Shh," Carter hissed.

"How many times do I need to repeat myself?" Waylan snapped. "I'm not going to the fucking Lazado."

"Waylan," Felix said, "be reasonable. It's where you and the lads will be safest."

"We're just as safe here. The guards don't know their faces; they're nothing more than a pair in thousands. Yours, however, they know, and you will leave. The sooner the better."

"It'll be as soon as Lucas can travel. Like I said, the lads are coming with me. You, I can't make do anything, but I'd encourage you to follow now."

"Who are you to tell me what's going to happen in my own home?"

"A fellow Pexatose."

"Do you think I care?" Waylan snapped. "Pexatose, human, British, I don't listen to—"

"Irish," Felix snarled. "I'm Irish, you goddamn Yankee."

"I ain't no Yankee," Waylan barked. "Take it back, you fucking leprechaun."

They continued to argue, going in circles.

Bracing himself, Lucas pushed himself upright, groaning.

Carter looked at him worried. "What are you doing?"

Lucas swung his legs over the edge of the bed. "Going down there."

"What? Why?"

"They don't decide what we do."

Getting to his feet was harder than anticipated and he swayed until Carter steadied him. Making his way down the stairs, he leaned heavily against the railing.

The two men stood across the room, arguing passionately.

"Enough," Lucas said just loud enough to get their attention.

"What are you doing out of bed?" Waylan growled.

He ignored the question. "Neither of you gets to tell us what to do. We're grown men."

Both Felix and Waylan laughed.

"You may be grown, but ye're not men," Felix told him. "Nonetheless, ye do have a say. What would ye like to do now?"

"We'll go to the Lazado with you," Carter said.

"No, we won't," Lucas argued.

"Yes, we will. That's what Father said to do. Jared and Nico are probably already there. I conceded to staying when grief clouded me, but no longer. We should've gone with Virgil, and Felix is offering to take us, so we're going."

"Good lad," Felix said with a grin.

"What if I won't go?" Lucas asked.

"I'll make you," Carter said bluntly.

"The only thing left is to convince you to come too," Felix said, returning his attention to the smith.

"No," Waylan growled. "I told you people I wanted nothing to do with you twenty years ago. My answer hasn't changed."

"We need you. The ability of a Pexatose, it… can change the tide of wars."

Waylan crossed his arms. "No."

"What's a Pexatose?" Lucas asked.

"A *very* special elemental," Felix answered. "A Pexatose is someone who shouldn't have powers, someone who shouldn't exist in this world, yet does."

Lucas and Carter gave him searching looks.

"Pexatoses come from another world. They're brought here by Nanagins and are granted great abilities. Waylan's an earth elemental."

The smith shifted uncomfortably.

"But it's not earth he controls, it's metal."

"Where's your proof?"

"He bears a mark, just like any other elemental. Waylan, will you show them now?"

The smith gave Felix a look of fury, but nonetheless showed them the underside of his wrist. The mark was striking against his black skin; the earthen symbol was a reflective silver, its outer boarder a stark white.

"What about you?" Lucas asked Felix. "You said you're a Pexatose, too."

"Good ears, lad. I'll have to be mindful of that now." He showed them the underside of his wrist. The mark scarring his skin was a simple black leaf. "I'm a life elemental, but I can't heal using magic."

"That makes no sense," Carter blurted.

"Let me finish," Felix said calmly. "When presented with an injury, I know exactly how to heal it with ordinary medicine."

A sudden overwhelming feeling overcame Lucas. Darkness covered his eyes, and he had the sensation of falling. Light returned and he shook his head, surprised to find himself back in bed, Carter sitting beside him.

"Lucas," Carter said relieved.

"What happened?" he asked groggily.

"You weren't ready to be on your feet," Waylan said.

✠✠✠

Jared struggled to keep his eyes open, and the setting sun was only making him feel drowsier. A few hours of rest had felt like the greatest reprieve, and he yearned to return to that state. It was his watch though. Rubbing his eyes, he began to pace.

The sun inched closer to the horizon and as soon as the fiery ball touched the leaves, he roused Kade and Aron. Before leaving, they swallowed a few pieces of stale bread and jerky.

He scooped Keegan into his arms, heartened to find her skin cooler to the touch. Jared wanted to believe the poison was fading but knew better than to hope for that.

Jared watched Kade clamber onto his horse in preparation to carry Keegan and he stared at him for a moment before making his way to Aron.

"What do you think you're doing?" Kade asked.

"Getting Keegan to the Lazado."

"W—"

"Enough!" he snapped. While Aron had arrived in an unorthodox manner, it didn't mean he couldn't be trusted. Besides, they'd all come together under strange circumstances. "He's given me no cause to doubt him. You have. He's only trying to help and it's time you let him."

"You have no say here."

"You'll find I do."

As Jared rode from the clearing, he could hear the curses behind him, but that was good; it meant Kade was following.

✝✝✝

Nico headed straight to bed and promptly fell asleep, boots still on.

Letting him be, Braxton lit a candle and pulled out the proper translation of the prophecy. His eyes glazed over as he stared at the page, having already memorized the words.

He knew he should tell his father, but something was stopping him. For days, he had tried to put his finger on the feeling, but it always slipped away. Maybe it was because the truth condemned Aron.

He was hard-pressed to find sleep that night. Since the griffins' release, he had not had one of his strange dreams and each morning he awoke refreshed, but he always went to bed with a feeling of unease.

When his eyes did close, he was thankfully sent into serene darkness. He remained in nothingness for a while before warm light filled the throne room. Forms materialized slowly until they became human—six people, with heads bowed.

A seventh person took shape and asked the first one, "Woth eya sesuna eyar kunyi?"

"Naya," the man responded, spitting on the shoes of the one standing before him.

Braxton watched as a sword separated the man's head from his body.

The man moved on to the next person and again asked, "Woth eya sesunar eyar kunyi?"

The reply was, "Avu."

That answer came four more times.

When it came to the last man, Braxton felt his heart catch. The grin on the prisoner's face made the question redundant; it was asked anyway.

"Woth eya sesuna eyar kunyi?"

"Naya," the man replied calmly. His demeanor did not change, even when the blade was poised above his neck. "Astæm az woth sesuna ayþ bindiar darvesen."

The people faded, the light going with them. Outside the window, Braxton could make out the night sky and watched his father pacing across the room. A shadow moved in the corner, and it transformed into a man. Light was reflected off the knife he held.

He tried to warn his father, but no sound escaped his lips. Braxton watched as the man drove the knife into the back of Caius's neck, instantly felling him.

Braxton jerked up, suddenly aware he could move and make sound. Nico stood beside him, a look of relief on his face.

"What is going on?" Braxton questioned, frantically throwing back the covers.

Nico backed away. "You were screaming. A bad dream, I think."

"Yes, a bad dream," he said quietly. "Go back to bed."

Nico gave him a concerned look but did as told.

Braxton leaned back, his thoughts careening about his mind. He had just witnessed his father's death; he had to tell him about the prophecy now.

CHAPTER 44

Nico awoke to find Braxton sitting at his desk, so enraptured in what he was doing that he failed to notice him walk up behind him.

"It's quite good," Nico said, commenting on the rough sketch of a pine tree.

Braxton startled but tried to play it off. "Thank you. Not many people get to see me drawing."

"Is it a secret?"

"No," Braxton said, still focused on his task. "But it is something that does not oft follow me outside this room. Come, time for breakfast."

As they walked, Nico noticed how tense his tutor was, as well as the dark circles under his eyes. The nightmare must've been traumatic.

Breakfast was eaten quickly and immediately afterward they headed to the training field. Nico's muscles tensed knowing the day would be long if it was anything like the past few.

Braxton led him to an empty area, and they began.

Nico managed to remain standing after most of the attacks, but each one battered him. Finally, a rock hit him in the back, sending him sprawling.

"Attacks will not always be where you can see them," Braxton said.

"Some warning would've been nice," he snapped.

"An enemy is not going to tell you his next move."

Getting to his feet, Nico readied himself and, although he didn't expect the strike to come from the front, the stone that hit his left leg produced pins and needles.

At midday, Braxton passed him along to Eamon, the earth training master, saying he had other matters to attend to.

"What was Braxton working on with you?" Eamon

"Attacks from all directions."

"You mastered the shield already?" Eamon said with a raised brow; the shield had been his first lesson.

"Braxton says so."

Eamon shot a rock at him, and he quickly brought up a shield.

"Good. Close your eyes."

"How am I supposed to see anything coming?"

"You're not. You'll hear the attack, feel it. You can't always rely on your sight and must learn to sense changes in your surroundings, to rely on your instincts."

Grinding his teeth, Nico closed his eyes. There was an instant before a rock hit his chest where he could hear it whistling through the air. Maybe Eamon was brighter than he thought.

✝✝✝

Braxton gulped as he neared his father's office, his heart racing, and he almost turned away again. So far, he had spent the entire afternoon trying to work up the nerve to divulge what he knew—and subsequently explain why he had kept it secret.

Taking a deep breath, he approached the door again and, before he could let himself think, knocked. There was a moment of silence and he found himself praying his father was elsewhere.

"Enter." Caius sat at his desk, looking over a sheaf of papers. "What do you need?"

"The Child of Prophecy…" Braxton started.

Caius glanced up, curiosity and concern written across his face.

"What can you tell me about it?" Braxton asked.

"It—*she* is the only person more powerful than me. The Vosjnik found her twenty years ago—"

"But Rosh Broyker saved her, and she experienced a Nanagin."

"Correct. And we now know Keegan is this child."

"Are you aware of Angela's last prophecy?"

"Of course."

"What did it say?"

"A careless pageboy dropped ink all over the sheet, making it difficult to read. But the essence of it is that a child will come to defeat me."

"So, it read something like this," Braxton stated, handing over one of the pages he had brought with him.

Caius read it carefully. "Yes."

He handed another page over. "Here it is in its entirety."

"Where did you get this?"

"I would rather not say. But you can see the inkblots made it easy to mistranslate."

His father read it over and mumbled, "It was never one…"

"No, it is four."

"Do you, by chance, know who they are?" Caius pressed angrily.

"Yes." His heart pounded. "You were right about Keegan. The other three are Jared Sieme, Kade Tavin—"

Caius cursed at Kade's name, muttering, "Bastard was hiding under my nose the whole time."

"And…"

"Out with it!"

He gulped. "Aron Alagard."

Caius's face paled and he was silent for a long time.

Braxton was aware of the Death Deal that had been made; Aron was untouchable, as were he and Kolt.

"Train with the griffins," Caius said finally. "Ready them for battle."

"How are you going to get past the border?"

Slamming his hand on the desk, his father roared, "Just do as I say!" As Braxton started to leave, Caius continued, "Continue to train with the boy, I want him to trust you. He will be key in turning his brother."

"Why would Nico be what convinces Jared to submit?"

"You would be amazed what people will do to protect their brothers."

Something in the words made Braxton believe he was speaking from experience.

✢✢✢

Walking upstairs, Lucas saw Waylan sitting on the edge of the bed, holding a small piece of parchment.

"What's that?" he asked.

"A photo," Waylan responded.

He sat beside the smith. "What's a photo?"

"Think of it like a painting."

The photo was worn and yellowed, but still looked hyper-realistic, as if someone had stopped time and placed it on a page. There were three people: a man, a woman, and a child.

The man looked like a younger version of Waylan. The woman was a head shorter and held the child in her arms. All three bore the whites of their teeth in their smiles.

"That's my wife, Ilene, and I," Waylan said, "and our foster child, Arthur."

"They look nice." He cursed himself for sounding so dumb.

"They were. Ilene used to always tell Arthur a bedtime story—before he died. She worked hard, did her best to help as many people as she could… She was the one who wanted to foster."

"What happened to the child?"

"He got hit by a car."

Lucas was going to ask what a car was, but seeing Waylan's melancholy, decided not to press.

Waylan tucked the photo away in a pocket as Felix appeared at the top of the stairs, asking, "Have you changed your mind?"

The smith gave him an aggravated look. "Unfortunately."

"Excellent. We'll leave tomorrow."

"What changed your mind?" Lucas asked.

"You and my wife," the smithy answered.

"How so?"

"Ilene always said if you take the time to help someone, you see they get where they're goin'. I took you and Carter in; I need to make sure you get to where you need to be, which just so happens to be the Lazado."

"Virgil was right about you. You might be headstrong, but you've got a good heart. Thank you, Waylan, for everything."

CHAPTER 45

Lucas pulled the hood of his cloak low over his face. The pack felt heavy, and he winced with every step. Felix had declared him fit to travel, but he didn't share the opinion. The sun was barely casting light across the street and was still well below the city walls.

They reached the gates as the portcullis rose. A man was waiting outside the gate, a donkey in tow, and he was allowed in without a word.

As they approached the gate, the guards stopped them. "Show your faces."

Lucas gritted his teeth, waiting to see what Felix would do. There was no doubt Felix was a wanted man, but he'd taken precautions to avoid being recognized by shaving his beard and trimming his shaggy hair. Now, he looked like any other graying, middle-aged man.

"Whatever for now?" Felix questioned.

"Because I said so," the guard snapped, reaching forward to throw Felix's hood back.

"Satisfied? You've exposed an agin' man to the mornin' mist."

"Remove your hoods," the guard instructed the rest of them.

Lucas let the hood fall onto his shoulders and the guard scrutinized him lazily before waving them through.

They were a good way down the road before Waylan dared to speak. "Do you intend for us to walk across the country?"

"Only a portion of it," Felix responded. "I hope to buy—or steal—horses in the next town."

"Is that wise? You're already a wanted man—as are we all, I suppose."

"Caius has bigger problems than a renegade, a long-forgotten Pexatose, and two troublesome youths."

"What bigger problems?" Carter asked.

"There've been rumors of an immensely powerful elemental that's been running amok," Felix answered.

"Keegan," Lucas growled.

"Who?"

Scowling, Lucas told him, "An elemental my brother took in. She's the one who brought soldiers to our doorstep."

"Do you know where she is, lad?"

Lucas loathed admitting he was going to have to see Keegan again. "With any luck, the same place we're headed."

‡‡‡

Nico groaned as he opened his eyes; every part of his body ached.

Braxton was at his desk drawing and some steps blinded Nico with a dull pain as he came to look over the prince's shoulder.

"Do you start every morning like this?"

"No, I have just had a bit of inspiration of late." Braxton moved his arm so Nico could see—it was a portrait of him with an earthen shield half raised. Turning to look at him, Braxton gave a low whistle. "Eamon did a number on you. We will not train today."

"Why?"

Braxton raised an eyebrow. "I would think you would be glad for a reprieve, but if you wish to train, we can."

"No," Nico said hastily.

"Go to the bathhouse—"

Nico cut him off, sniffing his shirt. "Do I smell?"

Braxton laughed. "No. One of the healing tubs should be able to take the sting out of those bruises. Get some breakfast before you go."

"What about Kolt?"

"Kolt has no power over you. Now go, before I change my mind."

Taking his cue, Nico headed towards the dining hall. Servants and pages bustled by, most paying him no heed, but those who did pointed and whispered; he hated that.

Coming into the dining hall, he was spotted by Kolt, who broke into a wide grin. "Learning your lessons, boy?"

He averted his eyes. "Yes."

A servant put a plate before him, piled high with eggs and a few links of sausage.

"Yes, *sir*," Kolt snapped. "Though, you may also call me Your Grace."

Coldly, Caius corrected, "You are no king, nor shall you be."

Nico couldn't help but smile, which made Kolt reach for his mug—likely to throw it.

"Put it down," Caius commanded.

Shoveling in a few mouthfuls of food and taking the sausage, Nico made his exit. It was better to not try his luck.

The bathhouse was well below the lowest windowed level of the castle and several soldiers and guards were already soaking in the large pools. There were six, each a different color, with varying pungent smells. The attendant, after hearing his ailments, directed him to the blue pool.

Four men were already lounging in it, talking and laughing loudly. He stripped quickly and slipped into the water.

"This is the soldiers' bathhouse," a man snarled at him. "Servants are to bathe elsewhere."

"I was told to come here," Nico said, suddenly feeling small and vulnerable.

"By whom?"

"Braxton Alagard."

"Ah, you're the crown prince's bwint." The man leaned back, placing his arms along the wall of the pool. "It's a wonder you have any cock at all."

Nico clenched his fists, knowing this wasn't a fight he'd win.

"Tell me, how is it you became the prince's student? How many times did you have to lie with him?"

Let them say what they will, he told himself. *None of it's true.*

The men laughed when he made no attempt to contradict them.

"Do you think if I had my way with the prince the king would make him *my* student?" another asked.

The others laughed malevolently.

"Now that's the best way for the crown prince to take your head," Eamon said, slipping into the pool beside Nico.

"We weren't talking to you," the first man snapped.

"No," Eamon said calmly, "but it never does well to speak poorly of the royal family."

That shut them up and soon the soldiers pulled themselves from the water, looks of loathing directed towards Nico.

"You're not well-loved by many people in this castle," Eamon told him, "but you have friends in high places."

"What do they have against me?"

"Most of these men were trained under Evard and other cruel tutors. None are strangers to brutality and pain. Yet, somehow, you were given to Braxton. He may put on a mean front, but behind closed doors we all know he's gentle."

"I didn't ask for that."

"No one asks for the fate they must endure. Yet we always envy those whose path is kinder than ours."

✠✠✠

Thaddeus waited patiently to be pulled from the wagon and brought before the king, knowing today was going to end in at least one death. As a group, he and the others were herded into the castle, the cool interior a welcome reprieve from the summer sun. In his heart, he could feel his Calling humming happily; he was where he belonged.

The marching of their feet created a discord that resonated off the walls. They were taken to what Thaddeus assumed was the throne room. They were made to kneel and only one man resisted, relenting when struck in the back of the knees.

They waited for quite some time—long enough for his knees ach. When the doors banged open behind him, Thaddeus did not jump like the others. Four men came into view, and he recognized the king and his kin instantly. One of his sons had hair black as a bruise while the other took after his father, his hair as yellow as dirty sunshine.

The fourth man stood rigidly, his dark eyes staring at them with contempt, a hand resting on the pommel of his sword. He came to the first prisoner.

"Will you serve the king?"

The man spat on the soldier's shoes. "No."

The soldier calmly drew his sword and brought it down across the man's neck. He then repeated the question to the others.

All answered, "Yes."

Thaddeus smiled as the soldier came to stand before him.

"Will you serve your king?"

He looked up. "No, but I will serve the Blind Prophet."

A hush settled over the room and Caius growled, "Leave." When the soldier looked at him perplexed, he roared, "Leave! And take the others."

Slowly, the king's newest elementals filed from the room, stealing fervent glances at Thaddeus.

"How do you know about the Blind Prophet?" Caius asked tersely once the doors had shut.

"It is my job." When the king gave him a questioning look, he said, "I am surprised you are unaware of Angela's second bloodline."

The muscles in Caius's jaw tightened. "Leave," he hissed at his sons.

They exchanged a glance before walking past Thaddeus.

"Who are you?"

"Thaddeus Broyker."

"I know that name."

"You should; you had the *honor* of murdering my son."

"I may give you the same honor."

"It will hurt you more than help you."

"How so?"

"I am one of the last Keepers of Prophecy. Do you know their history?"

"No, nor do I care to."

"And that will be your downfall; knowledge is power."

Caius's lips pulled into an aggravated smile. "Then enlighten me."

"Angela Alga, as you know, was the first Blind Prophet. She had three children. Two were endowed with the magic that would allow either to become the Blind Prophet if necessary and became the Alagards. The third was born without magic. This child stayed with Angela and, as the visions made it harder for her to keep hold of reality, helped her to make sense of the world, thus becoming a translator of her visions. His name became Broyker."

"You might prove useful yet."

"I hope to be," Thaddeus said, bowing his head. Knowing Caius was about to dismiss him, he decided to use his only chance to save Reven. "Though, I should warn you about my family's curse." It was a lie, but he could not lose his grandson.

Caius gave a disconcerted frown. "What curse?"

"The Broykers are only afforded one child per generation."

"You are the last then… since I killed your son."

"No, I have a grandson."

"Where is he?"

"Somewhere outside your grasp and he will never serve you. I just thought I should warn you to not kill him unless you want to spend the rest of your life harried by double meanings and twisted words."

"He will serve me. Everyone does, sooner or later."

"Only if you can find them."

Thaddeus gave a slight bow to the king, as was expected of him, before a guard took him to the Blind Prophet.

His knees ached from kneeling for so long, but it was for the good of many; telling the king most of what he knew ensured he got exactly what he needed: access to the Blind Prophet and the library.

He was shocked to discover the Blind Prophet was holed away in the depths of the castle like some plague. The door was unadorned, simple, inconspicuous; no one would guess one of the most important people in the world resided behind it.

The torches along the wall of the room provided less than adequate light—something he would fix.

A man emerged from a chamber whose the entrance hidden in the gloom. "I was not expecting you today, brother."

"I am most definitely not your brother," Thaddeus informed him, "though we are distantly related."

"To whom do I have the pleasure of speaking with?"

"Thaddeus Broyker."

"Thaddeus, it is a pleasure to meet you. I am sorry about your son, but he was the only one who could have done it."

"I understand," he said, a pang in his heart. "And how should I address you? I assume *oh wise one* is too formal."

The Blind Prophet gave a hearty laugh. "I like you already. I am Alyck. Now, Thaddeus—do you go by Thad? I am going to call you Thad—I have a few questions as to what you know."

"I would like to rest now; it has been a grueling few weeks and a tiresome past few hours. I will answer all your questions later, just as I know you will answer mine."

‡‡‡

Kade kicked Aron's leg and once sure he was awake, stalked away and gave himself up to sleep.

Aron rubbed his eyes, wishing he were still dreaming.

Time passed slowly and the only way he knew the night had not come to a standstill was the movement of the moon. It sluggishly crept across the sky and his eyelids sagged, threatening to send him careening into dreamland. Shaking his head, he got to his feet and began to pace.

After so many days of hard riding, it felt good to stretch his muscles. Someone began to cough, but he thought nothing of it. When the sound became raspy and pained, he turned his attention to Keegan. She struggled to catch a breath, chest rising and falling heavily, blood coloring the spittle coming from her mouth.

He yelled to wake the others, "Kade!" Sola and Lunos he was terrified. "Jared!"

They awoke groggily, fearing the worst. Kade stumbled to his feet, endeavoring to draw his sword. Jared tried to rise and pull a dagger from his boot, which caused him to ram his head into the tree he had been sleeping against.

Realizing there were no attackers, Kade snapped, "Why did you wake us?"

"Keegan," he answered.

The sword in Kade's hand dropped as he rushed over. "No. We should have more time."

"What does this mean?" Jared questioned, joining them. Blood ran down his face from a deep scrape along his forehead.

"We have less time than we thought," Kade answered darkly. "The poison's beginning to eat at her organs."

"What do we do?"

"Ride," Kade said, picking Keegan up, "and pray to Sola and Lunos we reach the Lazado in time." There was a pause. "Or we turn around."

CHAPTER 46

Caius paced across the throne room. As Braxton watched, he noticed inconsistencies in his father's behavior—the short stride, the wringing of hands, the fearful look in his eyes. Why did his father look so nervous? Caius never showed emotions—aside from anger or hubris.

A shadow moved across the room and formed into a man with hateful blue eyes and wild hair. He raised a knife and plunged it into Caius's neck.

Light blinded his pupils and Braxton realized he was awake, still sitting at his desk, a half-finished drawing before him. He placed the sketch in a drawer and shook Nico awake. He knew—hoped—there was time before his vision came to pass. Maybe he could find a way to prevent it.

Together, they silently made their way to breakfast.

"Why was the boy not training yesterday?" Caius queried as they sat down.

"I gave him leave to rest," Braxton answered. Dark bruises still covered Nico's arms and legs, though he no longer complained of soreness. "And I was looking into the business with the griffins."

Beside him, Nico choked, spitting egg halfway across the table.

"Did you find the culprit?"

"No, sir. Whoever it was covered their tracks well."

"And Aron; any news on his whereabouts?"

"No." Considering all that had happened, Braxton had completely forgotten about him.

"He will come back sooner or later. The boy will never survive on his own."

Braxton had his doubts.

When they left, Nico asked excitedly, "You have griffins here?"

"Yes," he answered, for a moment remembering their purple blood splashed across his body.

"I though they only existed in lore."

If only. "No, they are as real as dragons and just as vicious."

Nico's eyes widened.

"Would you like to see them?" Braxton regretted the words as soon as he said them; few were supposed to know of them and even fewer of their whereabouts.

"Can we?"

"Sure. But you cannot breathe a word of this to anyone."

"Deal!"

"Come on." Making sure they were alone in the hall, he opened the passage to the griffin stable. He knew the way well enough, but Nico struggled in the dark. They came out into the anterior room, and he could hear the griffins stirring.

Pulling a torch from its sconce, he took Nico into the main chamber. Where the wall had once opened into nothingness, a heavy iron grate now barred the way. The five remaining griffins looked at him and gave snorts of anger.

The traitor returns, Niyth seethed.

He approached Myrish cautiously, the griffin's dark bronze feathers refracting the torch's light. *You know I tried to avoid bloodshed.*

Myrish snapped at him and Braxton drew back. Slowly, he came to stand just outside the griffin's reach and stood his ground.

We know, Crowlin admitted.

Braxton noticed Myrish held his wing awkwardly. "Is your wing broken, Myrish?"

From when your chains grounded me.

"You named them?" Nico questioned, taking a step towards the wounded beast.

"Whoa." Braxton thrust out an arm to stop him. "Griffins are... particular. Let him get a sense of you." *I will send someone to mend that later.*

Nico held still while Myrish strained against the iron links to sniff at him.

Pulling away, he said, *I would sooner you not.*

"Now you can approach," Braxton told Nico, "and I did not name them; they named themselves." *I was not asking,* he told the griffin.

"How?" Nico asked. "They're just beasts"

Myrish clicked his beak and gave a low hiss.

Beasts he calls us, Phynex raged. *Tell him we are no more beasts than the little beast before us.*

"They are no more beast than you or I," Braxton said, rubbing Myrish's head. "They are intelligent, smart as any human."

"How do you know their names?"

"Telepathy. Myrish might talk to you if he is in a good mood."

"What are the others' names?" Nico asked.

He pointed them out. "Crowlin, Niyth, Phynex, and Oxren."

Who is this boy? Myrish asked.

My student.

Myrish gave what Braxton had learned was a laugh. *You took a student? I can only wonder what possessed you.*

It was to save him.

I can see. You have always had a good heart for a human. But I fear you will turn it to stone in the future.

"What do you use them for?" Nico asked.

"Nothing," Braxton said. He almost added "at the moment". He needed to mention his father's plan to use them in battle but was afraid of how the griffins might react.

This one is innocent, Niyth commented, as Nico continued to marvel at them. *Such a shame.*

Braxton felt a twang of guilt. After a while, he said, "Time to go. You have to do some training today."

"Can we come see them again?" Nico asked as they headed towards the anterior room.

"Maybe." Braxton looked back at Myrish, and a thought crossed his mind. *Do you know who released you?*

No, Myrish answered. *But he smelled like you—of anger, of sadness, of Seleena, of Alyck.*

✝✝✝

The trees were sparse now, barely more than twigs. Night had long since fallen and Jared was insisting they stop. The horses breathed heavily and all of them were sleep deprived. If he could, he had no doubt he'd sleep for many hours.

Jared shook his head to clear his mind and noticed Kade slumped forward on his horse, no doubt asleep. He spurred Brewer forward and grabbed Aros's reins.

Kade awoke with a jerk, snarling, "What are you doing?"

"You fell asleep," Jared explained. "We *need* to stop."

"We can't."

"We have to. None of us will do Keegan any good dead."

"You can stay," Kade said, taking the reins back, "but I'm continuing."

"Do not make me hurt you," Aron said.

Jared turned to see Aron had drawn his bow. "What do you think you're doing?"

"What I have to. We must stop. It will only be for a few hours."

Kade bore a look of fury as he spat, "Shoot me. It won't change anything."

An arrow whizzed past Jared. At first, he thought it hadn't struck, but when he looked at Kade saw a thin line of red across his cheek.

"That was a warning," Aron stated.

The muscles in Kade's jaw tightened and swung his leg over Aros. Sliding to the ground, he stumbled, almost dropping Keegan.

"You could've hurt her," Jared seethed, also dismounting.

"Could've but didn't."

"Let me take her."

"She's not yours to protect."

"Yes, she is. She's all of ours to protect."

"No, she isn't," Kade roared. "She's not your sister; she's not yours to protect!" He breathed heavily, defensively holding Keegan close.

"Did you just say *sister*?" Aron asked.

Kade took a breath. "Yes."

"How—" Jared started.

Kade headed him off. "It's a long story."

"Then you had better take a seat and tell us," Aron said.

"We don't have time for this."

"We're making time," Jared said, nodding at Aron as a signal that he should notch another arrow.

Kade glowered but did as instructed. "I didn't know any of this until a few weeks ago. Someone was sent to save her when she was born. Well… he could've taken either of us, but he chose her. She was taken away and somehow ended up in her world. Twenty years later, she managed to come back."

The brief explanation left Jared angry and with only more questions.

Kade was slow to answer their queries at first, but the more he spoke, the easier the answers came.

When done, Jared was speechless. Now that he looked at them, he could see the resemblance.

"We should get some sleep. There's still a good distance between us and safety," he finally said.

Besides, if Kade did any more talking, he was liable to have a go at him then and there. Some secrets were yours to keep; this wasn't one of them.

CHAPTER 47

Soft light spilled over the horizon when Kade stirred. Jared and Aron had already packed up camp. The only thing left was the embers.

"We thought we'd let you rest as long as possible," Jared told him when asked why they hadn't woken him earlier.

Kade knew the real reason; they were still donpox he'd kept a secret. But he didn't regret it. Within his heart he knew staying his tongue had protected Keegan. And he realized he couldn't lose another person he cared about without falling apart as the larimar stone in his pocket seemed to weigh him down.

As they traveled, the trees grew sparser with every passing mile and by midday disappeared entirely, opening into a desolate zone. He'd never seen the Borderlands before, but it was as bleak as descripted. The ground was gray, like a sick skin over the earth. No living thing prospered here, and the blight stretched for as far as he could see. He could feel pain and suffering radiating from the land.

"What happened here?" Jared asked quietly.

"War," Kade answered. "When Caius crowned himself king, the other races banded together to fight him. When they couldn't defeat him, they used a spell to create a border that would stand for as long as he remains in this world. No one wishing harm to those on the other side may cross."

"Things should have regrown," Aron stated, jumping down from his horse. He took a handful of dirt and let the fine particles fall through his fingers.

"The land's cursed with the blood of the dead," Kade said.

"I do not like this."

Kade urged Aros forward. "No one does."

Aros gave a snort and pawed at the ground, only reluctantly starting forward when Kade dug his heels into his side. The other horses were just as wary.

The sun was hot with nothing to shade them and sweat beaded on their foreheads to roll down their faces. It wasn't long before the sad excuses for trees were lost in the gray waste.

"How far is it across the Borderlands?" Jared asked stiffly.

"Ten miles to the border, twenty miles total," Kade answered grimly. "That is *if* we can get across the border."

Ahead, he could already espy the opaque blue wall denoting the boundary. It went up as high as he could see, well into the clouds and beyond. Soon, they were at its face.

Aros shook his head nervously, but tentatively stepped beyond the border when pressed. As they passed through, a light feeling of electricity ran over Kade's body.

"Almost there," he told Keegan. "Be strong."

‡‡‡

He smelled like you—of anger, of sadness, of Seleena, of Alyck. The words had been playing in Braxton's head for days, almost to the point of obsession. Finally, he decided a visit to Alyck was due and Nico was left in Eamon's capable hands.

When he went to unlock Alyck's door, there was no telltale click of the lock. Had Alyck finally taken leave of his duty? He pushed the door open and was disheartened to find the chair void.

A man emerged from one of the other chambers. "Ah, you must be Braxton."

He stared and was about to ask what the man was doing there when he recalled this was the man who had agreed to serve the Blind Prophet.

"I never caught your name," Braxton said.

"Thaddeus Broyker." He gave a polite smile.

"Hello, Braxton, come to ask some questions?" Alyck said, finally emerging.

"Yes…" he said, warily eyeing Thaddeus.

"No need to worry about Thad. He will no more spill information than I."

"I wanted to talk to you about something the griffins said. They said whoever released them smelled like me—of anger, of sadness, of Seleena, of you."

Alyck seemed taken aback by the last item. "Curious. Well, let us think, I am sure with a little thought you can solve this riddle. Firstly, what purpose would releasing the griffins serve?"

"To render them useless, cause us pain," Braxton said, growing frustrated that Alyck never made things simple. "To distract us…"

"See, all you had to do was put a little thought into it."

"How did he even know where the griffins were?" Braxton said, trying to convince himself the perpetrator was not whom he thought. "How could he have smelled like me?"

"Aron often made visits to me, much like you do."

"How?"

Alyck gave him a concerned looked. "I assumed that was fairly evident—with a key."

Braxton's head reeled with all the questions that arose. "I have to tell Father. You know that, right?"

"Of course," Alyck said, tilting his head forward in a nod, "but no one can touch him now."

"I know Aron is a Child of Prophecy."

"As do I."

"You promised he would live a long life."

"And he will."

✠✠✠

The Yarav forest had been visible on the horizon for hours now, slowly growing closer. They reached the tree line as night settled.

We made it, Aron thought to himself, relief washing over him. It was a moment before he realized the world was deathly quiet.

"Something's not right," Jared muttered.

If Kade intended to respond, he was not given the chance as light exploded into existence.

Aron's horse reared in fright, and he fought to remain in the saddle. Once the palfrey landed, hands took ahold of him, pulling him to the ground. He dropped heavily, his wrist getting caught beneath his body and bending painfully. Aron fumbled to draw a weapon and got tangled in his cloak. Hands grabbed his arms and, once he was subdued, he found Jared was similarly restrained.

Kade had managed to stay on his horse, though an archer had an arrow aimed at his chest.

"Who are you?" the archer asked.

"Kade… Digore, son of Kagen, ward of Thaddeus Broyker, subject of none," he answered calmly.

Aron knew that was not Kade's family name, but did not dare correct him.

"Where do you come from?"

"A land of subjugation and hate."

"Why should we admit you?"

"War cannot be fought only in the minds of men. It must be fought on the field, with payment of blood, in the hopes Sola and Lunos will see us through."

"And your companions, who are they?"

"Jared Sieme, son of the dead; Aron no name, son of a bastard; and Keegan Tavin, daughter of Korissa."

407

The archer lowered his bow and the men holding Aron and Jared withdrew. "You seek refuge."

"Yes, and help. My friend's been poisoned with a dagger dipped in Ramilla."

The men around them gave a collective groan.

The archer placed a hand on Keegan's forehead. "How long ago?"

"About a week," Kade answered, dismounting.

"The poison's far advanced; we may not be able to save her. Edreba's another four days from here."

Kade paled and Aron's heart skipped a beat. All had been for naught.

The archer called for one of his men. "Take our fastest horse and get her to the city."

"Please, hurry," Kade said. "I can't lose her."

✟✟✟

They reached the town at nightfall. A torrential downpour had started a few hours past and had yet to let up. Lucas was soaked to the skin and quite unhappy, the deluge only serving to further aggravate his wound.

Their feet sunk into the muck as they walked down the main street and only a few brave souls dashed through the rain.

Ahead, a door opened, spilling warm light, the sound of chatter and laughter coming like a whisper through the storm. Felix ushered them into the tavern where the tables were crowded and a large fire roared in the hearth, making Lucas long to sit beside it.

"Room for four," Felix said to the barman.

"Gold coin," the man grunted. Felix slid it to him and was given a key in exchange. "First room on the third floor."

They went upstairs and Lucas dumped his pack and clutched at his side. Waylan helped him change the bandages and afterwards they slipped back downstairs.

They chose a table near the fire to let the heat warm and dry them. A wench soon brought them food and drink. Carter practically inhaled both, giving a burp when his plate was cleared. At least some things never changed.

In a low voice, Waylan said, "Those men in the corner have been eyeing us since we sat down."

Lucas glanced at them. Both were young, but their faces were hard and weathered.

"They've been watching us since we got here," Felix said unconcernedly.

"I don't like the looks of them," Waylan said.

Felix shrugged. "I'm sure they'd say the same about you."

The men shared a look before downing their ale and heading towards their table.

Waylan reached for the dagger at his waist.

"I don't think that'll be necessary," Felix told him.

One man stood at the head of the table while the other leaned between Felix and Carter, pressing a dirk against Carter's side. Lucas took ahold of his tankard, preparing to leap across the table at the man who dared threaten his brother.

"I wouldn't do that, boy," the one at the head of the table sneered, grabbing the tankard from him, and downing it. "Or Oslin sees how deep he can stick that blade."

Lucas clenched his fists, slowly rising to his feet.

"Sit down."

Carter flinched as Oslin dug the steel harder against his side.

"I suggest you do so, lad," Felix said, easily taking a sip of ale. "Can I help you, gents?"

"You're supposed to be rotting in a cell," the man said.

"With Nox and Indol. Yes, Caeyl, I should be."

"Where are they?"

"Decomposing—unless they were burned."

"Make no jests, Felix," Oslin snarled. "They were good men."

"That they were," Felix said with an air of sorrow. "But so are these men you've seen fit to threaten now."

"I see two boys and a nobody," Caeyl said.

"I see something quite different."

"And what's that?"

"Two stubborn young men who want revenge as much as you and a very well-trained blacksmith."

"Recruits?" Oslin questioned.

"If they so choose."

"Let's find out?" Oslin asked, digging the dirk further into Carter's side.

"Come now," Felix said, "you know decisions made under duress aren't decisions at all. And we fight for the same cause. Oslin, put your weapon away, share a drink."

"Not a very convincing argument," Oslin said, withdrawing, "but I do love a good pint."

Caeyl smiled and, grabbing a chair from another table, sat down. "Tell us, old man, how did you escape?"

"These two here," Felix said, motioning to Lucas and Carter.

Once it became clear Oslin and Caeyl were done with them, Lucas and Carter—sporting a spot of red where the dirk had pierced his skin—took their leave. Lucas ground his teeth to keep from flying at Oslin and seeing how he liked a knife in the ribs.

✠✠✠

Alyck gave a pained sigh, opening his eyes. "Caius is going to die."

"I cannot see how that is a bad thing," Thaddeus said. "The world has been crying for his death for centuries."

"That is not the problem. Keegan is not the one to kill him."

"That contradicts your previous visions."

"I know. Nothing has changed surrounding the girl, but there is another player in my brother's demise now."

"As long as his death comes to pass, why does it matter who does the deed?"

"If it is by any hand other than Keegan's I see my brother rising from the grave."

The dead rising was an impossible and frightening idea. "Can you see more about this figure who will kill Caius?"

"No," Alyck rubbed his eyes, "he is too shrouded in shadow and hate for me to turn my attentions to him."

The door opened and Caius entered.

Call his name and he shall come, Thaddeus thought.

"Are you going to tell me?" the king asked.

Alyck gave Caius a conniving smirk. "Yes."

"Where should I go to experience a Nanagin?"

"To the place where it all began. To the place where you cast our stones. To the place you fear the most. To the place we said goodbye."

The color drained from Caius's face. "You do not… you cannot… no. I cannot go there. Find another place!"

Alyck shrugged. "To get what you so desperately want, you must face your demons."

"I cannot do that. You know why I cannot do that."

"Yet, you must. It is the only way to get what you desire."

The king remained rooted in place for a heartbeat before he all but fled.

"Where did you tell him to go?" Thaddeus asked.

"Home. He has to go home."

CHAPTER 48

How are you feeling?" Lyerlly asked the boy lying in the bed. He was a gaunt little thing, but hopefully with the tumor removed he would be able to flourish.

"Better," he answered, pressing at his side. "I can hardly feel the tumor."

"Get some rest and we should have it gone by tomorrow." She closed the curtains around his bed and headed towards her office.

The door to the hospital slammed open and Lyerlly cringed at the sound of breaking glass. That was the third window this month.

"She needs help," a voice called.

"Put her on the bed," one of the nurses said.

"It's Ramilla," the man said.

"Get the antidote," Lyerlly commanded, taking over.

Elia rushed to the storeroom and the nurses who were not with patients hurried to help.

"Go get my husband, please," Lyerlly said to the soldier.

The girl's clothes were in ruins, torn and coated in dirt and blood. Her face was sallow and covered in a sheen of sweat. She was struggling to breathe and coughing blood.

"Henley, Ty, keep her heart and lungs going." She yelled, "Elia, hurry with that antidote!"

The girl seized and gave a cough that splattered her cheeks in a mist of red.

"There's a block," Ty said, pulling away.

She placed a hand on the girl's stomach and lent her own power. Ty was right, something pushed back against her magic, making it difficult to assist. This was no simple case of Ramilla poisoning; it was in an altered state with a resistance to healing. Pushing through the block, she found her ears were filled with the sound of the girl's beating heart. It was slow, giving a painful flutter every few seconds.

Elia returned, breathless, a bottle of pale pink liquid in her hands.

Lyerlly opened the stopper, and the sickly-sweet scent quickly filled the air. Carefully, she dripped the antidote into the girl's mouth. Immediately, the coughing subsided, and her body eased.

"Rebuild her organs." Lyerlly stepped back. "Once she can survive without your help, take a break."

"Yes, ma'am," Henley said.

Someone placed a hand on the small of her back and Lyerlly jumped.

"Will she live?" Bernot asked.

"Yes," she sighed, "but only if she wants to. A few more hours and the poison would have taken her. But even at this point, she can still go to the void."

Bernot gave a small nod, studying the girl, eyebrows knitted together in concentration. He only got that look when he was planning something.

"Do we know her name?" she asked.

"Keegan Tavin. But I suspect it is an alias."

"Why would she do that?"

"Her companions gave it to her. Kade Digore, Jared Sieme, and Aron no name."

"Are those names supposed to mean something?"

"No. But Tavin… that is a name I have known for quite some time. One of the Vosjnik was named Tavin."

"Are you trying to tell me *she* is one of the Vosjnik?"

"No. More likely someone gave her their name to shift suspicion from himself." Bernot reached forward and turned

Keegan's wrist over to reveal five white marks. "Please keep me updated. And if Mahogen comes by, give him something to do. The longer we can keep his father from getting involved, the better."

With Bernot gone, she examined the girl's wrist. Power exuded from the marks, signifying they were not imitations.

She stared, uncomprehending. *Who are you and your companions?*

✟✟✟

Fire surrounded her, roaring, eating at everything. The wood of the building crackled and groaned in pain and a hiccupped cry came from within the flames. Keegan saw a baby in the center of the blaze.

She desperately wanted to grab the infant and flee, but her body refused to listen. Helplessly, she watched as the flames began to singe the swaddling blanket, smoke curling around the child. But the fire never seeming to touch the child's skin.

Beginning to feel hot, she saw the flames climbing her legs. She told her feet to move, but they were rooted in place, no matter how hard she strained. Yellow and orange distorted her vision and was soon joined by gray. She could barely see through her tears of pain.

Come to me, a voice from the fire said.

"Who's there?" she called.

Come to me. Come to me.

She recognized the voice; it belonged to Caius.

"No!"

Come to me. Come to me. Come to me.

The baby began to scream, and a hole formed under it. A wind picked up and the flames danced and spun about every corner, sucking the breath from her lungs. Suddenly, the wind exploded outward, quenching the flames.

Come to me. Come to me.

414

She was thrown backwards, head striking the wall, her body dropping heavily. Darkness quickly followed.

The voice began to laugh. *You will come back to me, child, and, when you do, I will kill you. Come to me.*

✠✠✠

Caius paced across the throne room, wringing his hands all the while.

The shadows shifted across the room, creeping along, and taking the form of a man with wild hair and sharp blue eyes. Nearing Caius, the man jabbed a knife into his neck and the king gave a muted scream, crumpling.

It felt like Braxton stood there forever, watching the killer hover over the body. He blinked and the world around him filled with a soft light. Sitting up, he realized he was in his chambers, Nico snoring loudly across the room.

He dressed and prepared to wake Nico, then changed his mind. He left the boy a note instructing him to eat and then report to Eamon.

When he entered Alyck's chambers, he found his uncle waiting expectantly.

"Do you know what I am going to ask or are you simply hoping I will accidentally tell you?" Braxton said, remembering Alyck could see nothing of his future.

Alyck's customary grin faltered, "Unfortunately, the latter. What is it you need to know?"

"Why am I having these dreams? Why can I see the future?" He spied Thaddeus hiding in the shadows, a crease between the old man's eyebrows.

"I wish I knew."

Frustration rose in his throat and there was a cracking sound that made them all jump.

Alyck slowly rose from the chair and Braxton turned to see what his uncle was staring at. The stones above the doorway were cracked, a few pieces crumbling to the floor.

415

His heart began to race; it had been years since he had lost control of his magic. Embarrassment rose in his chest while a blanket of worry settled over his shoulders.

Dust began to shake from the new cracks; he was losing control again. Braxton rushed from the room before he could bring the ceiling down on them. Control over his magic was something he had mastered as a child. Why was this happening?

Pushing the event from his mind, he refused to believe he was regressing and made his way to the training field to work with Nico—to prove to himself that he was still in control, that everything was as it should be.

‡‡‡

Thaddeus slipped into the main chamber to hear Alyck's exchange with Braxton. The questions the prince asked were… interesting.

How could Alyck, the man who put on a show of knowing everything—and oftentimes did—be unaware? He could see Braxton was becoming frustrated and watched as the stones above the doorway split, sending webbed cracks across their surface. After a moment, more dust spilled into the room and Braxton fled.

Alyck turned to Thaddeus, concern plastered on his face. "You seem to know the things I do not."

"Well…" he answered. "There are a few things I need to investigate first."

"Do it quickly."

Thaddeus bowed his head. "When did you start having visions of the future?"

"The day my brother cursed me to." Anger dripped from his words.

"You were not meant to become the Blind Prophet?"

"No."

"Caius… *he* was supposed to become the Blind Prophet then?"

"Not as far as I know. He became overzealous and power-hungry after returning to this world and, when he overthrew Seleena, forgot someone needed to fill Angela's role. With him as king, I was the only choice."

Thaddeus nodded, formulating his thoughts. Alyck was never meant to be the Blind Prophet, but neither was Caius—which went against all logic.

"I have much more investigating to do than I thought."

✠✠✠

Tiredly, Lyerlly stepped away. Night had long since fallen and while she had dismissed the nurses hours ago, she was not ready to give up. The Ramilla had been neutralized a day ago and there was marked improvement—granted, they had fought tooth and nail. Keegan could survive without assistance now, but should she wake anytime soon, she would be hard pressed to even stand on her own.

While her friends had attended to her hurts in the field, none had healed because of the Ramilla. Lyerlly had left the little cuts and bruises to mend on their own, starting with the major injuries. Hours had passed and she had only just finished properly setting her broken leg. As it was, any applied pressure would rebreak the tibia.

"How is she?" a voice said from the shadows as she gently pulled the covers over Keegan.

Lyerlly jumped, heart pounding against her chest as an Alvor emerged from the shadows.

"Better," she answered. "You know as well as I that you should not be here."

"I was curious about the girl," Mahogen said. "My father has yet to learn of her, but it will not be long before he does."

"Even so, Prince—"

"You have known me for far too many years. No need for formalities."

"Even so, *Mahogen*, we are trying to keep her existence secret save for a select few."

"Little good *that* has done. Half the city knows she is here, though most can only guess at who she really is."

Lyerlly sighed. "The trees really do whisper."

"Not as much as the people in their branches."

Lyerlly crossed her arms. "I hoped to avoid this. No doubt Caius has a bounty on her head—one that might even tempt our best men."

Mahogen turned Keegan's wrist over. "Then put a guard on her."

"Would you care to volunteer?"

"I would," Mahogen said, taking the chair beside the bed. "There is great power in this one and I am curious to see how she will use it."

"Let us know when you tire."

He gave her a devilish smile. "By that time, you may no longer be running the hospital."

In the office, Elia was looking through a stack of papers. "Headed home?"

"Yes," Lyerlly responded, removing her apron. "Try to rebuild some of her muscle mass every few hours. Use Mahogen if you grow weary."

"Would it not be better to finish mending the injuries first?"

"She will not be leaving that bed anytime soon, but she needs muscle to support herself if she is to make a well-timed recovery."

The night was pleasant and, high up in the trees, Lyerlly could make out some of the lights of the city. The ladder was not far from the hospital, but in the dark it could be challenging to find.

The way up was monotonous but calming and, the higher she rose, the more she settled. Lyerlly had been born in these trees and she trusted them more than solid ground. In the treetops, bridges connected the canopy and houses nestled into the branches, a few even finding places inside the massive trunks. Only a few people strode along the walkways at this hour.

Their house was larger than its neighbors and peeked over the canopy. During the day, it offered a spectacular view of the rolling forest. Inside, she found Bernot sitting at the kitchen table.

Upon her entrance, he came to kiss her. "How is she?"

"Fine," Lyerlly said. "Hopefully she will wake soon. But it seems half the city knows of her."

Bernot sighed. "So, it does. We should put a guard on her to be safe."

"Mahogen has already volunteered."

Her husband was quiet for a moment.

"He has been your friend your entire life, do not distrust him because of who his father is. And you wanted to keep him there anyway."

"You are right, of course we can trust Mahogen. I do not know why I worried."

"The blight of running a nation of rebels," Lyerlly said, kissing his brow.

CHAPTER 49

Kade could see no buildings, yet they were supposedly in Edreba. Laughter floated in the breeze, but he couldn't find the source. A large part of him wondered if sleeplessness had finally made him mad.

They stopped beside a massive tree and their escorts dismounted.

"We want to see our friend," Aron demanded, swinging down from his palfrey.

"After," their Alvor guard, Hickor, said.

"After what?" Jared questioned.

"After you've seen our commander," Halcyon, one of the human soldiers, said.

"He can wait," Aron refuted.

"We've been instructed to bring you to our commander as soon as you reached the city."

"There is nothing here," Aron huffed.

"If you are going to live with us, you must learn to see past the bark on the tree," Hickor said with a huff.

Kade was just as confused as the others, but knew it was best to watch and wait.

Hickor approached the tree and placed his hand on the trunk. Slowly, a doorknob protruded.

Inside, the tree was completely hollow, a spiral staircase hugging the inner wall. The wood was worn smooth, yet the tree was still living.

"What is this?" Jared asked in wonder.

"The Gortlin Tree," Halcyon answered. "In every Alvor city, the tallest tree is dedicated to its citizens. They contain libraries and the offices of city officials."

"Where's your commander's office?" Kade dared to ask.

"Do not fatigue yourself," Hickor mocked, "you will only have to climb to the first floor. Bernot is not important enough to the city itself to have a higher place."

Kade was unsure of how to take that.

Halcyon initiated the ascent. While the stairs weren't steep, by the time they reached the first landing, even Kade was breathing hard. He glanced over the edge to see they'd gone up nearly sixty feet.

Halcyon ushered them into the office, and they found a man—younger than Kade had expected, maybe twenty-eight years of age—sitting at the desk. His eyes were like obsidian and his black hair fell to just brush his jaw. His skin was swarthy and dark and, when he rose, he was looking down on all of them.

Kade didn't give him a chance to speak, "I want to see—"

"Your sister," the man finished. "I bet you do."

His lips pulled into a snarl.

"Calm, I have not intruded into your mind."

"Then how did you know?"

"I can see it in the shape of the face, the high forehead, the slight upturn in the nose, the hazel eyes, and rust hair. The truth is there if you are willing to see it." The man motioned towards three chairs. "Please."

They sat cautiously.

"Let us start with names," the man said, coming to lean on the side of the desk nearest them, "I am Bernot Bællar."

"I'm sure you've been told our names," Kade growled.

"I have, but I would like to hear you name yourselves."

"I'm Kade Digore, this is Jared Sieme, and Aron no name."

Bernot leaned back in his chair. "Kade, I would appreciate if you did not try to deceive me. I will give you another chance to tell me who you are."

"I already did."

"You think me a lack-wit? You have plagued the nations for many years, Kade Tavin, and I must say, I never imagined you would come here—willingly. You will have to create a better lie if you wish to fool me. But you must really care for your sister to risk finding your death here."

"I may have slept with the enemy, but it was only so I could slit their throats."

"Your parents were good people," Bernot said. Before Kade could say anything else, Bernot turned to Aron. "And Aron Alagard, who would have thought the king's son would seek us out?"

Jared reacted in utter shock. "What?"

Kade bellowed, "That's why I don't trust him!"

"You knew?" Jared bit.

"Even if he wanted to, he could not have told you," Bernot explained. "The king places a spell on his men which keeps them from talking about any aspect of his sons in the presence of the oblivious."

"A spell?"

"Yes, a spell. Spellcasters are rare, but they do exist. By saying a string of words in the Old Language it is possible to do some amazing things."

"Too many lies," Jared snarled, lunging at Kade.

Bernot held out a hand to stay him. "Take a seat, Jared."

"And if I don't?"

"Take a seat."

Jared reached for the knife he kept in his boot, but, noting its absence, did as instructed. "How were you able to tell us?"

"Do I look like one of the king's men?" Bernot answered sardonically.

"A better question would be, how did you find out?" Aron probed.

Bernot ignored him, turning his attention to Kade. "Tell me, Kade, is your sister truly the Child of Prophecy?"

"Yes," Kade answered, looking him straight in the eye. "As are Jared and I."

"There is only supposed to be one."

"Four," Jared corrected.

"How would you know this?" Bernot questioned.

"Thaddeus told us."

"Thaddeus Broyker?"

Jared nodded.

"I have found you board in a children's home," Bernot said, as Hickor opened the door.

"Take us to Keegan," Kade demanded.

"In due time. But first, eat, sleep, and try not to kill each other." As they left, Bernot added, "And next time, do not lie to me."

‡‡‡

Blood was what Jared wanted most—Kade's specifically. Too much had his "friend" kept from him. Given access to a weapon, he'd gladly dig some steel into Kade. He'd probably not aim to kill but definitely to maim and cause pain—actually, he might kill him if the fancy struck. Fortunately for Kade, the Lazado had taken their weapons.

When they emerged from the Gortlin Tree, they were dismayed to discover their horses had vanished.

"You will not need them where you are going," Hickor said.

Even Halcyon sensed the threatening undertone in his comment and made to ease their alarm. "Your horses have been stabled and your belongings have gone to the children's home."

"And where would that be?" Kade snapped.

423

"In the city," Hickor said, walking away.

They followed the Alvor through the giant trees, twigs and dead leaves crunching underfoot. Under different circumstances, Jared would've marveled at the forest. Woodland creatures hopped between the trunks, looking like miniatures of their true forms; most creatures would've run at the sight of people, yet these beasts were at ease, completely ignoring them.

Hickor approached one of the trees and placed a hand on its side. Jared expected another door to reveal itself; instead, a series of ladder rungs appeared.

Halfway up, Jared made the mistake of looking down and the world became a dizzyingly fog far below.

"Climb," Kade snapped when he froze in momentary fear.

At the top, wooden walkways linked the trees and houses rested in the high branches.

"A city in the trees," Aron said, taking in the view. "How does no one fall from the walkways?"

"They have better sense than you ground-dwellers," Hickor responded sharply.

"And there are nets for those who don't," Halcyon added.

The walkways were bustling, and children darted between them, giggles abound. Jared noticed a few boys with wooden swords clutching in hand. He hated to think this play might one day soon save their lives. Soon, they reached a tree that's leaves were a strange cream color, and they were led inside.

Halcyon took them into a kitchen where they found a plump, little woman scolding a boy. She was about the same height as Keegan—and a very similar personality it seemed. Seeing them, the woman sent the boy scampering with a playful kick to the backside.

"More charges for me, Halcyon?" she said.

"As usual. Though, I doubt these three will be as mischievous as the rest."

"But trouble they will cause nonetheless." She eyed them for a moment before dismissing Halcyon.

"Prepare room for a fourth," the guard said.

"We require better accommodations," Kade said at once.

The woman put her hands on her hips. "Oh, is Behthany Rhyen's not good enough for ya? Do tell why?"

"We aren't children."

"How old are you?"

"Twenty."

She laughed. "A mere child."

"You're not much older than us."

Behthany gave another laugh and Jared saw a flash of silver in her mouth. "Your eyes deceive you, boy. I am well past my hundredth year."

"How?" Aron said incredulously.

Kade took a guess. "Half Alvor, half human?"

"Correct."

"Would explain your longevity and the silver in your mouth, but the lack of horns," Kade expanded.

"And why I am stuck with you lot. Anyway, your rooms are on the top floor. It is reserved for you *adults* who are still yet children. None of the youngins should bother you up there."

"I'd prefer to be housed away from *him*," Jared said, referring to Kade.

"And what makes you think I'd like to be forced to spend any more time with you or the bastard?" Kade argued.

It was hard to hear the words that came next as they all resorted to shouting.

Behthany roared, "Enough! You will act civil in this house, lest I need beat you with a belt." They looked sourly at each other. "You will act politely towards your companions and there will be no bloodshed in here or so help me. Am I understood?" When they declined to answer, she said louder, "Am I understood?"

"Yes, ma'am," they chorused.

"Good. Like I said, top floor. Dinner is at sunset. See you are not late." She dismissed them with a wave. Under her breath, she muttered, "Bovestun well act like children but have the gall to call themselves men."

‡‡‡

True to his word, Mahogen watched Keegan through the night.

Lyerlly had tried to dismiss him come morn, but he deflected her instructions. He made no nuisance of himself, so she allowed him to stay.

"Mahogen," she eventually said sternly, "make yourself useful, or leave." There was little room for bystanders in her hospital.

Mahogen smiled. "How can I be of service?"

"Help Ty clean the bedpans."

"I would sooner aid in healing."

"Bedpans."

Mahogen raised an eyebrow but left to do as instructed.

Lyerlly turned her attention to Keegan. All that was left of the broken leg was a hairline fracture, which should have taken no time to heal, but with the Ramilla's lingering block, took the rest of the day. Mahogen wisely did not return until she was done.

As she pulled the covers over Keegan, Bernot appeared and shared a few words with Mahogen. The Alvor quickly slipped into the office.

"How does she fare?" her husband asked.

"Better than before."

"Is there anything we can do to wake her?"

"Not that I know of. Nor would I."

"I need her awake."

"Why?"

Bernot gave her a solemn look. "Because she has a part to play in the war."

"*What* war?"

"The one I intend to wage," he said, walking away.

War—the one thing her husband wanted yet could not have; the barrier saw to that. The border had been raised to keep Caius and his militants out, but the spell also kept them from crossing.

"Bernot knows, as well as any, war cannot be waged," Mahogen said, retaking his seat beside the bed.

"Does not mean he is not going to try," Lyerlly told the prince, walking way.

She left quietly, leaving the hospital in Henley's capable hands for the night. The journey home was not as enjoyable as usual, her mind elsewhere. On the walkways, wind pulled at her skirt, sending it whirling about her ankles.

Bernot was sat at the kitchen table when she arrived home, maps and papers scattered across the tabletop.

"You know you cannot start a war," she reminded him.

"I am going to," he said stubbornly.

"How? No warring nation can get past the border."

"I will find a way. Otherwise, what use is having the most powerful elemental the world has ever seen?"

She took a seat across from him. "I am not sure."

Bernot reached across the table and took her hand.

"In time," she continued, "Sola and Lunos will reveal all."

"We don't have time. The world is dying under Caius's thumb. The border was meant to stand forever, but sooner or later everything falls. I mean for us to cause that."

"How?"

Bernot leaned back. "I am working on that. But Keegan is the key. That much I know."

‡‡‡

Thaddeus closed the book he had been reading and set it back on the shelf. The guards behind him shifted, preparing to follow him. He had spent the last two days in the king's private library, hunting for information on the Blind Prophets.

Thus far, his search had uncovered only two tomes. The larger one contained all of Angela's prophecies and a few of Alyck's. This he would be keeping in their chambers and was going to endeavor to make Alyck recall previous predictions to record them, as well as enter any new ones.

The second was tiny in comparison and covered in dark moleskin. It gave the origins of the Blind Prophet but did not tell him much he did not already know. There was also nothing on how the next Prophet was to be chosen, as Seleena had been the only queen to rule under Angela's guidance. There was, however, a spell scribbled in the first few pages that appeared to be able to create a Blind Prophet and it told an interesting story. The handwriting, given the hints of old-style script he recognized from several notes sent to Alyck, told him it was Caius's work. While few had access to the king's personal library, a part of Thaddeus wondered why Caius left this precious information out in the open. Then he realized why: spellcasters were so rare and without them, the information was useless; and not many people could speak or even read the Old Language these days.

The tale the spell described was multifold. He could see where it extended and intertwined the Prophet's life with the ruling bloodline, where it took the Prophet's sight, and limited their powers to foresight. He re-examined that segment of the spell and suddenly understood—or at least had a theory. Thaddeus closed the books, took them back to his chambers, and immediately left again.

He struggled to find his way through the castle, surprising even himself when he reached his destination.

Looking out the window next to the door, he watched the sun near the horizon, casting magnificent hues across the sky.

He knocked quietly on the door, entering once given permission. Thaddeus had expected a lavish interior, fit for a king; it was anything but. The room was austere, with only the necessities and a single, small portrait hanging on the wall. The woman depicted was gorgeous, her lustrous black hair tumbling across the canvas in gentle waves. Her blue eyes held an air of despondency and the hint of a secret.

"Your wife I take it," Thaddeus said as Caius entered the room from an adjacent chamber.

"Yes, Seleena" Caius answered in a light growl. "My wife and the queen, daughter of the Dragon King. What are you doing here? You are only supposed to come when Alyck makes a pertinent prophecy."

"It is something of that nature. Or at least it relates to the Blind Prophet. You were supposed to become the next Blind Prophet."

Caius's features darkened.

"But you forced your brother to take your place. Why?"

"I did what I did for a reason, and it is none of your concern."

"I fear it is."

"Get out."

"As you wish, but I will continue to ask until you tell me what I need to know."

"You will lose your voice."

"But never my mind," Thaddeus refuted.

‡‡‡

The children's home was larger than Aron first presumed as much of it hidden by the branches it was constructed within. They had climbed sets of narrow stairs until they reached the upper floor.

Their windows looked over the sprawling forest outside, the sun creating a fire of green as it touched the leaves. The layout followed the points of a compass, a pair of bedrooms and shared washroom at three of the points and a kitchen at the fourth. In the center was a sitting area with a few couches and a dining table.

Jared and Kade took rooms on opposite sides after snatching their bags from the table. Having no desire to deal with either, Aron took a room in the third wing. It was smaller than his bedchambers in Agrielha, but still roomy, the bed able to sleep two people comfortably and covered in a pale, yellow comforter. It was worn and old, most likely a donation, but that would not make it any less useable.

Dumping his bag on the floor, he went to the window. Roosting birds dropped onto branches as twilight overcame the sky. Despite everything, he smiled; it just felt right. He was where he belonged.

Going to the washroom, he was assaulted by his reflection in the mirror, which looked strange compared to how he remembered himself. A scruffy beard covered his jaw and combined with unkempt hair, made him look wild. His usually black-as-night hair had taken on subtle hues of a deep brown. The only thing unchanged were his indigo-colored eyes.

Not wanting to miss dinner, he promised himself he would shave afterwards. He doubted Jared and Kade would wait for him and made the trip downstairs alone. The table was crowded with rowdy children of various ages, from barely waddling behind older siblings to looking at most a year or two younger than he.

Taking a seat, he glanced at Behthany, who seemed to be ignoring the fact Jared and Kade were absent. There was enough food on the table to cater a feast by all standards. Dishes were piled high with chicken, the meat removed from the bone to likely prevent the little ones from choking on accident, bowls were filled with mashed potatoes and peas, and loaves of bread were placed intermittently along the table.

Following the children's lead, he piled his plate high and dug in. As he ate, the only noise came from clattering forks and knives. As the food diminished, voices began to join the clangor.

He felt a tug on his sleeve.

"Where are your brothers?" a little girl asked.

"Uhh…" Aron faltered. "My brothers are far away in Agrielha."

"Not those brothers. Your other brothers."

"I have no other brothers."

"Yes, you do," a boy across the table added. "The ones you came in with earlier."

Aron gripped his fork tightly. "They are *not* my brothers."

"Of course they are," the boy continued. "We leave our families behind when we come here, but we gain new ones."

"Yeah," another child chimed in. "Hugie and I share no blood, but we're siblings. We have to look after each other."

It was hard to tell who was speaking next as all the children at once proclaimed who their siblings were.

"Enough," Behthany said from the head of the table. "Aron, Kade, and Jared have just arrived, and it may take them some time to recognize themselves as brothers. No one is to pester them about it."

"Yes, ma'am," the children chorused.

"Good. Now, get to cleaning."

The children took the dirty plates and cutlery into the kitchen, leaving him with Behthany and he hoped to make a quiet exit.

"Tomorrow, you will help with clean up," Behthany informed him. "And make sure your brothers know not to miss meals. I cannot have you boys starving."

‡‡‡

The wall scraped open, and Braxton stepped into the dimly lit stable. The griffins were already stirring, their chains clinking as they moved.

Where is your student? Crowlin questioned.

"Sleeping."

Should you not be doing the same? she asked. Her feathers were dark gray, bordering on black, and reminded him of the night.

Probably, but I have been finding it hard to sleep. "Too much to think about."

"About what?" a voice asked from the shadows.

Braxton nearly jumped out of his skin. Pulling his dagger, he brandished it at the area where the voice had come from.

"No need for that," the voice said, stepping into the dim torchlight.

"Thaddeus? What are you doing here?"

"Talking to you."

"How did you even know I would be here?"

"A mutual friend."

Sheathing his knife, Braxton gave him a sour look. "What do you need?"

"I want to talk about what happened earlier."

The muscles in his shoulders tightened. "There is nothing to talk about."

Clearly not, Crowlin said, nudging him towards Thaddeus. *Listen to this man; he bears the air of knowledge.*

"You can tell me. I promise I will keep it between us."

Braxton took a moment. "There is not much to tell. I… have been dreaming the future."

"That is not nothing, my dear boy. How long has this been occurring?"

He had to think, "A few months—since Keegan arrived."

"Ah, our ever-elusive Keegan. She seems to leave a wake of disturbance, does she not?"

"I suppose…"

"Describe your visions."

"Repetitive. I keep having the same dream until it actually happens. Or I figure out the meaning."

"What do you mean?"

"They are always in the Old Language."

"Are you fluent in the Old Language?"

Braxton shook his head.

Thaddeus muttered, "Interesting."

"We should both be going," Braxton said after a short silence.

"Of course, the paths set before us are arduous. But before we leave, I do have one more question. Why did you lose control?"

Braxton's stomach worked into a knot. "I did not lose control," he stammered. "It… must have been something else."

Braxton, Myrish said.

"What?" he snapped, turning to the griffin. As he did, the few loose pebbles that could be found in the stables clattered back to the ground.

"You are not aware when it happens, are you? How long has this been happening?" Thaddeus asked.

The words were sticky in his throat. "Today was the first time. Or at least the first time I noticed."

Thaddeus placed a hand on his shoulder. "Everything will be fine. I will try to give you an answer—when I myself know something for sure; you have my word. Now, go back to bed."

Braxton nodded tiredly and opened the door to the secret passageway. He turned to let Thaddeus through first and was shocked to find the old man had disappeared.

He left via the door, Phynex told him, giving a slight shuffling of his wings, which was as close to a shrug as he could give.

Walking through the darkness was easy—dealing with his thoughts was not and he did his best to push them aside, to let himself believe that things were normal and fine.

CHAPTER 50

A persistent knock pulled her from sleep. Its insistence carried a kind of direness in its tone. Whatever news was waiting for them, it was likely important it be dealt with quickly.

Lyerlly ran her fingers along Bernot's back to rouse him. "Want to get the door?"

"Not particularly," he mumbled.

"Please," she said sleepily, giving him a gentle push.

He grumbled but rose off the mattress. It was not long before she heard muted voices downstairs.

She expected Bernot to return shortly; when he did not, grew curious. Wrapping a shawl around her shoulders, she went to investigate, and found Bernot talking to a soldier; although minutes previously he had been fast asleep, he looked quite alert now.

"What is going on?" she asked.

"Keegan."

"Is she alright?"

"Yes, but we are both needed at the hospital, *immediately*," Bernot told her, grabbing a jacket from the closet.

Dying candles lit the windows of a few houses and owls watched curiously as they made their way through the city. The climb down the ladder and the walk across the forest floor seemed to take longer than she remembered. Outside the hospital, the patients who could leave their beds were huddled in the night.

"What are they doing out here?" Lyerlly snapped at the soldiers standing around.

"We couldn't make them stay in there with the body," one stammered.

"Body…?" She pushed past the man.

The floor near Keegan's bed was stained in a sickening crimson. Henley's body lay face up, her eyes glassy and staring blankly at the ceiling.

"Who did this?" Lyerlly demanded.

"We're looking into it now," a soldier told her.

Mahogen sat beside Keegan's bed, dabbing a cloth to her head where a gash spilled red blood over the side of her face.

"What happened?" Lyerlly asked furiously. "You were supposed to be watching her!"

"I was," Mahogen said calmly. "Henley thought she heard something outside, so I went to check. When I came back, she was dead, and Keegan was on the floor across the hospital."

"Did you see who it was?"

"No."

"Did you sense who it was?"

"No."

"Why would someone try to take the girl and then leave her behind?" her husband asked.

"My guess is they got scared," Mahogen replied.

"Lyerlly, I need to speak to you in the office," Bernot said, drawing her away. With the door shut, he told her, "I always knew we had spies, but I hoped none would be this bold. I am going to put a full guard rotation on the hospital, and someone is to be with Keegan at all times."

"If you must."

"How much longer until she comes to?"

"If only I knew."

"She needs to be moved. Somewhere safer."

"We cannot move her until she wakes. If she were elsewhere and something happened, no one would be at hand to help."

Bernot sighed, pinching the bridge of his nose. So much rested on this girl and it appeared she would never make things easy.

✠✠✠

There was a soft rap on his door.

"What?" Kade groaned blearily.

It'd been easy to forget he was exhausted during their breakneck flight across the country. He'd meant to go to dinner, but once he'd sat on the bed, he'd fallen asleep and not moved until now. Coming to fully, he realized he was holding Cassidy's larimar pendent in his fist. Something inside him started to bend and he only stopped it from breaking by shoving the necklace into his pocket.

"Bernot wishes to speak to you," Behthany called.

"Tell him he can go roy—"

"I am *not* a messenger and that *was not* a request."

Scowling, he threw back the covers. They had yet to be given back their weapons and he felt bare without his sword. He didn't know what Bernot wanted, but he had no intention of giving it to him.

Kade found Bernot sitting in the common room with a woman. She sat elegantly, looking like a highborn lady. Her skin was unmarred—smooth and pale. Chestnut colored hair hung freely about her shoulders and brown eyes gazed at him with a strange kind of knowing while a warm power emanated from her.

"My lady," he said, remembering his manners.

"This is my wife, Lyerlly," Bernot said, a coy smirk playing on his lips. He motioned to an empty chair. "Take a seat."

He did so, then realized Aron and Jared were also present.

"I want to see Keegan," Jared demanded, likely not for the first time.

"In time," Bernot told him. "I want to know how all of you met Keegan."

"Why?" Kade snapped.

Aron decided to guess. "He wants to know if she really is the Child of Prophecy."

"You mean if *we* are the Children of Prophecy," Kade corrected.

"Correct," Bernot said. "Is she? Are you?"

"She is," Aron responded.

Jared added, "And we are. At least Kade and I are."

"How did she come to meet all of you?"

Aron took a moment to answer. "I freed her from my father's dungeon."

Bernot's brows twitched, and he turned to Jared.

"She found me," Jared told him.

"I saved her from the Vosjnik," Kade said.

Liar, Jared snarled.

"Kade, what have I told you about lying? And, no, I have not entered your mind. But I cannot ignore the emotions coming from your brother telling me otherwise."

"We are not *brothers*," Jared bit.

"You came here together," Lyerlly said. "By all rights, the second you stepped over the border, you became family."

"How did you come to know Keegan?" Bernot repeated.

"A long story, that you'd best hear from Keegan," Kade said, trying to redirect the question.

"I am not asking Keegan. But it does seem there is much all of you are not telling me. So, start at the beginning. Aron, I believe the first part belongs to you."

Kade glanced down the table, realizing he didn't actually know much of Keegan's first days in Arciol, except how damaging her entrance had been to the throne room.

Aron began with how she was found in the throne room, destruction all around her, then spoke of his visits with Alyck and all he'd been told. Aron ended with Keegan riding off on Darkheart, now Bastille.

"Kade has the next part," the prince said.

"There's not much to tell," Kade said, keeping his face neutral. "The Vosjnik chased her towards Lake Romann. When we caught up to her, there was a light, wind, and explosion, and she disappeared. Jared."

Bernot held up a hand to stay Jared. "Describe the explosion."

Kade shifted uncomfortably in the chair. "It was like there were three suns and we were on the outskirts of a gale storm. The light and wind were pulling inwards, towards Keegan. Then, at its climax, it exploded outward. None of us were harmed, but Keegan was gone."

"You know what that was."

"Yes," Kade answered, "a Nanagin." He could see the wheels turning in Bernot's head, he just didn't know what conclusions he was coming to.

"Jared," Bernot invited, turning his attention to him.

"There was an explosion just before her horse brought her into my camp," Jared began. He told them how he'd taken her home, how she'd come down with some sickness, and how her magic had suddenly manifested. He then talked about the early days of their training, growing quieter as he neared the time his family was killed.

Something possessed Kade and he jumped in. He didn't look at Jared, but knew he was grateful; the subject still caused him heartache.

Jared took up the telling of their journey from Suttan, leaving most details about Cassidy out. Kade knew he was settling his debt. Even so, the larimar in his pocket seemed to become infinitely heavier. After their capture by the Vosjnik, Aron backtracked to tell of his own flight from

Agrielha, and they were content to let him bring the story to a close.

By the end of it, both Bernot and Lyerlly bore looks of incredulity.

"This has been most informative. Is there anything else you *want* to tell us?" Bernot asked.

"No," Kade told him emphatically.

Silently, Bernot and Lyerlly stood.

"Hold on," Aron said, "we told you what you wanted to know. Now let us see Keegan."

"Not just yet. There is still the matter of testing your skills."

"When can we do that?" Kade asked, clenching his fists.

"On the morrow. I will send someone to take you to the training grounds."

✢✢✢

Jared only had to look at Kade to see his frustration matched his own. However, he was in no mood to reconcile and commiserate. Going downstairs to get lunch, he found Behthany playing the maiden in distress in the common room. Seeing him, she picked her way across the chaos. A few of the younger children pulled away from their battles to chase after her, wrapping themselves in her skirts, giggling as she dragged them over.

"Wanting lunch, I presume," she said, hands on her hips.

"Yes," he answered.

"*Please.*"

"Yes, *please.*"

She reached down, tickling a little girl. "There is bread and cheese in the kitchen. Help yourself."

Jared helped himself to a large slice of bread and a few blocks of cheese, washing it down with a cup of water.

Deciding he needed to get out for a bit, he followed the path to the walkways out front, the sun high above, warm and pleasant. He shoved his hands in his pockets and walked until he came to a large junction between several trees where a market was set up.

Children ran through the crowd happily while adults haggled. He chose a random vendor and enquired where he could find the Gortlin Tree. The vendor obliged and armed with a set of directions, Jared pushed across the market.

It was some time before he found the tree, its top even higher than the ones that held the rest of the city. A motley assortment of greens colored its leaves, causing it to seem as if it was an indecisive chameleon—they didn't have that creature in this world, but Keegan had explained it to him once. He set a hand against the tree like Hickor had done to open the door.

"It will not work for you," a voice said behind him. As he spun around, Bernot queried, "May I ask why you are here?"

"There are a few more things I want to tell you."

Bernot kept a straight face and opened the door into the tree. "We will take the lift down."

The lift was little more than an expansive basket that lurched as they stepped into its confines and swung as they rode down.

"Why wouldn't the door open for me?" Jared asked.

"You are neither an Alvor nor an agent of the Lazado. Yet."

They didn't talk the rest of the way and the lift creaked and groaned, making him wonder if it'd hold. Near the bottom, it jerked to a stop, and they stepped onto the landing. He was glad to have solid footing again.

Bernot opened the door to his office, ushering him in. "What is it you want to tell me?"

"Kade's a murderer and a liar."

"Nothing I am not aware of. If you want me to expel your brother, you will have to give me a better reason. His good outweighs the misdeeds."

"He's not my brother," Jared hissed. "Kade killed my family, then failed to mention he'd given my little brother to the king."

"Why would he not tell you this?"

"To make us come here," he said with disgust.

"Us?"

"Keegan and me. She would've gone back for Nico regardless of the danger to herself. And I would've followed."

"Then the lie was told in your best interest. Is that such a damning thing?"

"Yes, when in conjunction with everything else."

"Such as?"

"He knew who Aron was and Keegan was his sister yet didn't tell us."

"In regard to Aron, he could not tell you any more than he could control the changing of the seasons. Caius spells his men so they cannot mention his offspring in most contexts."

"You already told me this."

"I did and the reasoning has not changed. I believe Kade, in his own way, tried to warn you."

Jared thought about how Kade had voiced his mistrust of Aron. Maybe he should've listened—and fought harder against Kade at the start.

"Keegan," he continued, "doesn't know."

"Know what?"

"That she's Kade's twin."

"And you would have me tell her, so it does not look like you betrayed Kade?"

"No. I couldn't care less what he thinks of me. I'd rather she not be told."

"Why?"

"I know how people will take to Kade. Let her deny any relation besides a forced one so she won't be treated as a monster, like him."

‡‡‡

Lyerlly slowly climbed the ladder to the city, fireflies sputtering into existence around her like fleeting stars. On the walkways, children raced to catch the glowing insects.

At home, she found Bernot waiting for her. "Any change?"

She shook her head.

"I cannot keep them away forever. What am I to do?"

"Let them see her," she said. "Why did you have me come earlier?"

"Because, whereas I hear the person the words come from, you hear the words that come from the person. I know who they are and that clouds how I judge what they say."

Lyerlly took a seat. "What is it you heard them say?"

"Many things. The only commonality is how much they care for their sister."

"It would take a blind man to not see that. What else did you learn?"

"Several things. Some offered insight into Caius and others explained some of the mysteries surrounding Keegan, while giving rise to yet more questions."

Lyerlly leaned forward on an elbow. "Do tell."

"Keegan is the Child of Prophecy."

"We already knew that."

"But so are her brothers."

She tilted her head. "I did want to ask about that; I thought there was only one."

"No, that is what Angela wanted Caius to believe." He pulled a piece of parchment from his pocket and handed it to her. "Angela's last prophecy."

"Why did you pretend you were unaware of this?"

He shrugged. "I felt the deception might offer more insight."

Turning her attention to the parchment, she read: Four children shall defeat the despot. To rouse, drive, intercede,

443

and assuage his companions is one's self-given duty. A life of displacement one must lead. To right the wrong is one's ambition. To sit upon the throne is one's right by ancient blood. Black and white yet compelled to stand in spite. To each their own misfortune: forbidden love shall be the ruin of the first, the light before the thunder shall be the second's demise, the steel of the blade shall cast down the third, the lies of the mother shall condemn the fourth. Twenty fingers from their birth must we count until revolution is sparked by the one of all elements.

"Four," she said, "and you think they are…"

"It all fits. Though, I do not believe Aron knows."

"Why would he not?"

"Because he was not with them in Suttan. The only person who knew about this prophecy, besides me, is the man who told me about it—Thaddeus Broyker. Keegan knows she is special—*knows* she is a Child of Prophecy. And I have no doubt she is aware we are placing the fate of us all on her shoulders. But she does not know who she truly is in respect to this world and how she came to be as she is."

"Do you intend to tell her?"

"In time. The rest has only led to theories I need to investigate."

Lyerlly stood and cupped her husband's face in her hands. "You are going to rid us of Caius."

"No, they are. They will be the ones to swing the sword. Go to bed, my dear, we have a long path ahead of us. I have called a Council of the Nations and they should be here within the turn of the moon."

"Is that wise?"

"Necessary."

"They will tear the poor girl apart fighting over her."

"Something tells me it is not Keegan that will be torn apart. If she stands true to how her brothers describe her, it will be she who decides the terms of this war."

CHAPTER 51

Aron awoke to someone pounding on his door. Rising, he dressed and went to the common area to find Kade and Jared waiting, the silence between them chilling.

Hickor escorted them to the forest floor and, somehow, the descent managed to be more racking than the climb up.

They were led through the forest in silence, and he let his mind wander. After a time, he realized it was the beginning of his twentieth year. Braxton and Kolt had thrown extravagant feasts and balls to mark their twentieth birthdays. He doubted the same would have been done for him and was simply glad to be beyond his father's reach. In his wildest dreams, he could not have asked for a better gift on his birthday.

The training field was a fair distance from where they had descended. The men were segregated into classes depending on weapon of choice. Most of the space was given to swordsmen and elementals while archers and those with maces and pikes were on the outskirts. Towards the far back, a few men fought with fists.

Bernot was waiting for them. "What are your weapons of choice?"

"Sword and magic," Kade answered.

He was sent off with Halcyon.

"Magic," Jared answered.

Hickor went with him.

"Bow and arrow," Aron answered.

Bernot led him to where the archers were practicing, rows of straw stuffed dummies acting as targets. Arrows stuck from them like quills, yet, despite that, they grinned devilishly.

He was handed a bow and a tube of arrows was set on the ground next to him.

"Start easy," Bernot instructed, "take a shot to the chest."

Aron notched and arrow and pulled the bowstring back, feeling the muscles in his arms working to maintain the tension. As he breathed out, he let the arrow fly. It pierced the dummy's eye.

The archer next to him gave a disconcerted look.

"Impressive" Bernot commented, "but not what I asked for."

"No," Aron admitted. "This is what you asked for." He notched another arrow and let it go. It went through the target's heart. "When can I see Keegan?"

"As soon as we are done here." Bernot surveyed the training field behind him. "Do you see Kade?"

Aron strained to find him in the flurry of motion. "Yes."

"I want you to shoot an arrow at him in such a way that it tears his clothing but leaves his skin unmarked."

Aron paused—what Bernot asked was a test. He could either do as asked, showing he could follow directions, and that he was a good shot. *Or…*

Slowly, he pulled the bowstring back. As he was about to release, he spun and loosed the arrow at the target. It sheared through its side, spilling a few golden rods of hay onto the ground.

"I am a good shot," he announced, "and as much as I dislike Kade, I will not do something that could potentially harm him."

"We might make use of you yet."

Aron did not like the implication, but kept his mouth shut.

"As soon as your brothers are done, we shall go see your sister."

‡‡‡

Come to me.

Nothing but blackness existed.

Come to me.

Unbelievably, the world was getting darker.

Come to me.

Keegan was beginning to fade.

Be strong, came another voice, hardly more than a whisper. *Be strong.*

Come to me. There was a hint of worry in Caius's words now.

Be strong, be strong, be strong. Each repetition was louder than the last.

The darkness began to fade and there was light in the distance.

The voice was practically yelling now, *Be strong!*

Light rushed at Keegan like a bolt. Her eyes opened and strained at the overabundance of white. At first, it was all she could see, but slowly colors appeared. Her head felt like it was full of cotton and there was a dull ache in her muscles. Studying her surroundings, she saw a man in the chair beside the bed.

He looked human, save for the golden horns protruding from his head that peeked above his brown, bark-colored hair. He stared ahead, unblinkingly, like a statue.

She couldn't place where in time and space she was and, eyeing the man, quietly threw back the covers. Realizing she was in nothing but a long shirt that reached her knees, she eased herself off the bed, the tiled floor cool on her bare feet. She stood for no more than a few seconds before her legs buckled, sending her crashing to the floor.

"Keegan," the man said.

"Where am I?" she began, pushing to her feet.

"There is no need to fight."

The words made her feel that something was wrong, and she tried to take a step. Her legs spasmed and she fell, grabbing onto the curtain around the bed. The cloth pulled from its hangings, revealing the hospital. A few nurses looked at her curiously but made no attempt to help.

"Stay where you are," the man instructed.

Feeling defenseless, Keegan scrambled to her feet, only managing a few steps before collapsing onto her knees. She didn't know why her legs were so weak, but it only served to make her feel more unnerved.

"Stop," implored the man.

Ignoring him, Keegan made a final attempt to stand, crumpling onto the floor almost instantly. Realizing she wouldn't get anywhere that way, she scuttled backwards, saying, "Stay the fuck away from me."

The man followed after her, "Keegan—"

"Stay away," she said, holding her hands out.

The tile floor cracked, and rocks pulled themselves forth to float before her.

A woman in the background screamed and the world succumbed to pandemonium.

She could hear multiple voices yelling at her to yield and sensed someone trying to grab her from behind. She raised a column of earth and there was a loud "umph" as the person was hit in the stomach. Black spots began to float across her vision from a sudden exhaustion and it was all she could do to remain upright.

Soldiers rushed into the hospital, weapons drawn.

The man with the golden horns took a step towards her and she went to throw a projectile at him but only managed to crack the tiled floor before she feared she'd pass out.

"Enough," the said man, his forearms raised to shield his face preemptively. There was something calming about his voice, but she was still on edge. "Enough."

Slowly, the rocks began to lower, and it was all she could do to keep herself sitting upright.

There was a flurry of motion, and the horned man was sent stumbling. She couldn't see who'd attacked him, but others joined the fray.

Men and women in white aprons struggled to pull the fracas apart and Keegan sat in the background, forgotten momentarily.

"STOP!" a woman yelled.

Everyone froze and slowly they disentangled themselves as a man and a woman walked into their midst.

"What on earth do you think you are doing?" the woman demanded.

✠✠✠

What I would give to have wings, Braxton said, leaning against the cool stones.

Hmph, was Oxren's response. *They are freeing until someone clips them.*

You may find yourselves in the sky again sooner than you think, Braxton told him. *My father wants me to train you for battle.*

Myrish roared with laughter both mentally and audibly. *The only battle we will fight will be to destroy Caius.*

"Of course, you cannot make life easy."

An easy life is not worth living, Crowlin told him. *Have the Vosjnik captured the girl?*

"I have not heard anything." *I am not sure if that is good or bad.*

No news is good news, Niyth said. *Do you actually intend to train us?*

Guilt welled in his chest. *I would rather not. But if I do not, my father will find a way to force you to.*

Ever the man with the seemingly noble intentions.

"But good intentions are worth *nothing*." He pushed himself to his feet. "I should be going."

They are worth more than you think, Crowlin said. *You are kinder than most humans we have met.*

"You have only met horrible examples of humanity." His foot struck a loose pebble, sending it skittering across the room. There was a loud thump, and he followed the path the pebble had taken. It was now imbedded in the wall. He took a deep breath, forcing himself to maintain his composure.

There was a clicking of beaks as the griffins conversed.

You should talk to Alyck, Crowlin told him with concern. *Something is shifting with your magic.*

Braxton knew doing so would garner nothing but frustration; he was going to have to face whatever came without warning or advice.

‡‡‡

An ache was forming in Lyerlly's head. Keegan sat on the floor, anxious and confused, deep gouges cracking the tile floor around her, Ty was hunched over holding his stomach, Keegan's brothers were all in a lather, and poor Mahogen looked bewildered that someone had managed to hit him.

"What on earth do you think you are doing?" Lyerlly demanded.

"Keegan—" Aron stammered.

"Quiet."

Bernot placed a hand on Lyerlly's shoulder to waylay her anger. "Would one of you gentlemen help Keegan back into bed?"

The three brothers scrambled to help; Aron reached her first.

Keegan gave him a curious look, but consented to being scooped into his arms, looking tiny, frail, and fragile.

As they followed Aron, Mahogen wiped away a line of blood from his mouth. The Alvor took a moment to stare at

450

the red on his hand—as if it were the most peculiar thing he had ever seen.

Aron deposited Keegan and she began spewing questions. "Where are we? What's going on? How'd I get here? Why does he have h—"

"Calm," Bernot said soothingly.

"Where are we?" Keegan asked again.

"The Lazado," Aron answered, taking her hand.

Absentmindedly, she ran her thumb over his palm. "But we were in Revod. And Vitia… and Cassidy…"

Kade's breath seemed to hitch at the mention of the last person.

"Do you remember getting stabbed by Vitia?" Bernot said, making Keegan reach for her shoulder. "That blade was poisoned."

"How long?"

"Two weeks," Kade answered.

"And I'm gonna be fine?" she asked. "No lingering effects?"

"In time," Lyerlly told her. "The poison destroyed most of your muscle. We have been rebuilding them, but the Ramilla was modified to inhibit that."

"What does that mean for me?"

"We will continue to artificially rebuild your muscles, but ultimately it will be better for you to do so on your own."

"We shall let you and your brothers talk," Bernot said rising.

Keegan's brows knitted together. "*Brothers*?"

Bernot smiled. "Those who come to the Lazado together become family." *Office,* he said to Lyerlly.

He husband leaned against the edge of the desk. "I never imagined she would be that powerful."

Lyerlly huffed. "None of us did. I have never seen anyone do so much damage while still recovering from Ramilla."

"She is the ace up our sleeve, but also the thorn in our side. We will need to be careful how we proceed with her."

Lyerlly crossed her arms. "And there is your problem, you are treating her like an object. You will never control her, but you may be able to guide her."

Bernot took her face in his hands. "How did I end up with such a beautiful and intelligent wife?"

CHAPTER 52

Having been given the choice of staying in the hospital or going to a children's home, Keegan had chosen the latter. Mahogen had taken her to the Gortlin Tree, and they were currently ascending it in a primitive elevator.

The basket swung slightly as they rose. Keegan knew she looked like a star-struck child but couldn't care less. The Gortlin Tree was a sight to behold. It was so tall she wondered if it went on forever. A few people climbed the stairs spiraling the trunk, many calling greetings to Mahogen as they rose past.

"You're popular," she commented, still unsure of what to make of Mahogen. His horns felt menacing, but the kindness in his smiles reassured her.

"Princes tend to be," Mahogen returned.

"You're a prince?"

"Just like Aron, yes."

"*Aron*? He's not a… is he?"

"Did you not know? Aron is Caius's son."

Keegan looked over the edge of the basket. "Um… no, I didn't."

The basket stopped and Mahogen stepped onto the platform, offering a hand to help her.

Outside, the city was alive; large walkways were strung between the trees and houses nestled in the branches.

"Damn," she muttered. Even with the technology of her world, no one there would ever see the likes of this.

As they walked through the city, Mahogen pointed out places of interest. She feigned attentiveness, her mind preoccupied with Aron's ill-begotten secret. Soon they arrived at a tree with cream-colored leaves.

"The white leaves signify a children's home," Mahogen explained.

Inside was a large group of children—the youngest looking around three, the oldest seventeen or eighteen—sitting at a table, chattering over an evening meal.

"Behthany's in the kitchen," an older girl said preemptively.

In the kitchen, Bernot and the boys were talking to a woman with a rounded face that made her look as if she were a cheerful person and far too young to be running what was more or less an orphanage.

As Behthany was about to speak, a little boy ran into the kitchen, crying, "Bethsy, Bethsy!"

She gave them an apologetic look before dealing with the child, shortly sending him on his way. "Apologies 'bout that. You must be Keegan."

"Uh, yes, ma'am," Keegan responded. "And Bethsy, I presume."

"Bethsy is an annoying pet name from the children. I prefer Behthany."

"Yes, ma'am."

Bethsy lazily hit Bernot in the chest, walking away. "The manners on this one! Why can you not send me more like her?"

"She seems nice," Keegan commented.

"Just do not get on her bad side," Bernot warned. "The boys will show you to your accommodations. I will give you a few days to rest, but then I need to test your skills."

"Okey dokey."

Bernot gave her a perplexed look before giving a curt nod and walking out with Mahogen.

She was slow going up the stairs and, as soon as the door to their floor closed, she turned to the boys, a look of betrayal on her face.

"Why didn't you tell me?" she said, speaking to Aron specifically.

"Tell you what?" Aron asked.

"You're Caius's son."

"I told Jared not to trust him," Kade blurted.

"You knew and didn't say anything?" Keegan thundered.

"Well- I- there, there's this—" Kade stammered.

Aron came to his rescue. "He could not. My father spells his men so they cannot speak of me to those who do not already know of me and my brothers. Please do not hate me."

"I don't hate you," Keegan admitted. "It just would've been nice to know."

"Would you have trusted me?"

"When I first met you, no. But I didn't trust anyone then."

"How can you trust him now?" Kade seethed.

Coolly, Keegan turned to him. "The sins of the father are not the sins of the son."

A vein appeared in Kade's temple.

She shrugged. "And unless there's some other major secret he's not telling me, it is what it is."

Jared shot Kade a look.

Keegan put her hands on her hips. "Is there something *you* need to tell me, Kade?"

"No."

She gave him a skeptical look but didn't press. Noticing her saddlebag on the table, she asked, "So, where's my room?"

"Over here," Kade and Jared responded quicky. Too quicky.

Keegan scrutinized them. "Kade, you hate Aron, Aron, you hate Jared, and, Jared, you hate Kade. Do I have that right?"

"I don't hate either of them," Aron offered sheepishly.

"Brilliant. And let me guess, you each took a room in separate wings, so I have to choose between the three of you."

Silence.

Taking her bag, she walked away, choosing a random wing.

‡‡‡

"She is nothing like I expected," Mahogen declared as they walked.

"I cannot disagree," Bernot said. "The other leaders are going to have a field day with her."

"You summoned them?"

"What choice do I have? We need their support if we are going to wage and win this war."

"You have not told my father yet… I assume that is why you encouraged Lyerlly to keep me in the hospital?"

"Nothing gets past you." Bernot gave his friend a wry grin. "Tell the old man tonight, just keep her location to yourself. I do not need him messing up my plans."

Mahogen gave a hearty laugh. "What do you think he is going to do?"

"Try to marry her to you! I cannot save you again."

"The only person you did a favor for was yourself. You love her to bits and, I admit, you suit Lyerlly much better than I ever could."

It was Bernot's turn to laugh. "No woman has ever suited you."

"You know me too well."

"Why is he pushing you to marry anyway?"

"He wants me to get him a powerful pawn. And he wants to see grandchildren before his third century."

"Regardless of the fact you have not even reached your third decade?"

"That, and the other matter."

"Yes, well, tell him. And count on him not being happy."

Mahogen turned down a street, bidding him a fair evening.

Heading back to his office, Bernot considered taking the basket down. Instead, he took the stairs to prolong the inevitable. On his desk, he found four slips of paper. Essentially, they all read the same: the leaders of the other nations would be there within the fortnight.

‡‡‡

Lucas leaned against the wall, glaring at the others across the room. Against his warnings, all of them had consumed copious amounts of beer and were singing rowdily with the inn's other tenants. He brought his tankard to his lips, taking a small sip of the amber liquid.

A man he'd failed to notice took a seat opposite him.

"Go away."

"You should hear what I 'ave t' say first. I know your brother."

Lucas paused. "How?"

"He stayed with my grandfather an' I in Suttan. Came with a man named Kade and a girl named Keegan."

The mention of Keegan made Lucas pay attention. "Why should I care?"

The man shrugged. "I just thought you might like t' know he 's safe."

"Which brother?" Lucas questioned, noticing the singularity of the statement.

"Jared."

Nico was still unaccounted for—possibly dead. "Who are you?"

"Reven Broyker."

"You came over here for something other than to give me news of my brother."

457

"I also wanted t' offer you retribution."

"How?"

"With a single death."

"The king's?"

"Yes."

Lucas gave a loud laugh, earning a few curious looks. "Are you mad?"

"Hear me out. The castle 's riddled with secret passageways, most o' which the king 's unaware of. It 'll be easy t' sneak into his chambers and put a knife in 'im."

Lucas wanted to tell him no, that this was a *horrible* idea, but his mouth responded, "Yes."

"Can we count your other brother in?"

Lucas looked to Carter; Felix was helping him down another tankard. "No. We should leave now, while my companions will be none the wiser."

If he could rid the world of Caius, his family would be safe, would never have to run, never live in fear, never lose a friend again. He wanted to say goodbye, but someone would stop him, talk sense into him.

As he mounted his horse, laughter drifted from the inn; he forced himself to ignore it. He was out to make history, to make the world better.

‡‡‡

"I need something that will make your brother tell me what I need to know," Thaddeus said. "Something that suggests I already know or something to… shock him into giving up the information."

"You need to know about our parents' death."

Thaddeus took a seat across from Alyck.

"Before my brother experienced his Nanagin, we lived in the north. Our closest neighbors were miles away and we were self-reliant for the most part. Caius has always been a strong telepath with immense control over his powers, but, several months before his Nanagin, he began to lose that control and became moody and reserved. He never confided in me about what was happening.

"The day of his Nanagin, a group of bandits fell upon our house. Our parents were passive people and gave them what they wanted. But they wanted more and while our parents complied, my brother began to grow angry, and he lost control. The telepathic wave he released was painful..." Alyck gave an involuntary shudder. "That wave killed the bandits and our parents. It was only by some miracle I survived.

"Realizing what he had done, Caius relapsed and continued to lose more and more control. I do not remember most of what happened next, but I do recall a blinding light and a surge of wind. When I was finally able to focus, I was at our neighbor's house and had been babbling nonsense for a week straight. When I enquired about my brother, I was told his body had not been found. Caius was absent from our world for five months."

"What were your parents' names?" Thaddeus asked.

"Meloda and Braxten. Surprisingly, Caius is sentimental."

"What was he like after he returned?"

"Cold, calculating. And his control had returned."

"This has been most helpful; thank you," Thaddeus said softly.

CHAPTER 53

Lyerlly almost did not notice Okleiy Ustor—the Alvor king—slipping into the hospital. Bernot had told her he had been informed about Keegan, but she would not have guessed the king would come directly to her for information. Had she not known him so well, she might have assumed he was in a good mood.

"Lyerlly," Okleiy said, walking towards her with open arms to hug her. "Where is the girl?" he asked quietly into her ear.

Pulling away, she began making her rounds. "You will have to be more specific."

She did not need to look at him to know he was irritated.

"Keegan Digore. Where is she?"

"At a children's home I believe."

Okleiy grabbed her arm—not forcefully, but the threat was clear. "I tire of these games; where is she?"

Lyerlly shrugged out of his grip. "I don't know; you will have to ask Bernot. And even then, I cannot let you see her yet; she is much too weak still."

"If that were so, she would be here. Under your watchful gaze."

"Normally, yes. But circumstances have arisen to make us deviate. Okleiy, I know you want to use this girl for your own gains; I suggest you do not try to."

"Who are you to tell me what I can and cannot do in my own kingdom, *human*?"

"It was only a suggestion. Anything more you will need to take up with my husband." She did not give him a chance to refute her dismissal. *Bernot,* she tested.

Yes, darling, came his response.

Okleiy is coming.

✠✠✠

Bernot was quietly running figures for the upkeep of the Lazado when there was a rap on the door, mercifully pulling him from the work.

"Enter."

Okleiy Ustor traipsed in.

Though the Alvor king was like a second father to him, Bernot had found that did not stop him from trying to gain ground and power whenever he could.

"I assume you are here about Keegan," he said candidly.

Okleiy took a seat in one of the wooden chairs across from him. "Correct. Where is she?"

"I cannot disclose that currently."

"And why is that?"

"I am afraid you will try to sway her." As Okleiy began to speak, he played a dangerous game and cut him off. "I know what you will say, but a heavy burden weighs on her. It will do no good if someone has more hold than the others."

"At least until after the summoning."

"Yes, at least until then."

"But you have access to her."

"Only to test her skills in a few days hence. After which, contact will cease until the Council of Nations."

Okleiy looked at him skeptically before rising and leaving abruptly.

After the door had closed, Bernot leaned back in his chair, running a hand through his thick hair. He might have staved off the Alvor king for the moment, but he was tenacious; he would pry and search and bribe until he found the girl.

He rang the bell on his desk, prompting Olyver to come in.

"Please tell Hernando Barnsed I need him." He returned to his figures until the captain arrived.

Hernando was an older gentleman, his salt-and-pepper hair faded well back on his head. He had once been a strong as a bear, but a peaceful life and age had seen to the deterioration of his body. Though he might not be what he once was, Hernando was still one of the best swordsmen Bernot knew—and a trusted friend and advisor.

"Been ah long time since ya' called on me," Hernando said jovially.

"Times of peace make little use of soldiers. I take it you have heard of the mysterious girl who came into our midst about a week past."

"I 'ave. 'Ave heard a fair few rumors, too. Some say she is the king's renegade daughter. Others, an assassin sent for you, who was fool 'nough to fall on 'er own poisoned blade. 'N those 're just the sensible ones."

"None are true, but she is *very* important. I need you to place a guard on her. She is at Behthany Rhyen's with her three brothers."

"An' if the girl decides to leave the house?"

"Go with her. You are there to watch over her, not place her under house arrest. Who are your best men?"

"Halcyon Brygh, Rhyse Velaz, and Wexsley Grioux."

"Good, use them."

"May I ask why she is so important?"

"Yes, but I will decline to answer. Dismissed. Oh, ask Mahogen to help as well; I think he has taken a liking to the girl."

✝✝✝

"Why did you make Alyck become the Blind Prophet?" Thaddeus asked.

"Get out of my chambers," Caius barked exasperatedly, slamming his hands on his desk.

"I will if you tell me what I need to know. I would not be asking if it were not important," he persisted.

"There is absolutely no reason for you to know."

"You might be surprised," Thaddeus said. "Just so you know, Meloda and Braxten's deaths were not your fault."

The blood drained from Caius's face. "How… how do you know that?" He paused, cursing. "Alyck."

"Yes, but I am sure you have more to add to the story."

"It was this stupid bloodline."

Thaddeus nodded understandingly. Guilt had been eating at Caius. All Thaddeus had to do now was listen.

"Do you know how terrifying it is to see the future? How terrifying it is to see your mother's death? Your father's death? Your brother's death? The visions kept… playing in my head until they came true. Except for one—the only one I was able to prevent.

"Do you think I wanted to become king? I was more than happy with my life before all of *this* happened. I was content with being on the Council of Elders, content with being *normal*." Caius took a shuddering breath.

"Naturally, this has caused pent-up emotions. Start from the beginning, so I may understand," Thaddeus encouraged.

Caius looked like he wanted to be persistent in his unwillingness to talk, but the floodgates had already sprung a leak.

Taking the chair from his desk, he turned it to face Thaddeus. "Clearly, you already know how my parents died, but… there is a part of that story only I know: the reason I lost control. Several months before… the incident, I began having visions of the future. The first one was where I saw Alyck's death, though there were other trivial visions, like a slaughtered cow or a small injury. For months, I dreamt a bolt of lightning would cast him down. My nerves began to fray and at times I found myself losing control over my powers.

"The day the bandits attacked, that control was completely gone for a moment, and in that moment, I lost *everything*. The only thing that saved Alyck was my Nanagin.

"While in the other world, I was sure my brother was dead, and grief prevented me from using my powers. I survived and returned. My powers returned, along with the ability to cast spells. I eventually learned Alyck was alive, and I was so strong I was given a place on the Council of Elders.

"Everything was fine for a few years, but then *that* vision, amongst others, returned. I *had* to find a way to save Alyck—and myself, as I was beginning to lose control again. And I did. By making Alyck become the Blind Prophet, I ensured that he lived. That vision has never come to pass," Caius finished.

"Noble through and through," Thaddeus said kindly. Seeing there was nothing further to be said, he stood to take his leave.

"I expect you to keep this to yourself."

Thaddeus bowed his head, standing in the doorway. "Of course."

CHAPTER 54

The past three days had been long and boring, with Jared only emerging from his room at mealtimes—and even that was done begrudgingly.

Coming out for breakfast, he found Bernot and Mahogen sitting at the table.

"What do you want?" Jared asked, pouring a glass of water.

"I need to test Keegan's skills."

"Humph, I won't be the one to wake her."

"No need, she already knows we are here."

Jared paused. "I'm coming, too."

"Excellent. We will make an outing of it; Kade and Aron are coming too."

"All good," Keegan said coming from her room.

Downstairs, Wexsley, one of Keegan's guards, was waiting for them. He was a snively-looking man with watery eyes and large ears. Jared doubted he could do much in the way of fighting but supposed he wouldn't be there if that were true.

Wexsley took Keegan to the Gortlin Tree to descend in the basket, leaving the rest of them to climb down.

As they emerged from the trees onto the training field, a quiet overtook the practicing men. They slowly moved to the outskirts of the field, pushing against each other to ensure they had a good view.

"How many skill tests do you think you can do today?" Bernot asked Keegan.

She shrugged. "I dunno. I'll let you know when I've had enough. And I don't know how to do air, fire, or water."

Bernot scanned the crowd, before calling a man forward. "Do your best," was all he said to the man that would be Keegan's opponent before turning the field over.

Jared reached for his magic preemptively, should this go too far, and had the feeling Kade did likewise.

Keegan started slowly, lazily shooting a rock at her opponent, which he returned in kind. Rather than stopping his rock, she let it sail past; it wasn't her usual style, as she was more likely to try to show her strength.

Crossing his arms, Jared wondered what game she was playing.

Keegan raised the earth around her and idly began to shoot sections at the man. He focused on blocking the projectiles and failed to notice he was sinking into the ground. By the time he did, he was entrapped up to his knees. Seeing he'd realized her ploy, Keegan sunk him up to his shoulders instantly.

The man seemed surprised she'd defeated him so easily, though graciously accepted Keegan's hand when she reached out to help him up. As he melted back into the crowd, his faced turned to one of embarrassment. Snickers followed him and Jared felt a twinge of sympathy for the man. Had it been a fight that left both of them dripping in sweat, there would be no judgement; but Keegan had simply distracted and outsmarted the man.

Keegan's subsequent opponent was an Alvor. He could tell she knew she was beat, but in her usual stubborn manner, attempted to fight regardless. The match didn't last long.

Bernot stepped forward for the telepathy skill test. Jared was about to call for him to stop, as Keegan appeared to be at her threshold, but decided against it; she usually knew her limits—even if she liked to push them—and if he tried to save her, she'd surely have choice words later.

Bernot's face was calm while Keegan had her eyes screwed shut. She clenched her fists in determination and her eyes snapped open. Suddenly, Bernot was thrown across the field.

There was a hush as they all stared in shock before a few men rushed to help Bernot to his feet.

Bernot brushed them off and went to talk quietly to Keegan, her eyes wide as she shook her head and shrugged often. He offered her an arm, which she accepted, and they walked from the field.

Jared started to follow, but Wexsley stopped him. "I'm to walk you home."

"But… Keegan," Aron argued.

"Bernot will take her back later; there are things he wants to discuss with her."

Looking back to the field, he no longer could see her or Bernot. Aware that protesting was pointless, he followed Wexsley. He expected Kade to be fuming and it was then he realized he wasn't with them either.

"Where's Kade?" he hissed to Aron.

✝✝✝

"Are you Kade Tavin?" someone asked, pulling Kade away from Keegan's first skill test.

He turned to look at the man—the Alvor. He was tall, holding an air of grace. His brown hair was layered with leaf green streaks while large, while golden horns protruded from his head. "Who's asking?"

"The king of the Alvor."

His stomach dropped. It was never a good idea to insult an Alvor, even less if said Alvor was a king.

"Walk with me."

Kade stole a glance at Keegan.

"Do not worry, she is in good hands."

Feeling he had no choice, Kade followed.

Once they were away from the crowd, the king introduced himself. "I am Okleiy Ustor. I believe you know my son, Mahogen."

In no mood for pleasantries, he forgot who he was dealing with. "What do you want?"

"I want you to be a bit more gracious," Okleiy scolded.

He swallowed his pride. "Sorry, my… friends and I haven't been getting along of late."

"Yes, you and your brothers seem to be in discord over your sister. Though, you are the only one with the right to decide her fate as her *biological* brother."

"How do you know that?" he asked warily. "And Keegan decides her own fate."

"It is hard to miss," Okleiy huffed. "You look so much alike."

"Keep that observation to yourself. Please."

"Of course. Under one stipulation, you join me for dinner tonight."

There had to be something the king wanted; Alvor were notoriously tricky.

"Sure. We'll join you tonight."

"No, no, only you."

"Fine."

"Excellent, I will have Mahogen escort you."

Turning to head back to the training field, Kade found the tests had finished and changed his path to take him to a ladder. Once reaching where one should've been, he realized he had no way to access it.

"Let me," Okleiy said, appearing and placing a hand on the tree.

Kade didn't bother thanking him and began to climb. Once he had struggled to make his way back to the children's home, he found Jared and Aron sitting at the table anxiously.

"Where have you been?" Jared snapped.

"Places," he answered snidely. "Where's Keegan?"

"If you'd stayed, you would know," Jared fumed, storming to his room.

"Where is she?" he asked Aron.

"No idea; she went off with Bernot."

✞✞✞

Bernot took Keegan to the Gortlin Tree and was surprised she had no qualms leaving her brothers behind. His head was still pounding from the attack that had sent him across the field. Never had he seen, or experienced, something like that and he was curious to know how she had done it.

Reaching the tree, he was about to call down the basket when Keegan stopped him, insisting she was strong enough to climb the stairs. And she did manage, even if she was slow going.

Sitting at his desk, he took a long inhale before beginning. "I see you are well-versed in earth magic and have a good start on life magic. As for telepathy…"

"Yeah, sorry about that," she said, rubbing the back of her neck. "I'm not really sure how I did that."

She knows she is powerful but does not know just how much power she contains. "How did you come to this world?"

"Hell if I know. Magic probably."

"Do you trust Jared, Aron, and Kade?"

She raised an eyebrow. "What, you afraid they kidnapped me or something?"

He gave her an austere look.

"They might be childish and hard-headed, but they're good guys. Aron helped me escape from Caius, Jared took me in, and Kade, in his own twisted way, helped us avoid the Vosjnik."

"You still did not answer the question. Do you trust them?"

"I wouldn't've stuck with 'em if I didn't."

"You are free to roam the city after I give you your yewnes."

"Yewnes?"

"It is what will allow you to access the hidden ladders and doorways of the city."

"Ah."

"I do ask that you stay away from Okleiy Ustor until the Council of Nations."

Keegan gave him a muddled look. "Couple of questions; who is Okleiy Ustor and what's the Council of Nations?"

"Okleiy is the king of the Alvor. And the Council of Nations is where the leaders or representatives from every nation convene. In this case, our reason is you."

"'Cause we're the Children of Prophecy." She stifled a yawn. "If there isn't anything else, do you mind if I go? I'm beat."

"Beat?"

"Tired."

"Of course; let me walk you back." Bernot picked up the bag next to his desk, slinging it over his shoulder.

"What's in the bag?" she questioned as he ushered her through the door.

"Your weapons."

"I bet the boys'll be excited to get them back. They'll probably use 'em to stick each other."

Bernot chuckled to hide his worry at the potential verity.

Upstairs at the children's home, Aron sat at the table reading a book.

"There you are," he said with relief.

Bernot extracted Aron's bow, which he took excitedly.

"You can leave the rest," Keegan told him. "We'll distribute things."

"I still need to give you yewnes," Bernot reminded her, taking her hand. He muttered a few words in the Old Language and, when he pulled away, a small dot marked the side of her palm.

"What'd you do?" she asked, examining the mark. "That wasn't elemental magic."

"That was a spell," Bernot told her, repeating the process with Aron.

"But you would need to be a spellcaster…" Aron trailed off.

Bernot smiled, then went into Kade and Jared's rooms.

On his way out, he stopped to talk to Behthany. "If you see Okleiy around here, let me know."

"Sweetie, if my father comes 'round, the whole city is going to bovestun well know about it," she told him.

‡‡‡

For several days, Nico had noticed a strange scent on Braxton, and it'd taken him some time to place it. Once he'd realized Braxton smelled like the griffins, he decided to confront him about it. But to do so, he needed to catch him in the stables and had therefore spent the last few days looking for the secret passageway leading there.

So far, he'd found just about every other hidden corridor, as he only roughly recalled where the entrance was. Most of the passages led to empty rooms, though one led to the coffers. He was tempted to take as much gold as he could stuff into his pockets, then realized he had nothing to spend it on—and should he be caught, only bad things would come of it.

As always, he checked over his shoulder to make sure he was alone before he began running his hands along the wall, eventually finding a divot. The wall scraped along the floor and taking a torch from a sconce, he made his way through the passage.

The trip was much easier with light, and he wondered how Braxton navigated so well blind. Coming to the top of the stairs, he pulled a lever and another door opened smoothly. Peering around the stone, he saw Braxton sitting on the floor, stroking Myrish, who sat next to him.

Myrish turned to look at Nico, drawing Braxton's attention.

Lazily the prince said, "I knew your curiosity would hold you back only so long. Providing no one outside my family knows you're aware of the griffins, you are welcome to visit anytime."

Not the response he'd expected.

Closing the door, he came to sit next to Braxton. "I didn't come for the griffins."

Braxton raised an eyebrow.

"I came to see you."

"How did you figure I would be here?"

"You smelled like them. It took me a while to place the scent, but then I recognized it: feathers and dust with a hint of iron and wind."

Braxton laughed. "What does wind smell like?"

Freedom, a griffin with lackluster silver feathers answered.

"I'm sorry, but I don't remember your names," Nico said sheepishly.

Our introductions were hasty, feel no shame. I am Niyth.

The other griffins re-introduced themselves and Nico committed their names to heart. *I am glad to properly make your acquaintance,* he said, speaking to them telepathically for the first time.

We see your studies with the telepaths are going well, Oxren said. His feathers were black and mottled with white.

Though Nico was not a telepath, Braxton had deemed it important he know how to communicate with those who were, as well as how to safeguard his mind and secrets.

Nico was surprised they knew about his daily life, yet somehow not. "Why have you been spending all your time here?" he asked Braxton.

"Adult things," Braxton said, giving a sad smile. "Now, run along, tomorrow's training is going to be trying."

CHAPTER 55

It felt right having his sword belted around his waist again, but it was even more comforting to have the knife tucked in his boot. Kade walked beside Mahogen, dusk settling around them.

"Be courteous when talking to my father," Mahogen warned. "He can be a bit *touchy* with humans."

"He'll take what he gets from me," Kade said snidely. "I have no intention of playing games."

"Games may not be what you want, but games are what you will get. We Alvor live for plays on words, so be careful when accepting a deal. It may not be exactly what you think."

"Why aren't you like that?"

"I choose not to be. I find it only sows mistrust and animosity."

They stopped outside a massive house nestled in the fork of a tree.

"And here is where I leave you," Mahogen said, motioning to the door.

"Aren't you joining us?" Kade questioned, suddenly realizing how helpful the prince might be.

"No, I was not invited."

Apprehensively, Kade stepped forward and knocked on the door; it seemed an eternity before someone answered. He was greeted by a servant and shown to the dining room.

A massive chandelier hung from the ceiling, the crystals sending rainbows scattering across the walls. A long table was set for four, Okleiy sitting at the head with a woman on either side. One was older, whom Kade took to be Okleiy's wife. The other was young and stunning, her lips the color of a ruby. When she smiled, she revealed straight, pearly teeth. High cheekbones gave her an elegant look and long, honey-colored tresses were piled on her head, the tips of two golden horns protruded from her hair.

"Heh-hem," Okleiy said, bringing his attention back. "This is my wife Aster and my daughter Shyre."

"Pleasure to meet you," he said, more to Shyre than Aster.

"Take a seat."

He hurried to sit beside Shyre, the scent of pine emanating from her.

A plate of quail and vegetables was set before him, the smell making his mouth water. The quail tasted magnificent and after a few bites, he remembered to make small talk.

"Shyre… you…" His brain chose that moment to stop working.

Shyre looked to her father disappointed, "I hoped this one would remember how to speak."

"—are beautiful," Kade blurted. As soon as the words left his mouth, he regretted them. Cassidy was hardly with the old gods, and he was already admiring someone else.

"How sweet of you," she said.

Her voice had a hypnotic quality that somehow calmed him.

"I'm sure your husband tells you that every day."

"He would, if I had one."

Kade melted at the words.

"Make no rash promises," Aster said preemptively.

"I think it would be a fine match," Okleiy spoke up. "Of course, I will need something from you though."

There it was, the real reason for this dinner. "And what would that be?"

"I have been trying for some time to find Mahogen a wife. It has been a hard task, but it seems he has taken a liking to your sister. I would propose a union between them."

Kade laughed, causing the Alvors to frown. "She'll never accept."

"You can make her."

"Yeah, just like I can make the sun rise."

"I recommend you find a way."

"And if I don't?"

"There are numerous people who are calling for your head," Okleiy said calmly. "And I would feel bad if Caius was not reunited with his son. I know it is what I would want."

Kade wanted nothing more than to fly across the table. He couldn't care less about the threat to Aron, but those made to him weren't taken lightly.

"I protect my family fiercely," Okleiy continued.

"There's only so much I can do to convince her."

"You are her brother. As the head of your family, she must listen to you."

"But she—"

"Will listen to you. And, of course, this will stay between us until the vows are exchanged. I would have them said the day after the Council of Nations. Now, let us talk of other matters. How are you liking the city?"

He was forced to make idle chatter, answering questions curtly and with little enthusiasm. Beauty had lost its charm and he felt like a rat in a cage. None too soon he was saying goodnight. Shyre walked him to the door and gave him a parting kiss that felt like a punch.

The sky was dark, a quarter moon adding its pale light to the lanterns along the street, and he walked away from the house quickly, pulling at the collar of his shirt, already feeling steel against his throat. He had no idea what he was going to do, but he was going to need a massive stroke of luck to pull it off.

‡‡‡

If he thought Tratoleck was a big city, he was mistaken; the city of Agrielha was monstrous in comparison and Lucas was amazed so many people could fit in one place. Reven seemed unperturbed and had no qualms with the inn they were boarding in that possessed a certain criminal element.

They picked a dark corner of the taproom and settled in. Lucas hadn't asked much about Reven, and his companion had done likewise.

Reven glanced around, making sure no one was paying them any attention and pulled a piece of parchment from his pocket, flattening its creases on the table.

"Time t' come up with a plan."

"What's this?" Lucas probed, trying to decipher the squiggles.

"A map o' the castle's secret passageways."

"Where did you get this?"

"I drew it. My grandfather made me memorize these tunnels as a child. I despised 'im for it at the time, but who knew it 'd be useful?"

"Explains why it looks like vite," Lucas muttered, wondering what kind of family Reven came from.

"There 're several entrances outside the castle, but only one starting in the city." He pointed to a place on the map. "Here."

"You act like this means something to me. I can't make heads or tails of this royiken mess."

Reven gave him a frustrated look. "You do n't need t' be able to' read it. Now, the problem is, I do n't know where within this inn the entrance is."

"Wait, the entrance is *here*?"

"I just said that. For now, our problem 's finding the tunnel and doin' so without raising suspicion. Any ideas?"

Lucas's side began to throb as he was reminded of Elza's harebrained scheme. He got the feeling this might have a similar outcome. "I won't help you. This plan's going to get me killed."

"You can n't leave now."

"Why not?"

"You do n't know how t' get to the Lazado," Reven stated plainly, still looking over the map. "If you help me, I 'll take you there."

"I'm sure I can find a Kojote to take me."

Reven gave a snort of laughter. "Good luck. It 's hard enough t' find one in any other city; forget 'bout finding one here."

Lucas pulled the knife from his boot and held it against Reven's leg where he knew the big artery laid. "I won't help you." Dismay filled him when his hand, of its own accord, sheathed the knife.

Reven turned his wrist over, exposing his elemental mark. "Do n't threaten me. I will n't make you help me, but I would suggest it."

"Then you've played my hand for me," Lucas snarled.

"No, I 'ave simply presented you with the only option of getting to the Lazado—*and* back to your brothers."

"You'll pay for this."

"Not anytime soon."

✠✠✠

"Why does no one understand what causes a Blind Prophet to begin acquiring their powers?" Thaddeus fumed, leaning back heavily in the chair. Beside him the fire in the hearth crackled calmly.

"Possibly because no one understands the magic surrounding it," Alyck suggested.

Thaddeus agreed. "I might be able to figure it out if I had the original spell."

"I can help with that."

"You know the original spell used to create the Blind Prophet?"

Alyck gave him a wry smile. "No."

"Out with it," Thaddeus said, not in the mood for games. It was often hard to remember Alyck was centuries older than him—especially as he still acted the age, sometimes younger, that he looked.

Alyck went to the bedroom, returning with a piece of parchment. "I think this what you need."

"Where did you get it?"

"From a very dear friend." There was sorrow in the words. "Now, I think I shall retire for the night."

Thaddeus nodded in acknowledgement, his attention already on the spell. It was lengthy, taking up most of the page and well thought out; it took a few times of reading to fully understand all its facets.

He already knew the Blind Prophet was linked to the ruling bloodline, but the interesting bit was that as long as someone of the lineage remained alive, the Prophet would continue to live. Thaddeus thought about the implications; Caius could be removed without Alyck suffering the ramifications. And the next king did not have to be one of his sons either.

However, there was no mention of how the next Prophet was chosen, aside from the fact they would come from Angela's bloodline. And there was no mention of what factors caused them to begin obtaining their powers. From Caius's story, it seemed it had taken years, and, at one point, the process had ceased. He hoped the next monarch was years away from taking the throne, otherwise Braxton was in for a rude awakening. The fact Braxton was coming into his powers implied Caius and his kin would not be long for this world

‡‡‡

There was a knock and Keegan called, "Come in."

Aron poked his head through the doorway. "Want to go for a walk?"

She looked out the window to see sunset darkening the sky. "Why not?"

In the common room downstairs, Halcyon had to dislodge a few children to chase after them.

"Let's lose him," Keegan said mischievously.

Aron raised an eyebrow, but, taking her hand, began to run.

When they finally stopped, Keegan clutched at a stitch on her side, laughing, while fireflies danced around them like grounded stars. Pulling her hand from Aron's, she chased after the insects; after catching one, she showed it to him. The firefly crawled across her finger before taking flight with a parting flash.

"I used to do this all the time as a kid," she said happily. It was one of the few times she hadn't felt the weight of being an orphan.

"It looks like fun," Aron commented shyly.

"Wait, have you never caught fireflies before?"

Aron rubbed the back of his neck. "My father never allowed it."

"Oh, now you have to!"

He smiled sheepishly. "How do I do this?"

"See the bug and catch it. Just make sure you cup your hands, otherwise you're gonna have a squeeshed bug."

Stepping back, she watched Aron attempt to catch a lightning bug; he was close, though was unprepared for the light to disappear. Once he got the hang of it, he caught them as well as she.

They chased the fireflies until true stars replaced them and then started back to the children's home; it wasn't long before they could see the children's home. Out front, Halcyon paced, likely waiting for them.

Aron pulled Keegan into a side alley to avoid being spotted and she wound up pushed against the wall. Aron stood above her, his hands on the wall beside her shoulders. Under different circumstances, the situation might have felt threatening. But not with Aron. Never with Aron.

Keegan pressed her lips together to stifle a giggle. Mirth danced in Aron's eyes, and she suddenly found herself swimming in their blue depths. And maybe it was her imagination, but Aron seemed to be returning the expression.

A door slammed shut somewhere nearby, snapping Keegan out of her reverie. Her hands were resting on Aron's chest, and she gently pushed him away. Confusion registered in his eyes.

Not knowing what to say, Keegan ducked under his arm and ran back to the children's home, pausing in the doorway to see him staring after her. Halcyon had already started on a tirade, but she ignored him.

Leaving the door open, she hurried up the stairs, locking herself in her room. Sitting against the door, running her hands through her hair, conflicting emotions bubbled through her.

✝✝✝

How could she ever want someone like him? A liar, a son of Caius. That was all Aron could think. And it amazed him that Shiloh had seen past all his short comings. But something had changed recently, and now he was wondering how anyone else could do that too. And how could he let go of Shiloh so easily? *When* had he started to let her go?

Slowly, he returned to the children's home, taking a very round-about path. The branches holding the city were dark, but along the walkways lanterns had been lit for the night owls.

Halcyon reappeared as he reached the doorway, angrily asking, "Why the royik did you two run off?"

Aron shrugged. He had simply been following Keegan's whirlwind.

On their floor, all was quiet. Though all were not asleep from the light seeping underneath the doors of Kade and Jared's doors. Walking to Keegan's door, he raised a hand to knock, then paused. Turning on his heels, he went to his room and, with nothing better to do, crawled into bed.

He intended to sleep, but his mind had other ideas, replaying what could have been, both long ago and now. But even in his imagination he resented how much the thoughts brought him joy. He should still be mourning Shiloh. Shouldn't he? Did he even deserve happiness?

The door opened and a figure slipped in; he wondered if it was Kade finally coming to stick a knife in his chest.

"You awake?" Keegan whispered.

He breathed a sigh of relief. "Yes."

She crawled into the bed and sat cross-legged beside him. "Can we talk?" Without light, she was nothing more than a shadow. And he could not help but think of her as catlike—unabashed and shrouded in mystery.

"Sure," he mumbled, sitting up.

"Look," Keegan began, "I like you… as a friend." She almost sounded like she was trying to convince herself.

Aron was not sure what was being left unsaid. Yet, his heart soared that Keegan simply valued him—that she trusted him. It was… comforting to have someone again in his life who genuinely cared for him.

"I… understand."

A part of him longed for that something more he had had with Shiloh. But he doubted he would ever find that kind of connection again. Not with who he was. Not with who he was the son of.

He could not see the expression on Keegan's face, but he hoped it was soft.

"Who'd you leave behind?" she asked without warning.

"What do you mean?"

"I dunno. It just feels like… like you're missing someone."

"I did not leave her behind," he whispered. "She was murdered."

"I'm sorry," she said softly, her hands wrapping around his. "I understand. My family isn't dead, but they might as well be."

He was confused, then realized what she meant; she would never see her anyone from the other world again. "I never thought of you going through that."

Keegan quickly turned the subject away from herself. "What was her name?"

"Shiloh," Aron choked.

"Tell me about her."

"She was beautiful, and kind… and mine. Wonderfully mine."

They continued to talk well into the night, each word lifting a weight from his shoulders he had not known was there. By the time they fell into silence, the moon was no longer visible outside the window.

Aron was not sure when it happened, but Keegan fell asleep beside him.

"Thank you for letting me talk. You will never know what it means to me," he whispered, draping an arm over her stomach, and pulling her close.

In response, her fingers twined with his.

CHAPTER 56

Braxton looked away as his father was stabbed. When he opened his eyes again, he was in his room, morning light coming through the window—Caius presumably alive. Throwing back the covers, he dressed and made his way to his father's chambers.

"Enter," he was bid after knocking.

Braxton did so and paused; something was different. He could not put his finger on it, but this was not the man he knew.

Caius seemed nervous and gave him an unsure smile. "What do you need... son?"

"I... never mind."

"All right," Caius said, averting his gaze.

Out in the hall, Braxton lingered, brows knitted together. So much was not as it should be that he did not know where to begin. The wheels in his head turned, but nothing was coming of it.

When Caius had commanded him to train the griffins, he had been too afraid to fly with them. Somehow, they had cajoled him into promising to let them soar no later than July twenty-second. He had put it off as long as he could, but the day had come to live up to his word.

Inside the stable, the griffins were waiting excitedly, anticipation hanging in the air like static and poison.

"You promised to behave yourselves," Braxton said, approaching Myrish, his heart beating a fast pace against his ribs.

Believe me, I will, the bronze griffin replied.

The griffin stamped his feet impatiently as Braxton situated a saddle on his back. Likely Myrish was berating him for treating him like a horse, but Braxton needed something to hold onto. Something he could strap himself into so he would not fall. Before unlocking the chain from around the griffin's neck he pulled back the iron grate over the opening in the wall.

"No funny business," he said, as the shackle around Myrish's neck tumbled to the ground.

Myrish did not answer, but the waves of joy he felt were enough that Braxton knew he would do as promised. Taking a breath, he pulled himself into the saddle, feeling the beast's muscles tense. He quickly strapped his legs in before giving Myrish the go-ahead.

There was just enough time for him to wind his hands into the leather thongs at the crest of the saddle before the world froze for a moment. Then the griffin was running, his talons clacking against the floor like knives. Myrish leapt through the opening, thrusting them into nothingness, and Braxton's stomach rose into his chest, pushing against his throat.

The ground rushed towards them, and Braxton closed his eyes, terrified Myrish was too weak to stay aloft. There was a jerk as the griffin unfurled his wings and they soared on a current into the clouds.

You can let go now, Myrish told him.

Braxton slowly released his iron-clad grip on Myrish's feathers. When his hands had moved from the saddle to the griffin he could not say. Looking down, he was amazed by the beautiful scene below.

The grass was a magnificent green and spots of whites and yellow signified patches of wildflowers. Clouds floated through the sky, giving the blue a milky hue in the distance while the sun warmed his skin in a friendly embrace. Agrielha proper, up against its winding river, was a peaceful sight to the east—seemingly frozen in time for their perch on high.

Braxton's heart beat fast with excitement, threatening to leap from his chest, and the wind against his body was refreshing. There was something about flying that was exuberating, liberating. Here, the only prisons were the ones he created.

A humming sense of bliss came from Myrish, and he sank into the feeling.

When the castle became small behind them, he reluctantly told Myrish to turn back. All he had to do was let the griffin keep going and every bit of pain would melt away. But he could not leave the other griffins behind—nor Nico.

Upon their return, the other griffins excitedly talked to Myrish in their wild language of clicks and caws and chirps.

As he unsaddled Myrish, he noticed someone in the stable. "Nico?"

The boy came from one of the stalls.

"What are you doing here?"

"I wanted to see the griffins," the boy answered with only the barest hint of sheepishness.

"You care for them?"

He shrugged. "I suppose."

Braxton smiled. "Good, I have a job for you."

A spark flared in Nico's blue eyes. "What?"

"Come back tomorrow and see. Now, I am sure Eamon has something for you to practice. And if I catch you here again during training hours without permission, I will ban you."

The boy bit his cheek, seeming to doubt he would hold true to his threat, but left without another word.

What do you have planned for him? Crowlin asked.

Something you will like, was all he told her.

‡‡‡

Two weeks had passed quietly and Kade seldom saw the others. All interactions with Keegan were awkward, at least they felt like it for him, as he had yet to tell her she was going to marry Mahogen. There were times he tried to tell her, but the timing never felt right. And he dreaded the moment the time was right. Or when he had no other options.

When he was not hiding in his room, he was roaming the city or training. Swordplay was the best at helping him forget the predicament, but only so long as an opponent pressed him. The moment his weapon froze, all his worries came flooding back.

Emerging from his room, he had planned to go to the training field and was surprised to find Wexsley climbing the stairs. Usually the guards left them to their own devices and stayed on the lower floors.

"I'm here to take you to the summoning," Wexsley huffed. "Please dress in the clothes you were given."

His stomach dropped. He was out of time.

"I'll get Keegan," Kade managed to mutter.

He wiped his palms on his pants before knocking on her door. No response. He knocked again, louder. "Keegan." Nothing. "Keegan!"

She pulled open the door, rubbing the sleep from her eyes, and it appeared she was wearing one of Aron's shirts—without any trousers.

"What?" she snapped in the way people suddenly roused from sleep could.

His mind blanked as anger bubbled in his throat.

Keegan snapped her fingers. "Hellooo, Earth to Kade."

He pulled her into the room. "What are you doing with him?"

"What?"

"You're wearing Aron's shirt; why?"

"Dude, it's my pajamas. Bethsy gave it to me."

"Your what?"

"It's what I sleep in. What do you need?"

"It's time for the summoning."

The color faded from Keegan's features, leaving her freckles standing in contrast like reverse stars, as she stepped back, allowing him entry into the room. With a shaky breath, she pulled a pristine, white dress from the closet. Knowing her, it wouldn't remain that way for long.

"I need to talk to you," he said

"Can it wait?"

"Not really."

"Face the door."

He did so, heart beating wildly. "You know Mahogen?"

"Yeah…?"

"…You're going to marry him. Tomorrow."

She gave a nervous laugh.

"I'm not joking."

"What?" she exclaimed.

He turned to face her. "You have to marry him."

"Like hell I do! Who the fu—"

Kade came as close to pleading as he'd allow himself. "Keegan, please. You *have to* marry Mahogen."

"Why?" When he didn't respond, she snapped, "Kade!"

"Okleiy's going to hand Aron and I over to Caius if you don't."

Red flooded her face. "I'm gonna kill him. I swear to God, I'm gonna kill him." She eyed him. "How long have you known?"

"Couple of weeks."

"A couple of weeks!" Keegan shrieked.

"I'm sorry."

"Sorry ain't gonna cut it." She angrily pulled open the door. "Wexsley, I need to talk to Bernot. *Now*."

"He's unavailable until after the summoning," Wexsley told her, taken aback by her anger. "Kade, get dressed, the leaders don't like to be kept waiting."

"It's important," Keegan persisted.

"It's not possible until after the summoning."

Keegan turned back to Kade. "Get ready, we'll deal with this later. Provided I don't frickin' strangle you first. And keep this between us. Lord knows Aron and Jared'll only make matters worse."

‡‡‡

The leaders and their adjutants sat around the concentric table, talking quietly amongst themselves. Bernot studied them carefully, wondering who would cause the most trouble. None knew why they were here—except for himself, Okleiy, and their aides. He had no doubt the other leaders would trample each other to get to Keegan once they learned of her.

We're here, Wexsley informed him.

May we begin? Tahrin, the dragons' representative, said impatiently, speaking telepathically so all present could hear.

"We may." Bernot came to stand in the center of the congregation. "For centuries, we have hidden behind the border to evade Caius. We have all but given up on defeating him. Our only hope was—"

"The Child of Prophecy," Garne Skaagg, the Torrpeki representative finished, already beginning to understand.

"Precisely."

"Do you mean to tell us you found the Child of Prophecy?" Atlia Mahiako questioned, leaning forward.

The heir to the Merfolk throne was young and untried, and Bernot was interested to see if she possessed her mother's intellect. Siene had not given a reason as to why her daughter was present in her stead, but it might be a blessing if Atlia was willing to join the cause.

"Not just one," Bernot told her, "all four."

The other leaders looked at him skeptically, most trying to figure out the game he was playing.

I see no children, Tahrin stated tetchily.

489

Bernot called for the doors to open. Keegan took a moment, before shyly joining him in the center of the room, her brothers trailing behind her.

It was hard to believe these were the same people he had taken in just weeks past. The boys were clean-shaven and bathed, no longer frenzied-looking. Keegan was much stronger, a determined air about her—something that had not changed. He prayed *she* was not going to be the instigator today.

"May I present Keegan Digore, Kade Tavin, Jared Sieme, and Aron Alagard."

Kade and Aron received glares, their names being well-known.

What makes you think these are the Children of Prophecy? Tahrin said, speaking to only the leaders.

Keegan stared at Tahrin with a look of astonishment.

Close your mouth, the dragon snarled at her.

"I- I- I'm s-sorry," she stammered. "I've just never seen a dragon before. You're really fucking cool."

Tahrin held her head a little higher. *Where is your proof?* Her tone was softer now; flattery went a long way with dragons.

"Keegan," Bernot held out a hand for her arm.

Sighing, she gave it to him, and he showed the leaders the marks on her wrist.

The Buluo adjutant, a youth with wily, wolfish features, vaulted over the table and snatched her arm. Thankfully, Keegan refrained from clouting the boy, who began trying to remove the marks. When he could not, he snapped, "Prove it. Prove you can use all the elements."

Snatching her hand back, Keegan caused a column of earth to rise. She looked to the Buluo with a sly smile and a look of discomfort overtook the boy's face as he began scratching his armpits and hooting.

Garne chuckled unabashedly while Atlia was more tactful, only letting a grin flash across her features.

Once Keegan released him, the Buluo slinked back to his seat, eyes diverted towards the floor.

"That was two," Rangi, the Buluo representative said.

"I can't do any of the others yet," Keegan admitted.

"Then what use are you?"

"She can learn," Bernot said, rounding the table to retake his seat.

✠✠✠

They stood in the center of the room while the leaders talked, and it looked like things were just getting started. Each leader was vying for control of Keegan and seemed to have forgotten about him, Aron, and Kade. Once it was established that they obeyed the laws of magic, they became of little interest.

"She should train under us," Garne, the Torrpeki representative, argued. "She is obviously most advanced in earth magic. We should focus on perfecting this element."

"No," Atlia argued. "If she is already versed there, teach her something new."

Jared shifted on his feet beginning to feel anger—though it wasn't his own. Glancing at Keegan, her fists and jaw were clenched.

He nudged her, whispering, "Are you okay?"

"Shut up," she said through gritted teeth.

He gave her a questioning look but realized she hadn't been speaking to him.

"Shut up," she repeated slightly louder, then in a normal voice, "Shut up."

Bernot grew quiet, concern sparking in his obsidian eyes.

"Shut up," Keegan said loudly.

Tahrin heard and shifted her attention, *Excuse me?*

"Shut up!"

A snap of mental energy crashed into Jared and, from the looks on the leaders' faces, they'd felt it too.

"What gives any of you the right to decide what *I* do?" she yelled. "I'm getting real tired of being voluntold."

Lower— the dragon started.

"Shut up! None of you have any control over me," Keegan said, beginning a tirade. "I don't have to do jack-shit—let alone kill Caius. But it seems the goddamn universe has other ideas. So, here's what's gonna happen; y'all can't get across the border and, until you can, I'm useless. I'm gonna spend six months training in each element. Unless y'all can figure out a way across the border, at which time, we'll re-access and speed up the process. All y'all have do is decide which order it's in. I'd recommend going in a circle: earth, water, air, fire, life, or in reverse. Take your pick, I don't give a damn," she finished, storming off.

"Where do you think you are going?" Okleiy demanded.

"Away from you idiots. Oh, and I'm not marrying Mahogen. And Okleiy, if you *ever* threaten my friends again, I swear to God I'll rip your fucking head off."

"Do not threaten me," the Alvor snarled.

"That wasn't a threat, that was a goddamned promise." She didn't give them time to stop her again.

Mahogen gave the tension a moment before chasing after her.

When Jared started to go after her as well, Tahrin demanded, *Who gave you permission to leave?*

"Kee—" he started.

Stay where you are.

He considered disobeying, but the look the dragon gave him said it would be unwise.

‡‡‡

Inside the griffin stable, the griffins waited for them, along with two new additions, half the size of their compatriots and covered in dull brown feathers. In places, the fledglings were beginning to show with their true colors.

"Who are they?" Nico approached the newcomers, letting them smell his hand.

I am Ima, a feminine voice announced, coming from the griffin with the teal tint beginning to emerge.

I am Harker, said the one with dark golden feathers mingling within the brown.

"Why haven't I seen them before?"

"Ima and Harker are hatchlings," Braxton explained. "They were kept in the nursery until yesterday."

"What's the job you have for me?"

"I am too big to fly with the hatchlings, so I want you to train with them."

"*Me*?" Never in his wildest dreams had Nico imagined flying. "Of course; I'd be honored."

Braxton smiled. "Let us get them tacked up then."

Saddling the griffins was much like saddling Brewer, but easier, as the griffins didn't tower over him like the Clydesdale had. Harker tried to aid in his saddling, but often just made it more difficult. Yet, rather than getting frustrated, Nico found himself laughing.

When he climbed onto Harker's back, anticipation, dread, and excitement mixed with his blood. The griffin carefully made his way towards the ledge, sticking his head into the sky, sniffing the wind.

Oxren, Braxton on his back, barreled past. Keeping his wings tight, Oxren plummeted towards the ground. Just before crashing was imminent, he unfurled his wings, skimming over the grass.

Nico leaned forward carefully and, processing how far up they were, jerked back quickly. Gulping, he encouraged Harker to follow.

As they sank, Harker pumped his wings and, though they kept falling, it wasn't at an alarming rate. Still, Nico's heart bounced in his chest while his stomach sloshed about.

Oxren rushed past them, giving a caw, and Nico could hear Braxton laughing and realized how exuberating this must be—well, when not on the wings of a fledgling.

Harker did his best to keep up but was too inexperienced to manage all the graceful maneuvers. It wasn't long before he was exhausted and Braxton saw them returned safely to the griffin stables before Oxren darted away again.

As he sat with the griffins—Harker asleep and Ima with her head in his lap—Nico realized he'd gained that which he thought he'd lost forever: family. He might not be of the same race as the griffins or the same blood as Braxton, but they were family.

CHAPTER 57

Every time Keegan thought she'd pushed her anger back into its bottle, it broke free again. She was well beyond pissed.

"Keegan," Mahogen called.

"What?" she roared, turning on him.

"Walk with me," he invited, offering her his arm.

She crossed her arms tightly across her chest. "To where?"

"Find out."

To her own disbelief, she took his arm.

"Where are you going?" Rhyse, one of her guards, questioned breathlessly as he, Wexsley, and Halcyon caught up to her.

She pushed Mahogen as a cue to lead the way. "On a walk."

Her guards didn't argue, and she was glad, as she was dangerously close to slapping the next person who told her what to do.

Slowly the trees began to decrease in size, soon dropping away entirely. They were in a small clearing with a pond in the center. Fragile waterlilies floated on the surface and birds flitted between branches, singing soft melodies.

"Welcome to The Royal Koi Pond," Mahogen said once they reached the water's edge.

Large red, white, and orange fish swam serenely through the water, and she felt her ire draining away. She gently squeezed the Alvor's arm in a silent thanks.

Mahogen placed a hand on her head. "I am glad this has calmed you, but I need to get back to the summoning."

"Okay." She took a seat and returned her attention to the koi.

After a moment, the prince sat beside her. "Eh, they do not need me."

She smiled and together they watched the koi swim lazily. Keegan wasn't sure how long they sat, but a sudden tiredness overtook her. Finding she couldn't resist it, she lay down on the grass and slipped into an easy sleep.

✠✠✠

It had been ages since Keegan had stormed out—and the leaders were still deliberating. Aron was used to political proceedings, but even he was beginning to get frustrated.

"We should do as the child suggests," Atlia said coolly.

That was no suggestion, Tahrin stated angrily.

"Suggestion, demand, order," the Mermaid shrugged, "what difference does it make?"

"Her plan is the best idea we have," Bernot added. "I call for a vote. Those in favor." He raised his hand.

Atlia and Garne joined him.

Aron hoped the Alvor would be on their side, but Keegan's threat had dashed that.

"You do not have the majority," Rangi said.

Aron raised his hand. "Yes, he does."

"You have no say," Rangi sneered.

"I believe we do," he argued. "This is our fate as well and we still have the power to walk away."

You would not, Tahrin tested, a sliver of fear hidden in her booming voice.

"They would," Bernot said. "These three men would willingly give all they have and more to keep their sister safe. Do not underestimate them."

Garne smiled, revealing his fangs. "Then it appears we have reached a decision."

Aron gave a mocking bow before turning to leave but was surprised to find the doors would not open.

You are dismissed, Tahrin said in a needling tone.

Kade pushed him aside and began pulling at the door.

"It is not locked," Bernot said, joining them. "As you saw, your sister was able to leave."

Aron noticed a few symbols inscribed on the wall. "What are those?"

Bernot went to inspect them. "Spell runes." He cursed. "Someone has locked us in."

An ear-splitting scream resonated through Aron's head and, from the pained looks on everybody's faces, they had heard it too.

"What the royik was that?" Rangi asked, rubbing his temple.

"Keegan," Kade mumbled as the floor shook, sending Aron to his knees.

Move, Tahrin demanded as they scrambled back. She bashed her muscular tail against the door for several minutes before it exploded outwards.

Aron rushed through the cloud of debris, somehow expecting Keegan to be nearby. "Where is she?" he said frantically when met with only splintered wood and dust.

Okleiy pushed past him, fear and worry in his voice. "The Royal Koi Pond."

✠✠✠

Alyck stared blankly at the wall. Anyone else would have feared the worst, but Thaddeus knew better. Alyck was having a vision. The Blind Prophet twitched, and he moved closer.

"What did you see?" Thaddeus whispered.

"Same thing I have been seeing for the past few weeks," Alyck answered. Thaddeus knew he was referring to his brother's death. "But something was different. There was a raven this time."

"A raven?"

"Yes." Alyck rubbed his eyes. "Do you think it means anything?"

Thaddeus thought for a moment; ravens symbolized fate and deceit and were harbingers of change. Sometimes they were harbingers of death too. "It could… maybe… I am not sure. Why would the vision suddenly change?"

Alyck shrugged. "Because Sola and Lunos would rather play with my mind than give me answers. This does not usually happen, but when it does, the addition usually pertains to something vital."

"Describe the man to me."

"Dark hair, blue eyes, average looking."

"Did he have a scar across his face?"

"No."

He sighed deeply. For a moment he had feared the raven might represent his grandson given Kade's nickname for him. "I do not know what this change means."

"No one will until it comes to pass. I just wish it would happen soon."

Thaddeus considered advising against this, knowing it would lead to a new era—one without Alyck. Braxton was coming into his powers, meaning one of Caius's sons would not be ascending the throne.

They sat in silence until Alyck broke it, "I know my time is coming, I just wish I understood the mystery of how two people can kill my brother." He gave a sly smile. "Sparing my feelings does me no good. Since Keegan's return, my days have been numbered."

"I cannot solve the conundrum of your brother's death, but I do know what is happening to Braxton."

"Do tell me."

"He is becoming a Blind Prophet."

The color drained from Alyck's face. "No… the fates cannot be so cruel."

✟✟✟

Warm from lying in the sun, Keegan rolled onto her back, yawning and stretching her arms above her head. The grass was soft underneath her shoulders and she would have happily stayed there forever. But she knew she should head back; the boys would be fretting. Part of her wanted to let them stew while she enjoyed watching the clouds float by for once instead of worrying about everyone and everything.

There was a strangled gurgle and Keegan sat up cautiously. Mahogen was lying face down on the grass several yards away and Wexsley stood by a tree, his back to her, a pair of boots sticking from between his legs. Getting to her feet slowly, Keegan's gut told her to do anything but stay there.

Wexsley stepped aside, revealing Rhyse, crimson spilling down his chest from a gash in his throat. Seeing her, Wexsley pointed the bloodied knife at her.

She turned to run and collided with Halcyon, who took hold of her wrists. Keegan screamed and the sound was quickly smothered as Wexsley placed an ether-soaked rag over her mouth. It seared her throat and her knees buckled, refusing to hold her upright. After what seemed an aeon, Halcyon shoved her to the ground.

As she coughed, she managed to ask, "Why?"

"Because you are worth a fortune," Halcyon said bluntly. He turned to Wexsley. "Get the horses, I'll deal with these two."

Glancing at Mahogen, she realized he was alive, and relief flooded through her. She struggled to her feet, only to have Halcyon push her to the ground again.

"Don't do this," she pleaded, stubbornly struggling to her feet again.

"Quiet," Halcyon snapped, backhanding her across the face.

The sting brought back memories. She knew she'd never be able to beat him but was going to try anyway. Keegan tried to run and when Halcyon grabbed her, clawed at his eyes. He struck her, sending blue and yellow spots across her vision. When the colors disappeared, she was on the ground again.

Halcyon wrenched her arms behind her back, placing strain on her shoulders.

"Please," she begged, tears rolling down her cheeks.

The guard wrapped a rope around her wrists, then pulled out a long rag, drenching it in ether. "Have to take precautions," Halcyon said snidely, securing the gag. "I heard ether wears off quickly on you."

✠✠✠

As they sprinted into the clearing, Kade yelled, "Keegan." No response. "Keegan!"

"She is not here," Bernot said.

Something inside Kade cracked, and the panic that caused was nearly enough to send him on a rampage.

Garne pointed and Kade looked to see Rhyse's body slumped against a tree, blood staining the front of his shirt.

"Who was with her?" Atlia asked.

"Rhyse, Wexsley, and Halcyon," Bernot answered.

Okleiy added, "And my son."

"Find the other two," a soldier ordered in reference to Keegan's guards.

Okleiy stopped them. "They are not here."

"Did… whoever took Keegan, take them, too?" Aron questioned.

500

"I have a feeling Halcyon and Wexsley are the ones who did the taking," the Alvor king growled.

Kade clenched his fists. If—no, when—he found those bastards, he was going to kill them.

"Where would they take her?" Jared pressed.

"Them," Garne corrected. "Mahogen is missing as well."

"Most likely to the border," Bernot said, picking up a discarded rag from the ground. "Ether."

"Why would they do this?" Aron questioned.

"Money and titles, I assume. No doubt Caius will pay handsomely for Keegan. As for why they took Mahogen, I cannot pretend to understand. We must find them before they cross the border. Once they do, we cannot follow. Tahrin, fly ahead and see if you can spot them."

The dragon didn't look pleased at being given an order and showed it with a puff of smoke. Regardless, she spread her massive, red wings and took to the sky.

"The rest of us will follow on the ground," Bernot continued as a group of soldiers stormed into the clearing, extra horses in tow. He swung up onto a sable charger. "Hickor, can you track them?"

"Can I track them?" Hickor scoffed, spurring his horse into the forest.

Not waiting for an order, Kade spurred Aros after the Alvor.

After a time, Hickor slowed and dismounted, a look of confusion muddling his features. He paced in circles round trees and shrubs, often stopping to touch a branch or leaf. But the confused expression never faltered.

"Have you lost the trail?" Atlia asked.

"No," Hickor said. "There are two trails and no knowing which one leads to them."

"Then we split," Bernot announced calmly.

Kade was about to agree when he took a closer look at the hoof-prints. One set was perfectly stomped into the ground, each print a replica. "No, it's a ruse. We've done something similar before."

"Are you sure?" Garne questioned. He didn't need to add what the outcome would be if Kade were wrong.

He looked at the trails again and his confidence wavered.

His face must have showed this for Okleiy snarled, "You are wasting time," before beginning to give directions.

"He is right," Hickor said, re-emerging from the underbrush; Kade hadn't even noticed the Alvor slip away. "They went this way."

"How could you know that?" Okleiy snapped.

"Come see."

Jared gave Kade a perturbed look before following the Alvor through the brush.

The clearing they came in to was grotesque. Tree roots emerged from the ground like clawing arms and fear seemed to hang in the air.

"Who… what is this?" Okleiy muttered.

"This is Keegan," Kade answered quietly.

CHAPTER 58

It had been two days and they had yet to catch up to Halcyon and Wexsley. Tahrin had gone ahead but was unable to spot them from the sky and Bernot was beginning to worry.

They were able to get fresh horses at outposts along the way but were still pushing hard. Just ahead was the border outpost, where a set of fresh horses awaited and within minutes they were in the bleak Borderlands. Bernot could see out to the blue wall that divided them from Caius; not a living soul was in sight.

Any sign? he asked Tahrin.

The dragon was a red blur in the open sky. *No.* She dove towards them, sending great shivers through the earth as she landed.

"They came this way," Hickor said, working to calm his balking horse.

I have not seen them, Tahrin growled.

"Then you must be blind," Kade snarled impulsively.

Tahrin snapped at him, causing his horse to buck and give a frightened whinny.

"Easy, Tahrin," Bernot said. "I have a feeling they might have used an invisibility spell." After seeing the spell runes etched outside the meeting room, there was no other viable truth. While most spellcasters made themselves known, not all did. And with no visible way to know someone was a spellcaster, unlike elementals who bore symbols on their skin, they could live in anonymity. It was just such a shame

Halcyon or Wexsley, whichever one was the spellcaster, had chosen to use their magic for the wrong purpose.

"What do we do then?" Aron questioned.

"Nothing," Rangi said angrily. "They have crossed the border; we cannot touch them."

"I'm bringing her back," Kade said defiantly.

"Even if you could cross, we will not allow it," Garne spoke. "You are a Child of Prophecy; we need to—"

"We saved her before and we'll do it again," Jared cut him off.

A soldier from the back spoke up. "I might not make it across the border, but I'm willing to try."

Several others joined their cause.

"Why would you do this?" Bernot asked the first man to volunteer.

"Keegan helped my son with his sword fighting, giving pointers and offering to spar even when she could barely keep the blade up. I'd feel ashamed if I left her to Caius without at least trying."

"Well said." Bernot spoke to the other leaders, "I, for one, am going. You may wait here or come." He knew all would come—attempt to at least—for fear of losing what little hold each thought they had over the girl.

Dust-clouds rose behind them as they crossed the Borderlands and Kade plowed through the wall without hesitation, his brothers following. The rest of them stopped just short of the barrier.

Bernot's men took deep breaths before crossing, only a few getting stuck. None of Okleiy's men were able to pass. He looked to the other leaders and began forward. Abruptly, he was midair and falling, hitting the ground with an "oof".

The other leaders gave him worried looks, but each tried to pass. None made it. It seemed none of their intentions were not of the war faring agenda.

"Prepare for anything," Bernot instructed those who had crossed. "And bring her back."

‡‡‡

Keegan was dropped onto the ground unceremoniously, her shoulder ramming into a root. The blindfold was pushed up slightly and she could make out a few pairs of boots; enough to know there was no use in trying to escape just yet.

"As promised," Halcyon said. "Where's our money?"

"Here," a woman's voice said alongside the clinking coins.

"That's barely a fraction of what you promised," Halcyon balked. Suddenly, he was gasping, choking on something.

Wexsley began pleading and soon fell silent.

"Get her up," the woman instructed.

Keegan was yanked to her feet and the blindfold was torn away. She blinked, bringing her eyes into focus and recognized the Vosjnik. Guthrie held her and she frantically struggled against him.

He drew a knife, and she managed an audible hiccup through the gag. Guthrie cut the ropes binding her hands and her first instinct was to strike out.

"Stop," Vitia said, using her magic.

Keegan's body buzzed as it obeyed a will not her own. Slowly her arms lowered to her side.

Brennian reached for her other arm and removed the gag.

Vitia turned her attention to Mahogen, who had been pulled off his horse. "Not what I asked for, but still a prize," she sneered, grabbing one of his golden horns.

Mahogen gave no reaction.

"Why can't you people just leave me alone?" Keegan yelled.

"Nothing personal," Guthrie said, "but we have orders."

"And your brother won't be able to save you this time," Vitia jibed cruelly.

Keegan gave her an unwavering look. "Obviously; they're a world away."

Vitia looked momentarily confused. "No, the brother you have in this world."

"Don't have any. Unless you mean by Alvor stand—"

"I mean your biological brother, Kade."

"What?" Keegan snorted. "He's not my brother."

Vitia produced a crumpled paper from her pocket and pushed it into her hands.

By the end, Keegan could scarcely keep from shaking. "Where did you get this?"

"Your brother. Didn't he tell you?" Vitia said with a shrewd grin. "Let her go."

Keegan looked at her searchingly as Brennian and Guthrie obeyed.

"Run."

She didn't need to be told a second time and, in her rush, stumbled over a root. Glancing over her shoulder as she scrambled to her feet, she saw Vitia staring after her, Thahan beside her, bow strung and aimed.

There was a piercing pain in her shoulder and, tumbling to the ground, she screamed. As she lay there, feeling defeated, Keegan realized this was what Vitia wanted.

Think again, she thought to herself, pushing herself up. The look of surprise on Vitia's face was worth the pain.

When Keegan took off again, she turned herself into an erratic target, using the trees as barriers. Branches snapped behind her and an arrow grazed her side, but she barely felt it with the adrenaline coursing through her veins. A sudden pain radiating from her left thigh felled her. She knew if she looked back she'd find an arrow protruding from the muscle.

Keegan knew she couldn't outrun them but was still going to try. She had to—or she would have to face death. The pain in her leg and shoulder was searing as she struggled to her feet. She stumbled forward, placing a hand against a tree for support and the scream she emitted when the arrow pierced her palm seemed to come from somewhere far off. Sliding to her knees, her face scraped against the rough bark, tears mixing with droplets of blood.

She took deep breaths, doing her best to give Vitia as little satisfaction as possible. There was a snap, and someone pulled her hand down the broken shaft, the splinters at the end clawing at her flesh.

"The cavalry is here," Aron said, dragging her into his arms.

‡‡‡

While the Vosjnik were occupied, Aron knew he needed to get Keegan somewhere safe. He had meant to flee on horseback, but the thing had spooked and run off. The sounds of battle fell away and he stopped, gently leaning Keegan against a tree.

"I need to remove the arrows," he said calmly.

Keegan gritted her teeth, tear wetting her cheeks. "Do it quickly."

He began with the one in her shoulder and, once done, let her lean against the tree. The one in her leg was deeply imbedded and he did not bother telling her his intentions, quickly shoving it completely through her thigh.

Keegan yelped, beating her good hand against the tree. "You'll need to bind the wounds to stop the bleeding."

Tearing away the bottom of her once white dress, he ripped it into strips, winding several around her leg while she tended to her hand. There was no easy way to bandage her shoulder, so he left it alone.

Kade, he said, remembering the others, *I have her, but lost my horse.*

Stay where you are.

"Kade and the others are on their way."

At the mention of his name, Keegan looked away, a tightness in her throat. "Kade's… my brother."

"Who told you?"

Her eyes snapped back to his and hurt shone in them. "You knew?"

He sighed. "I wanted to tell you, but Kade would not let me."

"Why?"

"You will have to ask him."

Her eyes widened in fear. "Aron."

He looked over his shoulder to find Thahan aiming a bow at his chest.

"Step away," Thahan commanded as Aron stood slowly. "I'd rather not do you harm."

Aron tightened his grip on his sword. "If you want her, you have to go through me."

"So be it."

Thahan released the bowstring, and the arrow pierced his heart smoothly.

Looking at his chest, Aron calmly watched blood dye his shirt. A scream, not his own, filled his ears and the world lurched sideways.

✜✜✜

The Vosjnik had fled, leaving Keegan and Mahogen behind. Kade wasn't sure why, but Vitia must've somehow achieved her goal. He pushed out with his mind to find Aron and Keegan; they weren't much farther.

He arrived to find Keegan leaning against a tree, red splotches staining her dress and Aron standing in front of her protectively. Thahan had an arrow aimed at the prince's chest, which he released, and hit true to the intended mark.

As Kade revealed himself, Thahan reached for another arrow, but was too slow. In one clean motion, his head was rolling from his shoulders.

He was aware Keegan had screamed, but now the world was deathly quiet. Kade found her unconscious, the arrow that had been in Aron's chest clenched in her fist. Where there should have been a hole in Aron's breast was seamless flesh.

Aron jerked up, gasping. "What happened?"

"Nastor if I know," Kade answered. *Jared, you need to bring the horses. Keegan's done… something and needs immediate attention.*

On our way.

"You would've died for her," he said to Aron.

"Of course."

"Why?"

"Same reason you would, which is what I have been trying to show you this entire time. I may be Caius's blood, but I will never be him."

Kade would never admit it, but he had truly misjudged Aron. Maybe in time he could come to trust him. And maybe one day call him friend.

"What happened?" Jared asked, arriving with the others.

"Not sure," Aron said. "But I have a feeling I should be dead."

Mahogen examined Keegan. "She is still breathing. We need to get her back to the Lazado."

"You're a life elemental," Kade stated.

"Ether," Mahogen said plainly. "And I was never particularly good at healing. We need Lyerlly."

"Edreba's days away," Jared argued.

"By horseback," Mahogen said slyly.

✠✠✠

A gale buffeted the hospital, rattling the windows in their holdings, threatening to shake them loose. Lyerlly rushed outside to find Aron sliding from Tahrin's back, Keegan dirtied and bloodied in his arms.

"Where are the others?" she asked.

"Riding back from the border," Aron answered, allowing Ty to take Keegan from him.

"What happened?" Lyerlly questioned, undoing Keegan's field dressings.

"Thahan shot her several times before we got away. He found us again and shot me in the heart." He paused and Lyerlly noticed the bloodied hole in his shirt. "When I came to, she was like this."

Lyerlly pointed to his chest. "I assume that is why they sent you back with her."

"Yes," he answered almost ashamedly.

Returning her attention to Keegan, she could sense no poison—the only injuries were the evident ones. Yet the girl was barely hanging onto life. Lyerlly slowly began to transfer her own energy to see if there was a response; Keegan's heart beat faster and her body drew away from the brink.

"Aron," Lyerlly instructed, "I need to transfer energy to Keegan. Find some soldiers and bring them here."

"Use me."

"You do not have nearly enough."

"Start with me."

She really did not have time to argue. "Fine." Placing a hand on his arm, she was amazed at how much energy he had—enough for two people. Once she drew enough to leave Keegan in a deep sleep, she left Elia and Ty to attend to her injuries.

Taking Aron to another bed, she drew the curtains. "Remove your shirt."

Aron's chest was muscled and unscarred, with no sign an arrow had pierced him. Placing a hand on his chest to assess the internal damage, she found nothing wrong.

"It is like you were never injured."

"How?"

"I am not sure, but it *was* Keegan's doing. What truly concerns me is she did it in an instant, while still under the effects of ether. That should be impossible."

CHAPTER 59

The sounds were of a busy area. They started like a buzzing, faint and unrecognizable. Slowly the sounds filtered into coherent beings. People chatted though Keegan couldn't make out any words clearly. Shoes clicked on a tiled floor. There was the scrape of a chair. A curtain slid against a rod.

Her eyes opened slowly and looking around, Keegan realized she was in the hospital in Edreba. Kade and Jared sat beside the bed, talking quietly.

Jared noticed she was awake. "Hey, how are you feeling?"

"Confused," she answered truthfully, pushing herself upright. Wexsley and Halcyon's betrayal resurfaced. Kade was her brother. Vitia had let Thahan use her as target practice. Aron had rescued her... "Oh my god, Aron."

Kade and Jared looked at each other dumbfounded, neither doing anything to console her as tears fell wildly down her cheeks.

"What did you do?" Aron asked. "I walked away for a minute."

"Aron," she exclaimed, pulling him into an embrace. Tears still fell, but now they were of relief. "But..." She remembered the arrow piercing his chest and scrambled to lift his shirt. "The arrow..." His chest was smooth, unbroken, whole. "How?"

"You," Aron answered, taking her hand.

"*How?*"

"We are not sure; we were hoping you knew."

Lyerlly pulled the curtain open. "Shoo," she said, sending the boys away.

Keegan was given a detailed account of her injuries while Lyerlly checked her over.

"You can go to the children's home today if you wish," Lyerlly started. "But before you do, the leaders want to speak with you."

"Oh, *joy*. Let's get this over with."

Lyerlly returned with the leaders and Tahrin settled for observing through the window as she was too big to fit into the hospital.

"I don't know how I did it," Keegan said, heading them off.

So you say, the dragon responded.

Keegan shot her a glare. "Is that all y'all're here to talk about?"

"No," Bernot said calmly. "We thought you might like to know the path you will take."

"Ooh, do share," Keegan said, glad their games were over.

"You will start with the Torrpeki, then go to the Merfolk, Buluo, Dragons, and then back to us," Okleiy informed her.

"Good deal. Now," she said, swinging her legs over the edge of the bed. "I'm going home."

No one stopped her.

Lyerlly stood behind the group, arms folded across her chest. The order on the doctor's face was painfully clear.

"Yes ma'am," Keegan sighed, crawling back into bed.

Lyerlly's expression softened. "I believe that is what you all came here for. That being completed, I need to do a few more things before Miss Digore may leave. Should you need her for anything more, you may talk with her at the children's home. *Tomorrow*."

✠✠✠

513

Nico gave a yell of excitement as Ima dove towards the ground. The wind pulled his hair back, making it look like flame.

Crowlin followed them at a breakneck speed, the air cool against Braxton's skin. The griffin pulled out of the dive and returned to the clouds, leaving Ima struggling to follow.

You are doing much better, Braxton told the hatchling.

Ima gave a crow, diving towards the ground again and Braxton urged Crowlin to follow.

The griffin tucked in her wings, beginning a plummet towards the earth.

Suddenly, the world fell away and darkness was all around him. Braxton felt his stomach drop, finding himself in the throne room. A wild man snuck from the shadows, knife poised and ready. He jabbed the blade into the back of Caius's neck and his father gave a silent scream, falling to his knees.

The attacker's face transformed and a sneer pulled on his lips. Looking back at his father, Braxton saw it was now himself being stabbed. A scream filled his ears and the world burst into light.

The first thing he realized was that he was falling, the air ripping from his lungs. The next, was that Crowlin was chasing after him. She wrapped her claws around his biceps, stopping his free-fall, the jerk as his momentum was stopped making it feel like his shoulders were being pulled apart.

His feet touched the ground and Crowlin released him. As he rolled across the grass, his body somehow found every rock. When he came to a stop, he just lay there, body throbbing.

As Ima landed, Nico jumped off her back and raced to him. "Braxton! Braxton, are you alright?"

Worry emanated from the griffins, and he pushed himself upright. "Yes. What happened?"

Nico crouched beside him. "I'm not sure. You were fine one moment, then you fell… Did you faint?"

"No…" A shooting pain presented itself behind his eyes and he gasped in pain.

Braxton, Crowlin said worriedly.

"I am fine," he managed. "But let us stop for the day."

Climbing onto Crowlin's back, he found it took all his strength to not curl into a ball. Through the pain, he could see one thing clearly: Kolt stabbing him in the back.

✝✝✝

Once Lyerlly approved Keegan's departure, she was anxious to return to the children's home. Something was eating at her and Kade might've asked if he didn't have feeling it would blow up in his face.

When they reached the top floor of the children's home, Keegan turned to face them, a pained look on her face. "Can I talk to Kade, alone please?"

Aron and Jared shared a worried look before going to their rooms. No doubt both would press their ears to the door to try and listen.

"Wha—" Kade started.

"How could you keep that from me?" Anger and pain rode on her words.

"Keep what from you?" he asked, genuinely confused.

"We're siblings." Her voice wavered. "Were you ever gonna tell me?"

"Maybe."

"*Maybe*? You should've told me, so I didn't have to find out from *Vitia*."

"You were never supposed to know."

A look of complete betrayal overtook her features. "That's not something you get to keep from me. Do you know how many years I spent looking for a family?"

"I was just trying to protect you."

515

"From *what*?"

"From how people would treat you. From people using that relationship against us."

She gave him a disappointed look. "Like how you treated Aron because of who his father is? And sibling or not, I would've been treated like that for simply being your friend. Is there anything else you wanna own up to?"

"Nico's alive."

The color drained from her face. "What?"

"Nico's—"

"I heard you the first time! Nico's alive, and we could've saved him. What about the rest of Jared's family?"

"Alessandra's dead. I let it happen."

"What about Lucas, Carter, and Jude?"

"Who?"

Keegan took a step back, shaking her head, utter betrayal marring her features. "I don't think I want to associate with a liar and murderer."

He knew she wanted to say much more but was too angry to find the right words. Yet her eyes spoke what her mouth couldn't. And he didn't blame her.

✝✝✝

Bernot took his seat, looking at the men across from him. The older gentleman was dark-skinned, his coarse, wiry hair beginning to lose its color. He was a large man and Bernot did not doubt he was accustomed to strenuous labor. The other could hardly be considered more than a child, probably not past his sixteenth year. There was something familiar about him that he could not place.

"Why did you bring them here? Any of the Initiators could have dealt with them," Bernot said, not pleased that Felix was placing more work on his already overladen plate.

"You told us to bring Pexatoses straight to you," Felix said, motioning to the older gentleman.

Bernot looked towards the boy. "And what about…"

"Carter," the boy provided.

"Yes, what about Carter?"

"Carter has no magic," Felix explained, "but knows Keegan."

Of course, he knew to whom Felix referred but he had to erase any doubt. "There are numerous people named Keegan, you will have to be specific."

"Keegan Digore," Carter snapped. "The one who leaves a wake of destruction in her royiken path."

It was then Bernot realized who Carter was. "You must be a Sieme."

"How do you know that? Are my brothers here?"

"Jared is."

"What about Nico? Lucas?" Carter pressed, his hands gripping the chair's arm.

"I have heard nothing of Lucas; I do believe Jared thought he was traveling with you."

Carter gulped. "He was until a few weeks ago."

"The boy's headstrong and I have a feelin' he went to do something stupid, now," Felix spoke up. "Would you be willin' to let me take a few men to go look for the wanker?"

"No," Bernot said. "There have been some unfortunate events that require me to keep as many men as I can at hand. Also, there would be no way to find Lucas; he will have to come to us. And Felix, do not think you have gotten out of telling me what happened to you."

Felix leaned back against the wall. "Expected nothin' less, sir."

"What about Nico?" Carter pressed.

Bernot paused before answering. "Caius has him."

The color drained from Carter's face. "Are… you… what's being done to save him?"

"Nothing. As I said before, there have been some important things happening here." Before Carter could lash out in anger and pain, he added, "But I have no doubt Caius is keeping him alive. Have no worries." He cursed to himself; that was never the correct thing to say.

"How can you tell me not to worry? My brother, my *little* brother's being held hostage by the king, having Sola and Lunos knows what happen to him."

"We will rescue him. However, things like this take time. I cannot say he will be saved today, or tomorrow, or even a week from now, but it will happen. You have my word." He knew Carter wanted to argue, but the boy had the foresight to realize doing so would get him nowhere. He turned his attention to the Pexatose. "I apologize, but I seem to have not received your name."

"Waylan Piscol," the man answered, his large arms folded across his chest.

"Ah, I wondered when you would decide to join us. You are the metal elemental if I remember correctly."

"It was done begrudgingly. And yes."

"Do you use your powers in your line of work, which is…?"

Waylan answered, "I'm a blacksmith, and no."

Whatever Waylan's reasons were for not using his powers, they were his own.

"Excellent. You will be given work in a forge, and you can work towards having your own."

"When Lucas arrives, I'll require him as an assistant."

"That can be arranged," Bernot said, pulling some papers from his desk. "Will you be wanting Carter as an assistant as well?"

Carter spoke up, "I worked with a shoemaker."

"I may have a job for you," Bernot said, recalling the increased demand in carpenters of late. "It is a carpentry position though."

He did not bother to affirm Carter's approval before scanning the papers in his hands. "Carter, there is room for you at Zaire's children's home. Waylan, there should be room above the forge if that will suffice."

"That's fine," Waylan said gruffly.

"I take it Jared and Keegan are at Zaire's," Carter commented.

"No," Bernot said. "I cannot allow you to see your brother yet… it would create complications."

"What kind of complications?"

"Jared is set to leave in a few days, and I have no doubt your arrival would keep him here. That, and I am sure you would convince him to go search for Lucas and make a fool-hearted attempt to rescue Nico."

"What if I swore not to?"

"Even then I would say no. Jared cannot afford to be distracted—the world cannot afford for him to be distracted. Once he has left, I will inform him of your safe arrival."

"You can't keep me from him," Carter argued, his desperation evident.

"Unfortunately, I can, and I must."

Carter made to continue arguing, but Felix placed a hand on his shoulder, stopping him. "I know it's not what you want to hear, lad, but trust me, Bernot's doin' what he thinks is best now."

"Thank you," Bernot said. "Now, Felix will take you where you need to go and I promise, you will see all three of your brothers again. But you must be patient."

CHAPTER 60

His nerves were on edge, then again, they'd been that way for the past few weeks. *July twenty-seventh, the day history changes,* Lucas thought, following Reven into the inn's cellar.

Reven moved a crate, revealing a small hole in the wall.

"That'd better not be how we're getting into the castle," Lucas snapped.

Reven ignored him, dropping onto his stomach. Once Reven was through, Lucas considered moving the crate over the entrance and simply walking away.

"Do n't even try it," Reven hissed from the darkness.

Taking a deep breath, Lucas edged into the dusty and dark tunnel. "Let's get this over with."

Reven, torch in hand, led the way, and Lucas was more than happy to let him; it meant he wasn't the one walking through never-ending spider webs. Glancing back, he was disheartened to find he couldn't see the tunnel's opening; he was truly committed now. Touching the knife at his waist, he realized there was more than one way out of this.

"Why do you want to kill the king?" he asked.

"Now is n't the time for this."

"You seem to know my motivations, but I hardly know anything about you. Why is it you want to kill the king?"

""Cause of what he did to my family."

"What did he do to yours that he hasn't done to everyone else's?"

"Killed them."

"His soldiers do that every day."

"No, he wielded the blade. My father died saving a Child of Prophecy—Keegan. And you 'ave no idea what that did t' my family. My mother was never told my father 'd been murdered and thought he 'd left 'er. She turned to drink, and it killed her. My grandfather was an amazing spell-caster but, when my father died, grief overpowered everything. Now, he 's dead because o' a supposed friend's betrayal."

"Did you see your grandfather die?"

"No."

"Then he could still be alive."

"No one survives long in the Suttan dungeon. Especially not old men."

The walk through the tunnel was excruciating and with no sunlight to gauge time, it felt like forever. But eventually there was an end.

"We 'ill wait until dark," Reven said hunkering down.

"How do you know it's not night already?"

"I have my ways."

"Then why did we come so royiken early?"

"T' make people think we 'd left the inn." Their constant butting heads was beginning to wear down Reven's usually placid nature. "Sleep if you like, there 's not much else t' do."

✢✢✢

The room was blissfully dark and from his open window and Aron could hear owls hooting in the night. After Keegan and Kade's fight, she had disappeared; he had gone to check on her and found an empty room with an open window. Aron had debated telling the others, but she probably needed time alone. Sooner or later, she would come back—at least he hoped.

The air between Kade and Jared grew worse with the discovery that most of Jared's family had survived the

521

Vosjnik. Jared had immediately gone to Bernot to ask for leave to look for them. From the slamming of his door when he returned, Aron assumed he was refused.

He heard a rustling outside his window and a shadow climbed through.

"You up?" Keegan whispered.

"Yes," he responded, sitting up.

She climbed into the bed and sat quietly.

With the help of the small streams of moonlight pervading through the leaves, he could see something glistening on her face.

"What is wrong?" he asked, reaching for her hand.

"It's all too much," she answered. "I… I don't want to be part of this world. None of it makes sense."

"What does not make sense?"

"Everything," she hiccupped. "How can people keep so much from me? Why do I have to save everyone?"

"I cannot answer the latter," Aron said, wiping away a trail of tears. "But they—we—keep things from you because we are trying to protect you, because we care about you."

She pushed his hand away in anger. "It doesn't protect me!" Quietly, she said, "I should've never come here." She shifted, about to get up to leave.

He took her hand again. "Do not fault us because we are doing what we think is right."

"How do you know it's the right thing to do?"

"We do not." He pulled her into an embrace. "But we try, and that is what matters."

Her sobbing made it impossible to respond.

Aron stroked her hair in an effort to comfort her and slowly the tears subsided as exhaustion overtook her. Gently, he laid her down, covering her with the blanket.

He was about to head into the common room to sleep on the couch when she grabbed his hand. "Stay. Please."

Aron hesitated, then climbed back into the bed cradling her body against his.

Keegan nestled against him. "Thank you."
He waited until she was asleep to gently kiss her hair.

‡‡‡

Someone was shaking him. Reven pulled away just in time to avoid Lucas's flailing limbs as he jerked back to reality.

"Time t' go," Reven said, picking up the torch with one hand and feeling the wall with the other.

Lucas wondered what he was looking for until the wall sprang open. He crept past Reven, peering into the corridor.

"See anyone?"

"No," Lucas answered. Reven pushed past him, and he asked, "You know where you're going, right?" He was sure the "map" wasn't as accurate as Reven believed.

"Through the halls, no, through the secret passages, yes."

Lucas gritted his teeth, feeling exposed, and tiptoed after him.

Reven pressed another stone only a few hundred feet down the hallway, opening another hidden door. Lucas let him lead again and when they came across pitfalls, was glad he found them first. It wasn't long before they came to another dead-end. Reven quickly opened the door and the room they stepped into was plain but comfortable, aside from the painting of a woman with sad eyes.

As they explored, Lucas felt the painting's eyes follow him. Stalking towards the bed, he expecting to find the king fast asleep, but the covers were tangled and empty.

"Where is he?"

"How should I royiken know?" Reven snapped back.

"This is your noxþ plan, find him."

Reven stormed to the door and when he returned, was dragging a guard along. The man's eyes were wide with fear, but he didn't resist, clearly under Reven's control.

"Where 's the king?" Reven asked, throwing the guard to the floor.

"I don't know," the man answered, fighting Reven's control.

"Where is he?"

The guard gave a scream through gritted teeth. "He didn't tell me."

Reven drew his knife. "Where is he?"

The man eyed the blade before saying, "You'll kill me even if I tell; do your worst."

Reven crouched in front of him. "Oh, I was never going to kill you. But I 'll make it so you wish I had."

The guard gave him a cold stare, which Reven returned. Slowly pain washed over the man's features.

"This can end well if you tell me what I need t' know."

The guard only managed to stay steadfast for a few more moments. "In the throne room. He always goes there when he can't sleep."

✛✛✛

"This poses a problem," Rangi stated. "Caius will undoubtedly use the boy to turn his brother."

"I know," Bernot said calmly. "That is why I propose we send parties to extract the boy."

"That would be suicide for your men," Atlia stated. "Caius must understand his value and have him heavily guarded."

"Our men," Okleiy corrected the princess.

"No," Atlia said. "I agreed to train the Child of Prophecy, but I promised no help in the war you want to wage. I am not yet queen and cannot grant you the forces you ask for."

Bernot's stomach sank. He had assumed that when the leaders agreed to train Keegan they would support him in the war as well. "How many of you will stand with me in the war to come?"

Only Okleiy answered his call.

Bernot felt a weight fall on his shoulders. "I need your assistance if I am to overthrow Caius."

Caius is not wreaking havoc in our lands, Tahrin told him. *We have our own concerns. The dragons will gladly train Keegan, but we cannot offer more.*

There were similar answers from Rangi and Garne.

Bernot looked to Okleiy, hoping he might put his conniving skills towards a greater good, and for once was rewarded.

"Will you consent to give us use of your Pexatoses?" the Alvor asked.

"Pexatoses are allowed to make their own decisions as free people of Arciol," Rangi told them. "We will ask them to help; whether or not they do is up to them."

The door burst open, and a flustered soldier rushed in.

Tahrin bared her fangs. *What do you think you are doing?*

The man hardly spared her a glance. "I need to talk to Bernot; it's urgent."

Sighing, Bernot followed the man outside.

"The border... the border's gone," the man answered frantically.

"What do you mean *gone*?"

The man stammered, "Gone! It no longer exists. How is this possible?"

He ignored the man's question. "Tell Hernando Barnsed to increase the number of men at the border and make sure you tell no one else of this."

The man gulped, clearly wanting to argue. Clearly afraid of what the loss of the border meant for him and the other soldier of the Lazado. "Yes, sir."

He steadied himself before re-entering the room. "My apologizes. You must all forgive me, but there are some unforeseen events that require my immediate attention. May we finish this discussion on the morrow?"

Tahrin showed her irritation with a puff of smoke. *Courtesy aside, you leave us with little choice.*

Bernot bowed his head. "Thank you."

As the others stood and began making their way from the room, he called out to the Alvor.

Okleiy had the sense to wait until the doors closed before asking, "What has happened?"

"The border has fallen. Caius is dead."

"I have already agreed to join your cause."

Bernot knew to be wary of a gift from the Alvor, especially Okleiy. "But at what price?"

"I want the same thing I did before."

"And what would that be?" Bernot asked though he already knew.

"I want Mahogen to be matched to the Child of Prophecy."

Bernot took a deep breath to give himself time to think. For once, it was hard to keep the smile that pulled at his lips. "Fine, Mahogen will be matched with a Child of Prophecy."

An Alvor approached and whispered something in the king's ear. Bernot hoped the distraction was enough to make Okleiy forget his exact words.

Okleiy grinned, thinking he had won. "My men are yours. Use them wisely."

Bernot gave Okleiy a nod before walking away. Thankfully, he had left himself some leeway. He never promised when a union would take place, but that would stave off Okleiy only so long. The true ace was that while he had promised Mahogen would be matched with a Child of Prophecy, but he had never promised which one. Now, all he had to do was find the one that best suited Mahogen.

✜✜✜

"Are you sure this is the right one?" Lucas asked aggravated.

So far, Reven had taken them everywhere but the throne room. Apparently, his map of the secret passages wasn't as solid as he thought.

"It should be the right one," Reven answered, uncertainty in his voice as he opened the door.

They were finally rewarded, and the door spit them out into the shadows of the throne. The back of the throne was plain, with the words "The future is mine to make, break, and bend" inscribed on it.

Drawing his knife, Lucas slipped into the shadows lining the walls. Immediately, he spotted Caius; thankfully, the king didn't notice him. The man was nothing like he imagined. He was beginning to show the wear of age and a sense of anxiety surrounded him as he paced, eyes never leaving the floor.

Lucas waited until the king had his back turned before creeping forward. His heart pounded, pumping adrenaline through his veins as his nerves sat on edge. He was within feet now and he lunged forward, driving the knife into the back of Caius's neck.

The king gave a loud cry and collapsed to his knees. Lucas removed the knife and Caius fell forward, blood seeping from the fatal wound.

There was banging on the door. "Sir, is everything all right?"

"Lucas," Reven hissed, frantically motioning for him.

He stole a last glance at the felled king before sprinting across the room. As he was swallowed by the shadows, the doors burst open, guards spilling in.

Reven quickly shut the door and started running; Lucas didn't need to be told to follow.

They only stopped when they reached a dead-end that required them to move from one tunnel to another.

"Congratulations, you just killed the king," Reven said.

CHAPTER 61

The castle was in utter pandemonium. Everyone from servants to guards to cooks. Everywhere Nico looked was people.

Braxton was called upon, which meant Nico was roused too, and whatever the soldier had said to the prince was enough to drain the color from his face. They dressed quickly and all but ran to the throne room.

There were so many guards standing outside the door that Nico wondered if someone had died. None of the men would look at Braxton, as if ashamed.

Inside, they found the cause of the commotion: Caius's body. Nico recalled his mother's death and instantly knew what Braxton was going through. He also knew he should feel sadness, but his heart was singing.

Braxton went to stand above his father, face devoid of emotion.

Nico followed but gave him space so as not to make him feel intruded upon. He noticed the wound on Caius's neck, and something struck a chord. He knew it wasn't easy to stab someone through their spine and most people would've felled the king anywhere else. But there was one person he knew who insisted upon using a knife between the vertebrae to deliver death: Lucas.

His brother had always done this to kill whatever small farm animals they needed, saying it was painless and less bloody than slitting the animal's throat. He tried to convince himself there was no possible way Lucas could've done this—could've been in Agrielha—but the precision was too telltale.

The doors slammed open and Kolt stormed in. He was almost as pale as Braxton and, when he saw Caius, began screaming as if someone was trying to kill *him.*

Braxton didn't even seem to notice.

Nico looked between the brothers, trying to figure out how they could have such differing reactions.

Turning on his heels, Braxton walked from the room. As he passed the guards, he ordered, "Take my brother to his room. Drain his energy if he will not go quietly."

The guards gave each other concerned looks, before doing as told.

Kolt wasn't happy and threw a punch. Other soldiers quickly came to hold him back and someone sapped his energy.

Nico ran to catch up to Braxton. "Where are you going?"

"Back to bed."

"But—"

"But nothing."

✣✣✣

It was hard to believe, but it had happened, the dream had come to pass; his father was dead. Braxton stood over the body, Kolt beside him. A sheet covered Caius's body, but his face remained visible. Braxton knew he should feel sad, but all he felt was apprehension; he would be crowned king in a few days.

What he understood from the guards was that his father had been in the throne room—alone. There was no way someone could have snuck past them to murder the king, so his death had come at the hands of Sola and Lunos. But he knew better—man had dealt this death.

Kolt was surprisingly silent and sullen, and this was the only time Braxton could recall him showing emotions other than hate, arrogance, or contempt. He almost wanted to console him, forget the animosity and cruelty between them.

"The funeral should take place no later than tomorrow," a prioress said.

Braxton had not noticed her enter. Prioresses were uncommon in Arciol, with each city only having a few, but they played a major role in the burial of the dead—at least those who could afford their services—as most people still upheld some kind of belief in the old gods.

"And what about the coronation?" Braxton asked, suddenly realizing he had no one to guide him.

"Whenever you think would be best," she answered. "My duties only concern the dead."

"The funeral will be tomorrow," Kolt spoke up.

Braxton had no reason to argue and, for once, was content to let his brother decide.

"As you wish," the prioress said apathetically, covering Caius's face.

Braxton gave her a small nod of thanks and started to walk away.

Kolt lingered. "And the coronation the day after that? Would you like me to take care of the preparations?"

He stopped to scrutinize his brother and could see no signs of trickery—something he had learned to discern like a smile.

"That would be *incredibly* helpful." And, as much as he wanted to question Kolt's sudden kindness, he did not want to snap him out of his stupor.

There was so much he wanted to do—needed to do—but he could not muster the energy. Braxton dazedly made his way back to his chambers and sat on the bed, staring blankly. Eventually, he sank onto the mattress.

He was suddenly in the throne room, a mass of people standing around him, all facing the throne. Braxton turned his attention there and was disappointed when the person sitting in the gilded chair was unrecognizable.

A priest lowered a crown onto his head, saying, "Ell poyla ayþ kunyi."

The scene darkened and two men stood alone. He thought he was reliving his father's death until he realized the two were he and someone else. Braxton watched helplessly as the other man drove a knife into his back.

‡‡‡

A persistent knocking made Kade groggily opened his eyes. "What?"

"You're needed, immediately."

The voice was unfamiliar, and he was about to question it when he remembered what had happened to Keegan's old guards. He wasn't surprised Bernot had given them replacements, but he wasn't going to allow anyone near his sister. Not again.

Dressing quickly, he found Bernot and several men waiting for him in the common space.

"What's so urgent?" he asked.

"We should wait for the others," Bernot said.

Bernot was generally calm and collected, but today was clearly anxious.

"What happened?" he pushed.

"Many things. Many things."

He apprehensively took a seat. Jared was the next to show his face and it wasn't a pleasant one for him. The revelation that most of his family was alive had not worked to amend their distrust. It made no sense to him—he would have assume Jared would have been please at his and the Vosjnik's oversight.

Kade felt anger course through his veins when Keegan emerged from Aron's room and clenched his fists to keep from flying at the prince. Though Aron had proven his intentions were good, Kade still wasn't entirely willing to put all his trust him.

What are you doing with him? he snarled to Keegan.

Whatever the hell I want, she snapped back.

Sitting, Keegan pulled her knees to her chest, pressing her shins against the table.

"What's up?" she asked Bernot.

Bernot gave her a confused look before answering, "The ceiling…"

She chuckled. "No, I mean what happened?"

"Oh." He paused before continuing. "Caius is dead."

Keegan's feet dropped onto the floor, and she leaned over the table. "What! How do you know he's dead?"

"Last night, the border fell. And the only way that could happen is if he is… dead"

"How are the two correlated?"

"In their last stand, the Council of Elders wove an enchantment that would protect the rest of the world from Caius's tyranny. As long as he was in this world, it would stand."

"So, what does that mean for us?" Jared asked. "We're no longer needed if the king's dead."

"I believe Caius left safeguards so his sons will ascend the throne," Bernot told them. "I fear we will need you to aid in deposing them."

Aron spoke for the first time. "Braxton will not need to be deposed; he is nothing like our father."

"Yet the risk is too great," Bernot insisted.

"You want to get rid of him before he has a chance to even disprove your worst fear? I would wager that before you met me you assumed I was like my father."

"You would be right."

"Give Braxton a chance."

"The world cannot take the risk."

"He's not like Caius," Keegan said quietly.

Bernot sighed. "What is it you propose I do then?"

Aron thought for a moment. "Put your forces in place, but do not attack."

Bernot grinned.

"You were already planning on doing that."

"I was. But I needed to confirm it was the right course. By both your and Keegan's words, I've determined it would be against better judgment to not give Braxton a chance. But Keegan, I do want to ask why you vouch for him?"

She was pensive for a moment. "Because he didn't want to do the things he was forced to do. He always held back. So, where does that leave *me*?"

"I still want you to train in all the elements, but you cannot go to each nation to do so now. They will have to come to you. Kade, Aron, and Jared, your roles have not changed, and you must train to become warriors."

"Gladly," Kade said. "When can we begin?"

"Now, if you like," Bernot answered. "But Jared, I think there is someone you will want to see first."

Jared creased his brows together. "Who?"

"Carter."

Jared jumped out of his seat. "Carter's here?"

"He is."

"And Lucas?"

"I think you should hear that story from your brother."

‡‡‡

Following Bernot was pure torture; his pace was slow, and Jared wanted nothing more than to scream at him to run. His thoughts tumbled around themselves as he struggled to create an explanation as to why Lucas hadn't made it to the Lazado.

Bernot stopped outside another children's home, and they found Carter in the kitchen.

Shock and joy morphed his brother's features.

Jared rushed forward and pulled Carter into an embrace. There were so many things he wanted to ask, so many things he wanted to say, but his voice was stuck. It wasn't like losing his family all over but having to remember what they'd lost... it hurt tremendously. Carter returned the embrace and he realized they were both crying.

"I was sure I'd never see you again," Jared choked. "I thought you were dead."

Carter managed to laugh. "I'm glad I'm not."

Jared pulled away and studied him. Carter's childlike features had melted into the features of a man. There was wear on his face and there was no doubt he'd been tried and tested like the rest of them.

"Where's Lucas? And father?" he questioned, turning to the topic that was eating at him most now he knew Carter was safe.

Carter gave an aggravated sigh. "I wish I knew where Lucas was so I could slap him upside the head. And father... he died."

Jared felt like he'd been struck. "Do you have any idea where Lucas might've gone?" He couldn't mourn his father now; he couldn't take that kind of pain again. Not yet. And in a way, he had already grieved for him.

Carter shook his head and gulped before asking, "What happened to Nico?"

Jared turned away, emotions roiling within. "I don't know, but the Vosjnik have him. Or did. Braxton must have him now. I should've never let him stay home."

Carter placed a comforting hand on his shoulder. "You couldn't have known what would happen. What matters now is what we do to save him."

"I would give anything to do that, but right now there are things outside my control."

"What things?"

"The world needs me... here. I'm a Child of Prophecy."

"There's only one and that *one* is Keegan."

"A lie. There are four of us. Keegan and I are two. You can meet the others if you'd like."

"Then you can all help me rescue Nico?"

Jared's heart was splitting in two. He knew what he wanted to do, what he should do. "No. We'll never be allowed to."

The anger and distraught on Carter's face was heart wrenching. "He's our brother! Our baby brother!"

"You think I don't know that?" It took all of Jared's control to not yell. "I want nothing more than to get Keegan and go rescue him, but we can't. We'll find a way to save him, but we have to entrust the mission to someone else."

"You'd leave him to be tortured by the king?"

"The king's dead."

Carter's face became neutral before turning to shock. "That doesn't change anything."

"It might. The man to ascend the throne is supposedly a good person. We may not have to do much to get him back."

"You can't know that for sure."

"No, but I have faith Nico will return to us. Whether by force or otherwise, we'll get him back."

CHAPTER 62

Bernot waited patiently while the leaders trickled in. He had decided to inform the Children of Prophecy of Caius's demise first and was now wondering if that had been the right decision. Except for Okleiy, the leaders all looked annoyed. Atlia gave him a small smile in passing and he hoped he already had the Merprincess on his side. There was also something else in Atlia's look, something akin to sadness.

Tahrin did not bother to hide her distain. *Where did we leave off?*

"You promised to ask your Pexatoses if they would provide aid in the coming war," Bernot said. "I am going to ask for your help once more."

"We already gave you an answer," Rangi said.

"You did," Bernot admitted, "But the circumstances have changed. We will not be waging war against Caius Alagard; we will be waging it against Braxton Alagard."

The leaders gave him baffled looks.

"Last night the border fell, which can mean only one thing: Caius is dead."

"How?" Garne asked. "And by whose hand?"

"I am not sure," Bernot admitted. "The only thing I know is Caius is gone from this world."

"Do you have any operatives in Agrielha?" Rangi questioned.

"Not since Rosh Broyker," Bernot answered. "I ask now that you join forces with me. I intend to wait, see what kind of king Braxton will be, but should he prove to be like his father…"

"I will stand with you," Okleiy declared.

There was silence from the rest of the leaders as they shifted uncomfortably.

Only Tahrin had the nerve to look him in the eye. *No. This is still not our war.*

The others made similar statements.

Atlia had been holding her tongue but finally spoke, "I will join your crusade."

"You are but a representative for your mother," Rangi reminded her.

Atlia was mute for a moment, as if composing herself. "Unfortunately, as of this morning, that is not so. My mother has passed."

Bernot understood the look he had noticed before. "My deepest condolences."

Atlia gave a slight dip of her head. "I remember a world in which we did not feel threatened by Caius. My people are far beyond the reach of anyone but Sola and Lunos, so I cannot imagine what those under his rule feel. I have no reason besides compassion to give my support, but sometimes compassion is the best reason to do anything." When none of the others made a motion to add theirs, she concluded, "You are fools for believing our trials are over."

What would you know of waging war or ruling a nation? Tahrin seethed.

"Nothing," Atlia admitted. "But having watched my mother and learned from her mistakes, I *know* this is the right course of action."

"I cannot justify going to war," Garne said. "Not now at least."

"So be it," Atlia said. "I just pray to Sola and Lunos you come to your senses before it is too late."

She stood and Bernot thought she was going to storm from the room; he was pleasantly surprised when she did not.

"As per my people's custom, I have gifts for all the leaders here today. With what is to come, it is imperative we are able to contact each other quickly. Thus, I offer each of you a small Looking Glass."

They were indeed small for she pulled them from a hidden pocket in her dress and handed them out.

"To use them, speak the name of the race you wish to contact in the Old Language. Now, I do believe there is a Child of Prophecy who needs training." She smiled, baring her small, pointed incisors, and left.

Bernot wanted to chase after her, to thank her, for she had taken a bigger risk than he would have ever dared. Instead, he held his place and watched as resentment crossed the faces of the other leaders. Atlia's actions had simultaneously angered and shamed them. He just hoped her words and actions would push them into acting—sooner, rather than later.

✝✝✝

Keegan paced across the common room while the boys lounged, watching her anxiously. For the longest time after Bernot had left, no one said a word—as if they were afraid that if they spoke of Caius he would rise from the dead.

"Is he really dead?" she finally managed, her thoughts beginning to cohesively come together. "Like… nothing's ever *that* easy for us."

"Why would Bernot lie?" Aron countered.

"I dunno," she said. "Just… there's no way he's dead. Good things don't happen to me—to *us*."

"Good things do happen to us," Aron argued. "Maybe just not in the most straightforward way."

Keegan addressed Kade and Jared, "What'd y'all think?"

"If the border's down, Caius is dead," Kade said plainly. "There's no way to cheat the spell."

There was a knock at the door.

"It's open," Keegan called.

The Mermaid that entered was an ethereal creature, possessing more grace than Keegan could ever hope to. Her skin was a pale blue with hints of silver scales scattered across her body. From below the collar of her dress, she could make out the head of a shark tattoo swimming beneath her collarbone.

Caught off guard, Keegan struggled to remember the Mermaid's name, "Uhh… Atlia… right?"

"I am," she responded, gently closing the door. "Atlia Mahiako."

An awkward silence followed, and Keegan rocked on her heels. "Is there something we can help you with?"

"I was hoping to help you," Atlia said. "With Caius dead, Bernot wants to wage war and you are woefully unprepared. I am willing to train you in water magic."

Keegan shrugged. "When'd you wanna start?"

"Now."

"Eh, what the hell; ain't got nothing better to do."

Kade started to protest, and she shot him a glare. He still wasn't forgiven for his omissions. And until such time—if ever—he had no say in anything she did. "I don't think Atlia's gonna try to kidnap me."

"That's what we thought about Wexsley and Halcyon," Kade said audibly under his breath.

Ignoring him, she followed Atlia, expecting to go to some watery training field. Instead, the Mermaid took her to the kitchen downstairs, where she filled a glass with water and took a seat at the table.

"Do you know where the water paika is?" Atlia asked, leaning back in the chair.

"Reven told me once," Keegan said, racking her brain, "but I don't remember."

"In the right eye."

"Why's it there? It seems so…" she struggled to find the right word, irrelevant."

The Mermaid laughed. "So it does, and I have no answer."

"I assume water magic should be similar to earth and life magic."

"I would agree, but I am only a water elemental so I cannot confirm it."

"Right."

Keegan closed her eyes and searched for the paika. As per everything in Arciol, nothing made sense. The paika was bright orange, as if it were on fire. She took a breath and tried to smash it like she would the earth paika. Her hand passed through the gem, and she switched her approach to resemble how she'd gain access to the life paika, gently endeavoring to pick it up. Again, her hand passed through it.

"Why can't I get hold of it?"

Atlia smiled. "What element are we working with?"

"Water," Keegan answered, unsure of what she was getting at.

"Then treat the paika like water."

Having an idea of what Atlia wanted her to do, but not sure of its validity, she decided to try it, rather than look a fool and ask for direction. Re-entering her mind, she took a deep breath and reached towards the gem, simply letting her hand rest inside.

A rush of power surged through her, though, it was different from the way it felt to use earth or life magic. The power flooded over her and felt like a wave lapping at her seams. Like it was the most natural thing in the world for her. Ripples of magic shifted and coursed through her body like blood through her veins.

She sent the magic towards the water in the glass and imagined it rising. When she opened her eyes, the water had done exactly as she wanted. With a quick furrowing of her eyes, she willed the water to freeze. The effect was almost instantaneous. Pleased with herself, she melted the ice and returned the water to the glass.

Glancing at Atlia, she was concerned by the stare she was getting. "What?"

"You have never used water magic before?" Atlia said quietly. "Are you sure?"

"Positive. Why?"

"What you just did is not something most water elementals—even Merfolk—do within the first few minutes of practice. Something special you are. Well, I suppose this is a good start. We will continue tomorrow."

"Sounds good," she said, taking a sip from the glass. She watched Atlia leave, then slipped out the back door.

✚✚✚

"Good morning," Alyck said as Thaddeus entered the bedroom.

"Good morning. Any interesting visions?"

"I am not sure. The world is amuck today."

"What do you mean?"

"Nothing is clear," Alyck said, sitting up. "Clouds cover everything."

"I wish I knew how to help you." Looking at the Blind Prophets eyes, the cloudiness of his cataract seemed more prevalent.

"Me too. I see something about the coronation. Something… I am just not sure what though."

Thaddeus squatted beside the bed. "Do you want me to do something?"

"I am not sure." There was a pause. "Look after Braxton."

Thaddeus patted Alyck's knee. "I can do that."

Making his way through the castle, he did his best to blend in with the servants scurrying about. A few guards recognized him, but all knew he had free rein—at least he had during Caius's rule, and he assumed the courtesy would extend into Braxton's.

He first looked for Braxton in his chambers and ran into Nico. The child was alarmed to see him, and Thaddeus slipped away before he could do much questioning. The next place he checked was the dining hall, where he met Kolt. He was unsure if the boy knew who he was and his place within the castle, but was not about to ask, knowing his volatile reputation.

After that, he went to the griffin stables. The beasts eyed him eagerly, but there was nothing he could do to save these magnificent creatures from their fate; that was something only Sola and Lunos could do. He did, however, offer some small comfort.

"Caius has left this world," he said before disappearing back into the secret tunnels that he preferred to use.

Clicks from the griffins called after him, begging for more than those simple words.

He was about to return to Alyck's chambers when he realized where Braxton was. He would have done the same if the opportunity had been allowed him.

The doors to the Chapel of the Prioress were ornate and even more terrifying than those that guarded the throne room. One was a deep black with a pearl white dragon soaring across its inkiness. The other, white as the sun, had an onyx dragon facing its opposing counterpart. The expression shared between the two beasts was not one of hatred, but of love.

Thaddeus pushed open the white door and entered. If the doors were beautiful, he had no words to describe the Chapel itself. Colored windows scattered rainbows across the room, suggesting the opposite of death and shadows. Elegantly crafted statues of women crying out for lost loved ones circled the room. In the center was a stone altar, upon which a body lay; Braxton stood at its head.

Thaddeus carefully made his way over, noticing how no tears fell down Braxton's face, in spite of his look of utter shock.

"There was nothing you could have done," he said softly.

Braxton was slow to pull his eyes from his father's body. "What if there was?"

"How could you have known?" Thaddeus asked, placing a hand on his shoulder. Then he remembered he very well could have been aware of what was to come.

Braxton looked to him. "I did know. I have been… having visions."

"What did you see?"

Braxton looked back at his father.

"You can tell me," Thaddeus encouraged. "I will not tell another soul."

"I saw the future. It is hard to discern what the visions are at times. And I never know when they will come to pass."

"It is all right," Thaddeus said, forcing Braxton to look away from the body, pulling him into an embrace. He felt tears soaking the fabric of his shirt.

"Sometimes I wished him dead. Sometimes I wanted to kill him."

We all did, Thaddeus thought. "But *you* were not the one who killed him."

CHAPTER 63

Nico sat with his legs dangling over the precipice, Ima on his left, Harker to his right. The sky outside was a crystal blue that begged to be explored.

Are we going to fly today? Harker asked, looking at Nico with his glossy black eyes that exuded innocence.

"No, Braxton's burying Caius. Not much of anything's going to be happening besides falsely shed tears."

Was Caius a bad person? Ima asked.

Nico was about to scoff at her question then remembered how young she was—barely a year old. "Yes, he was a very bad person."

What about Braxton?

He had to think. Braxton was one of the few people who'd shown him kindness since his ordeal began, but he'd also heard the rumors.

"I'm not sure I can answer that."

They were silent and watched the sun make its path across the morning sky. He'd considered going to the funeral, but knew it'd bring up too many painful memories. Already thoughts of his mother were resurfacing, and he wiped his eyes to cover the evidence.

When can we fly again? Harker asked.

Nico smiled. "After Braxton's coronation." For as antsy as they were to return to the skies—to temporary freedom—he too felt their sentiments.

When is that? Ima said.

"Tomorrow."

Then what happens?

"I'm not sure. I hope things will return to the way they were before."

Including the Vosjnik using us as sky horses? Myrish said.

Nico whipped around to look at the bronze-tinted griffin. "I don't know Braxton's plans," he admitted. He wanted to say more, assure Myrish those monsters would never get to experience what it was like to fly.

Instead, he focused his attention on the horizon. With Braxton as king, there was a chance they'd be given back their freedom. There was a chance they could walk away from all of this.

But nothing was set in stone.

✠✠✠

The Chapel of the Prioress was filled to capacity and Braxton felt the hundreds of eyes that pretended to cry staring at him. This was nothing like the last funeral he had been to—the one for his mother. There, it had just been the four of them: Caius, Braxton, Kolt, and a mewling newborn Aron. The tears shed there had been genuine.

The chapel filled with incense, and he knew the funeral was about to begin in proper. A hymn drifted through the air, sweet and melodic, carrying feelings of sorrow. The words were in the Old Language, and he could pick out a few. Yet the true meaning of the song remained outside his grasp. Braxton knew he should be shedding tears of grief, but his eyes remained dry.

Caius was wrapped in white linen, a red sash tied around his torso. The sash was meant to represent the blood flowing through all men and the sin that came forth after death. He huffed, knowing so much more sin should be showing.

A line of prioresses reached the body, all garbed in dresses made of pale pink silk accented with blue, white

545

chiffon veils covering their faces and draped over their arms. They were beautiful, seraphs sent by Sola and Lunos.

The singing stopped and turned into a droning hum while the cloud of incense grew thicker, the smell clogging his nostrils.

The room became quiet, as if death himself had descended, and a single voice filled the atmosphere. It was ethereal and at first seemed to have no origin. Then Braxton realized it was the prioress he had spoken to the yesterday. Her face was unveiled, and painted ichor-colored tears streamed down her face. The air in the room seemed to instantly clear of the smell and smoke.

He then noticed his father's body—or, the place it had lain, for it had disappeared. Panic rose in his chest.

"Today, we have sent a king to an eternal life with Sola and Lunos," the prioress spoke. "His worldly body has been laid to rest within the earth. The elements that created him shall reclaim him. Blood and bones will turn to dust and water to replenish the earth. Death creates life."

The prioresses began to sing again, and Braxton felt something slide down his face. He reached up: tears. He willed them to cease, but they only fell quicker.

There was a hand on his shoulder, and he turned to find Kolt, tears also spilling from his eyes. They shared a look, and, for the first time, Braxton realized Kolt did care, did have a heart. He pulled his brother into an embrace, and they shared in their sorrow.

✝✝✝

Aron had been awake since before sunrise. He had woken in the middle of the night in a cold sweat and even now his father's face floated across his vision. Knowing he would never fall back asleep, he had crawled onto the roof. His father's death had finally sunk in.

It was barely midday, but the sun was hot and the sparse leaves at the crown of the tree offered little relief. Feeling a pang in his stomach, he recognized it as the same feeling he had felt after Shiloh died. Why? How could he feel anything but joy at Caius's departure?

"Hey," a voice called, and his attention snapped to Keegan as she climbed onto the roof and sat beside him. "What's wrong?"

"I… I am not sure."

She pulled him into a hug. "It's okay to be sad; he was your father."

He was unable to do or say anything for what seemed an eternity. Then slowly, and of their own accord, his arms wrapped around Keegan as tears began to fall.

"Why am I upset?"

"Because, regardless of how shitty a person was, he was family and he loved you. I kind of understand. It's why Kade did what he did—or at least in part, anyway."

"My father never loved me."

Keegan rubbed his back. "In his own twisted way, he did. Why else would he've kept your identity secret? Why else would he've let you live the life you did?"

"Because he had to." Aron wiped his eyes. "My father made a Death Deal with my mother when I was born; he could not kill or grievously hurt me."

"Seems a bit extreme."

He shrugged, returning his attention to the rolling forest. He knew Keegan wanted to do something, say something to comfort him, and he put a hand on her knee, giving it a gentle squeeze. Nothing but time would heal this wound.

"If there's anything I can do, let me know," she said.

When he did not respond, she clambered down from the roof.

He felt a lump in his throat and drew his knees up to his chest. Aron did not care about his father, not after everything he had done. Yet, he did care and there was nothing he could do about it.

✚✚✚

It felt good to be swinging a sword—even if it was only against a straw-stuffed dummy. Kade let his muscles lead and he fell into a rhythm: cut, slash, hack.

"That dummy must've donp you off," a voice behind him said.

Kade whipped around, instinct telling him to keep his weapon poised to attack. There was a clang as swords met.

"Watch it there, I don't pop back up like that dummy."

Kade quickly took in the man, who was shorter than himself by a few inches. He had brown eyes with a laugh about them, crinkles about the corners, and was missing half of his left eyebrow, presumably from a fight.

"Who are you?" Kade asked, stepping back.

The man dropped the point of his sword. "Elhyas Wealsh."

His usual desire to be left alone presented itself in his tone. "Can I help you?"

"Was just wondering if you wanted a proper sparring partner."

Kade felt bad for his gruffness. "Yes, I would appreciate a partner—a living one."

"Care to switch to sparring weapons, Kade? Or do you think you can best old Elhyas?"

He heard warning bells. "How do you know my name?"

Elhyas laughed. "Son, everyone here knows your name. And the name of that pretty sister of yours and two brothers to boot. You four are the celebrities of the town."

He was suddenly concerned the man might be seeking retribution. "Why do you want to spar?"

"I want to see if you're as good as everyone claims. People boast of the great Kade Tavin and his skill with a sword and magic. I think it's chalked up bulla vite."

"Let's put it to the test," Kade said, lunging.

Elhyas easily blocked and quickly parried. Back and forth they went, their swords clanking together as if in true battle. Sweat beaded on his skin and he pushed Elhyas harder. His muscles pleaded for him to give ground and give up, but his mind pushed, knowing there was much more left in him.

For a moment, he was distracted and that was all Elhyas needed. Elhyas struck the flat of his blade near the guard and the weapon slipped from his grip. Before Kade could comprehend what was happening, there was a sword at his throat.

"Not bad, sonny," Elhyas smiled and pulled away. "Not bad at all."

"Not bad?" Kade exclaimed. "I am—was one of the king's best swordsmen."

"I can see that." Elhyas took a long drink from a water-skin. "But you're used to fighting coerced men and peasants. Still, you're better than most of the men on this field."

"You say I'm good, but I'd wager you'd say I could become better."

"You'd be right." Elhyas flashed him a smile. "Would you care to do exactly that?"

"Of course," Kade said, crossing his arms. "But who's going to train me—you? You barely bested me."

"Tis true, but yet it was with my non-dominant hand."

"Then train me, oh master," he said sarcastically, giving a bow to enhance the statement.

"You got a mouth on you, sonny. We'll start tomorrow."

"Why not today?"

"I have things to do," Elhyas said, walking away. "Keep going at that dummy though; I'm sure he's done something to deserve it."

✝✝✝

It was hard to believe the bright cheerful halls Thaddeus now walked had been covered in black hangings only a few hours past. There had been a quick transition from funeral decorations to gay ones for the coronation. He was not surprised the world would rather rejoice.

The air was alit with laughter, though when he reached the level where the crown prince, soon to be king, resided, there was only gloom.

He gently knocked on the door, entering when given permission.

"What do you want?" Braxton asked quietly.

"I wanted to see if you were alright."

Braxton turned to face him; his eyes were red and puffy and there were wet splotches on his shirt. "What do you think?"

"I know what it is like to lose someone." He came to stand beside the prince. "I know how much it hurts."

"You lost your son."

"And my daughter-in-law, and potentially my grandson."

"How have you not drowned in tears by now?"

"Because it will not bring them back. I did my share of mourning, but there comes a time when you move on. Wear the loss like a badge and do something great with it. Make the lives of those around you better."

"How would you suggest I do that?"

"That is something you will have to figure out. But I do know taking the crown tomorrow and being a fair ruler will put you on the right path."

"What if I do not want to be king?"

"That is your choice."

"What if I want to be king, but it is not my fate?"

"Then there is nothing you or I can do except help he who does take the throne." A pause followed and Thaddeus felt there was cause behind the prompted questions. "Is there something you saw?"

"Yes. I saw myself—I think it was me—sitting on the throne. Then, someone stabbed me in the back."

"You were stabbed in the back?" He instantly knew there were two possible meanings.

"Yes." There was fear in Braxton's eyes. "I know others have always coveted the throne, but do you think they would be willing to kill for it? Will they be so bold?"

"I do not think so. The visions are not always what you think. Sometimes, they offer clues and symbols about the future."

Braxton looked like he wanted to argue. "I am sure you are right."

"Do not worry about tomorrow or even the day after. I know in my heart of hearts you will be one of the greatest kings this world has ever seen."

"Thank you. Would you do me a favor?"

"Of course."

"Will you present me to the gods tomorrow at the ceremony?"

"It would be an honor."

CHAPTER 64

The world around him was soft and comfortable. Aron arched his back and stretched. His arm brushed against something warm. Opening his eyes, he was assaulted with a riot of rust-colored hair splayed around someone's head like a halo. Guilt overwhelmed him as he racked his brain.

The woman gave a sleepy groan, rolling over, and his eyes widened. Keegan pulled close to him, nestling into the crook of his shoulder. He tried to recall the events of the previous night and some of it felt hazy and unreachable.

Aron had hidden on the roof for most of the day until the sun had heated the shingles to an unbearable temperature. At that point, he relocated to his room. Just before dinner, Keegan came to check on him and he had not managed to get a single word out before she fled. Feeling worse than before, he had skipped dinner.

Well past dusk, Keegan returned, a flask clutched in her hand and a mischievous grin that said she was up to no good.

"What is that?" he asked, referring to the flask.

Keegan simply opened the stopper. The pungent smell immediately gave the answer: alcohol.

She took a gulp before handing it to him. "I was hoping for something softer, maybe mead. But liquor is all I could get my hands on."

There were misgivings, but, seeing the gleam in her eyes, Aron drank. The alcohol burned as it traced down his throat, leaving a warm feeling behind. He coughed through the after-burn. "Where did you get this?"

"Let's just say I owe Behthany a favor."

After that, everything started to blur, his head feeling heavy. Most of what he remembered was bringing the flask to his lips several more times and the warm burning sensation that followed.

He watched as Keegan inched closer to him. Then, before he could pull himself away, their lips melded together. Her breath was warm and carried passion. His hands found themselves on her shoulders, intending to push her away, but instead pulled her closer.

Her clothes were soft under his fingers, but all he wanted was to feel her skin. He scrambled to pull her shirt off. She pushed him back, staring at him breathlessly as guilt washed over him. It took only a moment for the entire mood to change.

Then, she started to pull at him desperately, her hands pushing his shirt up. He pulled it off, throwing it to the side. Keegan's quickly followed and his hands roamed the smooth contours of her back. She pulled him towards the bed and together they fell onto it.

His mind had refused to think of anything other than what was happening, anything other than Keegan. Their bodies came together, like forgotten lovers, a lock and key, puzzle pieces… Nothing else in the world except them and then existed. The act was soon over but the air still coursed with electricity. Their breaths came heavily, his heart begging for more.

Keegan nestled against him, and it wasn't long before she was asleep.

He had whispered something into her hair—though didn't remember what—and kissed her head before he too fell asleep.

Aron ran a hand through his hair; how could he have let this happen? Gently, he lifted himself from the bed, doing his best to not wake Keegan. He quickly dressed, untangling his clothes from Keegan's, and all but fled the room.

How could he have done this with Keegan? How could he have done this *to* Keegan?

✞✞✞

Reven prodded Lucas with his boot. "Rise an' shine, arse face."

"Shut the royik up," Lucas grumbled.

Sitting up, Lucas saw the sun had yet to rise over the treetops and he rubbed the sleep from his eyes.

Reven tossed him some jerky. "Hurry up. We 're burning daylight."

He quickly packed his bedroll, and they left the clearing at an amiable trot.

"Wonder what the funeral was like," Reven said.

"What?" Lucas questioned.

"Caius's funeral—I wonder what it was like."

The mention of Caius brought back the memories of their escape from the castle. Or rather the lack thereof. Something in his mind had stopped working. Though his nose had become super sensitive.

The few drops of Caius's blood that had landed on his hands had smelled like a flood. The iron heavy and inescapable. And that was the only thing he remembered until suddenly they were back at the inn. Sneaking out of the tunnel and through the bar had been easy. Then they were in saddles, headed towards the Lazado.

"What difference does it make?" Lucas asked.

Reven shrugged. "Was just wondering if people cried or celebrated."

He supposed Caius had people who cared about him— though couldn't fathom who. As far as he knew, Caius had never married, never had children, so his parents might be the only people who grieved for him. But that was impossible, as the king had been over two centuries old.

His heart began to feel heavy as it continued down this path of thought. If he were to drop dead today, who would miss him? He wasn't even entirely sure Nico and Jared were alive. Carter likely already assumed him dead. Reven… *He* would probably be the only person to mark his passing. Lucas shuddered at the thought.

"How long until we reach the Lazado?" he blurted.

"Few weeks," Reven said. "Maybe less if we push."

"Let's push."

Reven laughed, "Got a girl to see?"

"No, family. Family to make sure that's still alive."

"Then let 's get going. Would n't want to keep 'em waiting."

‡‡‡

Thaddeus straightened the sash crossing Braxton's chest. "There. Perfect."

The prince gave him a weak grimace. "Thank you."

"Are you nervous?"

"My stomach is in knots."

"Good, remember that feeling. Use it to help you make good decisions."

Braxton gave a genuine smile. "Is that not what I have you and Alyck for?"

Trumpets sounded from the throne room.

"Are you ready?" Thaddeus asked

"No."

"That is alright." Thaddeus took a breath and pushed open the doors, the griffins carved into them eyeing them scornfully.

The first thing he noticed were the flowers accenting the room and the banners bearing the Alagard coat-of-arms hanging from the walls. Then, the hundreds of faces turning to get a glimpse of the prince to be turned king.

Bright colors covered everyone. Women wore elegant up-dos and priceless gems, while men were dashing in coats embroidered with silver, gold, and bronze. To him it was like living stained glass.

At the bottom of the dais, Thaddeus stopped, giving Braxton a reassuring nod, before letting him slowly ascended the steps alone.

"Long live the king."

Seeing the smile playing on Braxton's lips, Thaddeus knew he would be fine. Having no further place in the coronation, he exited the throne room. As he walked down the halls, he frowned; the corridors were completely empty—of guards, servants, everyone. He told himself it was nothing.

Reaching Alyck's chambers, he inhaled deeply, knowing as soon as he crossed the threshold, he re-entered a prison of sorts.

"Alyck, I am back. You should see the throne room." When there was no response on how that was impossible, he called again, "Alyck?"

In their sleeping quarters, he found Alyck sitting on the bed, staring emptily at his hands, looking nothing like he had when Thaddeus had left him. As the Blind Prophet, he was exempt from the ravages of time—so long as Caius and those of his blood remained on the throne. That time had passed and Alyck seemed to have aged thirty years. Gray hair covered his head, sunspots dappled his skin, and wrinkles pulled at his body.

Thaddeus rushed to him. "What is happening?"

"Change," Alyck answered, his voice hoarse and croaky with age.

"How do we stop it?"

Alyck smiled. "You do not."

Thaddeus watched as the transformation continued before his eyes. The now gray hair began to fall from Alyck's scalp, lying across the bed like macabre snowfall. Alyck's breaths started to come in raspy wheezes.

"There has to be a way to stop this."

"Oh, there is," Alyck said, sinking back onto the bed. "But I do not want to." He took a shuddering breath and stilled.

Thaddeus bawled, "No!"

Then, in a moment, Alyck returned to his former self. His face became youthful, the wrinkles ironing themselves out, and his black hair regrowing in an instant.

The Blind Prophet bolted upright, eyes wide and full of fear, "No. NO! This was not supposed to happen." He seethed, "The bastard!"

"What are you talking about?" Thaddeus pressed, simultaneously relieved and worried about this new threat.

"Go see our new king for your answers. Then tell him I will never serve him."

✠✠✠

Braxton's breath caught in his throat as he watched Thaddeus leave. Somehow, the Keeper of Prophecy had come to be a source of stability and comfort. He pushed the thought away and focused on the priest standing before him. Now was not supposed to be comfortable. It was supposed to be heavy with the duty he was about to accept.

"Are you ready?" the priest whispered.

He nodded, his stomach like a great snake tying itself into a knot.

"Citizens of Agrielha," the priest began.

Braxton droned out the words, his mind taking in everything else, from the decorations to the people—to the lack of Kolt. Try as he might, he could not locate his brother.

At first, he was disappointed, then an uneasy feeling settled in. But he had no time to dwell on it.

"Do you swear to uphold the laws of this nation?" The priest continued, "Do you swear to uphold justice for those who misstep? Do you swear to uphold faith in your people? Do you swear to lead this nation in peace and war? Do you swear to rule with wisdom and kindness?"

Braxton gulped, understanding the gravity of what was being asked of him. "I do. I swear to uphold the law strictly, but to show mercy to those who might be led from the path of violence. I swear to ride into battle with my soldiers should the time come but pray for peace and prosperity instead. I swear to rule with the wisdom of those before me and with the guidance of those who wish to give it. I swear to all of this so this nation and its people may prosper."

The priest picked up a bowl of ash and smeared it along Braxton's jaw. "Rule with the strength and fierceness of your father." Ash was smeared in a line that traced the bottom of his eyes and ran over the bridge of his nose. "Rule with the kindness and understanding of Seleena." Ash went on his eyebrows, "Rule with the courage and wisdom of The Dragon King." The priest turned to pick up the crown.

This one was different from the one that had graced Caius's head; each ruler had their own. The one Braxton would wear was a simple circlet made of red gold, a single ruby imbedded above the space between the brows. Kolt had designed it and he felt pride knowing his brother had done well.

His thoughts returned to the fact Kolt was absent and he forced himself to focus on the priest and the crown. Just as it was about to rest upon his head, the doors burst open, and soldiers flooded the room.

Braxton slowly got to his feet, spotting Kolt amidst the soldiers. Kolt might not have been well liked by most of the servants and laymen in the castle but had always seemed to endear himself to those in the guard. It was never something

Braxton had understood—and until today, it was never something he had feared.

"What is the meaning of this?" Braxton demanded.

"An excellent question, brother." Kolt slowly approached, the soldiers falling in behind him. "Did you think I would miss my own coronation?"

"This is not your coronation."

A signature sneer was plastered across his brother's face. "Are you sure?"

Before Braxton could get another word out, hands latched onto his arms. His first instinct was to reach for his magic. He had barely reached for the paika when he felt cold metal around his wrists. He lost the connection to his magic and, try as he might, could not regain it.

"What is this?" he demanded as soldiers pulled him to where his brother stood.

"Call it an overthrow," Kolt said, walking past him to take a seat upon the throne.

"You cannot do this."

"Just did. Take him away."

Braxton struggled against the soldiers. "You will pay for this!"

"Stop," Kolt said lazily.

The soldiers froze, though Braxton continued fighting.

"I want him to witness history." Kolt turned to the priest. "Do it or die where you stand."

The priest was clearly shaken as he picked up the bowl of ash and prepared to repeat the words he had said earlier. The bowl of ash trembled in his hands but his voice did not waiver.

"Skip the bulla vite," Kolt snarled.

The priest put the bowl down and picked up the crown. All too slowly, the crown descended. All too soon it was resting on Kolt's head.

The priest stepped back. "Long live the king."

"Long live the king," the people in the room echoed in warbled, fearful tones.

In a daze, Braxton no longer fought the soldiers as they dragged him away. The castle around him disappeared and he was thrown into his own mind. How could he have been so stupid to believe Kolt would do anything good? He should have known. He should have known and now everyone was going to suffer. He had known and now he was going to suffer.

CHAPTER 65

W hat is this?" Okleiy queried, holding up a package.

"We know as much as you," Atlia said. "Bernot and I have not opened ours yet."

The three parcels, one for each of them, had arrived that morning, ostensibly from Agrielha, waiting for them outside their bedroom doors—arriving via the work of a spellcaster. He had sent word to Braxton about creating a treaty only yesterday, so these had to have been prepared some time before, which made him wonder if they were from Caius.

Bernot undid the twine around his package. Inside was something wrapped in tissue paper and a note. He turned his attention to the note first.

7/31

Dear Bernot Bællar,

I assume you have sent me a message requesting a peace treaty. You will find one is unnecessary after I destroy you. However, there is a way for this to end peacefully. Surrender yourself, Keegan Digore, Kade Tavin, and Aron Alagard and I might pardon your people for fleeing from the crown. Deny me and I will annihilate you.

I will give you and the other races time to pledge your loyalty. I expect a response within a week. Bow down or die.

Kolt Alagard

King of this world

"Vite," he cursed.

"This is not good," Atlia said. "We have to go to war."

Bernot turned his attention to the… *present*. Folding back the thin paper, he revealed two golden bracelets. It took several before he realized what they were and quickly dropped them onto the desk.

Atlia glanced up, worry etched on her face. "What are they?"

"Slajor manacles."

"Impossible. We destroyed them all when Caius became king."

"Apparently not," Okleiy said. "Or they figured out how to make more."

"That spell was lost centuries ago," Atlia argued.

"Bernot," a voice called.

He looked around, trying to find the source.

Okleiy gave him a baffled look while Atlia struggled to hold back laughter.

"Where is it coming from?" Bernot asked the Merqueen.

"The Looking Glass," she said, nodding towards his desk drawer.

Bernot yanked open the drawer, almost pulling it from the desk, and rummaged around until he found it. The piece had the faces of Tahrin, Rangi, and Garne squashed onto its surface.

"Did you get a package?" Rangi asked, distressed.

"I did," Bernot answered. "Did you all get slajor manacles, too?"

"Yes," they responded.

Bernot paid attention to the voice that answered for Tahrin; it was not hers and belonged to a man. "Who is speaking for Tahrin?"

"I," the voice said, the Looking Glass shifting to show a face.

"Ah. What do you intend to do about this?" Bernot asked, hoping he would finally get what he wanted.

"War," the man answered.

Rangi and Garne were slow to answer, but said the same.

"We cannot allow Kolt to threaten us like this," Rangi said. "I will have his head. How dare he believe he could ever hold us in subjugation? Has he forgotten who created humans?"

"You may have created humans, but we are your equals, so do not think less of us."

"He is right," Atlia said loud enough to be heard by the other leaders, "but let us turn the conversation to the present dilemma."

"War is our answer now," Garne provided. "Have you begun preparing?"

"Partially," Bernot answered. "We were waiting for Atlia's men before marching past the forestline. Now we will wait for all of you. And we must be quick before Kolt decides to launch an attack of his own."

"We will move with haste," Tahrin's speaker said. "We dragons can be there within three weeks or so."

"The Buluo will need more time," Rangi said. "We are still nomads and it will take a while for to reach out to all the tribe leaders. I hope we can reach you in less than a month but realistically it will be longer—much longer."

"Expect a month or so for the Torrpeki," Garne told him.

Bernot nodded. "Until then. Meanwhile, we will stop Kolt from getting further than the Borderlands."

"We shall be seeing you soon," Tahrin's speaker said, disappearing, quickly followed by the others.

Atlia rose from the chair. "We have much to prepare for, I will tell my Commanders to hurry here."

"I will prepare mine," Okleiy said, following Atlia.

To war we go. To death we march, he thought.

Bernot walked with them to the landing, watching as they began the descent down the Gortlin Tree. A flash of red caught his eye at the bottom of the staircase. Keegan paused to looked up and even from up high he could see the terror in her eyes.

‡‡‡

Jared sat on the couch, trying to read, though his anger was making it difficult. Carter had gone to his job at the carpenter's, something he intended to put an end to; if the rest of them didn't have to work, why should he? Aron was sitting at the table, apathetically refletching his arrows.

The door to the common room crept open to reveal a white-faced Keegan. Both he and Aron stopped what they were doing.

"What the royik, Keegan?" Kade said, emerging from his room. "I've been able to sense your emotions since you left the forest floor." When he noticed her face, he muttered, "Vitt."

"Take a seat," Jared said, pulling out a chair.

There was pure terror in her eyes. "Kolt's king."

A dead silence enveloped them.

"Who told you that?" Kade asked quietly. There was something in his voice, not quite fear, but close to it.

"I overheard Bernot, Okleiy, and Atlia talking."

Aron gulped. "Did you hear anything about Braxton?"

Her eyebrows knitted together in sympathy. "No, I'm sorry."

Kade rubbed his jaw. "You were slated to kill Caius. Kolt will be child's work."

Keegan shook her head again. "He made something called slajor manacles."

Kade cursed. "You're still stronger than him."

"But I'm not. None of us are. Kolt has no problem throwing away his humanity."

Jared hated himself, but now wasn't the time for grudges against misguided good intentions. "Then we work together. The prophecy spoke about it taking four children to defeat

564

Caius." He glanced at Kade. "I can never forgive what you did to my family."

"I don't expect you to."

"But if working with you means my brothers live, I'll do it. And maybe in time I'll see you as a friend again."

"I won't hold my breath." Kade turned to Aron. "I appreciate what you've done for Keegan, but I still don't like you. But I respect you enough to fight alongside you."

Jared returned his attention to Keegan. Kneeling, he took her hands, "When we work together, nothing is impossible."

Four Days Earlier...

Caius reached the crest of the hill and surveyed the land around him. Much had changed since he had last seen this place. The wild had overtaken what man had claimed and the house he had once known every nook and cranny of was barely more than a few piles of stone. The only true marker that this place had ever been significant was the gravestones.

Caius made his way over to the graves, laying a hand on the now weathered surfaces. Though time had taken its toll on these last tokens, the engraved names were still legible. He muttered a quick spell to returned them to their original standing, then another to prevent their destruction.

"The place where it all began," he muttered.

Though no one was around, he kept his tumultuous emotions beneath the surface. Too many times had he wished he could change the past, too many times had he placed all the blame on himself, too many times had he shed tears. He knew it was futile—they could never respond—but something made him start talking to his parents.

"Alyck is doing well. He is the Blind Prophet, and recently we found the Keeper of Prophecy. You also had a daughter-in-law. She was beautiful—the most beautiful woman to ever walk this earth; aside from you, Mother.

"Seleena was wonderful and it saddens me Aron never had the chance to know her. I guess I should also tell you that you have three grandsons: Braxton, Kolt, and Aron. All are doing well. Braxton has a long way to go before he will be able to handle being king, but he has the potential."

Caius continued to talk as the sun made its way across the sky. He wanted to apologize for what had happened, for his lack of control, but every time he tried, the words stuck in his throat. Placing a hand on the stones, he said his goodbyes and stood, realizing his fear of this place was unfounded.

The sun was a breath above the horizon, casting stunning colors into the atmosphere. A light wind ruffled his hair and he smiled, the pleasant memories of childhood flooding back, no longer clouded by shame and remorse.

He looked up as a rumbling nearby began to grow. The sky above him, clear at first, became warped and blackened. A hole opened in the center and he could see the other world through it, filled with bright lights, brighter than anything natural. The hole descended towards him and the wind grew into a storm. He grinned as the void swallowed him.

He could survive the other world again. His double could stand in his place. He would not be defeated.

The journey was painless, but as soon as his feet touched solid ground, it felt as if all the energy was siphoned from him. He collapsed and could feel stones digging into his skin, but he was weak, too weak to even keep his eyes open.

Pronunciations and Translations

Characters

Alessandra Sieme [al-es-an-dra sigh-m]
Alivia Fulpe [ah-live-e-uh fulp]
Alyck Alagard [al-eck al-ah-guard]
Angela Alga [an-gel-a al-ga]
Aræghan Vælar [are-ah-gone vay-lar]
Arkav [ark-av]
Aron Alagard [a-ron al-ah-guard]
Aros [ar-ohs]
Arthur [are-thur]
Aster Ustor [as-ter oos-tore]
Atlia Mahiako [at-lee-uh mah-he-ack-o]
Bastille/Darkheart [bass-teal/dark-heart]
Behthany "Bethsy" Rhyen [beth-an-ee "beth-see" rye-en]
Bernot Bællar [bern-ot bay-lar]
Bevel Vælar [bev-ell vay-lar
Braxten Alagard [brax-ten al-ah-guard]
Braxton Alagard [brax-ton al-ah-guard]
Brennian Thandov [bren-ee-an than-dov]
Brewer [brew-er]
Caeyl [kale]
Caius Alagard [kai-us al-ah-guard]
Caldon Vælar [cal-don vay-lar]
Carter Sieme [car-ter sigh-m]
Cassidy Wungim [cass-ih-dee wung-im]
Clark Idar [clark i-dar]
Connery Sray [con-er-ee sr-ay]
Crowlin [crowh-lynn]
Dax Ockloun [dax ock-lown]
Dunkan Yaw [dun-can yaw]
Eamon Echols [ee-ah-mon ech-oles]
Elhyas Wealsh [e-lie-as well-sh]

Elia [ell-e-ah]
Elza [ell-za]
Esen Vælar [es-en bay-lar]
Evard Poukyn [ev-ard poke-in]
Felix Isaacs [fe-lix iz-acks]
Finlay Cralter [fin-lay cral-ter]
Fraisher Vælar [fraish-er vay-lar]
Garne Skaagg [garn-eh sk-ag]
Graw [graw]
Guthrie Urvent [guth-re ur-vent]
Halcyon Brygh [hal-see-on brig]
Hammond [ham-ond]
Harker [hark-er]
Henley [hen-lee]
Hernando Barnsed [hern-an-doe barn-said]
Hickor Gorell [hick-ore gore-ell]
Hynde [hind]
Ilene Piscol [i-lean pisk-cull]
Ima [e-mah]
Indol [in-doll]
Iwin [i-win]
Jai [jai]
Jameson [jame-es-son]
Jared Sieme [jare-ed sigh-m]
Jude Sieme [joo-d sigh-m]
Kade Tavin [kay-d tav-in]
Kagen Tavin [kay-gen tav-in]
Keegan Ilene Digore [key-ghan i-lean die-gore]
Kolt Alagard [koh-lt al-ah-guard]
Korissa Tavin [core-iss-ah tav-in]
Laiyla Fulpe [lay-lah fulp]
Lucas Sieme [loo-cuss sigh-m]
Lunos [loo-nohs]
Lyerlly Bællar [Lie-er-lee bay-lar]
Mahogen Ustor [mah-hog-en oos-tore]
Mara Foxire [mar-ah fox-ire]

Marka [mark-ah]
Maryn Arst [mare-en are-st]
Meloda Alagard [mel-oh-dah al-ah-guard]
Myrish [my-rish]
Nicandro Quolt [nick-an-dro qu-olt]
Nico Sieme [nee-kho sigh-m]
Niyth [ni-yth]
Noriss Ett [nor-is et]
Norm [norm]
Nox [knocks]
Ocea Vælar [oh-she-ah vay-lar]
Okleiy Ustor [oak-lee oos-tore]
Olyver [oll-iv-er]
Orville [or-vill]
Oslin [oz-lynn]
Oxren [ox-ren]
Phinne [fin-ay]
Phynex [phe-nex]
Rangi [rang-i]
Reven Broyker [rev-en broi-ker]
Rhyse Velaz [re-ss vell-az]
Rosh Broyker [rosh broi-ker]
Seleena Vælar [sell-ee-nuh vay-lar]
Shiloh Laund [shy-loh lau-nd]
Shyre Ustor [shy-er oos-tore]
Siene Mahiako [see-en mah-he-ack-o]
Sola [sol-ah]
Stefan [stef-an]
Suki Vælar [soo-key vay-lar]
Tahrin [tah-rin]
Taite Ault [tay-t auwlt]
Thaddeus Broyker [thad-e-us broi-ker]
Thahan Havidray [tha-han have-ih-dray]
Ty [tie]
Uri Vælar [ur-e vay-lar]
Varley [var-lee]

Virgil Fulpe [verge-ill fulp]
Vitia Gorell [vee-tee-ah gore-ell]
Waylan Piscol [way-lan pisk-cull]
Wexsley Grioux [wex-slee gri-ox]
Zaire [zih-air]

Places

Agrielha [ag-re-el-uh]
Arciol [are-see-ole]
Averit Volcanoes [av-er-it vol-cane-oh-s]
Aylentowne [aye-len-town]
Bouyne [boone]
Drath [drath]
Edreba [eh-dreb-uh]
Glensung Plains [glen-sung plains]
Gortlin Tree [gore-t-lin tree]
Gydrick's Inn and Tavern [guide-ricks in and tav-ern]
Illeria Mountains [i-leer-e-ah mount-ains]
Lake Romann [lay-ke roh-man]
Magnenpie [mag-nen-pie]
Móverth [mauve-earth]
Ohvenail [oh-ven-ail]
Revod [rev-odd]
Suilenroc [sull-en-rock]
Suttan [sut-tan]
Tatat River [tat-at riv-er]
Tratoleck [trat-o-leck]
Westerlies [west-er-lees]
Whendell [when-dell]
Yarav Forest [yar-av for-est]

Old Language

Æay [ay]- they
Æysc [ay-sc]- ash
Adæmno [ad-aim-no]- moment
Arse [are-s]- ass
Astæm [as-tame]- but
Avu [av-oo]- yes
Ayþ [ay-th]- the
Az [as]- I
Bastard [bass-tard]- bastard
Betrayer [be-tray-er]- betrayer
Bindiar [bin-dee-ar]- blind
Bovestun [bove-est-un]- bloody
Bulla vite [bull-ah vie-t]- bullshit
Buna [boo-nuh]- fire
Bwint [b-win-t]- bitch
Casne [cas-nay]- can
Caxone [cax-own]- barrier
Darvesen [dar-ves-en]- prophet
Drackyn [drack-in]- dragon
Du [do]- it
Egreþer [eg-reth-er]- know
Eya [ey-ah]- you
Eyar [ey-ar]- your
Fackyon [fack-ee-on]- false
Fayo [fay-oh]- by
Foylisha [foy-lish-ah]- foolishness
Ghæ [gay]- that
Hamoomph [ham-oom-f]- heal
Haxnug [hax-nug]- stop
Hayclen [hay-clen]- fate
Hiell [hi-ell]- hell (place)
Hynak [hi-knack]- whore
Ictotm [ict-ot-m]- lord
Iruh [ih-roo]- for

Jappec [jap-pec]- defeat
Jyken [jai-ken]- while
Kævoka [kay-voke-ah]- wicked
Kunyi [coon-yih]- king
Lunviyda [loon-vee-da]- slaughter
Luxyen [lux-yen]- exile
Marmarda [marm-ard-ah]- murderer
Meki [mek-e]- have
Nackh [nack-h]- rule
Nastor [nas-tore]- hell (phrase)
Naya [nay-ah]- no
Noxþ [knockx-th]- damn
Nuþ [nuth]- again
Okæpyio [oak-ap-ee-oh]- adversity
Opida [oh-pee-dah]- bitch (extremely offensive, used for
women only)
Oywn [oywn]- own
Payn [pain]- path
Plazde [plaz-day]- please
Proytyct [proy-t-i-ct]- protect
Psodæ [ps-ode-ay]- child/children
Qalx [o-a-lx]- from
Rhæpn [rap-n]- who
Ri [re]- of
Rimbor [rim-bore]- remember
Royik [roy-ick]- fuck
Ryla [rye-la]- am
Ryo [rye-oh]- be
Sarig [sar-ig]- sorry
Sesuna [ses-oo-na]- serve
Solcan [soul-can]- seal
Soucer [sou-ker]- hero
Unla [oon-la]- only
Viæn [vee-an]- rise
Vite [vie-t]- shit [as in "piece of trash"]/excrement
Vito [vee-toe]- shit (as in "jack shit"/"oh shit")

Vitot [vee-tot]- piece of shit
Waysne [way-sn-ay]- earth
Woth [woth]- will
Wye [why]- now
Yarv [yar-v]- come
Zæ [zay]- these
Þe [the]- do

Word Endings/Tenses

-alb- more ("great*er*")
-est- the most ("great*est*")
-ox- past tense ("play*ed*")
-en- present/future tense ("go*ing*")
-s- plural ("dog*s*")
-u- feminine noun/verb ending
-i- masculine noun/verb ending

Peoples

Alvor [al-vore]
Arciolan [are-see-ole-an]- someone from Arciol
Buluo [boo-loo-oh]
Lazado [laz-ah-do]
Pexatose [pex-ah-toe-s]- someone from the other world
Torrpeki [tore-pec-ee]
Vosjnik [voz-nick]- a group of the best in each of their fields

Other

Borzan [bore-zan]- coffee
Ether [eth-er]- agent used to temporarily inhibit magic use

Kojote [koh-joe-te]- a person who secrets elementals across the country
Nanagin [nuh-nah-gin]- magical portal between worlds, specific in time in place to each person
Paika [pie-kuh]- gem that contains a person's access to magic
Ramilla [ram-ill-uh]- a poison made from octopus venom and the nectar of the dogwood flower
Rimor [rim-or]- earth immobilization technique
Yewne [yew-nay]- marker that grants access to the hidden Alvor cities
Zoutsi [zout-see]- earth immobilization technique

9 798218 247836